BITTER BURN

SIERRA SIMONE

Published by Bloom Books, an imprint of Sourcebooks
1935 Brookdale RD, Naperville, IL 60563-2773
(630) 961-3900
sourcebooks.com

Cataloging-in-Publication data is on file with the Library of Congress.

Printed and bound in Canada.
MBP 10 9 8 7 6 5 4 3 2 1

CONTENT NOTE

This book contains brief, nonspecific references to historical clerical abuse, which isn't depicted and doesn't involve the central characters.

This book also references self-harm in a religious context, and Chapter Sixteen mentions but does not depict self-harm in a nonreligious context. In Chapter Twenty-Two, Mark uses a metaphor of stabbing to describe what he does to himself by courting his own jealousy. In Chapter Forty, Mark uses a metaphor of having buried himself to describe where his own decisions have led him.

Chapter Eighteen depicts an attempted assault and attempted kidnapping of a secondary character by her stalker, which is stopped by a central character. This attempted kidnapping includes a verbal threat of facial disfigurement.

Finally, this book deals with themes of religion and violence throughout.

When I came back from Lyonnesse
   With magic in my eyes,
    All marked with mute surmise
My radiance rare and fathomless,
When I came back from Lyonnesse
   With magic in my eyes!

—Thomas Hardy

prologue

EIGHT YEARS AGO

It was the opera music he remembered afterward.

It spilled out the open door in the back of the building and filled the alley and the grassy courtyard beyond, and it didn't stop, despite the gunshots, despite the screams—despite his world ending.

It was somehow indelible to the scene, as fixed to the moment as the cloud-black skies or the glassy puddles dotting the streets, and for a single, eternal second, Mark Trevena thought to himself: *the third option.*

Forget diplomacy, forget war. Just two dead Americans in an alleyway while his SSO yelled in his ear and *Turandot* threaded through the wet, thick air of Kraków at night.

One of those dead Americans was his husband, Eliot.

But Mark had not been recruited to the Rangers and later to the CIA because he was slow, because he was afraid, because he couldn't see the pieces on the board. He saw everything the instant it happened—Eliot meeting with an informant about a new arms dealer on the scene, the American soldiers on patrol, the informant thinking he'd been set up…the flying bullets.

And now the informant was dead and an American soldier was dead and Eliot was dead, and the other soldiers from the patrol were calling for backup.

It was imperative said backup didn't arrive to find a CIA operative meeting with a known arms dealer—a dealer who had just killed an active-duty soldier.

It was imperative that no one knew the CIA had been here at all.

It was a fast descent from the roof of the botanical library where he'd been watching through a thermal monocular, listening in on Eliot's conversation. Mark moved quietly, silently, except for the soft exhale he gave when he jumped the final distance from a covered balcony to the courtyard. The soldiers wouldn't hear him, he was sure of that; there was one soldier rendering aid to two wounded companions while still trying to cover the opening to the alley, and he was busy and bloody and occupied with heroism. And *Turandot* veiled almost every sound—breathing, footsteps, the choked noise Mark made when he turned Eliot's face to his own and saw the blue eyes he'd once signed his soul away for had gone lifeless.

Amid the soaring tenor of "Nessun dorma," Mark dragged the bodies of his husband and the informant into the darkness, deep into the shadows gathered near the library until his SSO could arrange for transportation.

For removal.

And when the soldiers finally got their backup and made it to the end of the alley, they found it empty of everything.

Everything but music and spatters of blood.

———

A few weeks later, Melody Trevena was standing in a cemetery while her brother walked toward her. The summer sun glinted off their hair, twin haloes of gold and platinum, and with their strong features and ocean-colored eyes, the resemblance was unmistakable. The Trevena twins had gained such a reputation a few years back that Langley no longer allowed them to work together; they were too easily recognized that way. If you were a criminal and you were approached by two preternaturally attractive blonds with flawless suits and sociopathic smiles, then you knew the twins had been sent after you. It put people on their guard unnecessarily; it made things complicated. It never resulted in a failed mission, but it had resulted in more bloodstained silk blouses than Melody had the patience for. So Langley had split the siblings up, and while she missed the silent communication and implicit trust, she also didn't miss the dry-cleaning bills.

"They didn't give you the flag," Melody said now. Below them and through the trees, the mourners were gradually breaking away from Eliot's grave. He'd been popular and well loved, and even though she knew Mark hadn't begrudged Eliot his many lovers, she also knew it stung to stand in a crowd and be just another face. To have his marriage with Eliot diluted into a long-term assignment, into a professional partnership, into convenient sex by the people they both knew.

Not that Melody thought Eliot himself had always treated the marriage much differently. Mark had always loved Eliot more than Eliot had loved him, and when Melody told Mark so, he'd only murmured a low *I know*. And what could she say to that?

"They gave his mother the flag," replied Mark. "It was the right thing to do. She didn't know that we—she thought I was his ex-boyfriend. That's what he'd told her the last time they talked."

Mark's eyes weren't on the grave but on the trees

3

beyond—a middle distance where she knew he was seeing a dark alley overlaid on the trees, pale hands flecked with dirt and broken blades of grass from being dragged to a pickup point. Melody felt pity for her brother and irritation with Eliot for leaving him like this…a lonely mourner, written off as nobody special. For finding one last way to remind Mark that their marriage had been an easily dropped toy.

"You have his watch," she noted, glancing down at Mark's wrist. "They let you take it?"

"I didn't ask."

She looked up at his face. His eyes were dry; she expected no less. But she caught the brief flex of his hand at the edge of her vision—a tell she knew he'd never been able to control as well as he wanted to.

"They're saying it happened in Košice," she commented, looking away.

"They would say that," he finally said. "Safer that way. Less connection to the dead soldier in Kraków."

McKenzie Reed. Melody didn't often mourn the dead—it would get exhausting in her line of work—but she did feel a splinter of regret over the soldier, queer and brave and loyal. McKenzie's girlfriend was a chatter analyst working the Russian beat at Langley, and when Melody had heard that McKenzie had died, Melody had gone to the analyst's desk and left a note under the keyboard with her phone number and a short note telling her to ask Melody for anything she needed: fighting the superiors for bereavement leave, untangling possessions and shared leases, or just someone who understood what she'd lost, anything.

"I'm sorry." Melody didn't touch her twin, but she did turn to face him fully. "I am so sorry."

He nodded, accepting her honesty, accepting also all the things that she would never say to him. *It's going to be okay; time heals all wounds; everything happens for a reason.*

She did say, "Everyone knows it wasn't your fault. Everyone knows Lackland facilitated the meeting and forgot to tell the army liaison after we gave it the green light. Everyone knows this is what happens when we let the goddamn NSA try to help."

Mark tore his eyes away from whatever memories he'd been staring at in the trees and looked at her. "Lackland didn't forget. He made sure that we'd be there, in a city crawling with patrolling soldiers, in an alley with a known adversary. I think he wanted that informant dead, and he wanted anyone who knew what the informant knew to die too."

Melody's eyes narrowed the slightest amount as she studied her brother. Neither of them was prone to conspiracies, but they didn't have any illusions about the serpentine and needlessly convoluted schemes intelligence agencies dreamed up either. Was it possible that John Lackland, feckless and nepotistic, had committed treason in some ill-advised bid for power? Absolutely. Was it possible that he could do it *successfully*?

That, Melody doubted.

"We'd know if that were the case," she responded. "He's not smart enough, firstly, and secondly, he's too lazy to put together something like this, and across two agencies no less. Why would he risk his position? Future promotions?"

"I don't think it was his idea. I think he's connected to the group the informant was working for."

Ys was a rumor. Nothing more than a handful of sentences spoken by a man in an alley before he died, and sentences that sounded barely credible at that. Shadowy arms deals, warmongering for profit, corruption at the highest levels of power—and centuries of it. "We don't know that Ys is anything yet, much less that anyone on our side is involved."

"But if they are…"

Melody felt the smallest twinge of alarm. She trusted

Mark more than she trusted anybody alive, but she also knew him better than she knew herself, and she knew he wouldn't let this go. If he thought Eliot died because they were set up, betrayed, *sacrificed*, Mark would never, ever forget it.

She realized that the question she was about to ask was the one she should have asked the moment she saw him walking toward her in a black suit, a stolen silver watch glinting on his wrist.

"Mark, what are you going to do?"

Her twin's gaze slid up to the cemetery path where one or two people still lingered, talking in low, solemn tones. Eliot's picture was on an easel by his gravestone, and white magnolia flowers were everywhere, making a garden of an open grave. Lowered out of sight was the black casket trimmed in silver, its gleaming top now dulled with handfuls of dirt.

"This is the third option," he said without looking at her. "This is where it got us. We didn't get a goodbye. We didn't make anything better. Nobody even knows the actual city my husband died in. What is it for, Melody? What did those three bodies buy?"

"I've never known you to be precious about death," Melody said. "How many people have you killed? How many people have you watched die?"

He slanted a look at her. "Are you suggesting that I take my husband's death less personally?"

"I'm suggesting that it shouldn't change your viewpoint of the mission. Of how intelligence and special operations work."

There was something like a smile on his face now. It wasn't a happy smile or a brotherly one. It was precarious and sharp. Curved lips, white incisors.

"Well, it does change it," he said. "I'm going to find the person responsible for Eliot's death, and I'm going to kill them. And when I kill them, I'll make sure their body buys something much more expensive than a death notice with the wrong city on it."

"And what is that?"

"A fourth option."

And his smile grew even sharper.

one

MARK

IN MY DREAM, I'M STANDING BETWEEN TWO GRAVES.

It's winter, a wet winter that blusters and howls, and the wind tearing off the sea is nakedly homicidal. I ignore it, because it's the same sea I've grown up beside, the same wind.

I know its moods, and today, its mood matches mine.

The graves are not in a graveyard but in a walled garden on a headland pressing out to the west, a clenched fist of rock striking at the setting sun. There is a formidable stronghold here, the seat of my power, fortifications and a great hall and a barracks, the spaces between filled with countless dwellings and the small Christian chapel I allowed to be built years ago.

In the summer, the turquoise water below the headland is filled with ships bringing wine and wealth, ready to bear away my tin and bronze. Across a narrow spit of stone is the mainland, where a large town thrives, smoke rising from its large houses and small halls. On Beltane night, you can see the torches and fires burning from here. Sometimes you can even hear their drums over the waves.

But it is winter now, and the headland is shrouded in mist, and there are no ships and there are no fires and there are no drums.

Even in this garden, with its high stone walls, with the memory of bright summers and full baskets bound for the kitchens, there is nothing. No light, no life. Just the wet and the wind and two grown-over graves.

Of course, there is some life here, and I know it as well as the dream version of myself knows it. The garden has gone to waste over the last several years, the roses dead and the herbs gone wild, but two things have thrived despite the neglect, despite the lack of gardeners, and despite the bitter watering of my grief.

A hazel tree and a twisting hunt of honeysuckle. Far larger than they have any right to be for how young they are.

The hazel tree, growing from a dead knight's grave, has already spread its branches wide, and the honeysuckle, growing from a dead queen's, has crept its way over to the tree and climbed, twined, wrapped itself around every branch it could. In the summer, it's nearly impossible to tell where one ends and the other begins, since it's all a thicket of vibrant green leaves and pink and yellow flowers, but in the winter, it's easier. Only the honeysuckle has held on to some of its green.

I move between the graves, and as I often do, I sink to my knees between them. Finger the dying leaves caught in the long grass. Leaves that were grown out of soil so precious I won't let anyone else near it.

My dead knight. *My* dead queen.

In this cold, empty garden because of me.

two

MARK

PRESENT DAY

I'M NOT SORRY. I THINK IT'S IMPORTANT THAT YOU KNOW this about me—that you understand this.

I'm not sorry. I'd do it again.

It's selfish to do what I'm doing, but everything I've done since I kissed my bodyguard on the roof of my club has been selfish. Everything since my engagement to Isolde Lawrence, since founding Lyonesse, since watching my husband bleed to death under the cover of night and opera music.

I can dress it up as justice; I can dress it up as revenge; maybe I can even dress it up as love…But I know the truth. I know myself. I *want*. I want like a hungry wolf; I want like the sea lashing at the rocks. I want senselessly and ceaselessly and entirely.

I want my wife back. I want my bodyguard.

I want a hand around their throats and the salt of their tears stinging my lips.

I don't take the usual way to Morois House but instead

park a few miles away in a private, unmarked lane and press through the snow-caught heather until I reach the edge of the woods and leave the moor behind. On the narrow path leading into the valley and to the house itself, I keep to the grass and the rocks as much as possible to avoid making tracks—an old habit. One I learned here, in fact, along-side Melody and our older sister, Blanche. My grandfather, retired MI6, would play long games of hide-and-seek with us in these woods, teaching us how to hide during a sunny day and during a rainy one, how to find cover when the light was good and when the light was bad. He taught us the names of the flowers and the birds, how you could use the latter to assess whether anyone was coming close, how you could throw sticks and rocks against the trees to confuse a pursuer, how you could double back, triple back, go in circles to make your trail impossible to follow.

One day, he took my sisters and me on a long walk to a stone circle, half fallen over and overgrown with grass and wildflowers. The trees were too thick for the local farmers to let their sheep graze, my grandfather explained, and aside from the occasional rambler hoping to end up in a pub, no one came there. It was on the Ordnance Survey maps, but it was difficult to get to, and with the photogenic shores of Tintagel so close, why would anyone bother? Cornwall has plenty of standing stones, dolmens, and cairns that come with more convenient parking and fewer brambles, and besides, most visitors weren't coming for the history; they were coming for the sea.

But we weren't visitors, not the Trevena family, not even the last American flowering of it, and Grandad wanted us to know. He insisted that the Trevenas had once used these stone circles in times gone by, that we came from the people that built them five thousand years ago, that his own grandad took him to this very spot and told him that Trevenas must never forget who they were: bronze, stone, sea.

Melody, even at that age, was too practical to care about something as intangible as an ancestral past, and Blanche immediately made a romance of it, but I knew what our grandfather was giving us that day, and it wasn't a homily about the beauty of Cornwall. It wasn't an invitation into a legacy.

It was a warning.

Trevenas *outlast*. Trevenas are cruel. We are salt-skinned and thorned with gorse, and we worshipped capricious gods long after the saints began crawling over our hills. We have hearts of tin and minds of slate, and we do not flinch.

Grandad was M16; *his* grandfather returned from the Great War with three German cavalry pennants and not a single ounce of shell shock; and his grandfather before him was the last of the great Cornish smugglers. My own mother had been a mergers and acquisitions shark in the City, carving up corporations and portfolios with clever, monstrous slices, a shark who made her husband take her name after their wedding because she refused to have a new plaque etched for her firm's office. The only softness we ever saw of her before she died was her love for our father, who was a gentle man. Blanche inherited his sweetness, his generosity, his goodness. Melody and I inherited his crooked pinkie fingers and nothing else; we twins were Trevena through and through.

It's something I think about often these days, who I am. What I am.

If I were a different man, would I be sneaking through the mostly naked trees toward my own house right now? Would I have a fine red ridge on my throat from the night my wife almost killed me? An ugly knot of scar tissue on my shoulder from the time I was stabbed?

Would I have played the game, moving piece after piece on a board I couldn't see the edges of, for years and years, just to have both of them in my power?

I exhale slowly. It doesn't matter. I'm not a different man, and I'm not about to become one.

Although as I hear a melody floating over the wet, snow-patched graveyard, I almost wish that weren't the case. I almost wish that I were good, *normal*, the kind of warmhearted and generous lover that could follow the sound of singing to its source and greet it with a smile and open arms.

Instead, I lean my shoulder against the trunk of a tree and close my eyes and listen.

Tristan is singing.

I've never heard anyone sing quite like Tristan, like his heart has slipped onto his tongue, like it's not really singing if you don't leave a little arterial spatter on the floor when you're done. And not in a tortured way, not in a way that implies labor or pain. More like someone offering their kidney without a second thought. Like someone taking off their coat in the cold and draping it over your shoulders instead.

It's too generous; I don't deserve it. Neither does Isolde. The two of us deserve chants of penance or half-muffled opera music in the dark. We are the same that way.

He's singing "Hallelujah," and it charms me to think he considers himself the baffled king, the overthrown Samson. There is something so piquant about a good person thinking they are bad, about a strong person thinking they are weak. It is a devil in me—a devil just like Saul himself had—that I want to encourage this. That I want to croon in Tristan's ear that he is so bad, so very bad, that he is so weak to let me do the things he lets me do.

I finally open my eyes, starved enough for the sight of my soldier that it hurts like a stuck blade, and see him moving at the edge of the graveyard. Gathering sticks—for a fire later tonight maybe. He's wearing one of my old coats, a wool thing Eliot bought me after complaining about my jacket and its pragmatic layers of recycled polyester. And seeing Tristan in that coat—*at Morois*, in this place that meant so much to me and Eliot… I almost have to close my eyes again.

It reminds me of this last spring, of coming here for the annual lament I've allowed myself over the years. Of looking up to see Tristan in the library, his green eyes brimming with concern, his lips parted enough to show the shine of his tongue.

God, what I'd felt then.

Anger, sawtooth anger, and a grief that wouldn't stop bleeding. Lust like razor wire in my belly.

I did warn him, you know, and you can't say that I didn't.

With the screen of the trees, I can only see fractions of him, subdivisions of dark, overgrown hair and wool-clad shoulders. Gloved hands—his unknowingly wicked hands. Cradled wood. I watch him bend one last time for a stick and then straighten. He goes toward the house still singing, and like a sailor after a siren, I follow, helpless to do otherwise.

She's in there, I know, waiting for him. With her honey hair and her unusual mouth, made while God was in a playful mood. With her turquoise eyes and her features so delicately shaped that you'd think she was part porcelain doll.

She is not a porcelain doll, obviously. Dolls don't murder people.

I move silently toward the house, keeping to the trees and then to the chapel. Dusk comes early during a Cornish winter, and it's easy to stay in the gloaming, in the cold obscurity of the shadows, until I'm looking into the conservatory. And there I see her, wearing a white shirt—mine—and linen pants—also mine—with my ring on her finger. The light inside the house trims her in shades of pearl and gold, and she could be a holy card right now, *Our Lady of Perpetual Knives*, a saint of masochism and lies. And Tristan—kissing her over the bundle of sticks before he carries them into the library—could be a knight in a stained glass window. Glowing with purity and carrying the weight of chivalry on his shoulders, drawn for a fairy tale but sculpted in war.

What do they think of me, I wonder, after a month away? Isolde, the loyal saint, Tristan, the valiant hero? Knowing what they know of me now? Having had time to put the pieces together…perhaps not all of them but enough. Enough of those bloody, jagged pieces.

At Lyonesse, they think me furious; they think me brokenhearted. Mark, the untouchable lord, the dominant of dominants, cuckolded in grand fashion by two *submissives*, his wife and his bodyguard if you can believe it. Mark, who sits in the hall at night with his inscrutable features, who hasn't touched anyone to play or to fuck since his wife left him for another man.

I guess it was too much to hope that their elopement would go unnoticed, not after I was found zip-tied to my office chair the morning after.

Sedge would have stayed silent, I think, preferring to let his dislike of my bride and bodyguard fill the quiet cracks of conversations and linger in the pale gray flicks of his gaze. But Andrea has always hated this part of the plan, the *Tristan and Isolde* part of the plan, and perhaps, given everything that's happened, she was right to.

At any rate, she saw no need to preserve either Isolde's reputation or Tristan's, and within a day, it had spread far past the club, past DC, all the way to the edges of the globe. Lyonesse members from São Paulo to Singapore knew. Other kink club owners knew; Isabella Beroul's dominant reached out to me from Montreal; Nimue called me with advice that felt like something from a fortune cookie or maybe one of Tristan's novels about dragons. *Good rulers are merciful, Mark, as well as just.*

The fucking president of the United States called me to offer his condolences. And he just laughed when I asked him through my teeth if he hadn't been the runaway bodyguard in this scenario. *Yes, but the difference is that Greer's husband would have never let us run away*, he'd purred.

So anyway, the entire world knows what happened that night.

I'm cuckolded. I'm spurned. I'm humiliated. The young bride and the bright-eyed bodyguard, always such strange choices for a man like me, have stolen themselves away in the night along with my pride and my heart (although I'd rather be zip-tied to my office chair again than admit that last part to anyone else).

So, my singing Tristan, who tied whom to the kitchen chair? Who stole the throne and cut the hair? I thought I was every villain, every Saul and every Delilah, and yet here I am, the broken one, the overthrown. Watching the two people I reluctantly—oh God, they have no idea *how fucking reluctantly*—offered my affection to while they kiss each other, while they wear my clothes, while they carry my sticks.

Isolde stands in the middle of the house as Tristan disappears into the library, her hand drifting to her collarbone as she seems to stare at nothing in particular. The T-shirt she wears is far too big for her, and it exposes her slender throat and the dip of her clavicle; it hangs from the compact curves of her shoulders. You'd have no idea that under those baggy clothes were the coiled muscles of a predator, that the elegant hand at the base of her throat is the same hand responsible for the scar on my own. The same hand that has severed arteries, started fires, poisoned drinks, and has unflinchingly done so. My little demon, my little murderess. A swell of fond pride surges in my chest when I think of how she fought me in my office the night she left. Tristan interrupted

16

us (and stole my attention for a crucial second), but I could have happily fought her for hours. The very first time we met, she was still learning how to hold a knife, how to face someone else holding one, and taking her down had been as easy as walking forward. And now look at her.

I step back into the gloom of a magnolia tree just as she lifts her eyes, abruptly alert. She searches the shadows through the conservatory's windows as she steps closer, every line of her taut and alert, and oh God, how I'd like to come closer just now and show my face, just to see what she does.

Would she fight? Flee?

She wouldn't freeze or fawn, not my wife.

Tristan would come and—and what? Help her run away again? Try to fight for her, which would be as adorable as it was unnecessary?

But I don't step forward. I stay cloaked in darkness, utterly still, until she closes her eyes and shakes her head once, like she's chastising herself for seeing things. She shouldn't—she is correct that danger lies outside her door— but this close, I can see the dark smudges under her eyes and the sharp cut to her jaw. The last month has worn away at her like it's worn away at me.

I don't bother to suppress the bitter satisfaction I take in that.

She goes into the library then, and I sigh up at the magnolia branches above me, low and sprawling, and lumped with half-melted snow. My hand goes to the small chess piece I've taken to carrying everywhere with me. A queen made of cold, hard crystal.

What am I doing here? What did I hope would happen? That I'd stroll inside and they'd drop to their knees and beg my forgiveness? That they'd apologize for the one thing worse than their infidelity, which was their absence?

That they'd accept that I had planned to kill Isolde's

uncle—that I planned to kill him still? That I'd manipulated them both, and in Isolde's case, that I'd done it for years?

No. Isolde might have spared my life, might even have meant it when she said she loved me, but she still ran. All those confessions of love from her and Tristan, all those promises of faithfulness, and all it took was one opened safe, and they were gone.

If Isolde had slit my throat, it would have hurt less.

No, I suppose I'm too realistic to have hoped for anything by coming here. I don't deserve their forgiveness or understanding, and I won't deserve it at any point in my life, because I would do it all again. I'm going to keep doing it.

I came to Morois because yesterday, I had a dream where I stood in a wind-haunted garden and stared at honeysuckle leaves caught in the dead grass. I can still smell the wet stone of the garden walls. I can feel the damp earth soaking through my clothes. I can feel the leaves between my fingers, brittle and light, so different from the velvet petals of summer.

So much for the honeysuckle. The bad luck came anyway.

I woke up from the dream and booked a flight to England. For no other reason than to reassure myself that they were still alive, my sweet adulterers. Than to see with my own eyes that they were not buried near the sea.

But now that I have seen them, I should go, I should leave. That's what a logical person would do. I don't have time to check on two people who think they're good at hiding.

In fairness, Morois was an inspired choice on their part, because it's unknown to my enemies, only vaguely known by my employees, and only personally known by Blanche and Melody. The security system is closed, so I don't have eyes on the property when I'm not there, and it's isolated enough that there are no neighbors to notice if it's occupied or not.

Unfortunately, all the inspired choices in the world

wouldn't have changed a thing. It wouldn't have changed the little blue dots on the screen of my phone…or the pretty rings on their pretty, perfect fingers tracking their every move.

I've known they were at Morois since the minute they boiled their first kettle of tea, but I resisted coming, because what would have been the point?

And there's still no point—except that I had a bad dream, and there was no sleeping, no eating, no *thinking*, until I knew they were both alive and that their traitorous little hearts still beat in their dear, duplicitous chests.

So I should slip back through the trees and over the moor to my car. If I'm already on the other side of the Atlantic, I might as well see to some business, and I should see to it quickly.

I'm afraid for her sake that I will have to kill him first. I'm afraid for the sake of all future love between us that I will enjoy it.

But I don't move. I stay where I'm at, watching the doorway Isolde went through, rooted like a tree. Rotting like old fruit.

From the library window, a fire flickers.

three

MARK

I SNEAK IN THROUGH A WINDOW ON THE NORTH SIDE, EASING through the messy slush of grass and snow to a window my grandfather added to the house as a younger man. It has a catch hidden in the frame, invisible unless you know it's there, and it allows one to unlock the window from the outside—perfect for paranoid spies.

Or spurned husbands.

I don't realize how cold I am until I'm inside, and I take a moment to warm myself before shucking my wet shoes, coat, and gloves and moving into the depths of the house. The flagged floors hide the weight of my steps, and I know exactly how to slip past the library doors to avoid being detected—even by Isolde. Her senses might be sharper than Tristan's, but my wife has never had to sneak cookies past a Cold War spy with a twin sister in tow.

The lovers have closed the library doors to keep in the heat, but no matter. The warped Jacobean paneling in the far corridor doubles as the back of a bookshelf, and a gap in the wood gives me a view into the room. It was how Melody and I would check to see if Grandad had fallen asleep in his chair before we crept into the kitchen, and now it shows me Isolde in that very same chair, although she's not asleep. Her borrowed linen pants are off, and my bodyguard's shoulders are wedged between her fair thighs.

Dancing firelight makes flashing glimpses of the scene. The strong grip of Tristan's hands on her knees; the dark curl of hair at the nape of his neck; Isolde's erect nipples poking through the white T-shirt.

Her pearl-colored hair is up in a messy knot on top of her head, fallen strands brushing against a shoulder that's been bared, and her throat is in a long arch as Tristan runs his tongue along her core.

He's taken off the wool coat from earlier, wearing just a henley and jeans, but his boots are still on, like he didn't have the patience to take them off before going down on my wife. Even with his clothes on, there's no hiding the shift and pull of his muscles as he moves at his work, as he spreads Isolde's thighs farther apart. As his hips flex unconsciously.

Heat thrums through me, blistering and shapeless, as I watch Isolde's fingers moving through Tristan's hair. His jeans are stretched over his hips and the firm curves of his backside. It's harrowing to see. Dangerous for me and for him.

It was in this very library that I had him for the first time. I'd tried to avoid it, I really did—because he's my sister Blanche's stepson and also for the sake of my plans. For the sake of the innocence still shining from his bright eyes, an innocence he'd clung to despite war and death and the stubborn belief of an entire country that being a hero is the best thing a person can be rather than the loneliest. It was bad enough that I'd hired Tristan at all, but to use him like a concubine felt wrong even to me.

I just…hadn't planned on liking him so much.

And when I'd been fucked up over Eliot, drunk and lost in the memories of marrying under falling magnolia petals—to have Tristan Thomas kneeling at my feet, lips parted, eyes greener than jewels—

I am only mortal, you understand. And I've never claimed to be a hero.

On the other side of the bookshelf, Isolde is having an orgasm against Tristan's mouth, a long, shivering climax that has her back arched and her eyes closed. Tristan has a thumb buried in the muscles of her thigh, and I can see the pain sizzling through her like a current. She believes she deserves it, pain, and because she believes she deserves it, it's the only thing that sets her free. Makes her clean of her sins, and she has so many of those, even I won't argue about that.

Tristan lifts his face to hers, his lips wet and shining in the fire, and says, so I can barely hear him, "What you did last night… Can you do it again?"

Isolde opens her eyes and slides both of her hands down to cup his jaw. Her expression is tender—Tristan is so hard not to be tender toward—but I see a new tension in her body. I don't think Tristan is aware of it, because he gives a relieved shudder when Isolde nods.

"Thank you," he whispers.

I'm genuinely curious now—more than the morbid curiosity of a betrayed husband, more than the abject lust of the spying cuckold—and I watch as Isolde leans back in the chair. Pantsless, in a too-large T-shirt, her cunt still exposed, she suddenly looks like a queen. All five foot two of her, with her doll face and her faint freckles. Her chin is lifted, and her upper lip holds the barest hint of a sneer.

"Undress," she says.

The change in Tristan is immediate, heartbreaking almost. His head drops, and his chest heaves, and how many times have I seen this before? The grateful submission, the mindless ache that only a firm hand can soothe?

With his eyes down, Tristan gets to his feet and efficiently pulls his shirt over his head and then toes off his boots and socks. The jeans and boxer briefs come last, worked off and then folded neatly with the shirt and socks, the boots perfectly parallel on top of the pile, like it's awaiting a sergeant's inspection. My darling West Point boy.

The clench deep in my gut becomes painful as I watch Tristan step in front of Isolde. It's not only the nakedness of him—the heavy limbs and flat navel, the dark hair on his thighs and the most beautiful part of him stretching out in swollen offering—but the space between the two of them, the vulnerability and authority rendered into a firelit silhouette. Isolde and Tristan are playing Dom and sub, and I've never imagined this, never even considered its possibility, and yet I am completely riveted by it, by Tristan's bowed head and Isolde's curled lip.

She's more than *playing* a dominant. She's doing it and doing it well, although I can see what Tristan cannot: the twitch of her fingers on the arms of the chair, the swallow before she speaks again. But when she does speak, her voice is level and a little hard.

"On the floor," she says. "Flat on your back."

The instruction—tame enough on its own—drips with disdain, and Tristan trembles. But he complies immediately, the quick, utilitarian movements of a soldier, and soon he's supine on the imported carpet in front of the fireplace, his hands by his sides, his cock lifting up from his body and leaving strings of precum caught between his tip and his stomach.

He sucks in a breath as Isolde stands and moves so that she's next to him. She lifts a dainty foot, and even though I can't see it from here, I know the motion exposes the secret

23

pink flesh between her legs. He can't breathe properly at all now, his fingers scratching at the carpet as she lowers her foot and presses it to his erection.

"Please," he begs. "Please."

"Look at you, pleading for this," she says. "You must need it so badly."

She grinds her foot against him as she speaks, and he arches into the humiliating friction, throat straining.

"I can't imagine how much it hurts," she tells him, grinding harder. "Craving something so much, especially after you were so good to me." Her voice is still cool, but the praise is sincere, and she's doing a marvelous job with him, threading the needle between stealing the power he wants so badly to be stolen and actual debasement.

Like all good soldiers, Tristan wants to obey. He wants to do a good job. He wants to be *made* to do a good job. Humiliation, punishment, pain—they are all in service of that one need, and it takes a perceptive dominant to see the subtle distinctions inside a submission like Tristan's. He craves the raw clarity of helplessness, of smallness, of being forced, but it doesn't mean he can go without seeing his top's satisfaction and pleasure in him. The *used* feeling only feels good when it's inside a place where he belongs, whether it's because he's signed some papers or because he's—however foolishly—surrendered his heart.

Some people want to have their dick stepped on but *not* be called a disgusting piece of shit while it's done to them. What can I say? The taxonomy of fucking is endless. Chacun à son goût and all that.

Tristan's thighs are splayed as his heels rub against the carpet, and I can see the space under his testicles, the shadows and firm curves of his ass. I'm hard inside my trousers, but I curl my hands into fists and press them against the paneling, refusing to touch myself. It was bad enough when the two of them were on the yacht, fucking every chance they got, and I could watch Tristan screw like a soldier on leave whenever I wanted. I could watch Isolde in all those pretty clothes I'd picked out for her, just as breathtaking during a thalassic romance as she'd been when I'd broken her hymen on her father's desk. For those strange ten days, I'd barely recognized myself, excusing myself from business, from the hall, sneaking off to watch my bodyguard and my bride fuck all over my yacht like Adam and Eve before the fall, like they'd never fucked before, even though I'd historically fucked both of them within an inch of their lives.

I nearly jerked myself raw that week.

Tristan is close to climax now, has probably been close since the moment he tasted Isolde, and he's twisting on the carpet like he's being tortured with hot coals. I can't see Isolde's eyes or even her face; from here, I can only see that her neck is curved, that her attention is completely on him, that it's effortless for her to balance on one leg while she chafes his erection with the sole of her foot.

And then, with a precision it takes some dominants years to learn, she lifts her foot in the crucial moment before Tristan erupts. His flesh gives an unhappy, enervated lurch, and then fluid drips from the end, leaving a small pool on his belly. Like a dab of pearlescent paint on a painter's palette.

I want to smear it up to his chest and watch it shine in the light of the fire.

Tristan's whimper is one of utter misery. I, of course, am an artist of misery, a priest of it. Hearing that whimper, I know he could give me so many more. I know I could push him, torment that blood-flushed cock of his until the skin is pulled so tight that it shines even when it's dry. I could have him sobbing.

But Isolde is still learning, maybe, or just impatient. She pounces on him like a cat on a mouse—if a cat could pounce on a mouse twice its size—and is over him on all fours, kissing him hard enough that he grunts.

I hear that grunt like I made it myself, and my fingers curl even harder against themselves. I won't masturbate watching the two of them, I *won't*. Even an unrighteous man has to have his dignity.

My body doesn't care about dignity, however, and I don't have to look down to see the tent in my trousers. Every part of me is stretched like a wire even before Isolde sits on top of Tristan's hips and strokes his penis with her slick cunt, and then by the time she's begun rocking on top of him, my forehead is pressed to the paneling, my arms braced above my head, my heart pounding.

Tristan tries to push inside her, but she doesn't let him at first, lifting away or leaning forward, a slow game of chess. Pressing, retreating, pressing, retreating.

Until he's begging, beautifully, pleading with her to let him inside, to make it stop hurting, to *please* let him make her feel good. She could torment him like this for as long as she pleased—God knows I could keep him trembling in this state for an entire night—but her own patience must be at its breaking point. She reaches between them and fits his length to the entrance of her body. And then slowly sinks down.

"Oh God," Tristan mumbles, his eyes squeezing closed, his fingers digging into the carpet. Every muscle under his sweat-damp skin is quivering and tense, and his teeth clench together in barely endured agony.

For Isolde's part, she seems to feel much the same, because her thighs are already gripping his sides; her head is dropped back. She rides him hard, just like I've done on this very carpet, the direction of penetration less important than who is using whom, than the power stolen right out of Tristan's big, strong hands. She's using him to get herself off, and he is squeezed in agonized bliss, desperate not to come until she does, but it's nearly past any controlling now. He reaches up with a shaking hand, pushes it under the T-shirt she still wears, and palms her breast.

Hard, I think, judging by the sharp cry Isolde gives.

She comes again, this time on his cock, and suddenly, I find that I'm no longer in control of my own hand. It's reaching down, it's unfastening my trousers, and then I'm working myself hard enough that it hurts. But there's no choice, I have no choice, because something about my wife having an orgasm on top of another man has me unable to do anything else but give in.

And even with the T-shirt hanging down past her backside, even with her back to me, I see enough of her to fire every jealous, obsessive fantasy I've ever had. The slope of her neck. The upturned soles of her feet where they're tucked by Tristan's thighs. The hair in shades of gold and bone, just like in the handle of her favorite knife, the one I gave her knowing it would one day be streaked with blood like her fervent little soul.

It's her left hand I fixate on as she rides Tristan with darkly selfish prerogative. As she rolls her hips and drives every last ounce of stolen pleasure to the surface. Her ring flashes in the fire, the rubies and the gold, the pattern of honeysuckle wrought in permanent form. Etched on the inside of her ring are two words, the two words I've scored into my mind over and over again.

Quarto optio.

Tristan can't hold back any longer, and his entire body bows into one slow, juddering arch. A noise tears free of him—half gasp, half sob—like the orgasm is a mean thing sent to afflict him, and you'd think from the way he scratches at the carpet that he's being flayed alive.

Sweet puppy, my darling hero, unraveled by only the gentlest pull of a string.

I don't stop stroking myself as Tristan goes still, but I tell myself I'm going to, that I'm going to zip up and then step away, but just then, Isolde lifts to her knees above Tristan's hips. His organ slips free, and semen drips out after, sliding from her body onto his. Slowly and catching the light of the fire as it does.

Isolde reaches down, and I only realize what she's done when her left hand emerges shining and slick. She has Tristan's cum all over her wedding ring.

She pushes her wet fingers against his lips, and he loses it, flipping her over and entering her again with an animal grunt that sends hunger burning all the way through me. I should be in there right now; I should have them both at my disposal; I should be able to see that defiled wedding ring in as much detail as I want. I should be punishing them for this; I should be punishing myself with how good it feels to have them tear off pieces of a heart that I thought stopped beating in a damp alley eight years ago.

Tristan stabs into her over and over again, hard enough that I can hear it, deep enough that this well-bred heiress is completely uncivilized underneath him. Perspiration shimmers on his back, on the toiling muscles there, and I recognize this version of him from the yacht, from the surveillance footage I watched with a compulsion akin to addiction. Whatever goodness and chivalry are in him are gone, and now there's nothing left but the primal urge to take, to have. To possess. To come as hard and as much as he possibly can.

Ah, my poor hero and his breeding kink.

Isolde's fingers twist through his hair, tight, tight, like she's trying to hold on, and it's her left hand, and her wedding ring is still slippery with another man's seed, and even with all the delicious skin on offer, with Tristan's firm backside and the glimpses of Isolde's pink cunt, it's the ring that I'm staring at when the climax slams into me like an enemy charge. I stagger sideways, sucking in a sharp breath as it rips through my groin.

Cum splatters on the four-hundred-year-old paneling—a month's worth, what feels like years' worth, more and more, too much, not enough, oh God, it's not enough. Even as I'm painting antique wood with thick rivulets of white release, I know I need more, harder, *worse*. It's not enough to feel it sizzling up my thighs and churning in my groin. I want it burning me alive, charring my bones. I want there to be nothing left of me when I'm done.

There's still too much left of me when I'm done.

Inside the library, the lovers are cresting again, together, Tristan grunting into Isolde's neck and Isolde's heels digging into the small of Tristan's back as she pants out his name. Tristan stays on top of her for a long time after, his limbs slack and his face in her neck. She strokes his hair as the fire hisses and pops.

"We should go to bed," she says.

He nods but doesn't move. She keeps stroking his hair.

Meanwhile, I'm in a quiet fugue of my own. I'm stunned at myself, at my lack of self-control. I stare at the semen rolling down my wall and think, *How did I get here? How did they get so much power over me?*

This was supposed to be a game in the beginning, a gambit, the left flank of a battle plan that had been in place for years. I thought I could stay above it somehow, above the two of them, and I thought I could watch them together with the same detachment I'd feel watching two strangers at Lyonesse play.

I thought I could watch them fall in love. I thought I'd be utterly unaffected by it.

I was wrong.

four

MARK

I WISH I COULD SAY THAT I DON'T KNOW HOW LONG I STAND there after I zip up my pants, but the clock on the mantel tallies my weakness in relentlessly measured increments. Half an hour. I stand and watch the firelight dance over their exposed skin, watch Isolde's fingernails card through Tristan's hair. I can almost feel it between my own fingers, thick and soft, strong and silky. I sometimes wonder if the barber at West Point wept as they shaved Tristan's hair on R-Day.

Finally, Tristan pushes himself off the floor and lifts Isolde in his arms. She slips her arms around his neck, her eyes hooded but a faint pulling between her eyebrows. She's troubled, I think, but already resigned to worrying about whatever it is tomorrow, and it's a shame I'm not in there, because I would have made her as loose-limbed as Tristan. I would have made it so you had to ladle her off the carpet.

Maybe all husbands like to think so.

I ease back into the shadows of the corridor as Tristan emerges with Isolde, but I needn't have bothered. Tristan carries her off to my bedroom without so much as a glance in the opposite direction. Which is a good thing because I very nearly follow them, a sudden swell of possessiveness making me step forward, my hand lifted, like I'm reaching for them.

I catch myself before I do anything stupid—well, anything *else* stupid—and wait until I hear the bedroom door close. I give it a few more moments and then slip into the library.

Once inside, I sit at my desk, pull out a piece of paper and one of the heavy fountain pens left behind by my grandfather. It's not a long letter that I write. It doesn't have to be—Isolde won't believe a word of it anyway, and Tristan will be by her side regardless of what she chooses. And I don't hope I can convince Isolde that everything I said on our wedding night was real. Why would she believe me when she knows I've been false about so much else?

But I write the letter anyway. I won't say that I deserve her forgiveness, but neither does her uncle, and if she's going to resume her work as a saint of the Church, then she should know who she's really working for. And if she's not going to resume her work as a saint, then she needs to run.

Or come home to me.

I finish the letter and return the pen to where I found it, a strange ache in my throat as I look at the thick wooden ruler tucked neatly inside the drawer. I'd used that ruler on Tristan this spring. I'd layered neat red welts up his thighs like a ladder, and then I'd shoved him to the floor and climbed that ladder to heaven.

I used to have some degree of control, I think. The moment I felt it slipping with Isolde, I stepped back. I refused Tristan when he first begged me to use him, because I knew it was dangerous. I knew it was flirting with a darkness that I've kept carefully fenced for a very long time. I learned control in the army, in the Rangers, in the agency. I learned it on Eliot's body as he learned it on mine. I mastered it in the years after, when revenge burned like a sun inside my chest, when it choked me, when all I wanted to do was fly across an ocean and make everyone pay. I had nothing if I didn't have control.

I think of the cum still sliding down the paneling on the other side of the wall and rub my forehead with my hand, closing my eyes.

Where is that vaunted control now?

I get up and break apart the last smoldering log in the fire, thinking that I might need to add a stern postscript to my letter about fire safety, which I should *not* have to tell Tristan with his half-rural childhood, *or* Isolde, who is a consummate arsonist.

Satisfied that there's nothing but cooling embers left on the grate, I tuck the letter into my pocket and go into the kitchen, where I find a rag under the sink, and then I go back into the hallway to clean the mostly dried streaks off the wood.

If only the cuckold fetishists at Lyonesse could see me now, witness the solitary and ridiculous reality of scrubbing your cum off a wall while your wife sleeps in someone else's arms. Hardly the stuff of fantasies…unless your fantasies include a trip to the laundry room and serious consideration as to whether you need to polish the antique wood you just scrubbed clean.

As for my fantasies, well, I already lived them, didn't I? On a wicked Samhain night, the three of us together, both my sweet toys at my disposal, my wife mine to give to the little soldier who was mine to take.

It was perfect. For one night, it was absolutely perfect.

The rag goes into the basket in the laundry room, and then I go toward my bedroom, knowing this is a very bad idea and doing it anyway. A wise man would leave the letter on the kitchen table or stick it to the front door like his own dark, accusatory theses. A wise man would go back home and accept what he can't change.

But I have to see them one last time.

I want them.

I hate them.

I love them.

I'm careful as I open the door—the latch sometimes catches on the strike plate—and push it open with infinite slowness. The night is quiet, aside from whatever scraps of wind manage to pour in from the moor, and I imagine I can hear the thud of my heart against my ribs as I step inside the room. I almost want them to be awake, to scream at me, attack me, fall to my feet and nuzzle their faces against my thigh, but once I'm standing at the foot of the bed and my eyes adjust fully to the faint moonlight, I can see that they're both fast asleep, facing each other. Tristan's hand is folded protectively over Isolde's where it's curled between them.

And the jealousy nearly cuts me in half it's so sudden and sharp, not a sword but an axe, not made of steel but of loneliness and obsession.

This, more than any number of orgasms on the library floor, makes me want to claw the hills apart and boil the sea. My Tristan and my Isolde curled toward each other like a set of beautiful parentheses, the heartbreaking clasp of hands, the tangle of feet under the blanket.

I could laugh if I could breathe. Mark Trevena, famously jaded, famously immoral, and he's furious over *cuddling*. And I should have known—I should have fucking known because I was seething when Andrea told me about Tristan and Isolde in Belgrade, when I learned that Isolde broke her promise to me. But it was the ensuing realization that they'd been pining for each other like characters in a fairy tale that broke me apart. That they've been slipping through each other's thoughts, that they've been catching glances across the room. That any unexpected blush on their cheeks might have come from a secret flame whose warmth never touched my skin.

I felt a reasonable envy when it came to their lust, but when it comes to this? I am unreasonable beyond compare. I am livid with distrust and spite; I am as resentfully possessive as one of those dragons Tristan is always reading about.

I am mortally wounded by them holding hands.

I step forward, managing to drag in a breath as I do, some kind of swelling recklessness making me dizzy with possibility, with impending disaster. *Me*, I'm the disaster, and I will bring the full force of myself upon them, I will remind them that they pledged themselves to me, promised their hearts to me—

I pull up short at the foot of the bed. Something is gleaming just below their linked hands. Isolde's knife, as cold as the sky outside, as sharp as my love for them. Inches away from Isolde's hand, as if she wanted to be able to grab it at any moment.

To defend against an intruder? To defend against me?

The thought does what no amount of logic can do, and it stops me. It arrests the crazed obsession still pumping through my veins.

She ran away from you. She chose Tristan and she ran away from you. With good reason.

Running away was smart; it's what anyone with any shred of sense should have done. And I'm glad she has Tristan with her, even if it hurts like hell to see her with someone trustworthy and honest and good, even if it means he chose her over me.

They should be wary of me. They should want nothing to do with me. I should be met with the point of a knife.

I breathe out. It's better this way, and I know it: this had been part of my original plan after all. The two of them

34

together, and me forgotten, existing to them only in scraps of memory and bad dreams.

I'll leave. They're safe here, they have each other, and they need not worry that I'll come drag them out of their idyll just for the sake of my pride or my revenge. I'll have revenge enough without them.

But...hopelessly, selfishly...I want one last piece of them. Something I can hold on to.

So I take Isolde's knife.

Deftly but silently, I reach over her sleeping form and replace the knife with the one I brought with me, a blade made of matte black nylon and glass fiber, sharp enough to cut paper. I leave the letter underneath it.

I don't dare to kiss them, so I let myself imagine it, a brush of my lips over a cheek or along a jaw. I imagine crawling between them and pulling them both into my arms and sleeping until the late, gray daybreak of December comes and I can afflict them with myself as I so love to do.

And then I leave the lovers sleeping at Morois House, my knife between them and the truth too, and I accept that my heart—as hard and pointed and resistant to light as the blade now on the bed—is left there too.

I find my coat and my shoes in the laundry room, and I see myself out, careful not to leave tracks in the snow-splotched yard. They don't need to know how I got in.

A husband should have some secrets yet.

five

MARK

Once I reach my car, I make a call with the burner I picked up once I got to the country. Afterward, the phone gets knocked back to factory settings and dropped in an electronics recycling box in Exeter, where I also leave the pseudonymously rented car and walk to a station to board a train bound for London. I have a stocking hat pulled over my head and the collar of a battered secondhand coat turned up, and there's a pebble in my right shoe to hobble my usual lengthy stride.

It's not a perfect disguise—nothing is in a place as surveilled as England—but it's enough to make someone work to find me when they comb through the CCTV footage. That's as much as I need at the moment.

The London clockmaker has a shop behind a shit-splattered sidewalk in Croydon, and she's expecting me when I walk in. Clockmakers aren't a chatty bunch, so I'm not surprised when she wordlessly disappears into the back before I can even reach the counter.

I poke around the cases of watches and tabletop timepieces, watch the clocks on the wall tick in perfect unison. Behind the desk, a neat row of clocks shows the times across the globe.

The shop is cluttered but sparkling, unlike the battered storefront outside, and when the clockmaker emerges from the back, I get a glimpse of a well-ordered room with stacks of notepads, a shelf of atlases, and a fax machine made of yellowing plastic.

The clockmaker hands me a piece of paper. The clockmaker in Singapore is fond of coordinates, but here in London, things are a little quainter, and I just get a name. *Place Seffarine.*

I look up at the clockmaker. Her expression tells me that she knows exactly what I'm about to ask and that I'd better not. But *Fez*? I might as well search for a needle in a haystack in the dark. With gloves on.

I glance up at the clocks on the wall and mentally triangulate how long this little detour might take and then decide it doesn't matter. It might be yet another dead end, one more wasted trip, but I'll regret it if I don't try to find this man.

"They said he was a priest," the clockmaker says unexpectedly, dipping her head toward the paper in my hand. Even though we're alone in the shop, I'm a little surprised. Getting anything approaching context or detail or explanation from a clockmaker is almost unheard of. An SIS relic from the Cold War, the clockmakers operate on an older set of rules, the chief rule being that the less everyone knows, the better. A rule that's kept the clockmaking operation ticking through the decades, as counterterrorism overtook all other concerns, as private actors slowly started filtering into the business of intelligence and covert action. The clockmakers will work with almost anyone for the right price—provided Vauxhall Cross doesn't consider them a threat—but there's a difference between the SIS titrating out tidbits of information and them handing over everything they know about a subject.

"He was," I say and fold the paper into a crisp square. "He worked in the archives of the Vatican."

Professional interest flickers in the clockmaker's eyes. I know she's imagining what she could do with only a day in those archives, the secrets she could find to write on little pieces of paper for ridiculous sums.

"He's been hopping cities every few months," she says. "He knows how to hide, and now he's in Fez. In the medina."

In other words, he's in one of the easiest places to hide in the world.

She seems to come to some kind of decision. "You should know that someone else was asking after him. Three days ago."

Fuck.

"Who were they?" I ask, knowing she won't answer, and she doesn't. Clockmakers don't stay in business by revealing the identities of their customers.

"Best of luck," she says, and then she disappears into the back.

———

Fez is hectic but picturesque as I navigate the medina—an eight-hundred-acre warren of souks, mosques, and dead-end lanes. The streets are packed with stalls, vendors, and pack mules; fountains gurgle from hidden corners and unseen courtyards; cats dart everywhere. When I hear the din of hammers against copper, I slow my gait and stroll into Place Seffarine, one hand in the pocket of my tan suit. I become the picture of a tourist at leisure. I stop at the shops and chat with the coppersmiths in British-accented French, and I gradually piece together a sense of the square.

Most of the nearby buildings are low, two or three stories at most, with shuttered windows and cafés wedged onto rooftops. There's a madrasa on one side, with the occasional clump of students entering or leaving via the horseshoe arch, and vendors have spread out their wares on the steps rising up to the far end of the square, calling out to locals and tourists alike.

It's a noisy, busy place. A place where you can pass through without standing out.

I buy a few trinkets I don't need and then find a spot in a café with a cup of black coffee and a discarded newspaper, which I pretend to read while I observe the square from above.

I haven't forgotten that this is the worst part of intelligence work. Waiting and watching. Beating off boredom with a stick, keeping my thoughts from drifting to the endless unknowns.

Unknowns like whether my runaway priest will wait to leave his bolt-hole when the shadows stretch over the streets of the medina, or whether he'll trust the bustle of the square and brazenly go about his business during the day. Whether he's changed physically since the last known photo of him was taken. Whether he's alone.

Whether he's dangerous.

The café is sheltered from the briskest of the December breezes, but I'm grateful for my jacket and the fresh coffee as morning rolls into afternoon. An orange tabby hops into the chair next to me and cleans his paws. I stroke his ears while I read and drink more coffee. I think about cappuccinos and my bodyguard. I think about espresso cups cradled in my wife's slender, deadly hands.

I had a plan once, and it went like this: get revenge, and probably die in the process. It was a thing of clarity and purpose, and for all its moving parts, the reason behind it was as present as a hatchet buried in my chest. They killed what I loved, so I would kill all of them.

But then came Isolde. Isolde who fainted after crawling

to me because subspace hit her so hard; Isolde who used the honeysuckle knife I gave her to kill wicked priests.

Then came Tristan, who only wanted one thing while he was deployed, and that was a kiss. Who went to Ireland to get my bride for me because I asked, even though it lacerated his heart to do it.

And now I don't even know what the hell to do with my plan. I was supposed to care about *nothing*, and now I care about *two* things, and it's a little fucking irritating, if I'm honest.

There's a flicker of movement from one of the doorways opening into the square, and it would be easy to ignore, to forget, except I see a hand come up, then down, then side to side. The sign of the cross.

Instantly alert, I watch as a white man wearing a zip-up and jeans—tourist clothes—drops his hand, steps into the square, and starts walking toward one of the narrow lanes leading out to the rest of the medina. Small drops gleam darkly in his wake—blood, dripping from the hem of his jeans.

I toss my newspaper on the table, wedge some dirhams under the coffee cup, and stride out of the café. I nearly lose him as I shoulder my way down the lane he chose, but I catch sight of the dark green zip-up and curly brown hair as we walk past the university. He's found a baseball cap—or he had it already—and is pulling it over his head as he makes a sharp left turn down an even busier lane. Carpet stores and clothing stores have their doors flung open, and vendors have parked their wheeled carts between, selling everything from bottled water to dried scorpions.

I'm decently good at following people, if I'm allowed the self-praise, but my quarry seems to be just as good at evading a tail. He turns often, he doesn't shy away from crowds, and he uses the narrow lanes and congested corners to his advantage. I'm staying on him, but only *just*, and that's when he throws a glance over his shoulder. Just the one, but it's long enough to see me, which shouldn't matter—the medina is full of tourists, and I'm able to play the role of feckless British tourist quite well—but it does matter. And I have a beat after he bolts down the next lane he comes upon to appreciate that he must know who I am. It doesn't narrow down the list of people who'd like to run away from me, but it gives me an idea of what I'm in for.

I sigh and then take off after him, wishing that for once, things could be easy. Haven't I earned that? Something easy? Jesus.

He's fast, but so am I, and I gain on him as we tear past cafés and bazaars and piles of cats sleeping in the sun. I'd rather not be running in a linen suit and leather shoes, but I've operated in tuxedos, in dress shoes—and once in a full Venetian carnival costume and volto mask—so this isn't too bad, and despite the pinch in my feet and despite having to fumble for the leather gloves in my pocket to pull them on as I run, I've almost caught up to him when he ducks down by a fountain, turns, and scoops up something from the ground to throw at me.

I have only a second to register ears and a bushed tail—that motherfucker *threw a cat at me*—before I manage to catch the animal against my chest. Claws sink into my biceps and above my ribs; I hear a frantic hiss. It takes me precious seconds to disentangle the stray cat from my suit jacket and set it carefully on the ground. As far as diversions go, it was an effective one, because now I'm bleeding from the arm, I can't see my quarry, and this cat is perfectly fucking unharmed, turning around to hiss at me as I start running again, like I'm the one at fault here.

It's luck that I see the flash of movement up ahead, just a dart through the crowd, and I shove past people trying to sell bouquets of mint or purses into a leather goods store, which is mostly empty. I emerge onto a terrace overlooking a tannery and choke on the foul air. Vats of cow urine, pigeon feces, and lime dot the courtyard below, and beyond them are deep wells of dye—henna, saffron, indigo—and everywhere are wet animal skins, some raw, some fully processed. Across the tanneries, I see a group of tourists heading back inside a store from their viewing terrace with handfuls of mint held to their faces, and then finally on the terrace below, I spot the man I'm chasing. He casts a quick look back at me before he hops the final half story down to the tannery itself.

I jump after him, landing with a flinch as my thirty-six-year-old knees absorb the shock, and then jump again until I'm down on the level with the vats and skins, among the fetid air of the tannery.

I'd kill for even a sprig of mint right now.

The man hoists himself onto the honeycombed array of dye vats, scurrying between the opaque pools of red and yellow and blue, and I follow, quicker than him by just enough to be within grabbing distance as we reach the edge. He surges toward a narrow, empty alley piled with colorful stacks of finished leather, and once I'm in the alley with him, I tackle him to the pungent skins with a heavy thud. We roll once, twice, and he's reaching for something, and so am I, and by the time we stop rolling, we're in a scatter of leather with Isolde's stolen knife to his throat and the tip of his knife digging into my ribs.

He hisses in my face, "I'm not afraid to die. But I plan to take you with me."

I believe him on both counts, but I'm also not interested in killing him—not at the moment at least. "Since you're so eager to reach heaven, maybe you'll know the person I'm looking for." I keep my tone conversational, but the honey-suckle blade remains unambiguously pressed to his throat. "A

Father Minch. He'd be a few years younger than you—short, British, very paranoid."

The man's eyes burn up at me. His face is well shaped, with a strong brow and a wide jaw, but the ferocity of his anger makes him look wrong. Twisted. "You're too late, Sea Hound."

It's been some time since I've heard my old CIA code name, and I'm a little charmed by it, even if I don't like what he's saying. "You've already found him then."

"He's been sent to God to answer for his sins."

"Sounds like something a saint would say," I say, but it's more to keep his attention on my words and not on the subtle shifting of my knees on the leather beneath us. I'm not surprised he's a saint—there aren't very many people who will cross themselves while leaving bloody footprints across a public square—and it makes sense they would be as interested in Father Minch as I am. But it's not ideal.

"You know nothing about what a saint would say," he says, and his voice—accentless until this point—is getting more Italian by the syllable. "You know nothing about—"

I don't care. I'm already wrenching myself sideways, away from his knife, and by the time he's rolling to follow me, I'm pouncing, slicing. Two quick cuts—a scream that's muffled by leather—and then I'm standing, flicking his blood off the blade with a few practiced motions. "I'm sorry about the tendons, but I'd rather you not follow me. I'm sure you understand."

The saint gives me a baleful glare. "God will punish you for this," he seethes through clenched teeth.

Grow up, I want to say. Suburban tennis players deal with Achilles injuries all the time. "You'll be fine. You won't be able to run for a few months, but I doubt Mortimer will put you down like a horse."

His eyes burn brighter at the mention of his boss's name. "You're too late anyway, you scarred, perverted drunk."

Good to know my reputation precedes me.

"You mentioned about being too late earlier. I guess I'll have to go see for myself." I step on his hand, pinning it and his knife to the ground. I bend down and pry the knife out from under his fingers and tuck it in my jacket. "I guess this is farewell," I say. "Give Cardinal Cashel my regards."

I'm stepping away, my mind already retracing our path through the medina, when he calls out, "God will punish her too, you know."

This stops me as surely as any knife. I turn to face him, this murderer belly down in an alley, his ankles bleeding onto the dusty cobbles.

"Excuse me?" I ask pleasantly. At least I think I sound pleasant. I think I sound like someone in control.

His face is folded in pain and righteous fury as he twists to look up at me. "Your wife. She's an apostate, and it doesn't matter how well you're hiding her. God will find her, and he will drag her weakness and her lack of faith into the light."

It doesn't matter how well you're hiding her… So the saints think I'm hiding Isolde? *Cashel* thinks I'm hiding Isolde?

Could it be that she hasn't spoken to her uncle since she ran away from Lyonesse?

"What does this punishing and dragging involve?" I ask, squatting down next to him. "You wouldn't be talking about hurting her, right? My wife? That seems extraordinarily stupid to do, even for a zealot."

"It is not up to me what will happen to her but up to God, and God has chosen me to find her and force her atonement, whether by purging her sins in this life or sending her to purgatory."

"God has chosen you to force her atonement?"

"Yes."

"Cashel condones this?"

"The cardinal only conveys the will of God. He doesn't choose it for himself."

I flip the knife in my hand, the inlaid rubies glittering in the scant light that's worked its way down into the alley, and I catch the knife in reverse grip.

"Thank you for your honesty," I say as I lean closer. "God would be so proud."

I make sure he doesn't bleed too much on the leather as I kill him. It doesn't seem fair to the tannery workers to ruin all their hard work.

six

MARK

When I reach the doorway that I presume leads to Father Minch's apartment, I take a moment to place a quick call to Andrea. I hadn't *planned* on doing any wet work, had only amended my plan after that sack of fanatical shit disclosed that he might kill my wife, so there is a fair chance I'll need to bribe my way out of any unpleasantness coming from a dead body in the tannery. Andrea will help me find something suitable in Lyonesse's vaults of information in case it's needed.

I also tell her what the saint said to me about Cashel's plans to kill Isolde. Andrea hates Isolde with a bitterness that I think will never be sweetened, but she still agrees to start shaking trees on her end to find out more.

"Will you bring her home?" Andrea asks. She doesn't want me to, I can tell.

"If I do, are you going to undermine my authority at my own club again?"

Andrea doesn't answer, wisely. Her exposing Tristan and

Isolde in the garden a month ago didn't just embarrass my bodyguard and wife but eroded trust in my power, in my control.

Worse, it forced my hand.

And Andrea knows it. She recognizes she fucked up. She just loathes Isolde enough that there's still some ROI in that fuckup for her.

"I want to bring her home," I say. "She'd be safest at Lyonesse."

But happiest? Better off? No. Not that.

I finish my call with Andrea and follow the drying blood to a low wooden door and let myself inside. The sounds of the busy square outside filter through the shuttered windows, and glowing slats of light come in through the shutters and from under the door. I can see well enough— enough to catch the blood leading to a curtained area in the back, enough to notice that there's no overturned furniture or signs of a struggle. Just a Bible open on a table with a cup of coffee nearby. When I press the back of a gloved knuckle to it, I feel warmth. Fading but there.

It hasn't been long since Father Minch was torn from his morning devotionals.

The blood pointing the way to the back of the apartment is dark and still shining in trails rather than drops, and I prepare myself to find any number of things when I duck around the curtain.

What I do not prepare for, however, is finding Father Minch alive.

Alive is being generous, I suppose, because the only reason he's upright is that he's propped against a wall. Blood is still dripping from the wounds in his wrists, but feebly, and when he rolls his head against the wall to look at me, there is almost no life left in his expression, no fear left for him to give.

A rosary dangles from one hand.

"Father," I say, kneeling next to him, careful of the blood puddling on the floor. "I'm sorry."

He draws in a weak breath, tries to lick his lips. "Do I know you?" he whispers.

"No," I say as I pull a sheet down from his bed and start wrapping one of his wrists as tightly as I can. I think it might be too late, but I hate the idea of Cashel claiming him, giving Father Minch a lonely, ugly death just because this poor priest had a conscience. "I know the one who tried to kill you."

"Not tried to," the priest says, and every word is a struggle of concentration and air. "I'm already dead."

I'm wrapping his other wrist now. "We'll get you to a hospital, and you're going to be fine, and we'll find an even better place to hide, somewhere the cardinal can't find you."

His eyes meet mine under weighted lids. "So you know then. Cashel."

"Yes, Father. I know."

"His saint wouldn't let me die in a state of grace," the priest murmurs. "But he did allow me the rosary. To try to atone for as much as I could."

"You have nothing to atone for," I say firmly. "You left the Vatican because you couldn't make yourself sin for Cashel. That is courage. That is holiness."

This last part is something of a guess, but the relief in his eyes tells me I've hit the mark. Good. I'm about to reach for my phone to call for medical help—they won't be able to get an ambulance into the medina, but maybe the paramedics would get here in time anyway—when he says faintly, "The archives."

I nod at him as I pull out my phone. Minch had been an archivist in the Vatican before he fled, and while I'm not sure of the exact circumstances, the bishop who delivered the information to me as part of his Lyonesse payment knew that Minch's flight had something to do with Mortimer Cashel. That there was *something* in the archives.

"It's not real," Minch whispers. "It's not real."

"Shh. You can tell me all about it once they help you." I dial 150 and hit the Call button.

"It's not real." The words are slurred, sleepy almost. Not a good sign.

He looks at me and then behind my shoulder to the kitchen, then to me again. His eyes move slowly, the lids fluttering. "Take it," he mumbles. "Inside... I wrote them down."

His eyes close, his lips going slack.

The dispatcher picks up the phone, and somewhere between my only-just-serviceable Arabic and the dispatcher's French, I'm able to convey that there's an emergency, that we're in the small apartment on the east side of Place Seffarine, that we need a hospital.

By the time I'm done talking, Father Minch is dead.

I hang up the phone and stare at him a moment. He is such a small man, someone who started going bald early, whose beard would never entirely behave. He was meant to be scuffling around dusty books and fussing with metadata; he should never have had to show the kind of courage he showed, refusing to be part of whatever Cashel was keeping hidden in the archives.

That is the beauty of bravery, I suppose. It doesn't care what we look like or the lives we should have led, only doing what should be done.

I make the sign of the cross over his body, hoping that God will feel as I do—that Minch has more than earned his place in the house with many rooms—and then stand up and look around. I might have twenty minutes before the medical services team gets here, or I might have five. I can't search the entire apartment and still be conveniently elsewhere when the authorities show up, so I'll need to be quick.

I check the spots that seem the most obvious to me—the inside of the leather pouf, the underside of the ancient sink, the backs of the drawers of his dresser—but I think the saint who killed Minch went through everything too, given the lumps in the pouf's filling and the crookedness of the drawers. I found nothing on the saint after I killed him, but that doesn't mean he didn't destroy whatever he found...

My eyes stray to Minch's Bible. It's the Bible of a faithful man, highlighted and worn, the gold on the edges worn off from frequent thumbing and turning. I go over and look at what it's open to: Genesis, Jacob and Esau. I know the story well; it was one of Grandad's favorites, and he would read it aloud in his rumbling voice whenever we asked him to read a story to us.

And by thy sword shalt thou live, and shalt serve thy brother...

Cheerful stuff.

And then I think of Father Minch's eyes, moving behind my shoulder.

Take it. I wrote them down.

I don't have time to consider that I'm wrong about what he meant, and I take the Bible with me when I go, marking the story with the ribbon before closing it. Jacob and Esau. Not the story I'd want to go out on if I had a choice. I'd want rods and staffs and comfort—maybe some talk of vines and branches—not tent stew and deception.

I leave the way I came, and no one pays me any mind as I stroll back into the warren of streets, a leather book tucked under my arm. I get back to my hotel late in the day, shower, pack my things, and then walk to the train station. My suit and gloves from earlier are neatly dispatched in a wood-fired bread oven—with some money given to the baker for his trouble—and it seems like so far, no one has drawn a connection between a tall, blond tourist and the two fresh corpses in the city.

I board a train to Tangier, tuck myself against the window, and fall asleep.

seven

MARK

I WAKE JUST BEFORE TANGIER WITH A TWINGE IN MY RIGHT knee and a cramp deep in my chest. I stretch my leg out carefully before standing and getting my things; I don't bother trying to do anything with my chest. I already know the two pretty reasons why it hurts.

There are two ways to disappear, or at least to disappear *well*. You can vanish—there one breath and gone the next, the kind of disappearing that either happens because you're very quick or because you have your fingers in a salient digital pie—or you can evanesce over the space of a few hours, dissipating like fog on glass, fading until there's nothing left for anyone to follow. For example, anyone who noted the well-heeled British tourist in Fez might have been able to find his name—Trevor Owens—and see that he boarded a train to Tangier. But the man who stepped off the train in Tangier is no longer blond or well dressed or even British… He is dark-haired in a worn T-shirt with the tired shuffle of a gig worker. He will not board a train or a plane or a ferry, and he will not linger, and by the time a red-haired man slips off a freighter docking at Algeciras to pay cash for a car and drive to the French border, Trevor Owens will be little better than a ghost.

I am still prepared to bribe my way out of the messes I left behind in Fez, but honestly, I'd rather not spend the secrets if I don't have to. I have a feeling I'll need everything in my treasury before I'm done bringing down Cashel and Ys.

On the freighter, I dye my hair again, change clothes, and slip some cash to the captain before I step onto Spanish soil and strike for the part of town where I'll be able to find a new phone and a car that doesn't require real paperwork. I don't have to go far—just that scabbed-over seam where the industrial section meets the actual town, the shore where the dockworkers and incoming crew eddy with the unhoused, the unemployed, and police looking for smuggled hashish. And that's where I see the news, blaring from a mounted television inside a narrow store selling T-shirts, cigarettes I'm certain are smuggled from Gibraltar, and, most importantly, cheap cell phones.

My Spanish is strong, but it still takes a moment for the chatter of the news anchors to sink in, for me to hear not just the news but the low tones of the people smoking on the steps outside the store.

The pope is dead.

Fuck.

The news report is low on details. They can only say that the pope died last night, lingering complications from a prior surgery—and that the funeral is four days from now. The papal conclave will follow quickly after, and then the cardinals will select the new pope from among their number.

The anchor talks about the pope's ailing health over the last year as the feed cuts over to the gathering crowds in St. Peter's Square. The camera focuses on a microphone,

53

presumably meant for an imminent statement. Behind it, the cardinals and bishops stand like a cloud of blackbirds trimmed in scarlet and amaranth red. I see Cashel at the very edge, conferring with a monsignor with their heads bent. Whatever Cashel is saying, he's saying it quickly, the monsignor nodding and nodding as he taps something onto his phone. When the monsignor inclines his head briefly and strides away, Cashel turns back to face the crowd, his expression one of beatific solemnity, of profound sadness and yet also humble reassurance.

Another monsignor scurries up to the group, all of them turning and shuffling to confer—there is no overstating how complicated the choreography is for a Holy Father's death, a constant tension of practical and ecumenical demands, all of them overlapping onto a modern media and legal ecosystem—and I watch as Cashel lifts a hand to his jaw and rubs while the monsignor gestures behind him at the basilica.

I don't need to see any more.

The pope is dead. Cashel has made his move.

I purchase my new phone, activate the eSIM, use the browser to access a surveillance portal protected by multiple layers of authentication. The same portal I used to track Tristan and Isolde to Morois.

I stare at the two dots moving at a train's speed eastward from Calais. In the direction of Rome.

Shit.

————

I call Andrea and explain why I won't be back at Lyonesse tomorrow as planned and ask her to let Dinah and Sedge know too. Then I call my twin.

"This is Trevena," Melody answers crisply. She's the newly sworn-in deputy director of the NSA and very busy now. I don't care.

"It's me."

She sighs. "Hold on."

I hear movement and then the closing of a door. I imagine her in her spacious office, the newly crowned monarch of Fort Meade, ready to shape the world with a flick of her fingertips.

"Okay," she says. "What is it—and before you tell me, please tell me that you're not on your way to Rome right now."

"I'm on my way to Rome right now."

I hear something between a scoff and a sigh.

"You know Cashel is behind this. *This* is his play. This is how he gets the ring."

"More than likely," Melody concedes, "but what can you do about it, short of assassination?"

I don't answer.

"Mark," she says, irritated, like I'm a cat trying to lie down on her keyboard. "*No.*"

"I'm not planning on killing him. Yet."

Another sigh. I think she knows that's as good as she's going to get from me. But waiting to kill Cashel is a practical decision, not an ethical one. Even I'm not good enough to strike at a Catholic cardinal in his own nest with no plan in place or support nearby. And I still don't know how to stop Ys from rolling on despite his death, especially without knowing the identity of the Scales.

I thought I had—

I thought I had longer to move one or two more pieces across the board, that's all. A young man's mistake, except I no longer have the excuse of being young.

"Tristan and Isolde are almost to Rome. I can't have them tangled up in this, right in the middle of Cashel's plans." My free hand flexes at my side—a nervous habit I've never entirely been able to extirpate—and I shake it in irritation.

I'm standing on the side of an empty French highway, staring at a bunch of dead trees and some pine trees that wish they were dead. "A saint in Morocco told me that Cashel plans to kill Isolde. But if Cashel thinks she's useful to him still, then maybe he'll spare her for the time being." And *the time being* is good enough for me—long enough for me to make Isolde permanently safe.

"I'm not going to ask how you got a saint in Morocco to tell you anything."

"You shouldn't."

"And I'm guessing you're hoping you can leverage yourself as this *usefulness* somehow?"

"Yes."

"She was told to kill you."

"That's right."

"Are you willing to risk her trying again?"

My fingers find the scar at the base of my throat. I like the way it feels. A truer sign of her devotion than a ring on her finger or a collar around her neck. A testament in the flesh to what I've seen in her eyes. She could have killed me—easily, with my blessing and consent—and she didn't.

"She won't."

"Okay, so you're going to Rome, you'll somehow... maneuver...Isolde into being useful to Cashel, and then after that? The florilegium?"

The *florilegium* is what Melody calls the meticulously assembled dossier and assorted documents on every member of Ys we can find. A florilegium is typically a medieval compilation of writings by Church fathers, a sort of Catholic anthology, but there is another meaning for the word: a collection of information and illustrations about flowers.

I rather like that idea. That Andrea and I are making a guidebook to all the poisonous, avaricious, and invasive flowers of the world.

"Yes, the florilegium. And Brittany Hill."

"Oh, yes, the long-standing hunt for Brittany Hill. How's that going?"

My silence is its own answer.

Melody tuts. "You realize when you punch a name out of someone, it's bound to be a fake one, right?"

"Okay. Well. My options have been limited lately, so I don't appreciate the judgmental tone."

It's technically true that the name Brittany Hill came after some *persuasion*, but I still think it's genuine. The source I'd been persuading had been hired muscle of Filip Drobny's—muscle that had been sloppily trained and not paid well enough for silence. Drobny—a Slovakian warlord who had an understandable, if annoying, vendetta against me—had been one of the power players on Ys's weapons smuggling side until I killed him in Belgrade a couple months ago. And it probably goes without saying that the lower levels of any criminal organization aren't generally filled with people known for their discipline or discretion...or courage...but that seemed to be especially true of Drobny's little enterprise. It didn't take much at all for Drobny's man to tell me everything he knew, and with the desperation of someone who didn't want to lose his molars for a boss who didn't give a shit about him.

"My unexpected friend told me that Drobny knew if he found someone named Brittany Hill, he could exploit some vital weakness of Cashel's," I add. "You know at this point that I can't ignore any information that might help me."

"Your unexpected *friend*," laughs Melody. "Okay, so you use the florilegium and the elusive Brittany Hill to bring down an invisible league of arms dealers and whoever else, and at the end of this, what? What happens to you and Lyonesse and your two cheating toys?"

I've never told Melody how I imagine the end of this

playing out, because I know she won't accept it. She doesn't see sacrifice in the same terms I do—she thinks it's stupid. I think sacrifice is stupid too, yet sometimes stupid is all we have.

I do tell her this: "My two toys would be happier together than they'd be with me. They're well within their rights to hate me forever, you know."

"Just because you've lied to them, manipulated them, and you plan to kill Isolde's uncle?" A knowing laugh. "Sounds like foreplay to me."

———

Rome is a wall of teeming grief when I arrive at the crest of late afternoon. The faithful have pressed themselves into Vatican City, holding vigil, praying, crying, while the rest of the city churns with an uneasy mix of decorum and opportunism. I spot black-veiled nonne shuffling between camera operators unpacking tripods and vendors selling coins and plates commemorating the newly exanimate pope. Someone is selling street waffles with his face burned onto one side. A young man sits on a low wall with tears streaming down his face.

I track Tristan and Isolde to a graffiti-splattered apartment block north of the papal complex, and I sit in my parked car for a moment, reminding myself that I cannot storm into this shithole and drag them back to Lyonesse where they belong. Tristan—maybe—would be biddable. But Isolde would be like a cat in a room full of furniture; one wrong move and she'd be darting into the most unreachable corner, hissing at every attempt to retrieve her. But my God, how I want to kick down their door and order them home.

(I am furious with myself for wanting this. You have no idea how much. *Everything* would be so much easier if I felt nothing for them.)

But why are they here in Rome? The only reason I

can think of is that Isolde is going to her uncle, and that is beyond worrisome for me. It's fucking terrifying.

I've parked a few blocks away from their building, and I don't bother going in that direction, thinking it better not to risk being seen. Instead, I find a café to sit at while I wait for the blue dots to move on my phone. Behind me, an Italian and a Hungarian argue about which country gets to claim the invention of the espresso machine, and at the far end of the café, a journalist is taking a call on her laptop—an interview about the logistics of the upcoming conclave.

I myself have brought Minch's Bible, and I page through it as I drink my coffee. Regret is a small burr in my chest as I run my fingertips over years of underlines and notes, in different colors of ink, in handwriting both rushed and thoughtful.

I wish I could have saved him; I wish I'd found him sooner. Faith like this…it's rare. I remember my father's Bible, marked up just like this. I remember my hand folded in his warm, dry one as we prayed at dinner. I remember how he'd always, without fail, use the Bibles tucked in the back of the pews to follow along with the readings. Like the words were that important—they couldn't only be heard, they had to be seen. They couldn't only be seen, but they had to be understood, felt, ingested.

I flip the page to Psalm 120 and see a list scratched out in black archival ink.

Revelata Scientia, 1682—National Central Library of Rome

Geschichte der Geheimbünde, 1761—Admont Abbey

A Treatise of Politicks Large and Small, 1697—Thornchapel (private collection)

Letter from Thomas Jefferson to Bishop James Madison, 1800—

Before I can finish reading, my phone on the table gives

a little buzz. One of my dots is on the move—Tristan. I close the Bible and follow.

My hair is red at the moment, and I'm wearing all black like a priest—even without an actual collar, I easily blend into the clerical swarm flooding the city—and so it's easy to lag behind Tristan and stay beyond the edge of his awareness. He's good, I don't mean to imply that he's not good, but becoming a bodyguard still hasn't removed him of a certain... soldierliness. He expects a fair fight. He expects enemies to act like enemies, and he doesn't expect his employer to trail him like a wolf in the woods.

And perhaps, sweetly—heartbreakingly—there is a part of Tristan that doesn't suspect that anyone would ever follow *him*, want *him*—only what he is guarding. Whether it's me, Isolde, or a patch of rocky scrub overlooking the Carpathian basin... In his mind, only these can be desirable targets, never himself. And right now, Isolde is safely secreted in their apartment, so he thinks there isn't a need for the alertness I know he's capable of.

It's only been four days since I last saw him, but the snarl in the pit of my stomach still tightens with every glimpse of a broad shoulder, of the pale skin between his ear and the collar of the hoodie he wears. If I thought my besmirching of the venerable wood paneling at Morois had been enough to stave off future desire, I'd been wildly wrong, and the hunger crawling up my guts to grip me by the throat is almost enough to make me stagger. I need to touch him. I need to smell him. A single lick of the skin below his ear might be enough to save my life.

He stops at a small grocery store but not for long, and when he emerges again, he has a cloth tote bag, barely filled. Some lumps at the bottom—apples, I think—and then crusty bread sticking up above the top. He doesn't turn back toward the apartment however. After a moment's hesitation, he starts in the opposite direction, striking west in the blooming twilight, his head down. Soon we lose the crowds of the town, and save for a handful of intrepid joggers and bicyclists daring the December evening, we're nearly alone as Tristan climbs a winding footpath up a steep hill. The cool air is made sharper still by the eucalyptus trees on either side of the path; I pull in lungfuls of the pleasantly crisp scent and recognize it immediately. It's in the simple aftershave that Tristan uses.

As good as the eucalyptus smells here, high above Rome after a day in the winter sun, I know it would smell even better on my puppy.

I keep well behind my bodyguard, far enough that my footsteps won't carry, that I'm just beyond this curve or that curve, until we reach the top of the hill. There, his perception of his surroundings belatedly grows sharper, and he finally looks over his shoulder. The red hair and the clothes—they're enough for an instant of doubt, but no longer than that. His pace falters, his cheeks go pale, and he turns.

eight

MARK

A BIKE ZIPS BY, AND THEN WE'RE ALONE—JUST US AND THE lights of the city below. Across the valley, the Vatican rears up in a wall of stone and stone pines, lights glowing from within and the massive dome of St. Peter's lit up like a jewel.

Dusk loves Tristan, even in a hoodie and jeans, and he is painted against the gloom like a knight from a painting, like a hero already snared by La Belle Dame Sans Merci. Except it's me, I'm La Belle Dame tonight, and I think I could gobble up the fading roses on his cheeks, lay him down on the cold hill's side, and show him *such* a dream.

"Sir," he says, shock all over him.

"Oh, come now, baby. You really didn't think I'd find you?"

He shakes his head wordlessly.

He's stopped walking, but I haven't. I move closer and closer until I can see the fading twilight in his eyes.

"Playing house?" I ask, nodding at the bag in his hand.

He flushes. I come even closer.

"I would have let you play house with my wife if you wanted, Tristan. All you had to do was ask."

His flush deepens, but the words are hard and protective when he speaks. He's angry, not embarrassed. Or not only embarrassed at least. "She's only your wife because you lied to her and to everybody else too. Forced her to marry you—"

That surprises a real laugh out of me. "*Forced*? Do you really think she's a damsel in distress? She chose to marry me because she planned on using me. She chose to marry me knowing that I'd use her right back. The only thing she didn't know was the extent of what *I* knew. What you should know now too."

He glances away. So he does know.

"That she's a saint of the Church," I prod. "Do you know what that means? It means she kills in the name of God. It means that her uncle gets to decide what *in the name of God* means. And I'll never pretend that I haven't lied or cheated to get what I want, but what Isolde *cannot* claim is that she wasn't warned."

A breath leaves his lips. He knows this too.

"You didn't just lie. You lied to her," he says finally.

"And to you. Or did you not open the third box you stole?"

He straightens his shoulders and looks back to me, like a schoolboy gathering courage to tell his teacher the truth. Oh, Tristan. Honest to a fault.

"I did open the third box," he says. "I saw…what was inside it."

"And?"

He swallows. "And yes. It was all about me. Pictures of me. Articles about me."

"Don't you want to know why?" I'm curious to know if *he's* curious. If he's put it together yet.

"It's—" A breath. "It's about Ys, isn't it?"

I'm surprised again. I study his face, his beautifully transparent face. "Why do you think that?"

"The only thing you'd marked in the box was an article about Aaron Sims. You circled the name of the prime minister elect he tried to kill."

A scrim of shame is now drawn over Tristan's gaze, that guilt about his dead friend that he can never seem to shake. I'd relieve him of it if I could, shake the truth into him until his bones rattled. *You saved everyone you could*, I want to tell him. *That's better than most people get.*

It's this lie we tell ourselves about heroes, about what heroism is, that heroes are apart from such choices, from triage, from discretion. It's a fucking cancer.

Tristan goes on. "His sister—I think you might remember that she was trying to get ahold of me—I called her in Belgrade, and she told me that Aaron wasn't bribed into trying to kill the prime minister elect and her family. He was blackmailed. Threatened by a group called Ys. The same group that came up in the security meeting at Lyonesse a while ago, the same group you told Isolde about in the letter you left at Morois House." He pauses. "The same group Isolde overheard you talking to your sister about at the engagement party."

"Oh?"

"Something along the lines of *Ys started the game. I'm only finishing it.*"

Isolde had overheard that, had she? Interesting.

"So I thought… Well, I guess it seems like the only reason you would have picked me. You're trying to do something with Ys, and I'm tangled up in it because of Sims."

Oh, Tristan. The only *reason I could have picked you?*

His eyes are on the ground, lifting to mine only briefly. "I don't understand exactly why though. I stopped whatever Ys wanted to do that day by stopping Sims. Why do I matter?"

I make a choice not to tell him the real reason the third box is dedicated solely to Tristan Thomas, American hero, and it's more cowardly than cruel. I'm not proud of myself, but as I've mentioned before, I never planned to care about Tristan. This is an unforeseen inconvenience, and I can't be blamed for it.

"Do you know why Ys was in Carpathia?" I ask. "Why they wanted to kill that politician?"

Tristan shakes his head. His hair—dark and thick and longer than I've ever seen it—catches against the collar of his hoodie. It would be cool to the touch at the ends, only warm at the nape of his neck and where your nails could scratch gently at his scalp. My fingers twitch. In proximity to him, focus is occasionally a runaway thing, something I first noticed at Blanche's wedding.

"There are two reasons, the first of which is that a destabilized Carpathia is much easier to move weapons and everything else through—a corridor from west to east and then back again." We are completely alone right now, but I still pitch my voice lower, softer, in the lee of the dome. "The second is maybe less obvious but maybe even more pernicious. Carpathia has struggled to get to its feet for years, and in the meantime, the Church has stepped in. Food, medical aid, housing, foster care, public education—all the infrastructure that should belong to Carpathia's government is in fact the Church's. The Church would say that it's holding these services in trust, that it's there only as a helping hand to Carpathia and nothing more. But of course, the Church isn't doing this at a deficit. Since Carpathia is outsourcing all this assistance, *delegating*, they are delegating all the funds to the Church as well. International aid money, UN-pledged money, their fledgling taxes. The Church is now an essential part of Carpathian governance and is getting paid handsomely to exist as such."

Understanding flickers over Tristan's face. "The prime minister," he says. "She was a threat to that."

"She *is* a threat to that. Because of you, Tristan. You saved her life and, in the process, created a huge challenge for the Church in Carpathia."

"But what does that have to do with Ys?" he asks, a notch dipping between his brows. "Is Ys exploiting Carpathia's reliance on the Church somehow? Using gaps between the Church and the government to move things around?"

I find his desire to keep good things good and bad things bad rather sweet. I've always been too willing to mix the two together, to search for one inside the other, to stain innocence and exonerate guilt, and look at where it's gotten me.

"You mentioned my letter to Isolde—you must have read it too. You must remember what I said: Mortimer Cashel is the head of Ys. All this happens at a lift of his fingers."

He gives me a look. "Yes, I read your letter, but I don't believe it. It can't be right."

"It can't be? Why not?"

"That's like—it's like some kind of nineteenth-century Protestant conspiracy or something. 'The papists are evil and want to take over the world.' The pope isn't trying to influence events through…I don't know, political puppets or something."

"I'm not talking about *the pope*," I make clear. "Ys has nothing to do with him. Or had nothing to do with him, rather. I'm sure you've heard the sad news about his passing."

Tristan's eyebrow lifts the tiniest amount. A drill sergeant would miss it, but a lover wouldn't. He's not in the mood for my irreverence today.

So I get back to the point. "A year of declining health, setbacks after surgeries and so on. A year for a cardinal to shore up support ahead of a conclave." I nod at the dome across the valley, lit against the dimming sky. "So no, it's not a papal conspiracy. *Yet*. Not until Cashel is elected pontiff."

Tristan is already shaking his head. "No. Isolde told her uncle what she overheard you saying to your sister at the engagement party, and after she told him, he asked her to find out what you knew about Ys. He wouldn't have done that if he already knew about it."

"Do you think he was asking her to learn what Ys was? Or do you think he was trying to figure out *how much I knew*? There's a difference." The first real surge of worry takes me, that I won't be able to convince Tristan of this in enough time to keep Isolde safe from her uncle. "And things have changed since then anyway. Cashel seems to think killing Isolde is the most expedient move right now."

An instinctive protectiveness ripples through him quickly, handsomely, straightening his shoulders and lifting his chin. Only the grocery bag hanging from his hand disrupts the portrait of the hero at work.

"No one is hurting Isolde," he says firmly.

"Isolde would slit the throat of anyone who tried," I reply. "Anyone she was ready for, that is."

Tristan's jaw works subtly to the side as he considers this. The implication of whom she *wouldn't* be ready for. And then: "I'm not saying I believe you."

"If I'm right, then it's the two of you here in Rome or maybe back at Morois, alone against a group that has evaded detection for centuries. If I'm right, then she's safer at Lyonesse than she would be anywhere else."

Tristan's gaze is piercing, righteous. "And why should Isolde believe you? Why should she trust you? After years of lying to her, why should she believe that you're telling her the truth now?"

"You stole three boxes of reasons for her not to trust me. She has four years of my lies stored up at her feet. I won't pretend otherwise. Nevertheless, it's still the truth."

"Why not tell her yourself? Why a letter and then showing up in Rome four days later?"

It's my turn to look away. I don't like the idea of Tristan

seeing what I can't hide. "I knew you two were at Morois from the moment you stepped under the magnolia trees to walk through the front door. I imagined you happy there, and I thought—" I corral my thoughts and start over. "It was a moment of weakness, coming there, but the moment I saw you both, I knew I'd leave you as I found you. I didn't have the appetite to play the tyrant husband just then. But Isolde still needed to know about her uncle. I hoped she'd have time to consider the facts and come to the truth on her own, but I've since learned of Cashel's plans for her. I learned the pope is dead. I'm here because she no longer has the luxury of time."

"Why not tell her that yourself?"

I step forward and find Tristan's free hand. His lips part as I take his fingers and press them to the raised scar on my neck. "She and I did not part well when we were together last. I'm sure you remember."

His hand is warm and strong, the fingertips on my neck gentle and careful as they explore the line of the wound Isolde left.

"You think I can convince her," he says.

"Have I convinced you?"

"Not yet." His eyes are on my neck too. I wish I could stand here forever and have him touch me. "But there is something about it all…" He shakes his head and looks at me. "I don't know. How can I say that I understand the secret agenda of Ys when I don't even know what *Ys* is? When I barely understand what it is that Isolde and her uncle do for the Church?"

Below us in the park, I see a red bicycle light moving down the trail, away from us, but it reminds me of how conspicuous we are, standing here, touching neck wounds. I take Tristan's hand and guide him to a low concrete wall facing the valley, both veiled in near darkness. He lets me lead him there, like we're boyfriends out enjoying the clear, empty night.

"Ys and the saints are two different things, or at least they were before Cashel, I think. The saints are like...like the CIA or MI6, except much older, I suppose. I've heard people say they're as old as the Church itself. I don't know how true that is, but they're certainly medieval at least. They're abided by other intelligence communities, since their concerns only rarely intersect with secular governments—Carpathia aside. They gather intelligence pertinent to the Church, and they act on it and occasionally they kill, which you've already guessed, even if you've been too shy to ask Isolde directly."

A drop of his gaze tells me I'm right. He hasn't asked her directly. Maybe he's afraid of the answers he'll hear and that he'll learn for certain he's a dove in a nest of kites.

"*Unlike* the saints, Ys hasn't been known to anyone in the intelligence community until the last decade or two. Even then, it was still mostly a rumor—that it had been around for centuries, that it could claim among its members the most powerful people in the world, et cetera, et cetera. The usual things claimed about secret societies, except Ys *is* supposed to be like some kind of un-Illuminati. Cashel's involvement, however, seems to be barely known, never spoken of, something I had to dig and dig and dig to find. Which I find extremely interesting. Because how secret is your secret web of warmongering and influence if it's on the lips of low-level arms dealers, and—I'm sorry to speak this way of Aaron Sims, Tristan—in the phone calls of soldiers vulnerable enough to get blackmailed into butchering children? It's not that secret at all, not as secret as everyone will swear up and down it is. But its leader...now that *is* quite secret. Quite difficult to piece together. Even for me, and I've dedicated my life to finding out."

We're sitting on the wall now, facing the valley and the

walled-off Vatican on the other side, its glow interrupted by tall, graceful trees and even more graceful rooftops. I've relinquished his hand, but I can feel it building in me, that shadow inside, and it won't be long before I'm taking his hand again, claiming a thigh to caress, or sliding my fingers into his mouth.

"So why have you dedicated your life to this?" he asks finally, and it is an important question, possibly the most important question, yet I think answering it honestly might eviscerate me.

Answering it and having to explain all the plans I once made in a seething, bleeding fury.

But he should know this much: "Because Ys killed Eliot. Cashel killed Eliot."

"You said Eliot died in a friendly fire accident. In Košice." His voice is careful.

"I did say that. Both things are true." The last sentence is a lie, but it can't be helped. The truth is too costly right now.

Tristan turns to face me. "Why? Why would a cardinal want a CIA officer dead?"

"Eliot, I believe, was very close to learning Cashel's identity, had been for weeks, and Mortimer knew it. So he had the Scales go through John Lackland before it could get any further."

"John Lackland. You killed him." He doesn't say it with disgust or surprise; he says it like it's something he already knew. "That night in Singapore. With the shower running and the room service you didn't eat."

"Yes." Killing the deputy director of the NSA took considerably more care than killing a random saint on the street, but believe me when I say I didn't mind at all. For John Lackland to die alone and screaming, I'd been willing to take all the care in the world.

"And the Scales," Tristan says slowly. "That would be Mortimer's second-in-command?"

70

"That is my best guess," I reply. "At first, I thought the Scales was a middle manager, and then maybe a consigliere, but now, I don't know. I don't even know if the Scales is one person or many. I don't know if it's a title that's passed on. I don't know if they're inside the Church or outside. Even the saints don't know. All I know is that the Scales seems to be part of the saints and a part of Ys and essential to the function of both."

Tristan passes a hand over his face. "Okay. So Ys killed Eliot," he says. "And you have been searching for revenge ever since."

I don't need to answer that, so I don't.

"And you started Lyonesse because of that, didn't you? To gather the information you needed to hurt everyone who'd hurt the man you loved."

"Yes."

"You learned that Mortimer was ultimately responsible for Ys, and then you realized his niece was being trained as a saint, so she would be doubly useful to you. Leverage against Mortimer and possibly even a source of information at the same time. Except he was leveraging her back, which you also knew. You knew and you still married her."

"Yes."

"And now what, sir?" Tristan asks, and it gives me a little curl of satisfaction to hear that *sir*. It always does. "What is the end of this? What happens to Isolde?"

It's nearly the same question as everyone else asks— *What happens next? Where does your retribution end and the normal course of the world begin?*—but of course, Tristan's chief concern is Isolde. I'd even planned it that way.

"She will be safe. You will be safe. I promise that to you." I pivot so that I'm straddling the wall, facing him directly, and I move close enough that my legs frame his knee on one side and his ass on the other. I take the bag from his hand

and set it aside, and he pulls in a breath as my hands find his waist under his hoodie. Goose bumps spring up on his otherwise warm skin as I stroke his spine on one side and his stomach on the other.

"How can you know that, sir?" he murmurs. "It's a promise you can't make."

"Watch me."

"It feels like that's all I can do sometimes," he answers helplessly, and then he shudders as the hand on his stomach drops to the button of his jeans and then to the zipper. "Sir…"

"Yes?"

"I—we shouldn't—"

"According to the deal we made before you ran away, I have two more times left with you, and that's not even counting the entire month you've had free access to my wife. Although you are *so hard*, puppy. Are you sure you've been making good use of her?"

I've got ahold of him now, running my thumb along the swollen head, finding the sweet little slit by feel alone. He makes a choked noise as I dip my hand lower, and he obediently spreads his thighs so I can cup his testicles. I have to fight the denim, but soon everything is worked farther down his hips, and I can use both hands to play with him. To cradle below as I tease the rigid inches above.

He bucks at the first real stroke I give him, and then embarrassment blossoms on his cheeks.

"It's been so long since I've touched you," I soothe. "It's okay. It's okay."

He's breathless. "I'm afraid I won't—I can't last—"

"It's okay. Just let me, my sweet knight. Just let me."

His lashes, as long as a doll's, rest on his cheeks as he closes his eyes, and when I murmur, *you're doing so well, you're so pretty like this, look at how wet it's getting*, he starts shivering like a fevered patient, flushed cheeks and open mouth. When he lifts his lashes, his eyes are glassy.

Like most soldiers, it doesn't occur to Tristan to move obliquely, sinuously, to meander to a finish. Detours and delays might be inevitable, but they should always be extrinsic; soldiers rarely take the scenic route for the hell of it. It's the same with pleasure, with fucking—when Tristan jerks himself off alone, he moves himself efficiently to the finish. The parts leading up to release are never savored or studied for their own sake.

So whenever I toy with him—explore all the subtle lines and curves of him, dangle him from the edge of orgasm and yank him back—he is helpless, baffled even, like it's never occurred to him that pleasure can be greater for having been skirted, unfurled, mapped to the minutest contours. When I stop jerking him to trace the seam of his balls, when I stop tracing to rub my thumb over his head and smear slick arousal across his frenulum, when I stop smearing and lean down to blow a puff of air—every shift in pace or intention has him arching, whimpering, casting me wounded glances, weaponizing a pout that would soften a granite wall.

I'll take payment for the adultery in wounded glances. I'll eat his pouts until I'm full.

But he is so starved for it, so desperate to be handled and controlled, that he's in complete agony before more than a few minutes of this. The skin is stretched so tight on his swollen organ that I can see it gleam faintly in the dark, and he's so engorged now that I could take a clinical reading of his pulse just from circling him with my fingers.

"Hands behind you," I murmur as he gets daring, seeking me out. I love and hate his hands. They are strong and beautiful and remarkably graceful for a man of Tristan's profession; I resent that I crave them at all, these graceful hands that still appear in my nightmares. "I've told you before: touching is earned, and you're a long way from earning anything yet. Be still for this part."

I shift myself enough that I can bend down and put my lips to the tip of his cock. He freezes, his breath caught right at the expansion of an inhale, and his erection jerks and jerks, just at the barest pressure.

"You've never—I didn't think—"

"Hush."

And then I take him into my mouth.

"Oh God," he breathes. His hands scrabble behind him on the concrete. "What the fuck. What the fuck."

Delight curls in my belly; I am smug, yes, satisfied in a way that I recognize as vaguely immoral, but also the delight is just...*him*. Just Tristan, sweet and brave and eternally defenseless in the face of his own desire.

It's been a long time since I've done this, since Eliot, and I've missed it. The ownership of it. The tender manipulation. A swirl of a tongue and he hunches over me. A suck and he arches away. A long pull into the back of my throat and he jerks his hips forward without meaning to. He's a ship of muscle and loyalty with nothing but my tongue as the rudder.

He is swelling and swelling, already at the edge, and if we had time, if we weren't in the open, if I wasn't in the shadow of my enemy's palace—ah, the things I would do. The razor-thin misery I would dance him along, the sweaty, palpitating, unendurable bliss I would wring from him.

But for now: pity. I brace my hands on his thighs, enjoying their flexing and trembling under my touch, and take him all the way in, a long, swallowing slide that undoes him. A jagged moan tears from his throat as he ejaculates, and he moans again when he realizes he can't work his way any deeper into my mouth—my hands on his thighs prevent him moving much at all. Not that I'm averse to having him fuck my throat one day—I think it would be fun, actually—but right now, it's also fun to deny him a little. Fun to leave him wanting something more.

I pull off and give him a pragmatic lick or two to make sure I've gotten everything and then straighten up to look at him. I could laugh if everything else weren't so dire—he's giving a better performance as a drunk than I ever have.

He sways a little as I tuck him away and hand him his bag of apples.

He blinks with glassed-over eyes, words seeming hard to come by. "Why—but—what about you?"

I glance down at my groin, which is tented with a displeased erection, and then look up to Tristan and shrug. "It'll keep."

There's a flicker of something along his jaw, and he jerks his head to the side. It reminds me of an unhappy horse tossing its head in protest of something.

"Something wrong, Tristan? Are you that offended that I'm not forcing you to your knees right now?"

He doesn't move his head, but his eyes do slide back to mine. "Just wondering what *it'll keep* means. It'll keep until you get home? Does that mean you have someone at Lyonesse who's—" Another jump of muscle in his jaw. "Is Isabella Beroul back?"

I'm amused and I'm pissed too. "Are you concerned about my fidelity, Tristan? Worried that I'll break my vows perhaps? How generous of you. I'll accept your prayers for my soul gladly."

Even in the lamplit dark, I can see the flush rising on his cheeks. But to his credit, I suppose, he doesn't allow me to force him away from his jealousy. "We have a right to know," he says stubbornly. "If there are others."

His jealousy is lovely, even if it's the rankest hypocrisy, and I relent. "No others, Tristan. I've slept alone this last month. Sat in the hall untouched. Heartbreak has that effect, you see."

He looks surprised at the word *heartbreak*, although how, I don't know, and as I stand up, he jumps to his feet too.

"How can you be heartbroken when you were the one who lied? Who deceived us all?"

"Even Judas was heartbroken," I say, "and I wasn't the only Judas in my marriage anyway."

He shakes his head slowly. "I'll never understand you. How you can be so certain of yourself after everything you've done."

Well. This I can make him understand. "When you've been where I've been, on those roads, in those pits of hell, you come to know that you can *only* be certain of yourself. You have nothing else to hold on to, not a flag or a creed, not the history you've been taught or the politics you've been given. You only have what you've seen and maybe, if you're lucky, a sense of right and wrong to go with it all. You can't rely on certainty to come from elsewhere, because it almost always comes as a lie from the mouths of the people who want to use you most."

"I don't want to use you," Tristan says softly, and I have no good response to that. Because it's true.

Because I did want to use him, and I still do.

When I don't answer, his eyes drift upward. "Why is your hair red?" he asks.

"Felt like a change. Why are you two in Rome?"

Tristan's laugh has a bitter note to it. "Felt like a change."

The darkness has thoroughly come for the city now, and Isolde will be wondering where her paramour is. I take a step backward into the shadows. "Bring my wife back, Tristan. I can keep her safer at Lyonesse, with all its flaws, than anywhere else."

Tristan chews on his lip. "What if I can't convince her to come back?"

"She has a way into the server rooms now, doesn't she? Tell her I'll let her use it if she comes back. She can even tell Cashel so."

He rubs his eyes with his free hand but then nods. "I'll see what I can do. I don't like—I don't like any of it. The saints. Ys. Her uncle. It feels too much like power for power's sake."

Oh, Tristan, I think. *That's where all power ends up if it's left alone long enough.*

"You never answered my question from earlier," he says suddenly. "Why hire me when I barely had anything to do with Ys?"

I decide to give him a little of the truth then, a silver thread of it, perhaps the one bright part in the twist of secrets and lies. "Because you did the right thing when you killed Aaron Sims. Because I knew that if you could do the right thing even when it meant killing your best friend, then you could do the right thing while working for me. I knew that I could trust you with Isolde's safety. I know that I still can."

And before he can respond—before he can plead or fret or argue—I melt into the dark and leave him standing alone. Under a halo of lamplight like the tragic hero he is.

nine

ISOLDE

Night still clings to the corners and arches of the Palazzo San Callisto, and I move as silently as the gray dawn currently sighing over the city as I slip into the courtyard behind my uncle's Roman apartment.

Light spills from the tower of the butter-colored basilica next door, and I move a little faster through the shadows. They will be preparing for morning Mass. I need to be gone before then, before the piazza is full of the grieving faithful who've found no room to pray closer to the Holy See.

The front door is locked, but that's not a problem. There's a grate above the front door, an easy handhold, and then a balcony above that with a nice little railing I can use to heave myself upward. I inch the teal shutters open enough to get inside and find myself in the central stairwell. From there, I can reach the roof, and from the roof, the open window of the penthouse apartment.

The floors are tile—standard in Rome and the preference of any man with enemies, since carpet too easily muffles footsteps—and I slide out of the window as languorously and quietly as a cat stretching in the sun. There is a blink of light from down the hall, like headlights passing by, but we are on the top floor, so it's not a car. And anyway, I already know what the light is.

I've never been here before but can immediately recognize the hallmarks of my uncle's style. Sparse but tasteful antique furnishings. Tall ceilings with their original plasterwork and occasional frescoes, all of which are distinctly pagan in subject matter. A scattered rug or two that almost certainly has some complicated backstory, as a gift from such and such diplomat or a rescue from such and such villa that the Church sold off. Small pieces of art in a mix of cheap and expensive frames. Next to a crucifix, I see a picture of my mother—his sister—smiling in front of Cashel House with her blond hair blowing around her face, her gapped front teeth on display. Like me, she had a faint dash of freckles across her nose and an upper lip that forgot to dip in the middle. Like Mortimer, she had those distinctive teeth and eyes that didn't quite match. She had smile lines so, so young because she was always smiling, like there was never a reason to stop.

Under that photograph is a picture I drew for him when I was in kindergarten, a church with little stick figures kneeling and praying outside it. It was beyond my childish skill to draw the praying figures *inside* the church, but I had known to bow their little stick heads and draw the ends of their little stick arms together, like folded hands. In blue crayon, I've given them all tears.

Why are they crying, little mouse? my uncle had asked when I'd bashfully given it to him.

Because they love Jesus, I'd told him. I'd been confused by the question. If you'd asked me to draw what it looked like to love God in any other way, I wouldn't have understood. I wouldn't have drawn hearts or large eyes. I wouldn't have drawn their hands up in the air in adoration or them locking arms in their shared love. Love was kneeling. Love was tears.

My uncle framed the picture with its stick figures rendered in crayon with a heavy gilt frame fit for a Titian or a Rubens.

It abruptly unnerves me, and I'm not sure why. It should be evidence that my uncle treasured a gift from his little niece, the closest to a child of his body he'd ever have. But right now, in the near darkness, the weeping figures in their overwrought frame look more like the suffering sinners in Dante's inferno, like an unhappy corner from a Bosch painting.

The art underneath my drawing is a copy in a simple frame: Caravaggio's *Sacrifice of Isaac*. Abraham has Isaac shoved to the altar, a knife poised to fall on his son, stopped only by the angel grabbing his wrist. Isaac's mouth is open in a soundless scream, his eyes wild with horror. Because there is no part of Abraham that suggests he wasn't going to do the unthinkable and call it blessed and right to do so.

I think of what Tristan told me before I came here and close my eyes. Then I shake my head. I'm seeing darkness where there isn't any, and there is plenty of darkness for the taking as it is.

I move through the large office toward the rest of the apartment, guided only by my memory of the floor plan Mark had in his safe, the floor plan I stole, among many other things, when I left Lyonesse.

Again, my uncle's taste is evident. Restraint in everything, but of course, the restraint is purely to highlight the utter spaciousness of the residence, the restored plaster, the centuries-old art pressed into the ceiling itself. You do not need to crowd your rooms with furniture to show your wealth and taste when they are rooms like these.

A dim light at the end of the hallway and a voice: prayer in a swaying Irish lilt. I reach the bedroom door—it is open enough for me to slip inside, which is ideal, since my uncle would never keep a door well oiled, for the same reason he would never sleep in a fully carpeted house, and then I'm standing behind him as he prays a chaplet at his prie-dieu. He's only in a collar and a jacket now, not his simar yet, although he's wearing his pectoral cross and his ecclesiastical ring. The sapphire glints in the light from the small candle he has lit nearby.

He finishes praying St. Faustina's closing prayer—*for Jesus is our Hope: through His merciful Heart, as through an open gate, we pass through to Heaven*—and without turning says, "Very good, Isolde. Now how did I know you were coming?"

"Two cameras in the courtyard, one in the stairwell," I say, expecting the question. "A motion sensor in the office."

"If not for those precautions, it would have been very well done. I didn't hear a thing." He crosses himself and stands, turns to face me. He smiles, my mother's smile, the smile of the grandparents I barely knew, and then beckons me forward into a hug.

I allow this, and I even embrace him in return, pressing my face down into his shoulder and smelling the smells of Rome. Incense and sunshine.

"I'm glad to see you, child. It's not your custom to disappear after you've been given a mission. I was worried that Mark had hurt you. Trapped you somewhere."

There's no sense in wondering why, if he'd thought this, he hadn't tried to send help. That's not how things are done—if a saint falls, then they are a martyr and a new voice in heaven to intercede for the saints below. The will of God is a greater imperative than a single life, even if that single life is your niece's.

I remember Mark's note at Morois, the stark brevity of the first line. *Your uncle is the head of Ys, and he is using the saints for Ys's ends now, not God's.*

And then his warning to Tristan last night, that my uncle wanted me dead, that even now, my fellow saints have been ordered to kill me. I have been declared an apostate.

I laughed when Tristan told me, felt like Mark was a boy telling scarier and scarier stories to frighten the girls on the playground.

Mortimer, the head of Ys?

Mortimer, kill me?

I pull back and say, "There was a struggle, All Saints' Eve. I had my knife to Mark's throat and nearly killed him, but I was stopped." I don't mention that *I* stopped myself. "I had no choice but to run afterward. I've been hiding in England with Tristan Thomas."

His brows, a mix of red and silver, pull together. "The bodyguard?"

"Yes."

He searches my face. "Tell me that you have not been foolish. Tell me that you have not been weak."

I bow my head against the hand holding my chin. "I'm sorry, Uncle. It was not...planned."

He examines me a moment more, then fully releases me to go sit in a chair in the corner. Blue-gray light is leaking deeper and deeper into the room now. "So you have tried to kill Mark and failed. It seems likely that you have committed adultery and run away with your lover. You have hidden all these weeks from both Mark and me, and now you have reappeared. Why, Isolde?"

His voice is brisker than it usually is with me. The briskness of a man with another meeting on the books, a man ready to have something over and dealt with.

It stings, that briskness. Funny that it should sting after Mark's note, his warning delivered through Tristan, but somehow it does.

"When I heard the Holy Father had died, I knew I

needed to find you and see if you required me." I must be careful here but not so careful that what I'm *not* revealing is just as apparent. "And Mark found Tristan. He says all will be forgiven if I come home."

"All will be forgiven…such as your attempted murder of him?"

This requires no artifice, no care at all. It's the whole, unvarnished truth. "I'm almost certain my husband sees a knife at his throat as a novel way to flirt."

Mortimer's mouth flashes down into a frown of distaste and then levels out again. "But he could certainly never trust you as he has before. You've lost any chance of an easy kill."

It's been years since I've fidgeted when speaking in front of him, but now I'm struggling to stay still. I'm asking for too much at once. I'm betting chips I don't even have. On the heels of failure and adultery, I will not be granted anything so uncomplicated as blanket permission to do what I need to do.

Tristan knew this. He begged me not to come this morning, thought it was beyond dangerous. But I had to. I had to have a moment alone with my uncle so I could look at his face and see for myself if any of what Mark claims could be true.

"I have the key to his server rooms," I say calmly. "I took it the night I left. Everything in Lyonesse, we can have. I'll be watched at first. My connection with Tristan was known at the end, so there will be more than Mark's suspicion to deal with. It will be the club's suspicion as well. But when the suspicion eases, as it must over time, I'll find my chance, and the Lyonesse treasury will belong to the saints at last."

I see something I never thought I'd see.

Greed, plain as anything, on my uncle's face.

He buries it quickly, a thoughtful expression and a half turn away from me, but I saw it. It was real. Mortimer

Cashel, the famous cipher, the smiling, inscrutable puppe-teer, undone by this singular desire.

"The Scales told us Mark is moving against the Church, but we don't know his timeline yet, and we might outrun him—or we might be able to stop him. It's a risk, I know, but whatever is in those vaults, Uncle, if it could be yours…"

"All of it," he murmurs, more to himself than to me, I think. "I could finally have all of it."

"Let me atone for my failure," I plead. "Let me return and deliver what you'd asked for. It's not certain, and it will take time—"

"And you will kill Mark at the end?" Mortimer asks. The mask is back, his eyes giving nothing away. "Perhaps it would be unwise to kill him before you get into the server vaults, because your access as a widow or as a murder suspect will be limited, but after… He cannot live, Isolde. He will destroy us if he does."

"Yes." I bow my head again to show my sincerity and to hide my face. "I will make sure I kill him this time."

A finger touches my chin. I look up into green-blue eyes, the right different from the left in its speckling and color composition. "You must," he commands. "You must make sure. If you fail again, if you are *weak* again, God will find a better tool, a sharper blade. Do you understand?"

Did you declare me an apostate? I want to ask. *Did you order my death like you once ordered an evil archbishop's? Like you ordered Mark's?*

These shouldn't be the questions choking my throat right now, not at all. I should want to ask about Ys, I should interrogate him about his plans, his activities, Drobny and Carpathia and if he's hoping to become the pope so he can shape the world even more explicitly to his desires.

But he is the father I wished I had, the only adult in my life who'd ever come close to understanding my grave, desperate, self-scourging heart. My actual father sold me into marriage, and now I want to know if my spiritual father sold me into death.

Because of my failures? Because of my lack of faith? Because he thought I'd been corrupted by Mark?

Or, my mind supplies, *turned by him.*

Turned into a double agent, pretending to work for the Church while I help Mark bring down Ys and my uncle with it.

But I see no answers in my uncle's face now; they are too well hidden. What is clear is the threat about failure and weakness he is making now…which is perhaps its own answer.

"Yes, Uncle," I say, swallowing against the creeping clench of betrayal at the base of my throat. I think of that painting of Abraham and Isaac hanging in the other room, of the terror in Isaac's face. He knew that Abraham wasn't about to stay his own knife. "I understand."

ten

MARK

I don't have time, and it's beyond defensible—just a twinge, really, at the nape of my neck and the pit of my stomach—but I stop at the National Central Library before I skulk out of the city.

For this, I wear a collar (purchased honestly at Gammarelli, like a good Roman priest) so that my nosing around is written off as pre-conclave boredom or as holy scholarly duty. I get into the library and guilt the librarian into honoring my request without any undue curiosity.

I sit in the glossy and echoing rarities room as the old volume is brought out and set on a cradle in front of me. I've already been asked to wash my hands; the rarities room doesn't require gloves for this particular book as a glove's fibers could catch on the brittle paper. They leave me with a few dire warnings in Italian and retreat to their desk on the other side of the room, and then I begin carefully lifting the cover.

When you work for the agency for too long, you develop a condition Melody calls spy brain, which is a sort of paranoid inverse of Occam's razor. It means that when I look at a book, as I am right now, my mind goes to tags or chips hidden in the spine or maybe documents pasted under the endpapers rather than what the pages actually say.

But a subtle scan with my phone reveals nothing at all, and I detect no seams or bumps under the endpapers or the cover of the book.

So then I stop thinking like an old spy and start thinking like an archivist. Like Father Minch would have if he were still alive. I begin to read.

Or rather, I pretend to read, because the *Revelata Scientia* is entirely in Latin. I only know a bare handful of Latin, two scratched-out semesters of high school before I dropped it for Spanish, and it was only enough to toil through Aesop's *Fables*, not enough to decipher whatever passed for "science" in 1682, when this was published.

Luckily, it's a slim volume, and I decide to cheat. I surreptitiously take pictures of each page with my phone, page after page of unevenly printed Latin with the occasional inset drawing, and then I gently close the book and stare at it for a moment, knowing I've wasted time I don't have on a feeling I can't prove.

Why did Father Minch have you written in the margins of his Bible? I ask the book.

It doesn't answer, and no possibilities come to me. I drum my fingers once on the table and then get up to tell the librarian I'm finished.

Three hours later, a favor from Lyonesse's treasury used, and I'm on a U.S. Air Force flight to DC, red hair, collar, and all.

———

"—asking to see you, one about the pope's death and his secrets, and three members about ongoing concerns with your wife and bodyguard missing. One is having a dispute with another member over a private room—sounds like an unauthorized subletting situation gone awry—and then we have an NDA issue to resolve. Andrea knows a little more about that than me, so I've scheduled a meeting between the three of us this afternoon. As you've requested, we're not opening the club on Christmas Eve or Christmas, although we will have a larger gathering the last day of Saturnalia, and then of course, our usual fete on New Year's Eve. Also are you going to explain the priest collar, or is this your latest bid to seem daring and mysterious?"

I look over at Dinah, my club manager, who's followed me into my apartment as I start shucking off my coat. "*Seem daring and mysterious?*" I ask, affronted.

She's not concerned for my hurt pride in the least. "And the hair? I'm sorry, Mark, but you make a terrible redhead."

I finish with my coat and drape it over a kitchen chair. Tiredness pulls at me, reminding me that I'm no longer a dashing young CIA officer. I really need to focus on getting a solid six or seven hours a night. "It'll wash out in a day or two. It was expedient not to be so overtly...*me* while abroad."

A dark, perfectly shaped brow lifts. But Dinah doesn't press; she knows it's for her own sake that I keep my activities close to the chest, and it's the same for Goran and Sedge too. Only Andrea has a slightly clearer picture of how I spend my time away from the club, and even then, it's still not complete.

"Sir," comes Sedge's soft voice from my door. "I thought you might want to set the week's agenda."

"Come in," I say, just as Dinah gives an *I'm going to get some work done* wave and starts to leave. "Dinah, I'll see you this afternoon when we meet with Andrea about the NDA violation."

"Yes, yes, see you later," she says, passing Sedge as he steps into the apartment.

His eyes catch on the collar at my neck, and a flush threatens at his freckled cheeks. "I, ah." He clears his throat and shuts the door, and when he turns back to me, his expression is devoid of anything telling. "I'm glad to see you back, sir. About this week's schedule, I kept it light in case your trip was extended once again. You'll meet this afternoon with Andrea and Dinah, and then on Sunday, you have a scheduled call with POTUS. That would be tricky to move if you needed to move it, but if you need a little more time to adjust from the jet lag, we can."

"No, no, keep the call with Moore." I think for a moment. "I'd like to meet with Goran and Nat tomorrow to follow up on the security changes since Drobny's attack."

"Sir." Sedge is using a stylus to write on his tablet now.

"And Lox. Can we put in a call to her? I can talk anytime that I'm not in the meeting this afternoon, including tonight. I'll be absent from the hall." I need time to wash out the dye. My club employees are one thing, but I don't need members at large seeing me with the same red hair I used to hop around Rome before a conclave.

"Yes, sir."

As he makes some notes, I unbutton the long-sleeved black shirt I'm wearing and roll up the sleeves. Sedge's gaze darts to my forearms and then, with some effort, pulls away. I politely pretend not to notice.

I kick off my shoes, stretch my back, and consider whether I have time for a shower and a nap before my meeting or just a shower when my assistant steps closer.

"Sir," he starts and then pauses. Looks down at his tablet but seems to see nothing. "I…"

I wait. I've had Sedge with me for less than two years,

but I've always found that his cautious insights are worth my patience.

"Did you find them? In Europe? Is that why you left?" The question seems to leave his lips despite himself—and there's no question who he means by *them*—and I'm unprepared for this from Sedge. From Andrea, certainly, and maybe this kind of probing from Dinah, when she's in a no-bullshit mood, but Sedge has always, always kept his opinions to himself, expressing them only with flicks of those silver eyes.

I don't think there's harm in telling him the truth, so long as it's not specific. "I did. And yes, that's why I left."

"But she's not here with you. She's not back."

"No," I exhale. "No, she's not back."

There is a furtive sort of ache to his face now, a compressed longing around his mouth and eyes, and I don't entirely understand what's happening until he steps forward again and sinks to his knees. Right in front of me.

"Sedge…"

"Sir, please. I am here for you. *Only* for you. If you need me."

I let out a long breath. I've fucked two bodyguards in a row—and Isabella Beroul and a few other subs besides—all while I was engaged to Isolde. I can hardly claim to be a picky man when it comes to fucking, so how can I explain to myself or anyone else all the subtle contours and gradations of obsession and possession and yearning? The love negotiated over adultery and secrets and lies? The betrayals turned into proof of devotion by the raised red line on my neck?

I love you, Isolde said with a knife pressing into my skin. *I love you*. And she meant it.

No, of course Sedge doesn't understand. He, like everyone, thinks I'm a hedonist with a bent toward sadism and imagines no barrier between me and my own shortsighted gratification now that I've been so publicly cuckolded.

Not to say that the idea of using my assistant in such a way would *never* have held any appeal for me. Sedge is beautiful and well made, his mouth a thing of temptation, his features delicate and symmetrical. The finely wrought face and the nearly colorless eyes give him an otherworldly look, and who wouldn't want to study those freckles? Watch those eyes change from silver to black as you cajoled pleasure out of his guarded body?

Before I can (gently) refuse him, he leans forward and presses his face between my hips. I freeze, but he doesn't, some kind of long-held control unraveling into loops and piles around him as he rubs against my groin, needily, hungrily, mouth open and whimpering. His entire body is shaking, and he's dropped his tablet on the floor, and when I slide my fingers into his flaxen hair, he presses even harder against me, seeking and mouthing.

"Please," he begs. "Please, sir. Only for you. I'll be only for you."

Blood and heat pool, and I swell against the attention. It would be easy, I think, to unbuckle my belt, pull myself out, and make my pliant assistant give me some relief. To grant myself satisfaction for all the times Tristan and Isolde have made a fool of me. To clear my head so I can *think*, so I can feel for a moment like the man I was before Tristan Thomas came and knocked down every palisade I'd built around my innermost being.

But bodyguards aside, I've been reluctant to fuck my employees, and it would be dangerous for me and someone like Sedge to be together anyway, because he is trembling with something that feels almost like self-hatred, and I would—

I would not be responsible with that.

91

It doesn't matter anyhow. As easily stirred as my flesh is right now, my mind and spirit are still in a Cornish forest watching my deceitful ones hold hands in their sleep.

"Sedge," I say with as much kindness as I can muster.

Contrary to what you might have heard about me, I try to soften my cruelties where I can. I understand Sedge's lust. I know what it feels like to have a yawning void in your belly, to feel like the ache in your chest and the ache between your legs are the same, the same throbbing grief.

"Sedge," I say again, and I pull his hair, tilting his face up toward mine. I am too firm with my grip, I think, because arousal whips through him as he registers the pain, and his hips move in the air. "You are everything someone like me could want. But I can't."

"You want it," he breathes. His cheeks are flushed, and his velvety lips are too. "You're so hard, sir. I can help. Let me help." He reaches up to squeeze the undeniable erection I'm sporting. Fuck.

I tighten my grip enough that the hand on me falters.

"I can't," I say, my voice as sympathetic as the hand in his hair isn't. "My body and my mind aren't in agreement. I still miss—I still wish they were—"

I blow out a long breath, let go of Sedge's hair, and then step back. His hand, where it had been fondling me, hovers in the empty air.

"I'm sorry. I am grateful for this, Sedge, but I'm not ready."

He ducks his head, his hand falling slowly to his side. "For her. You deny yourself for her, when she has denied herself nothing."

"I have not denied myself Tristan either," I reply. "Surely, the gossip at Lyonesse isn't so feeble that you haven't heard."

"They've chosen each other. They've left. How long will you starve yourself?" His voice is a miserable whisper now, and it makes me miserable too. That is the nature of unhappiness. It spreads like ink in water.

I move forward and press my hand to the side of his face. He turns toward the warmth instinctively, a flower to the sun. "In another life, you'd be very wanted. And in this life, I can help you find what you're looking for."

"You," he says, his eyes closed. "I'm always looking for you. And at you. Sir."

"I wish that things were otherwise," I say, which is barely true. There is no *otherwise* that's worth living through.

But the words seem to revive Sedge. "They will be eventually," he murmurs, opening his eyes to look up into mine. "I can wait, sir. For your broken heart to heal."

It won't, but there is no point in telling him so. I don't want to bruise this rare, vulnerable courage any more than I have to.

"That's kind of you," I answer, and then I kiss his head. "Will you be okay? Do you need a break from me after this?"

His teeth catch his lower lip as a new flush stains his skin. "I'll never need a break from serving you, sir."

———

I do have time for a shower before my afternoon meeting, and then right after, Lox calls me.

"Do you have more contractors exploiting my perfectly safe security systems using the log-ins you gave them?" she asks after I say *hello*. Just because one time a contractor managed to use our background check system to allow for Drobny's men to attack the club, endanger my guests, and stab me.

"I'll let you know during New Year's Eve," I say, turning in my desk chair to face the window. The Potomac is a tired gray, and even though the capital is doing its best to put on a festive show for the holidays, it looks tired and gray too. "But I appreciate the fixes you made."

I hear the reluctance in her reply. "However they got in, I wasn't happy they were able to fool the system with the fake profiles. I take pride in my work, and it pissed me off. I was glad to fix it."

"I have another project for you."

"Is there money in it, and will it piss off the NSA?"

"Don't worry about the NSA," I say, waving a hand she can't see. "We have a friend there now."

Lox snorts. "You want me to trust your sister? I was in intelligence too, Mark. I heard the stories about her."

"Then trust me."

"Absolutely not."

"Fair. But I'll pay double your usual rate." I quickly explain about Father Minch's Bible and my little library excursion in Rome.

Lox is immediately interested. "A Vatican archivist? Killed by a saint?"

"On Cashel's orders. And I feel like it isn't saint business but Ys business. I have no evidence for this, however. Only a gut feeling."

"And you think the scribbles in the priest's Bible are the evidence you need?" She doesn't sound skeptical, more like a mathematician drawing up an equation and tagging the unknowns.

"I can't even say *think*, because it implies some logic behind it. But he wanted me to have the Bible. He made it sound like what he'd written in there was important."

"Okay," she says. "So what do we need to do?"

"I'll send the pictures of the book over to you and the other titles Minch wrote down. I can't read Latin but…"

A snort. "I'll have it translated."

"Thank you."

"What do you think it will say?" she asks. "What could any of these books say that would have made Minch run away?"

"Something about Ys. Maybe something that connects Ys to the Catholic Church. Perhaps he went to Cashel, or perhaps he was smart enough to run away the minute he realized."

"Makes sense. Okay, I'll call once I have something."

"And, Lox?" I ask before she can hang up.

She groans. "What now?"

"Could you find someone for me too?"

"Possibly," she says warily. "Who?"

I stare out at the river. "Cara Sims."

"I'll do my best," replies Lox.

"I'll pay you double for that too."

"You better." And the call ends.

With a sigh, I turn back to my desk, where I see my prepared folder for the day, unopened from earlier this morning. I flip it open, seeing Sedge's neat and organized mind all over it, and let out a long, regretful exhale.

In another life, maybe. I dislike causing him pain in this one though.

There's a printed news article in the folder too with a brief note from Andrea. I thought you'd find this interesting, she's written.

Disgraced Carpathian Leader Melwas Kocur Dies in Prison; Preliminary Investigation Points to Heart Medication

As it happens, I do find it interesting. There will be an inquiry, an investigation into the Carpathian prison's health-care services, but he was an unhealthy man at the end, or at least that's what one hears through the grapevine.

I tap my thumb against the paper, granting myself a small breath of satisfaction. This at least has gone to plan.

Under the very satisfying article is a one-page

report—from Andrea—detailing a search for any mention of the name Brittany Hill in our treasury. There is none, so Andrea naturally asked Lox to shake some digital trees. As far as anyone can tell, Brittany Hill doesn't exist, at least online.

And then finally, there's a quick report about an email that was sent out to the college of cardinals in advance of the conclave.

Sent anonymously, it succinctly described the various Ys-related sins of Mortimer Cashel and then offered as much verifiable proof as we have—any proof that doesn't directly expose myself or a Lyonesse member as the source.

If the cardinals are really going to elect Cashel, then I don't want them to say they weren't warned.

That said, my hopes for this particular gambit are limited. Most of the cardinals aren't reading their own email, and the odds of an anonymous, conspiratorial message getting in front of a cardinal's eyes are low. Still, it would only take one chatty member of the Sacred College to ignite gossip, and if anything slows down the conclave, it's worth it. I make a mental note to tell Andrea to hold off on sending our florilegium just yet—the conclave will start any day now, and then nothing will be able to penetrate the hallowed halls of the Sistine Chapel. I'd rather save that card for a later, stronger play.

I flip the folder closed just as my phone lights up. A text from a number I don't recognize, six words to set my heart pounding.

We're coming back to you, sir.

eleven

TRISTAN

I'M MORE NERVOUS THAN I THINK I'VE EVER BEEN, INCLUDing going to war, including running away from Lyonesse with a furious Mark lashed to a chair. Those were nothing in hindsight, just the unconscious flexure of skill, a blend of panic and courage.

But returning *to* Mark...

I would be a very stupid person not to be scared right now.

Mark won't hurt Isolde. I am certain of this much at least. I also think he won't hurt me, not the kind of hurting that usually inspires fear.

It's only that the danger isn't in his violence but in his love. In the crushing, churning star-fusing burn of it.

If he still loves us, that is. And despite his wicked mouth in Rome, I have my doubts. What kind of love can survive this? *Us?*

There aren't any guests in the lobby this early, but Ms. Lim is behind the desk, a ring of keys at her waist. Her expression doesn't change as we approach, but she does step out to greet us.

"Mr. Trevena is expecting you," she says. "Follow me."

I glance over as we follow Ms. Lim up the stairs. Isolde doesn't need the railing, climbing the stairs with that prep school poise of hers, and like everyone I've chosen to surround myself with these days, her face betrays nothing at all. She looks like she's walking into Lyonesse after a morning spent in those expensive stores where they keep almost nothing on the shelves. Like she never left.

I wish I had her mettle. Her certainty.

What is it that Mark said to me? *When you've been where I've been, on those roads, in those pits of hell, you come to know that you can* only *be certain of yourself.*

Perhaps Isolde feels the same. She must. She's been walking very similar roads to Mark since she was nineteen.

Embarrassment snaps at my belly as I think of the martial arts on the yacht, the cherished knife, the meetings in Belgrade. I hadn't seen *what* she was until Samhain—I hadn't understood that I'd prostrated myself at the feet of yet another killer. I'd thought her a princess, a lonely queen, a kindred spirit, but all along, she'd been kindred to Mark's spirit, not mine. Her loneliness had been chosen with blood, and her crown was soldered with sin and set with the jewels of heaven…and until Samhain, I'd thought she priced old bowls for a living.

But I love her.

I can do nothing else.

Like the first time I walked through this club, I keep my eyes on Ms. Lim's heels as they click up the stairs and down the corridor leading to the hall's first tier of balconies. That time, it had been good manners. This time, it's to fight the urge to check on Isolde. To stare at her with worry or possessiveness or anything else that might set tongues wagging.

As if that will make a difference. I glance up to see a group of guests descending the staircase from the speakeasy-style bar above, presumably from a late lunch, and I watch as awareness of her festers through the guests like an infection.

Isolde's wearing a wool dress today—navy—with long sleeves, a high neck, and a skirt that flutters below her calves. Her hair is in a loose braid of pearl and gold, pulled over one shoulder, and her stockinged feet are clad in black heels, tall enough to be stylish, short enough to be appropriate in all but the most particular of churches. She is above all else completely unobjectionable, the Laurence heiress, the unflashily but tastefully clad daughter of a banker, and I know she chose this dress as armor, as a statement.

You cannot make me into the whore of your imagination, the clothes and hair say. *Try to accuse me of all the sins you think I've committed. Just try.*

But it doesn't make a difference. That only her hands are exposed simply eroticizes them, draws attention to the slender fingers and the now-tainted wedding ring. The dress hugs the tidy lines of her shoulders and pert curves of her chest. The braid—messy and soft and gleaming and tuggable—is patently obscene. If she were naked, she could hardly stir a person more.

The club members seem to agree, because under the glances of disgust or distrust or mockery, there is leering hunger. She's no longer Mark's darling pet. She's clearly unfaithful and therefore valueless to Mark, so why can't they have a turn with her?

It's reflexive and stupid of me, but I step between the members and Isolde and block their view. I give them the blank look I've learned to wear as Mark's bodyguard and gesture for Isolde to go on.

They stop gawking, but I don't miss that they clock me, my protectiveness, and I know by tonight, the club will be churning. Mark's wife is back, *with* the bodyguard, and you won't believe how audaciously they were acting around each other, in broad daylight no less…

I can't control it, and I don't know if Mark will even care, but it makes me clench my teeth all the same. They don't know anything about what's between Mark and Isolde or Isolde and me. They don't know that on Samhain, we'd held a fragile, glimmering possibility between the three of us. That for a few hours, it felt like we were the only people in the world.

On our way to the hall, we pass two employees and three members coming from a playroom, and it's the same story. They all look at me, a skimming of mild disapproval, and then look at Isolde with an antipathy that is no less carnal for how censorious it is. The blame of it all, the stain of adultery and betrayal, have settled on her.

Not me. Not Mark, whose secrets and lies lit the fuse just as surely as anything else. Oh no. Only her.

And I know it won't get any better after we get to the hall itself and I hear two very unwelcome voices: Andrea's and Sedge's.

Mark, who's standing with them and Dinah in his usual nook, looks over to see us approaching. When he notices how I move between him and his wife, his hand flexes at his side.

"Sir, Mr. Thomas and Mrs. Trevena are here," Ms. Lim says crisply.

Andrea stares at us with open dislike. Sedge doesn't look at us at all, his face a freckled cipher, angled toward his tablet as he writes something down.

"Thank you, Ms. Lim," Mark says. His voice is serious, his face serious too. He's wearing all black today, just like he was in that Roman park, and in the silver daylight coming in through the glassed roof, his eyes are blue enough to glow.

It's only been three days, but the shock of those

eyes—that gold hair, those forearms exposed by rolled-up sleeves—is nearly enough to make me turn and run in the other direction. It's one thing to meet in the twilight, already sundered, already hopeless, but to be here in daylight, hopeful, *hoping*—it's like walking right at the enemy with nothing in your hands but a white flag.

Ms. Lim leaves in a jingling of keys and a tattoo of heels on concrete, and then Mark looks out over the floor of the hall. Turned like this and with the benefit of daylight, I can see the things I couldn't in Rome: a hollow curve under his cheekbones, a new shadow under his eyes. The last six weeks have taken a toll on him, and I can't scoff at the word *heart-break* now, can I? Not when he looks like this.

Guilt is a hook behind my ribs. We had no choice on Samhain, but all those justifications feel strangely distant right now. Like they couldn't have been worth this.

"I know we're not finished with the Saturnalia planning," he says, "but I'd like a few moments alone with Mrs. Trevena, if I may."

I start to move, but he stops me.

"You stay, Tristan."

I don't know what would be easier to bear, the jealousy if I was sent away or the dread I feel now at being asked to remain, but either way, Dinah gives me a small, encouraging smile as she moves past. Sedge looks at neither of us as he leaves, and Andrea saves her venomous glare for Isolde. So much animosity rolls off the treasurer's blazer-clad shoulders that I think she might throw Isolde off the balcony as she passes.

And then we're alone, save for the staff downstairs currently unwinding protective padding on some very convincing Roman statues.

Mark braces his hands on the railing. "So," he says to the hall and not to us. "You've returned. I'm glad."

Before I can talk myself out of it, I ask, "Are you, sir? I'd rather be hiding from you for the rest of our lives than leave Isolde here if she's going to be treated like she's been treated so far today. So tell me that you *are* glad, that you aren't just offering her a haven but a home too."

Isolde draws a deep breath next to me but doesn't speak. I can't tell if she's relieved I've dragged this into the open or if she wishes I'd shut up.

For his part, Mark turns and leans his side against the railing, crossing his feet at the ankles so that one dress-shoed foot is propped up on its toe. I catch the very faint, very fast flicker of amusement around his mouth. "Hiding from me for the rest of your lives?"

He doesn't have to say the rest. *As if you could* is written all over his face.

I won't squirm, even if he's right. Waking up to his knife between us, the note tucked neatly underneath it, was like waking up to yellow eyes in the dark. The mammalian parts of my brain could only process it as the most immediate kind of danger, as a failure of vigilance. I slept through my watch, the wolf crept in, and now we would surely die.

"How did you find us?" Isolde asks. Her voice is pitched low so that it won't carry any farther than the balcony railing.

"I have my ways, and to answer your earlier question, Tristan, *I am glad.*" A catch on the word *glad*, and then a flicker of muscle along the side of his jaw. Like gladness isn't the only feeling burning inside him. He meets Isolde's eyes. "I take your presence here to mean that Tristan passed along my warnings about your uncle?"

Isolde's posture is as upright and graceful as Mark's is careless and slouching, but I know them well enough now to know that they would be circling each other if they could, a skeptical lioness and an arrogant lion scenting the air.

She lifts a hand in a gesture that I take to mean *to an*

extent. "What you told me in your note...what you told Tristan. You understand that it's nearly impossible for me to believe. That my uncle is the head of some secret society while also being the Vatican's head of intelligence. That my uncle would plan to *kill* me." Her voice doesn't shake, but I hear the wavering at the far edges of her words. She pulls in a deep breath. "You are asking me to believe the very worst of someone who was a father to me in every way that mattered and with no evidence save for your word. Your *word*, Mark, and you know how cheap a currency that is right now."

"But you're here now," Mark observes in a soft, silky voice. "So really, how cheap can it be, little wife?"

Isolde clamps down on whatever emotion ripples through her before it can do more than rouge her cheeks. She looks down and to the side, and I can practically feel her fighting inside herself.

"I went to see him," she says. Mark doesn't bother to hide his displeasure at that, and she looks up and laughs joylessly. "Tristan wasn't happy about it either. And funnily enough, my uncle wasn't happy about Tristan. He called me foolish and weak for running away with him, so there's unhappiness all around, it turns out. I told him that I wanted a second chance to rob your treasury. That it would take some time to regain your trust and that of course you'd need to stay alive until the prize was stolen. He wants what you have badly enough that he'll change his plans to get it, so he agreed."

Mark watches her. "And you believe him? You don't think that he said what he needed to say to maneuver his lamb back into the pen for slaughter?"

"I do believe him," she says, "because he strongly implied that same slaughter if my time here resulted in any more failures."

Mark doesn't reply, and I can offer nothing, because I'm just as clenched with anger and ferocious vigilance as I was when Isolde first told me. I want to build an outpost around her right now. I want air support and an entire company of troops on the way. I want to patrol her perimeter, and I also want to find her uncle and end this.

"So as you see, I'm here," she says tightly. "I don't want to believe you, and yet I'm here. I can barely stomach the idea that everything I've known to be true about my family, my faith, and my work as a saint is wrong, and yet I'm here. You've lied to me from the moment I met you, but my uncle has been lying to me since I was born, and I suppose that has to be worse."

Mark straightens and walks toward Isolde, who stays completely still. He takes her hand. "You betrayed my only request. You left me and took the sole other person I love with you when you went. You are the niece of my enemy and the one person in this world who can do me the greatest harm. And yet I'm here too."

Her lips tremble as he drops his mouth to the backs of her fingers. It's a cold kiss, I think. More like the kiss of an enemy than a husband.

"I'm not your uncle or your God, Isolde. I don't need your faith. Just stay until the gates of hell are shut. We can make it that long, I think."

twelve

TRISTAN

Footsteps come from behind me, and I turn to see a staff member wheeling in a dolly loaded with crates of wax candles, enough candles to make a firefighter whimper.

"Saturnalia," Mark says, as if that clears anything up, and then he sighs. His fingers tighten around Isolde's. "We should go up to my office for the next part."

The next part?

There's something grave in his tone, something that seeds worry in my gut. "Sir," I say, and I lead the way upstairs.

For six weeks, I have quietly dreamed of the three of us together, reunited somehow by an elegant twist of love or by some undeniable atonement, restored to what we were on Samhain. Adultery forgiven, lies forgiven, everything come to terms. But when I shut the door to Mark's office and the three of us are truly, completely alone, I don't feel joy or relief.

I feel like I've just buried us alive.

"Sit," Mark says into the hushed silence of the room, nodding at the two chairs in front of his desk. We do, me sitting with my feet flat on the floor and my hands on my thighs, Isolde crossing one leg over the other with her hands folded in her lap. Mark himself leans back against the front of his desk, half sitting on the edge, his hands in his pockets. His eyes, when they meet mine, are the blue of a glacier's underwater heart. Lovely, unfeeling.

The air is so thick in here I think I'm choking on it.

"Tristan, I can't have you at Lyonesse."

His words take time to create meaning inside my mind. At first, they are only sound, and then they are language, and then they are—

Exile. Death.

Damnation.

I think I make a noise maybe, a soft one, the instinctive inhale you take before a fall.

Isolde sits forward, features going bloodless with indignation. "If you want to punish someone, look to yourself first. We only left because of what I found in your safe, because you planned to kill my uncle—"

"Who planned to kill me, via yourself," Mark interjects.

"—and if this is a matter of adultery, of *fidelity*, I thought this was decided on Samhain, I thought we were in agreement. *I want you both to be mine, and I also want you to be each other's.* Sound familiar?"

"The 'mine' part was rather stripped from the equation when you zip-tied me to a chair and fled the country," says Mark, a little bitterly.

"So this is revenge? For six weeks' worth of separation?"

"Or for four years of lying to me about the real reason you agreed to this marriage," Mark suggests but then sighs. "I lied for the same length of time about the same thing, so we'll leave that one as a draw, shall we?"

Isolde's lips are white at the edges. "I thought my punishment for cheating was to know that you'd claim a right to

Tristan's bed as well. If we're going back to retribution, why not return to precedent?"

"I'd love to, believe me," Mark replies in a husky voice that I can feel on the nape of my neck and on the insides of my palms. "I'd like to itemize every lost hour—every excruciating moment apart—on your disloyal little bodies. I'd record my tolls and taxes with bite marks and splatters of wax."

I shudder. But I'm still falling, only barely listening past the blood whooshing in my ears and the rush of the ground coming up to meet me.

Mark is making me leave Lyonesse. Mark doesn't want me here with him, with Isolde.

"However," Mark goes on before Isolde can interrupt, "we have a…" He moves a hand from his pocket, as if to indicate the forthcoming linguistic imprecision. "A challenge."

"Is that so?" demands Isolde.

He's unfazed by her anger. "Two challenges, in fact, but they are linked. I'm sure you remember that Andrea was responsible for the revelation of your infidelity, first to me alone and then later to the club at large?"

The narrowing of Isolde's aquamarine eyes is the only response Mark gets.

It's enough for him. "I don't think there's currently a Lyonesse member who doesn't know what happened in the garden before Samhain, and while I'd like to think that there could have been some amelioration of the facts if we'd had time after that as a—as the three of us together…alas. The club knows I was discovered tied to that very chair with my neck bleeding and the safe hanging open. This has created uncertainty around the security of the club's secrets, and I am the first to admit that from a member's vantage, it all looks very messy and frangible."

"I presume it was Andrea who made sure this version of events spread through the club?"

Mark's gaze is cool on Isolde's face. "Am I to presume that you find Andrea bearing tales about my being zip-tied to a chair more objectionable than the being zip-tied to a chair itself?"

Her eyebrow arches ever so slightly. "I'm presuming that you know where to start cleaning your *messy and frangible* house, Mark. Your own subordinate is more preoccupied with her hatred of me than the integrity of the club. Or you could simply tell her why Tristan and I found it necessary to leave so quickly?"

"Oh, she knows," Mark replies. "It does little to change her opinion, of course, but opinions are resistant that way. But we're drifting from the point: it doesn't matter how the club learned of anything. The problem is that they did."

"And now the problem is us," I say numbly. "If you welcome us back after what we did…"

"I look like a terrible judge of character at best. At worst, I look like I'm again putting the club's security at risk. The security of the secrets beneath our feet." Mark's voice is as stark and cold as the glass surrounding us. "If I'm to keep you safe, Isolde, and if I'm to fight Ys, I need the club stable and reaping secrets at its usual rate. I can't afford for Lyonesse to fall apart before I'm finished."

I look down at my hands. The logic is sound. It still hurts.

Isolde takes a moment to speak. "The second challenge?" she finally asks.

"I don't know if your uncle is sincere in his endorsement of you returning, but I do know that if you're back here and Tristan remains by your side, it will undermine the illusion that you need time to win back my trust. Allowing your lover to remain here with you will look like I'm entirely too forgiving—and therefore you'd be able to exploit that forgiveness and furnish results for him right away. Or it'll look like you're not trying to win back my trust at all."

"If you claimed Tristan publicly…" She trails off, and Mark nods after it becomes clear that she isn't going to say more.

"I'm guessing you've spotted the problem? Claiming Tristan as my own lover might make a kind of sense if we were only performing for your uncle, but it won't quiet the whispers of Lyonesse. It will look like I'm keeping *two* duplicitous lovers close, which is much worse than attempting to repair a marriage with only one."

Isolde stands suddenly, not to leave but to pace. I look over my shoulder to watch her.

"It's not fair," she says, looking at me. "That you should be sent away in exile when you among the three of us have sinned the least."

"You have to be the one to stay," I say. I might be falling, all my bones might break when I hit the ground, but this much is true: "You need to be here. You'll be safer at Lyonesse than anywhere else."

"I hate this," she hisses. Her dress swings and swirls around her calves as she walks. "I hate the idea that I have to hide in a bower while Tristan is sent away in shame. That I have to stay here and be judged and reviled when it's not—not that simple—" Her voice is tight, and she turns away from both of us, too proud to let us see.

"I will do everything I can to preserve your dignity here," Mark says, and that cold authority of his is layered in every word. "No one will speak ill of you in my presence."

"Everything you can," Isolde echoes doubtfully. "Then will you fire Andrea?"

Mark takes a moment to answer. "I will not."

She turns to face him. "*Why?* She hates me. She undermines the strength of the club. Are you saying that there is no one else who can be the treasurer? No one else at all?"

"Andrea knows about Ys," he explains. "This is her fight

too. She was the first person aside from Melody to know what I planned to do."

We both look at Mark, and I think of his words on the roof several weeks ago. *She hates the same people I hate.*

"That's why you trust her," I say. "Because she wants to take down Ys."

"She needs the club functioning just as much as I do," he agrees. "And I need *her*, because the true nature of her job is curating and connecting information that has to do with Ys. Everything we've pieced together over the years, that's been me, yes, but her and Lox too. I'm sorry, Isolde, but she has to stay."

Isolde starts pacing again, unsatisfied.

"Sir," I venture, again trying to keep the misery out of my voice. "Am I fired? Evicted? How long do I have to find another job?"

Pity notches the space between Mark's brows. "I should have explained things better, Tristan, I'm sorry. You're not fired, and you're not evicted, but I have found a place for you elsewhere—with a friend of mine, Hugo. He owns a kink club called Armorica, and he's having some security issues around one of his submissives, something about an ex-member stalking her. You remember her. Isabella Beroul?"

Isolde paces even faster, and I give a short, tight nod. Yes, obviously I remember Isabella. Remember Mark fucking her atop the very desk he's leaning against now.

"You'll like Hugo," he's saying. "He's friendlier than me, which will be a welcome change, and his co-owner, Kayden, is about your age and also a former service member. Of the Canadian Army though. Naturally."

I can't keep up. "Naturally?"

"Well, they are Canadian. Armorica is in Montreal." Mark straightens and walks over to his credenza and makes himself a drink, like I'm not quietly panicking.

Montreal. *Canada.* I won't just be in a different city than the people I love but a different country altogether. The word *exile* suddenly doesn't feel strong enough.

"No gin?" Isolde asks acerbically as Mark knocks back a deep swallow of scotch.

A raspy laugh. "No, my queen. I assumed from the glass you left out on Samhain that my little habit had been thoroughly autopsied."

Okay, now I really can't keep up. "What habit?" I ask.

Isolde gives me a guilty look. "I didn't tell you because it seemed—well, it seemed obvious once I figured it out."

"Clearly, it's not obvious," I mutter. Petulance is strung through every word, but I can't help it. I know they're married, and now I know that they are more alike to each other than either of them is to me, but I hate the idea of all this private knowledge between them. I have no right to jealousy, but what does it matter now? We are all constantly, viciously jealous of each other, and I'm jealous of a glass of gin. Great.

"Isolde has learned that I'm not quite the dipsomaniac I've pretended to be," Mark says, as if the glass of scotch in his hand doesn't testify to the opposite. "My gin intake over the past several years has been more like…" A gesture with the glass that sends the whisky rolling inside. "Water. With some gin syrup added in, lest anyone get close enough to smell it. Or in case I kiss any bodyguards."

"Water?" I echo faintly. "Are you fucking kidding me?"

My language takes both Isolde and Mark by surprise. Isolde pauses midpace, and both of Mark's eyebrows lift.

"I am not fucking kidding you," he responds. "How do you go from the great and terrible Mark Trevena, the Sea Hound, to someone barely worth remembering? Barely worth thinking about? You turn into someone sloppy and slow. You remind them that you're no longer a young man. You show them a man so consumed with vice that he's forgotten to look over his shoulder. So I learned to tolerate the taste of gin-flavored water. It's not so bad, you know—it tastes like drinking from a Christmas tree stand. Or how I imagine that would taste. I haven't personally done it."

Isolde is moving again. "*Montreal*. How long?"

"I don't know." He does sound sorry about that at least. "As long as it takes." Isolde seems ready to prosecute him over this, and then he adds casually, "As long as it takes to make sure we have no perceived gap between us and that there won't be any more failures."

She stops, something struggling to break free in her face. Her hands move in her skirt, fisting the fabric and then letting go. I know that phrase, *perceived gap*—Isolde spoke those very words on the yacht when she was explaining the nature of her arranged marriage to me. Something about it seems to be affecting her deeply now.

Why? A ghost of past promises? Of vows unkept or intentions bent backward?

Mark is already staring at her when she looks over at him, his expression as casual as his tone, but when she meets his gaze, something decidedly uncasual passes between them.

Ah, that jealousy again.

"Right," she says, and there's a new tension around her eyes and mouth. "As long as it takes then."

"Sir," I break in, "I will go wherever I need to go, for however long, but will this mean that we can't…see each other at all? That we can't speak?"

Mark seems to want to say something and manages to wrench himself back from the edge. But guessing from the glass-draining swallow he takes and the twist of his mouth, it's something along the lines of *You didn't speak to me for six weeks. Clearly, you've been practicing for it.*

"It's smarter to keep our communication limited," says Isolde.

I can't keep the shock from my face. She didn't want me to leave a moment ago. Now she's saying we shouldn't even talk while I'm gone?

She meets my gaze levelly, although her hands are bunched in her skirt again. "We don't know who we can trust at Lyonesse, Tristan. I still think Andrea—"

"We are not putting Andrea's loyalty on trial again," Mark interrupts with some irritation.

"I don't care that she claims to hate Ys, Mark. She was at Drobny's favorite club, and she has no problem sowing discord inside yours."

Mark responds by pouring himself another scotch.

"As I was saying," Isolde says after a deep inhale, "I don't know how safe any communication would be, either because of a plant here at Lyonesse or because of one at Armorica. We have to assume that anything might leak out to the club at large and render all our careful sacrifices useless."

Well, fuck, I don't want that either. Leaving the two of them alone to re-create even the facsimile of a healing marriage will cleave me down to the bone, but the idea of my semi-banishment ultimately being for nothing is unendurable. I'd rather go back to being a ghost in my father's farmhouse. I'd rather go back to Carpathia.

"Right," I say around the ache in my throat. "We don't want that." And then to cover the new thickness in my voice, I say, "And when should I go, sir?"

Mark doesn't answer right away, and when he does, it's with the kind of precision that comes with a rehearsed apology…or a death sentence. "Your plane leaves tonight, Tristan."

thirteen

TRISTAN

TONIGHT.

I leave tonight.

"What time tonight?" Isolde asks for me, as if she knows I can't speak right now.

"Jago will escort Tristan to the airport in two hours. Goran will go too so he can give Tristan a quick briefing on Armorica on the way there."

So it's already been arranged, all of it settled. I should have known—Mark would never have broached the subject if he didn't have a course charted and the sails trimmed awaiting a tilt of the rudder. Sea Hound indeed.

"It's discourteous of me to separate the two of you with so little preparation, I admit, but I believe it's the safest course of action for Isolde."

"*And* your vendetta against Ys," I say, the acrimony seeping up from my stomach and stinging my tongue. But I can't stop myself. "That's what it's all been for, right? Marrying Isolde? And now splitting us apart? It's all for your revenge. *Yours.* Even though none of it would've been necessary if you had just left the two of us alone in the first place."

"I regret that I've put the two of you in this position." The words are diplomatic, but his bloodless knuckles around his glass are anything but. He looks like he wants to hurl his drink at the window and then demand I square up. "And I regret that any of this was necessary to avenge Eliot."

"You don't regret it," I say, getting to my feet. Not to fight but so that he can hear this properly before I go. "Not enough that you'd do it differently if given another chance."

A merciless smile. "How well you read me, Tristan. How well you know my mind, because *you are correct.* I would not do it differently, not if I thought there was no other way to find Ys and strangle it to death. But this is why you stayed a soldier and why they pulled me out of a war to do the things even generals blush to think about. Because I am willing to put three hearts on the scale and offer them in payment for the destruction of a shadow that has stolen from me, from you, from Aaron Sims and Cara Sims, from the people of Carpathia, and on and on and on. I have watched people pay far greater prices than heartbreak for far, far fucking less, so yes, I would do it again, because I think it's a goddamn *bargain.*"

The glass makes a sharp *crack* as Mark sets it on the credenza. He doesn't look like a man who's found a bargain at all. He looks like we're robbing him and leaving him for dead, like a traveler from Jerusalem on his way to Jericho. Like he'll never have a Good Samaritan pass by no matter how long he waits.

It doesn't cut my anger, but the joyless resignation in his face complicates it. I think Mark believes what he says, but I think he hates it too.

I think he has to remind himself to believe it sometimes, because it hurts so much.

"Did you mean that as a kind of comfort?" inquires Isolde, and there's scorn in every curve and angle of her body. She wears it well, like a designer dress. "We're supposed to hear that we're cheap tender for a debt we didn't know existed and *be glad*?"

Mark looks at her sidelong. He taps his fingertips on top of the credenza.

"No," he says finally. "I wouldn't ask that. Hate me as much as you wish."

There is a candelabra at the edge of the credenza, something that I've never seen before in his office, with its sumptuousness of minimalism and richness of emptiness. But the candles appear to be the same ones that were being wheeled into the hall earlier. Supplies for Saturnalia, whatever that means.

They are all half-burned, maybe as a test to see how long they lasted or how much wax they dripped, and Mark produces a matchbox from the cabinet next to the place where the liquor is stored.

"I imagine you'll want to say goodbye," he says. The match catches with a tear and a hiss, and he uses it to light the candle in the middle of the candelabra. And then a second one. "I'm afraid you don't have long, only until this burns down." He takes the second candle from the holder. "I'll have its twin with me here. You take the candelabra into the apartment. I'm sure you remember how soundproofed it is. Your privacy until the flame dies is complete."

And with that, he carries his candle over to the window and looks out at the water, deliberately giving us his back. Giving us the chance to say goodbye.

I don't even care if it's a trap. I stride over to the candelabra and then offer my hand to Isolde. With a conflicted look at Mark's back—the candle sending gold dancing in his hair, making his reflection in the window flicker—she takes my hand and allows me to lead her into the apartment. But she doesn't close the door behind her.

I also don't move to close the door. I'm not entirely sure why, and I'm not sure why she doesn't either. Privacy should be all we want—separation the best gift we could be given. But *should* has never had much power around Mark Trevena. Even angry, even hurting, I want to be near him. That a man so cold has somehow become the sun of my life is a very bleak thing, but that doesn't make it untrue.

I set the candelabra down on the kitchen counter and follow Isolde to where she's drifted to a small table near a window framing choppy water and ruffled gray sky. Her fingers light on the chessboard on the table, the quartz and crystal practically glowing in the silver light and the obsidian glinting darkly. She drags a finger to the empty square where the queen used to be; Mark hasn't replaced it on the board.

There's a large armchair by the window, and I take a seat. Isolde comes to my lap immediately, sliding an arm around my neck. She reaches up with her other hand to toy with my hair a little—it grew out at Morois, and it's started to curl at the edges. I'll need a haircut when I get to Montreal.

Our eyes meet, and I know we won't need words for this. What more can we say that we haven't already said? We love each other, and it's hopeless.

She shifts so that she's got her head against my chest, and I stroke a hand down her back, feeling the subtle interplay of her muscles. I found her so strange when I met her, this princess who pretended violence in her dojo, and now I find her stranger still, because she's more like violence that pretends at being a princess. Blood and death, the burbling, foamy hell of it, the chemical change from the quick to the dead—I tried so hard to run away from it. I left the army, took a job in a building where hurt and harm were separate things, and none of it mattered, because death found me anyway. Blond-haired and lethal and secretly tender, destruction both tall and short, a husband and a wife.

I wish it felt worse to hold Isolde knowing what she's done. I wish that it bothered me more knowing what Mark plans to do.

But now all I feel is my old sickness, an obsession marrow-deep.

We're arranged so that we're both facing the door, and I know we're both hoping for the same thing. That he'll come in, that he'll sweep his frigid ocean eyes over us and then make the farewell that we truly want. That he'll take his still burning candle and drip his name onto my skin with scalding wax.

The idea of it, the *hope*, makes me thicken and swell. I know Isolde feels my response underneath her, and I can guess that she feels much the same, given the careful way she presses her thighs together, but neither of us do anything more. To thwart Mark's obvious assumptions or to silently cajole him in, I don't know, but we don't do anything more than sit together. There's no frantic, heedless fucking of the forbidden lovers about to part. Because even holding Isolde is painful right now, even feeling her listening to my heart. Screwing her while Mark's within earshot, while he gives us permission to screw, like someone allowing a habitual drinker to drain the last of his liquor before calling it quits… that's never been what this love is.

This love is aching for him on a yacht in the middle of the ocean. This love is the moonlight catching on Isolde's tears.

This love is nightmares and the way she talks about lumpy old bowls and the way she looks standing over me, grinding her foot into my cock while her graceful, effortless balance betrays years of creeping across rooftops under the stars.

We weren't real in the dark, but now we're more than real in the light. We're doomed in it.

I toy with Isolde's braid, finding a strand that's worked its way loose and rubbing it between my fingertips, reveling in its softness and its shine. There's an old story from a collection of fairy tales I found at Morois about a king who'd vowed not to marry. He went outside his castle walls and saw a perched bird with three strands of lustrous hair caught in its beak, and the hair was so unusual, so beautiful, that the king amended his vow. He'd consent to marry so long as he married whomever the hair belonged to.

I can't remember how the story ends now, but it doesn't matter. I know how the king must have felt as I look at Isolde's hair. The color and gleam of nacre, the feeling of silk. I also would have broken a vow for it.

I suppose I broke someone else's instead.

The candle is burning low when Isolde finally says in a whisper, "I'll miss you, Tristan."

"I'll miss you too."

"I'll miss the way your heart beats so steadily. Like it was made for the rest of us to keep time to."

I kiss the top of her head. "Mark's beats just as steadily." And I flinch a little, having unintentionally wounded myself with my comfort, because now I am remembering, viscerally, how it felt to use his chest as a pillow. How it felt to be gathered up in his arms after whatever display of absolute depravity and hear the beautiful *lub-dub, lub-dub* of his heartbeat.

"It won't be forever," she says quietly, almost to herself. "Just until Ys is gone."

"And your uncle?" I ask in a gentle murmur. "Will you let Mark kill him?"

She looks down at where her free hand rests in her lap. Her honeysuckle engagement ring is a shimmer of ruby and gold from the deep navy of her skirt. "I don't know," she says bleakly.

But I think she does. I hope she does. I might be angry that Mark has used us, and I might be hurt that his single-minded need for revenge will always come first, but I'll never be upset about a world where Mortimer Cashel can't reach Isolde any longer.

The candle flame flickers once but rears up again, not quite done. Hot wax slides down the sconce of the candelabra, and I look away before my thoughts are no longer under my control.

"Promise me that you will stay here," I ask. "Promise me that you won't take missions for your uncle, that you won't take risks you don't need to take. I know you're not sure what you believe right now, and I know Mark has deceived you before, but I—I don't think he's lying about this."

She lets out a breath, one I can't hear, can only feel.

"I used to want nothing more than to be kept in a cloister, to have my days and nights hemmed in by prayer and routine. How peculiar that I'm to be cloistered now, yet it's the last thing I could ever want."

"None of us are doing what we want right now, Isolde. Not even Mark."

The flame is playing hide-and-seek now, dipping low and surging high and then almost disappearing again.

"Then you make a promise to me," she says. "If I'm to obey and become a meek little nun of Lyonesse, then I want something in return."

"Anything."

She pulls back to look at me, and there's fond exasperation on her face. "You are too trusting. Do *not* promise me anything."

"I can't help it." I offer her a weak smile. It's who I am. It's how I love. With a sickness I've never been able to cure.

She huffs a soundless laugh. "Fine then. I want you to call for me if you need me. I mean it, Tristan. I know you're the bodyguard, used to keeping everyone safe, and I know you're used to a certain loneliness and left-behind-ness, and you think you don't deserve anything else. But promise me that if you need me, you'll tell me. And I'll come. I don't care if it means my uncle tries to kill me or if it destroys the club—I'm yours the moment you ask."

I kiss the side of her mouth. "Is that all?" I ask. "That's such a small thing."

She sighs. "Did you think I was going to demand that you sneak back to Lyonesse every chance you can? Or command you to do everything that's asked of you in my name? I just don't want you to face something awful without someone by your side, that's all."

The flame finally, finally gives up, winking out as a thread of smoke twirls up from the charred wick.

We both hold our breath. Now that the moment is here, it feels impossible, wrong. Combat was like this—with a stillness and a quiet and an emptiness of action that began to feel permanent, felt like the truth of things, no matter how uneasy. Until the moment it wasn't, until it was time to move from an outpost or kick down a door, and suddenly there was no longer any such thing as truth or reality, and everything took on the blur of a hideous dream.

But like with combat, you can't wait for the moment to come to you. You must meet it, and meet it as well as you can. I set Isolde on her feet, and then I stand too. I take her hand in mine.

"Will you see me off?" I ask, guessing the answer from the slowly shrouding light in her gaze. She's already closing the doors on herself, clamping down on the wound.

"I think it's better if I stay here," she says. "You should have a chance to say goodbye to Mark privately as well. And

I…" A self-deprecating smile. "I might try to sneak into your suitcase if given half a chance."

I want to kiss her. I want to feel the plump give of her lips against mine, lick gently at them until she opens up for me, and then I want to taste her mouth one last time. Who knows how long it will be before we can be together again?

And even after Ys is gone…then what? Will Mark allow us all to be together, like we were so briefly on Samhain? Or will he be too wounded by everything that's happened, too jealous to try again?

I don't kiss her mouth. It feels too final somehow, too scripted. Lovers parting in a stage-directed tragedy. Instead, I kiss her fingers, pressing my lips to her knuckles and closing my eyes for the space of a single breath.

"I love you," I murmur, casting my eyes up from where I still hover over her hand. "I'll love you past death itself. Into heaven."

"If only I believed I could meet you there," she whispers. "I love you with whatever eternity is left inside me. I—"

Tears are caught on her eyelashes like dew, and she sucks in a breath and whirls away, yanking her hand free of mine in the process. She strides away from me, toward Mark's bedroom, and closes the door without looking back.

I can still feel the lingering warmth of her fingers on my lips.

fourteen

TRISTAN

When I walk into Mark's office, he's still staring at
the river, an extinguished candle stump hanging from his
fingers. He looks back at me and blinks, clearly expecting to
see both of us.

"Isolde didn't feel up to seeing me off," I explain, and he
nods briefly.

"Well then. You have about thirty minutes left before
Jago pulls the car around. I've taken the liberty of having
Sedge pack your things. Hugo is not as particular about suits
as I am, but he is quite fussy about Armorica employees
looking dowdy or cheap, so I've also asked Sedge to make
sure your street clothes are up to Hugo's standards."

"Yes, sir."

"We will have to make a little show of walking you
down. Don't give me that pout. It won't be your own
personal Via Dolorosa, just enough of a display to kick off
some speculation that I can later feed." He waves a hand in a
circle to indicate the strategy. "*Yes*, I've temporarily sent my

bodyguard away. *Yes*, even as my wife remains here. *No*, I don't want to talk about it. That sort of thing."

"You always have everything planned," I note. Not spitefully, not mournfully. Stated as a fact, which it is.

He gives a humorless laugh. "No, Tristan. I do not. Not when it comes to you or Isolde or the two of you together." He steps away from the window and comes toward me, the candle stump left on his desk and his hands in his pockets. "Was it a farewell worthy of your love?" he asks.

Did you fuck her? feels like the subtext, and it's the subtext I answer. "We left the door open, sir. You were welcome to come witness our farewell anytime you wanted."

"How noble," he says. "So pure."

I don't want to do this, not as I'm being sent away. I don't want him to retreat into his barbs and his bitterness, his handsome malice. I don't want to retreat into martyred obedience either.

It's my turn to step toward him. "Nothing's changed, sir. We still love you. I still love you."

He stares at me, eyes hard, his jaw flexed. Even in his pocket, I can see his hand twitch. I think he might respond, might argue with me at least, or show me a little bit of the man I've glimpsed at Morois or on Samhain. The one who mixes his cruelty with tenderness and makes his possessiveness feel like play. Whose coldest parts are the hottest to the touch.

But he doesn't speak, not even for some cutting rebuttal. He just starts walking toward the door of his office. "Let's get downstairs," he says. "It won't hurt to be early."

Yes, it will. It will hurt me. Please let me have every last second with you, please, please.

But I won't beg. Not like this.

We leave his office, and I try not to think about how every step toward the elevator is a step away from Isolde, a step closer to banishment. Banishment with Isabella Beroul of all people. God's way of punishing me for that old envy, I suppose.

We get into the elevator, and he reaches past me to press the button for the ground floor. The smell of petrichor and wet, wet greenery—Morois after a spring storm—envelops me. I breathe it in, a last gasp of oxygen before going under, and Mark goes still next to me.

We start sinking down to the ground floor, and it hasn't even been a year since I first stepped into an elevator with him, but it feels like my entire life now, the only life that matters, and how quickly that life is ending. Now there is only the afterlife, the limbo.

The elevator comes to a smooth stop, and the doors open. To our right is a hallway leading out into the open lobby, and this late in the afternoon, I can hear the din of many, many voices. Guests arriving, most of them blending business with pleasure in the low gloaming of winter twilight. Dinner will turn to drinks, which will turn to time in the hall or in a playroom, and the line between work and wickedness will blur until it seems like there has never been one without the other.

I know how to force myself into danger, even if it's the lobby of Lyonesse and not an abandoned gas station filled with insurgents, so with an inhale and a brief touch of the black and silver ring on my forefinger for reassurance, I walk out of the elevator. I get a single step outside the doors when I hear Mark's shattered groan, and then I'm yanked by my coat in the opposite direction of the lobby, around the corner and into a storage room that's filled with even more candles and wax figures and strange disks made of terra-cotta and wood.

The door closes with a slam, plunging us into darkness, and then I'm shoved back against it and kissed. Hard enough that it nearly hurts, but I like it. I like the hurting. I open my mouth for him, scrabble to touch the hard body trapping mine.

For a moment, he lets me explore him, his waist and hips and ribs, and the sheer pleasure of freely touching Mark Trevena is enough to wreck me. My knees soften; my mouth goes slack under his. I slide my hands up the rungs of muscle and bone and then down again to the barely perceptible dip of his waist. I can feel the heat of his skin through the expensive cotton of his shirt, and when I grab his hips to pull him closer, I feel the brush of his erection against mine. We both shudder together, burning with the same fever.

He reaches for my hands, seizing them, stopping them. His mouth breaks from mine on an uneven exhale.

I think I'm about to be lectured on *touching* and *earning*, and I'm ready to fight about it, ready to inform him that if my banishment to Armorica can't earn me the right to run my hands up his clothed torso, then the currency of earning is inflated past all reason… But no lecture comes. No mock chastisements, nothing cold or mean to freeze me out. Instead, he presses his forehead to mine, still holding my hands. Slowly, so slowly, it feels like I must be making it up, his grip changes and his hands move. He is no longer caging my hands but holding them. And then, with a sigh so soft that it belongs in the blue hours of morning and not in the pitch black of a storage closet, his fingers lace with mine.

"This was never supposed to happen," he says softly.

I can feel the words against my lips as they're spoken. I can feel the trembling in his hands.

"You weren't supposed to happen. Not to me."

"*You* happen to everyone," I reply a little peevishly, and it garners me a quiet laugh.

"I don't want to." There's a scoured honesty to the words. A truth that had to be scrubbed clean of grime before it could be recognized at all. "I don't want this life."

126

I don't know what to make of this. "You chose this life," I say. "You built it from the ground up. What can you possibly not want about it?"

Despair haunts the words when he answers. "I don't want to be spoken of in whispers. I don't want to think in schemes and tricks. I don't want a mind that works in angles rather than straight lines. I hate that night has always made more sense to me than day. I *can't stand* what I can stand to do. I want to be like you, Tristan. I want to be good. I want to fight my enemies on a grassy field with the sun blazing down and everyone wearing their livery and the terms agreed on in advance. I want to die knowing I was a just and merciful man. Candid and kind and true, like you are. Like Maxen Colchester is."

Like Maxen Colchester was, I nearly say but I don't correct him. Mark so rarely illuminates himself—it's like a full moon suddenly breaking through the clouds, and all I can do is witness the unveiling. Stand and gaze in fascination at the world I'm almost never permitted to see. Not that I can *see* anything in this closet, but maybe that's why he's speaking at all. Maybe this is a confessional or a tomb, a place where sins and secrets are extinguished. Maybe it's just easier to tell the truth when no one can see your face and when you can't see theirs.

We're not real in the dark.

Mark rolls his forehead against mine, back and forth. He's shaking his head.

"Even now, I can't pretend to myself," he murmurs. "I think of you and Colchester, I think of that grassy field, and all I can think about is how I'd throw dirt in my enemy's face and jam a blade between his ribs while he was still scrubbing at his eyes. I think of what a waste bravery and courage are if they don't get the job done. I think of how justice and empathy and generosity are absolutely fucking worthless if we think the rules of engagement are more important than the outcome. I think the meek can only inherit the earth if we demand the will is read first, and I want to do more than read it. I want to be its executor. I don't just want to keep watch against our foes. I want to lay traps. I want to follow them to their dens. I want my enemies to have everything taken from them before they die, and I want to be the one to light their pyres and watch them burn in the dark. I want to be the one to bury the embers at dawn."

His hands have stopped shaking now, and though his inhales still come in jagged intervals, there's a growing clarity with every word he speaks.

Certainty in himself, that's what he'd told me in Rome that he trusted above all else, and as he goes on through his dark litany, I can hear his conviction unfurl and bloom.

"So you see why it doesn't matter what I want. You see why this was always a bad idea: you and me. The knight who thinks he's serving a king but is kneeling on the clanking, charred spoils of a dragon instead."

I move my hand, and he still hangs on to it, so I end up pressing both our hands against my chest. Letting him feel my heart pump blood and obsession. "Then let the dragon add me to his hoard," I say quietly. "I still pledge to his service."

We stand there in the dark for a century, a millennium, my heart squeezing and swelling against our hands.

A kiss comes gently, deliberately. A trace of his lips over mine, a press. A linger. And then warm air as he pulls away.

"You cannot," he says. "You can't pledge your service to me any more than you can stop being honest and kind and somehow still afraid that you are not enough of either of those things. Knights slay dragons, Tristan. Night watchmen drive the wolves away from town. I'm counting on that. You have no idea how much."

My hands are freed, and cool air rushes between us, unwelcome.

"Sir, with all due respect, you don't get to say whom I pledge myself to or what dragons I slay." A deep breath, and then one last pathetic attempt. "Please don't make me go. I'll hide. I'll fake my own death. Anything. Just don't send me so far away."

"Now you're the one throwing dirt in my eyes," he says tiredly. "You already know I'm weak for you, and only one other person alive can say that. Take that victory and claim your purple, but don't ask for more. I can't weigh your love against Isolde's safety and have either of you be the better off for it."

"My love against Isolde's safety...along with your revenge against Cardinal Cashel. Right?"

"Did I not admit as much during all my rambles a moment ago? I'm sorry, but I can't change who I am or what I've done, and both of those things mean I can't change what I must do next. Not to mention that my love and my revenge are now bound together far past what can be cut through in the time we have left. Alea iacta est."

I feel something brush against the sleeve of my coat—he's reaching past me to turn the handle of the door. A wedge of light, diffuse and golden, blinds me briefly. But he stays there, his hand wrapped around the door, not making me move so he can open it fully, his head bent.

He braces his foot between the door and the jamb. "Let me see your hand." His voice is strange. A little rushed, like he can't believe what he's about to do.

I do as he asks, and when his fingertips find my ring, the black and silver one he gave me before I went to Ireland to fetch his bride, my stomach falls to somewhere between my feet. And my heart hurts, it literally hurts, an ache that feels medical above all else.

He's taking back his gift. Stripping me of his ring, like I'm an unworthy thane.

Mark works the ring over my knuckles with smooth, careful movements, easing it over the joints in my finger until it's off.

"Don't," I say thickly. "Don't do that. Leave me—leave me a memento at least."

He looks up from my hand, and what I see there is so forceful, so terrifyingly intense, that I have to look away. I'm not sure what it is I see, if it's empathy or anger or pain, but it's so raw that I can now guess what his face looked like when he told me that he both wanted to be good and be the one to bury the embers at dawn.

He seems to realize he's revealed too much, and he ducks his head again. If I did that, it would look bashful, I think, but when he does it, it still manages to look haughty. A little dangerous.

And when I dare to look down at my hand again, I see something so dangerous that my body responds like I'm under attack. Thumping heart, diminished hearing, tunneled vision.

Mark has taken off his wedding ring, the one Isolde gave him in a cathedral piled with peonies and hyssop, and he's now working it onto the ring finger of my left hand.

Senseless and speechless, I let him.

"There," he murmurs, the ring reaching the base of my finger. It's warm from his own hand and just the tiniest bit loose. Not enough to move on its own but enough that I could twirl it easily around my finger if I wanted.

I stare down at it. "There," I say faintly.

There's an aching surrender in his voice when he says, "Now you have a piece of the dragon's hoard."

"And you, sir?" I ask, looking up to his face. The corners of his mouth are blanched as he stares down at my hand. "What will you have?"

He draws in a deep breath and then slips my ring onto his finger, in the same spot where his wedding ring was just a moment ago. "I'll have a piece of something good," he says.

It looks right on his hand, the black and silver of my ring, like it's belonged on his finger from the beginning. I don't know what it means to exchange rings like this— whether it's something like a vow or a farewell so permanent that all we can do is hold on to these small, inert pieces of each other—but whatever it means to Mark has him blinking and looking away.

His throat moves once before he says, "I got the idea from an old friend. Changing the rings, I mean. Jago will be waiting outside by now. We should go."

I don't argue. I just curl my fingers around the warm wedding ring now on my finger and nod. "Yes, sir."

Together, we leave the closet and round the corner. I know we don't look untoward—we both smoothed our clothes before stepping into the lobby, and we didn't kiss *that* hard—but I can feel the hush rippling through the space as we walk through it. The openly curious stares of the members, the hard gazes of the staff, eternally loyal to Mark and thinking of me as a Judas, a stealer of wives, a fox in the henhouse. A cruel joke, because who could steal someone as deadly as Isolde? Who could outfox Mark Trevena?

Mark walks just ahead of me, his stride brisk and his head up in that absolute arrogance I find irresistible. I understand why he detests himself for it, because arrogance is detestable, or at least it should be. But somehow on him it doesn't feel like anything other than a sword cutting through a knot. A dragon flying above his mountain. I'm in a building of rich and powerful people—all of them used to moving the world with a single email, with a lifted finger—and they, to a one, make room for Mark as he passes by. They watch him for cues. They admire and respect him, and if they hate him, they hate him with a fear that borders on awe.

Thank God he's not a different man. He wouldn't have been able to build Lyonesse otherwise, much less sustain it.

The doors open for us, and then we're walking across the pedestrian bridge to where Jago waits in the Maybach. The wind isn't bitter, but it's unpleasant, with small flurries dancing in the air, and I have to tilt my chin down so they don't catch on my eyelashes. I see the gold of Mark's wedding ring, unfamiliar on my hand, as I do. But I like it there.

Mark wore it, and before that, Isolde chose it and gave it to him. It's like both of them are there on my finger, bound into a talisman of all I've gained and lost here at Lyonesse.

Mark's face is neutral as we reach the car and I open the back door. I didn't expect anything different—we're being watched from the lobby of course—but I still wish for... for I don't even know what. Anything less than a stay of execution wouldn't be enough. But it stings to part like this, in full view of the club, acting out the part of a disgraced bodyguard when the disgrace is a lot more complicated than mere infidelity.

Mark extends his hand for me to shake, and beggar that I am, I take the final chance to touch him, even if it's calculated to look like a polite termination of employment and not a true farewell.

It's only because I'm watching his face so closely, so hungrily, that I see the infinitesimal reaction as my fingertips slide over the palm of his right hand. I look down and see in the fading daylight what I couldn't see in the storage closet—the angry red splotch of a burn. Mark quickly turns his hand so that I can't look at it any closer, but it doesn't matter. I saw.

Mark says, "Take care of yourself, Tristan," and walks back to the club. The flurries catch on his shoulders and on the tops of his shoes.

I don't have a chance to say anything else, but I don't know what I would say to a man with an injury like that. To a man who'd held a candle in his hand and let it burn all the way down to the skin.

fifteen

ISOLDE

"HE'S GONE," COMES A VOICE FROM BEHIND ME.

I turn from the glass railing and see Mark approaching the balcony from the shadows of his room. Even with his jacket off and his sleeves rolled up, he looks collected and crisp, an investment portfolio with blue graphs, an ad for leather luggage stitched by hand in Italy. His face gives me nothing of how he feels, and neither does his voice.

He is, however, holding a glass of scotch and not water masquerading as gin, so he's not as collected as he might appear.

I look back to the river and the city beyond, the crouched stubbiness of it, barely softened by twilight and the glow of the streetlights deeper in. Only the Potomac's bridges and the spires of Georgetown make the view bearable.

Sometimes I miss Manhattan so much it's like a suppurated wound tucked away in my mind. Even London—the city that always felt more like my father's than mine—I would take a thousand times over this place.

Mark joins me at the railing, bracing his forearms on it,

the drink cradled between both of his hands. Tiny snowflakes flutter around us; they melt and die the moment they touch the amber liquid inside Mark's glass.

I return my eyes to the grim, utilitarian city in front of me. "Did you tell him that my uncle would kill him if he stayed?"

"You know as well as I do that telling him such a thing would've only have made it harder for him to go."

He's right. It's why I didn't tell Tristan either, in all that time I spent curled in his lap, allowing myself a half candle's worth of make-believe. Because Tristan would have felt compelled to stay at the mere hint of further danger from my uncle, even if the danger was directed toward himself. Because Tristan would hear about someone trying to kill him, say *oh, only that?* and think it a small trade for staying here at Lyonesse.

Because Tristan—for his medals and his combat badges, for that Bronze Star nomination still working its way through the cubicled guts of Fort Knox—doesn't actually believe his life is worth very much at all.

"He'll put it together soon," I say a little tiredly. I'm not usually beholden to jet lag, but today has been about more than time zones. "Although even I didn't think of it until your office. The 'any more failures.'"

"I'd suspected your uncle would see Tristan as a distraction—or worse, as a liability, given what he might know. But if what you relayed about your conversation with your uncle was accurate, then it's better for him to think of Tristan as harmless and forgotten and certainly not important enough for you to keep close or confide in. My other reasons for sending Tristan to Armorica were important too, but this was the most compelling one."

He moves his hand toward me, and I realize he's offering me his scotch. My hesitation is brief, an instant at most, but he notices. Of course he does.

"Poison's not my style," he says with amusement, and I cast him a brief glance so that he knows that I think that's probably bullshit, historically speaking.

"Okay, okay," he amends. "It's not *usually* my style."

I take the glass and treat myself to a long drink. I don't actually think he'd poison me, at least not right now, but distrusting him is reflexive now. As it should have been from the very beginning.

It's when I hand the glass back to him that I see it: the ring he's wearing on his left hand. It's not the ring I gave him at our wedding.

Mark sees me looking, but he doesn't offer an explanation, and I don't ask. And I don't bother trying to straighten the deep, wrenching twist in my stomach. Whatever happened with the rings…they deserve that. The two of them.

But the memory of Samhain burns like a faraway fire on a hill, because there was a version of us that didn't need rings or candles or glasses of scotch. There was a version of us that wasn't atomized, blown apart, splintered with loneliness and spite. For one night, we had it.

For one night, we had everything.

"I'm having my things moved into Tristan's apartment," Mark says casually. "You may keep the use of this one. I thought it would be more comfortable for you."

More comfortable…without chess games, without Mark deftly chopping aromatics under a canopy of copper pots, without waking up inside the heavy, warm, perfect circle of his arms.

I suddenly wish for another swill of his drink. "And why are you moving downstairs?" I ask.

"We are presenting the image of a fractured partnership, Isolde. The more fractured it appears, the more time we buy back from your uncle's impatience."

I am careful not to move too much, to keep my face

the way I want it—a mannequin, a portrait of a queen who seems to display whatever emotion or quality the viewer wants her to display. "Is that all it is, Mark? A presentation? An appearance?"

"Are you asking if our marriage is fractured for real?" His voice could be made of the Potomac in December for how much warmth there is in it. "Or would you like to know if there's a point to repairing it?"

I look at him, the scar near his temple, the slightly uneven bridge of his nose. The mouth that can do more damage than anything else in this island shrine to sadism and pain. "I won't beg," I tell him. "I know how this works. We've done it before, the night you took my virginity, remember?"

He glances away and finishes his drink. "If that's how you like to think of it."

"And if we're doing this all over again, then what? Am I still expected to sit with you in the hall? Am I supposed to perform contrition? Present myself for spanking at every turn, knowing you detest me? What, Mark?"

"All you have to perform is whatever will give your uncle the idea that it's better not to have you killed for the time being. Do the spankings or not, Isolde, it's your choice, but at least apportion your antipathy in equal measure, not forgetting your uncle or yourself." He cuts me a look. "But you'll need to be better about performing contrition if you expect any of the serpents of Lyonesse to believe it."

"So that's it," I exhale. "You lied to me for years, manipulated me, used me against my uncle, and somehow it's my job to convince your serpents that I'm so very, very sorry. Somehow I have to stand here and listen to you imply that I've broken our marriage with the sin of…of what? Discovering the truth? Refusing to kill you for it like I should have? Daring to love the same man you do?"

His eyes narrow, his mouth pressing together, and he

angles toward me, leaning in, all tailored clothes and muscled threat.

And then he stops. His eyes are caught on my braid, on the flurries netting my hair, and then he drags his gaze up to mine.

"Our marriage should have never existed in the first place," says Mark. "Broken is all it ever was. And you should go inside. The snow has stopped melting in your hair."

He leaves without another word and also without a sound, the noiseless tread of a killer. The damp footprints and the sting of whisky in my throat are the only proof that he was here at all.

sixteen

ISOLDE

MARK MAKES GOOD ON HIS WORD, AND WITHIN THE HOUR, Lyonesse staff members are in his closet, in the bathroom, even in the kitchen, selecting knives and cutting boards and pots that are apparently preferable to whatever Tristan has in his apartment.

And then it's done. Some things remain—a handful of tuxedos, a few folded pairs of jeans, his books—but the things he uses daily are gone. I check the drawer on his side of the bed and see that the wedding rings from his first marriage are untouched though. Like me, they're a relic of a union long since robbed of breath.

I don't go down to the hall, and I don't call for food. I take the small bag that I brought with me from Europe and unpack the three outfits, the toothbrush, the holy card given to me by my uncle when I first killed for the Church. The knife Mark left at Morois in place of mine, sleek and light and sharp. Four pairs of underwear, four pairs of socks, three bras. The server room access chip I stole from Mark's watch before I left, tucked into a small, clear bag. A jumble of floor plans, article clippings, pictures, reports, all from the boxes we stole from Mark's safe.

I put the knife and chip on top of the jumble, and I put it all in Mark's drawer, careful not to disturb the wedding rings as I set everything on top. I'll never know Eliot, but I feel a sort of respect for him, a kinship maybe. He too loved Mark Trevena. It's not for the faint of heart.

And then I curl up on the bed, still in my dress, still wearing my heels. I twist my fingers into the blanket, just below where Mark's heart would be if he were lying next to me. But he's not, and the blanket is cold, and the sheets are cold underneath it.

I try to pray. I try to remember the words that made me feel less alone whenever I spoke them, but they come in fragments, brittle and flaking at the edges, disintegrating as soon as I murmur them aloud.

As a child, I thought loving God meant that I'd never be alone. But God has left me, either because of what I've done in His name or because of my doubts about what I've done, and my remaining family consists of two old men who care more about what I can do for them than about me as a person.

Tristan is gone. If my husband has any feelings for me left at all, it's against his will.

So I'm alone. As I always knew I was and as I always knew I would be.

In the lonely dark of a lonely apartment, my hand still clutching at Mark's side of the bed, I finally let myself cry.

———

Saturnalia comes to Lyonesse with unalloyed gusto, and if I'd hoped for a subtle return to the public life of Lyonesse, all of that is dashed the moment a submissive named Christopher is named the Saturnalicius princeps, the mock king. The first night of the festival, I come into the hall after the festivities have begun, right after Mark makes a speech that has the crowd roaring. My plan is to go to his usual chair and sit next to it, as if I've been there all evening, but I'm spotted by Christopher before I can.

"My lady!" he shouts, coming toward me at a full run and sliding to his knees just as he reaches me. "All hail my lady!"

All around us, heads turn, even from the floor above, even with the raucous crowd and the music playing, and I have no time to gather myself, to remind myself of the existential reasons I have to play the part. It's instinct I rely on, and the very real agonies of both pride and humiliation. The acid vise of loneliness gripping and eating my heart.

I look down at the puckish man kneeling at my feet. Like half the people here, he's wearing a colorful robe—his a rather short chiton, which is Greek rather than Roman, but I think even the most easily scandalized Roman wouldn't have complained about seeing those supple thighs of his.

His red hair is tousled and already a little damp at the roots from cavorting around the hall, and the hundreds of candles catch every scarlet and gold tress and make his copper-dusted legs shimmer.

I lift a hand and cup his cheek. The barest hint of stubble, fine lines around his mouth and eyes. He's in his midthirties, and I remember now that he does some kind of botany or ecology and spends his days looking into microscopes. *An unrepentant brat*, Mark had once told me about him. Perfect for the princeps of the feast.

"Stand up," I tell him, and then for the benefit of the Saturnalians around me, I add, "my lord."

"I *am*, aren't I?" Christopher grins as he pops up. "In that case, you are my queen. And I demand a dance."

He grabs my hand and would be yanking me

enthusiastically toward the stairs if he were a taller man or I weren't prepared. But I am prepared, and I can keep pace with him evenly, so I look as if I'm utterly unbothered by displaying myself in such a manner. As if it makes no difference to me whether I'm allowed to hide in a corner or if I dance in the middle of a room filled with gossiping club members who think I'm a cheating whore.

As we descend the stairs, the guests move aside, creating a sort of hole in the middle of the room. Stillness washes through the crowd like a tide. The music—a pastiche of lyres, lutes, horns, pipes, and drums—goes on, but the conversations, the rattle of jugs and goblets along the crescent-shaped tables, the stirrings on the low sofas and cushions, all stop.

I make the mistake of looking. Of seeing the faces, the sneers. The lewd grins and etched scowls.

And I stumble.

It's just a catch of my sandal on the floor, a flapping of my hem, but it's enough to summon my devil, I suppose, because when I steady myself, I see him standing at the nearest table to the dance floor. He has chosen to wear the garb of a Roman emperor, which, like everything else, looks absurdly good on him. A snow-white tunic, a toga of Tyrian purple trimmed in gold, and a laurel crown in his already gilded hair. Even his bare feet in laced-up sandals look magisterial.

He hasn't stepped forward, hasn't broken free of the crowd enough that it'll attract attention, but when our eyes meet, I see that he's poised to step in. To rescue me, even if rescue would come with the coldest blue eyes and the tightest jaw I've ever seen.

I will do everything I can to preserve your dignity here.

As a matter of principle? As part of some mysterious strategy that I can't see yet?

It doesn't matter. Nothing would diminish my dignity

more than my estranged husband having to rescue me from a red-haired sprite who has a fondness for ice cubes. I remember our hand signals—the ones he taught me when we were first engaged and I was meant to *pretend* to be his submissive—and I press my thumb and forefinger of my free hand together.

Stop.

Mark dips his chin the smallest amount, letting me know he understands, but he doesn't move away as Christopher sweeps me into the middle of the room and pulls me into an awful facsimile of a waltz.

I am beyond grateful for how I dressed tonight, in an indigo gown with the cut of a Roman stola, opaque and hanging to the floor. My hair is bound up in a braided circle, and my makeup is almost nothing except for some dark blue lipstick to match my dress. I am as serious as midnight, as solemn as the winter outside. If I have to be stared at right now, then this is what I want them to stare at, the opposite of whatever they've made me in their heads.

As a PR move, it's rather conspicuous, but it's a mistake to think conspicuous moves don't work as well as inconspicuous ones. Sometimes they work even better.

With the drums guiding my feet and the pipes tickling my shoulder blades, I manage to corral us into something with rhythm at least, something with a pattern. Christopher's amber eyes meet mine with surprise after we make our first turn around the space.

"You really know how to dance," he says.

I don't think he dragged me down here to embarrass me, not necessarily, but I do think he wouldn't have *minded* my embarrassment. It would have been a game to him, just more chaos for the newly minted king of chaos. But there's a faint gleam of admiration in his gaze when he glances around the space and sees that we've turned a potential farce into something else. What that something else is, I don't know, but it's enough to salvage my pride for the night.

Christopher spins me a final time with enough flourish that my gown twists around my feet and then lets me go with a deep bow.

I curtsy effortlessly and then rise.

Mark is gone, lost in the crowd, when I do.

———

The second night is the same, with a dress in a lighter shade of blue and without a waltz. Mark doesn't sit in the nook with me, but Arjun and Evander are there and treat me with kindness, as does Dinah when she stops by.

Christopher finds me and makes me drink a toast with him.

I feel the place Tristan would normally stand behind me like the sucking, screaming vacuum of outer space, and I feel the tiredness from my fractured, nightmare-filled sleep last night hanging like cobwebs from my bones.

Below us in the hall is an excess of togas and stolas, for those who aren't in costume, suits and lingerie, wine and flesh. Moans begin filling the hall, the whack of riding crops and paddles, shrieks of pain or delight or both.

I don't see my husband anywhere.

———

The third night. The fourth night.

The same, the same.

———

The fifth night, I'm in pink, my hair half down, and I'm listening to Arjun tell a visiting English earl and his wife about the growth of the boutique hotel market when I see Mark waved onto the stage by a mischievous Christopher. A doe-eyed sub with her hands bound is led out by Dinah—a sacrifice being escorted to the feet of Saturn himself. I've seen her before but only in passing; she's one of the club submissives. Which means this is probably a planned performance. It probably won't go further than a light flogging…or maybe some clamping if Mark decides the crowd has earned a treat.

But she *is* pretty, with pale bronze skin and wavy, onyx hair that's been pulled up and banded with white ribbons. She's curvy, with a body that moves and forms against the St. Andrew's cross as she's cuffed to it. The length of white silk that tied her hands together still trails from one of her wrists, matching the ribbon in her hair. When Mark steps closer to speak to her, his mouth to her ear, she curves toward him like a heliotrope. And when he runs a finger down her spine, from the nape of her neck to just above the small of her back, she quakes and shivers, undone by this smallest attention. A perfect sub.

My hands are clenched so hard in my lap that I can feel my fingernails digging into my skin.

"Careful," says a smoky voice. I look up to see Lady Anguish in a long chiton with vines stitched along one side, and a golden armband in the shape of a snake twined around an upper arm. Her dark hair is up and braided in a circle.

"Bona Dea?" I ask.

"Good eye," she replies as she sits in the empty chair next to me—Mark's empty chair. "I suppose a career in antiquities gives you an unfair advantage when it comes to iconography. Now, you must stop that before anyone sees." She presses a cool hand over one of my balled fists.

"Right," I exhale.

On the stage, Mark has stripped off his toga with all its cumbersome drapes and handed it to Dinah. The lights on the stage make a mockery of his long white tunic and then a mockery of us all, because we can see the silhouette of his strong thighs and narrow hips and powerful shoulders, and he's the opposite of reduced for being so revealed.

"Your jealousy should have the flavor of shame and repentance, not anger," Anguish advises in a low voice. It's so husky that it barely carries at all. "Unless you want word to reach your uncle that you're choosing your temper—or worse, the memory of your lover—over doing the job assigned to you."

Mark is picking up two floggers from a tray offered by another submissive and giving them a few test swings. He seems to like how they feel, because he nods, and the person holding the tray melts into the wings of the stage.

"You are genuinely jealous though, aren't you?" I can feel Anguish looking at me. "You'd walk down those stairs and drag Mark back to your rooms by that ridiculous golden hair of his if you thought you could get away with it."

"I think it's normal for a wife to be unhappy while her husband's with a naked woman." My voice is tighter than I'd like.

"You're not normal, and neither is Mark," Anguish points out with some amusement. "Tristan might be the closest thing to normal you know, but he won't be by the time the both of you are done with him."

I ignore this. Try to ignore the way Mark leans in to speak to the submissive again. I know he's just checking her safeword, asking about any old injuries or areas to avoid, but it looks unduly intimate, his mouth so close to the shell of her ear.

"Do you really think word would reach my uncle?" I ask. I don't doubt it's possible, given that the Scales was able to smuggle in messages to me earlier this year—surely that means there is a line back to my uncle. But my uncle also didn't seem to know everything when I talked to him in Rome, which means that line might be circumstantial. Or untrustworthy.

"Are you asking me as part owner of the club?" she asks back. "Or as the sister to Vivienne Moore, the aunt of the current president, and the wife of Merlin Rhys?"

I haven't forgotten how well connected Anguish is, but I hadn't considered that her connections might make her more insightful when it comes to a question like this. "All of it, I suppose."

"As an owner of Lyonesse, I'd say that the NDAs are ironclad, the staff is better vetted than most national intelligence agencies, and you have the unique benefit of a community that does not want to fuck up the cone of silence for all their perverted sakes. As someone who's been reluctantly watching politics since she was a teenager, I'll tell you that nowhere is watertight, not really. Lyonesse is close, but I suspect your uncle is still able to catch enough drips to keep him satisfied."

"So you know what my uncle is. What he does, I mean."

"Anyone who matters knows that Mortimer Cashel runs the intelligence arm of the Holy See."

I look over at her without speaking.

"But you mean Ys," she states. Not a question.

On the stage, Mark starts swinging the floggers. Figure eights, in tandem, a steady brush against the submissive's shoulder blades and then down to her backside. She arches for it above and below.

"It seems like everyone knows about Ys," I say. "For it supposedly being secret."

Anguish makes a *hmm* in the back of her throat. "Makes you wonder, doesn't it? About how secret they want to be?"

Mark had said something similar to Drobny when he killed him a couple months ago.

I think Ys wants to be feared, and you can't be feared if you're unknown.

"But very, very few people know about Mortimer Cashel's connection with Ys," she continues. "You, me. Mark and his twin sister. Andrea, Lox, and Lox's boyfriend, Rafe de Lacy. My nephew and my husband. But the CIA and NSA at large do not know. My nephew's cabinet does not know. It's a small group. If we all died, no one would know what we died trying to end."

"Are you trying to end Ys too? Why?"

Anguish looks down at her lap, plucks at her dress. "I made a mistake once, a lifetime ago. I've been trying to atone for it by doing some good in the world."

On the stage, Mark's flogging is a thing of elegance, light and glancing, with brief brushes of pain that have the submissive whimpering. And then, without warning, the lights go off, leaving only the candles and the tips of the floggers' falls, which are now glowing orange and red and yellow. It looks like Mark is flogging her with flames.

"Can I trust you?" I ask Anguish. "I haven't in the past. I don't like the way you convinced Mark to sell you half the club, and I think anyone who routinely tops Merlin Rhys is probably very dangerous. And you have no reason to help me."

"So cynical," Anguish replies, and it's hard to see her face with only the candles on stage, but it sounds like there's a smile in her voice. "*I* wouldn't trust me in your shoes. But I do care about Mark. I knew him when we were younger, and you've never seen a man do so much with so little. It was alchemy, like he was a magician, except the magic was his cunning, his ruthlessness. His determination. Like right now. He is doing exactly what he should be, which is looking like he wants to make you jealous. Like he wants to punish you, and not with fiber optic floggers but with relegation. Now you need to play your part, speak your lines."

"The shame and repentance," I say dully. I hate it. I do feel shame, but it's too intricate and too filigreed with self-righteousness and sewn on top of the betrayals that have been done *to me*—and it's not at all what the club wants to see.

But isn't it miserable enough to be rejected by Mark privately and publicly? Why do I have to chase after him too? All I want to do is hide in a corner and lick my wounds. For years.

The submissive on the stage is beginning to sway and slump now, her curves flashing in the moving light of the floggers.

"You'll have to go to him," advises Anguish. "The club would see him coming to you as weakness on his part. They think you robbed him and ran away with his bodyguard. What self-respecting person would make the first move in that case?"

The lights come up as Mark finishes with a controlled flurry of strikes, ending with a sharp flick between her legs.

My hands fist again.

But Mark doesn't touch her, doesn't step behind her and rub his cock against her or reward her with large, skilled fingers. Instead, he looks up at the balcony, up at me, and he does it so obviously that the rest of the crowd looks too.

I don't need Anguish to tell me to relax my hands this time. I don't even have to pretend to look miserable.

Mark doesn't react to whatever he sees in my face, but after he hands off care of the submissive to Dinah, he walks off the stage and disappears for the rest of the night.

You'll have to go to him.

Fuck.

The next night, I'm in orange silk, modest in front but draping lower in the back, my hair around my shoulders in sculpted curls. I'm a little agitated by the time I get to the hall, because I've been stewing all day about Mark flogging that submissive, and it's not even the flogging I'm upset about but that single caress down her spine. It was for my benefit

149

and for the benefit of the crowd, but I don't care. His caresses belong to me and Tristan, *absolutely* no one else, and I'd like to tell him so. Preferably while I'm yanking his belt open.

But I can't tell him so, because he's in meetings all day, and then he's already been claimed by the usual sycophants and serial networkers when I step onto the floor of the hall.

The mood is darker tonight, turned a little dangerous from the merriment of the first few days. There's an edge to the drinking and colloquy now, to the fucking and kink happening on scattered sofas and cushions, and it only takes me a minute on the floor to identify it.

Boredom.

Seven days is a long time for a festival, and these are people who already live like they're Romans at the court of Elagabalus. So even with wine and sex on the proverbial— and literal—table, they've grown restless. Bloodthirsty.

And now I'm in the middle of them, looking for Mark but as yet alone. Whispers tickle at my exposed shoulder blades as I move toward the stage, suddenly too nervous to approach Mark where he's trapped in conversation near a statue of Saturn.

"...can tell she misses him..."

"I heard Mark threatened to kill them both if they ever saw each other again..."

"...a trial by iron."

The last snippet is followed by a wave of shocked laughter, and unease burrows in my belly. If I'm not going to take Anguish's advice and go to Mark, then I should retreat to the safety of the nook. I'm not in control of my face tonight, or my body or my heart, and maybe that's the difference between being cuffed on stage and fucked in a torn wedding dress and being quite happy about it and then standing here fully clothed and feeling like my ribs are about to splinter from the atmospheric pressure of being watched.

I turn for the stairs, discretion being the better part of valor, and then two women holding goblets of wine step in front of me. They aren't wearing costumes; they're in pantsuits with cropped pants and stilettos, but their expressions are every bit as feral as the other Saturnalians. I've seen them with Andrea before, not just in the hall but having lunch and drinks.

So her friends then.

"How good of you to celebrate with us," the first woman says as she lifts her drink to her mouth.

My nervous system doesn't betray me now at least. I'm able to keep myself as cool as they are.

"I wouldn't have missed it," I say. They've crowded close enough that I have to look up at them, but I won't give them the satisfaction of stepping backward. I wish I'd put on heels though. I wish I were able to sleep by myself without waking up screaming so I didn't have exhausted bruises under my eyes. I wish I were back in the apartment staring at nothing.

The second woman tilts her head. "You did seem comfortable with Christopher that first night. Practiced dancing with him before?"

My fingertips tingle as my body decides that we need to shift from *calm* to *alert*.

I should have seen this coming. We sent Tristan away thinking it would bandage my reputation, that the miasma of distance and time would blur the memories, but I hadn't even considered that the club might suspect that I'd *continue* to be unfaithful. Might suspect that cheating is such an indelible trait of mine that it doesn't even matter whom I'm cheating with, so long as I can tumble around in a bed with someone who isn't Mark.

And I'm such a goddamn fool, because not once had I ever considered that the club might spread *baseless* rumors about me.

151

At least I know this much—a denial will make things even worse, seem like a sure indication that their aim was true. But neither can I be dismissive. Neither can I wave it away.

I meet her gaze and smile. "If I'm comfortable at Lyonesse, it's because Mark's always gone out of his way to make it so. There's never been something I couldn't come to him with. He can be a little too eager to solve problems for me, when I think about it, but that might be the former CIA officer in him. When you have a hammer, everything looks like a nail, they say."

Her expression shifts as I speak, subtly, going from jeering mock congeniality to a hard smile, to eyes that glint with more than reflected candlelight.

"I suppose we'll see how many problems he'll want to solve for you now."

"Shall we find out?" I ask calmly.

Silence.

They both stare at me, outmatched by this last gambit and knowing it. And point made, I nod in a polite goodbye and go upstairs.

————

The final night of Saturnalia, I put on a filmy yellow gown, translucent in almost any lighting. I selected the clothes for Saturnalia months ago, having no idea what the autumn would bring, and had been pleased with my interpretation of the theme. Darkness to light, the story of the midwinter solstice told in dress form. And of course, the final dress I'd chosen assuming I'd be sitting in Mark's lap as I wore it.

I almost change dresses. I think of those two women last night—Gabrielle and Dena, I learned their names were—and I think of the whispers. If I go down there like this tonight, then I'm abandoning even the conceptual armor of clothes. I'm proving that I'm indeed no vestal.

But what does it matter in the end? I am an outcast either way. At least in this dress, I might get Mark to look at me for longer than a single inhale.

I leave my hair unbound and tumbling down my back. It's longer than I've ever had it, since long hair is a liability as a saint, but I'm not a saint right now, am I? And I like the way it looks. Long enough for Mark to wrap his fist around and around.

Tonight I try the balcony first, and I'm relieved to see Mark finally, *fucking finally*, sitting in his usual leather chair like it's the throne of the underworld. He's surrounded by people, including Andrea, but that's fine. It's more important that we start the illusion of coming together before the club decides I'm secretly fucking Christopher or Dinah or the DJ or something.

I make my way to Mark, and he doesn't pretend not to see me. He watches me with a cool, appraising look as I step closer, and then as I come to a stop and sink to my knees in front of him, I feel his gaze on me still.

A wolf whistle at my dress, and then a murmur—Andrea's. *Maybe she's going to offer him a trial by iron after all.*

Someone clears their throat in discomfort.

"Look," says my husband. "The sun has returned at last."

I can't parse his tone exactly, if it's edged with mockery or admiration… But then he slides his sandaled feet apart on the floor, making room for me between them.

I'm allowed to stay.

I adjust myself so that I'm still kneeling, still looking down, but turned so that I'm facing the stage. Even without looking, I know we're being stared at, that word is rippling through the hall.

I remind myself that I have faced worse than gossip and disgust; I remind myself that I *will* face worse, and so could Mark and so could Tristan if my uncle is unconvinced of my efforts to rob Lyonesse's vaults. All that matters is keeping the three of us alive, and anyway, I made my choice when I came back here. I need to live with it.

But I can't carry it, the weight of their loathsome whispers and bursts of hard laughter. A shiver rolls through me, from top to bottom, and my lungs won't inflate as deeply as they should.

I've faced worse. I've faced worse.

Except even when I faced worse, I felt like I had God on my side, and my uncle and the Church too. Even scrambling on rooftops, holding my breath as bullets snapped around me, fighting men two or three times my size—I wasn't alone. I was a saint, one of God's most necessary children. My sins were to save God's kingdom, which meant even my darkest, bloodiest moments brought me deeper into the heavenly fold.

And now...

Now I can't even pray and feel comforted. I don't have God or Tristan or Mark, and I don't have myself, because no one's known me for so long that I don't even know myself anymore.

I close my eyes. For the first time in months, since I told Mark in the predawn light that I wanted to be his submissive for real, I think about punishing myself. Atoning with my flesh, flogging my own back, planting myself in the gold garden until my lips are blue.

The fantasies are vivid, urgent, coaxing. I could feel better if I hurt myself, the fantasies promise. I'd feel cleaner and better, because I deserve to hurt, don't I? I *did* break my promises to Mark. I did fuck Tristan in Belgrade and again in the garden here. I am greedy and constantly unfaithful in my thoughts. Maybe running away to Morois was justified, but I can't pretend that I'm not an adulteress. I can't pretend that I wouldn't be one still.

But I'm scared of myself, because in these fantasies, God isn't with me. And the atonement is an offering to nothing, to the empty air. To my own agonizing loneliness.

This isn't corporal penance. I want to hurt myself simply to hurt myself, and here it is at last, the truth I've been fleeing since my mother's funeral:

We are all alone, each of our hearts floating in its own dark and endless sea.

And no one, *no one*, can ever get close enough to rescue you before you drown.

I list sideways, dizzy and faint with the hopeless clarity of it. The *of course*-ness of it. How stupid I've been that I ever thought otherwise.

My shoulder bumps against the inside of Mark's knee, and I know I need to straighten myself, that a good submissive doesn't lean and that Mark probably can't stand the feel of me touching him right now, but I can't seem to move myself. I can't seem to make my muscles respond. It's as if all the nerves threaded through my flesh have gone cold, already icing over in that endless sea.

It's only Mark's warm, toga-draped knee keeping me upright. But this too he allows, and not once for the rest of the night does he shift his weight or pull away.

seventeen

TRISTAN

"Ice again, Ms. Beroul, so please be careful," I say as I open the door for my new principal and then assist her down the glistening steps to the sidewalk.

Isabella Beroul wrinkles her nose at me, snowy fluff catching on her reddish-blond hair. In her wool coat, soft blue scarf, and perfectly applied pink lipstick, she looks adorable and also expensive, which I suppose she is as the most requested submissive at Hugo Budic's club.

I open the door to the car waiting by the snow-dotted curb, help her inside, and then close it behind her. I take a beat to scan the area, noting the cars around us in case one follows us a little too long later, double-checking the windows and the fire escapes of the buildings around us. I see nothing suspicious, nothing to note other than how lovely the silver-stoned buildings of Old Montreal look in the snow.

"I'm so tired of winter," Isabella sighs dramatically when I get into the car with her. She drops her head back and closes her eyes. "I wish I could hibernate for three months like a bear."

I haven't felt like smiling much lately, but I could almost smile at that. I've never met someone less likely to hibernate than Isabella. In the ten days since I've come here, we've left Armorica at least twice a day, sometimes three or four times a day, and it feels like we're out of the club more than we're in it. To eat, to get coffee, to shop. And even the word *shop* doesn't do justice to Isabella's habits. Isabella shops like the shops should have a safeword.

"What time do you need to be back to the club?" I ask, checking my watch. Isabella lives at Armorica, so there's essentially no commute for her sessions, but I've quickly learned that the time she needs to get ready can vary substantially depending on what she'll be doing. For Armorica's raunchier, more public sister club on rue Sainte-Catherine, she's glitter-painted and ready in thirty minutes. For a private session in one of Armorica's luxurious, wainscoted playrooms, she might take more than two hours.

"Mmm, let's say five o'clock," she hums as the driver rolls us over the snowy cobblestones. "I have the Banker tonight, and she likes me to be extra tidy for her."

All of Isabella's clients are called things like that—the Banker, the Family Man, the Florist. It's something of a custom at Armorica to defer to epithets whenever possible, I've noticed, a little flourish of privacy that is more about good manners than actual secrecy. Hugo is fond of manners.

It does give the flavor of tasteful discretion to everything, even Isabella's sessions, which are far more explicitly transactional than what goes on between guests and club employees at Lyonesse. I'm not sure if it's bribery, Hugo's connections, or perhaps the shared protection of such high-profile clientele, but Armorica is a little more direct—in Hugo's refined way—about what club employees will do with guests. (For a fee, of course.)

"Thank you again for coming here," Isabella says after

a moment, opening her eyes to look at me. They're a bright gold-brown, large and fringed with thick lashes several shades darker than her hair. She has the kind of eyes that look sweet and soft in almost every light, paired with any expression. Those soft eyes are one of the many reasons why she's the jewel of Armorica's crown.

"It's my honor," I tell her. I've been vague about my expulsion from Lyonesse, but it hardly matters. The web of gossip between Lyonesse and Armorica is spun thickly enough that everyone already knows. "It feels nice to be helpful. And…wanted."

She puts a hand on my knee. Her coat sleeve has pulled up enough to expose the edge of her leather glove, and underneath that, the line of a nitrile glove, the kind she wears always, even to bed. It's a stark white against the pinky cream of her skin.

"You're very wanted here and beyond helpful." A shadow passes over her usually sunny face. "It's nice not to have to look over my shoulder when I leave the club. Or to—to wake up and wonder—"

She stops abruptly.

I put my hand over hers to let her know that she doesn't have to finish if she doesn't want to. I already know what she's afraid of when she wakes up in the middle of the night. A club member who'd purchased weekly sessions with her had grown dangerously obsessed, and after a scene that left Isabella uncomfortable, Hugo permanently revoked the man's membership and barred him from Armorica for life.

Three weeks ago, the ex-member had broken into her apartment at the club and left a disturbing note on her bathroom mirror, written in Hermès lipstick. He'd wedged a Polaroid of her sleeping into the mirror frame in case the meaning of the violation wasn't clear enough.

Hugo shared all this with Mark, told him that he wanted

additional security for Isabella. Luckily for everyone, Mark had a bodyguard he needed rid of and quickly.

That I long for my two blond criminals with a nerve-deep itch is a given; that I think of them constantly and worry about them and also resent their being together while I'm gone—that is a given too.

But even in my unhappiness, I can admit that there would have been no better exile for me. Armorica is a club fit for princes—opulent in a restrained, in-the-know way, outfitted with hand-sawn parquet floors, custom-mixed paint, and wall sconces imported from some workshop in the Cotswolds. Hugo is as genial as he is polished, and his co-owner Kayden Howell is a cheerful former soldier who's gone out of his way to make me feel welcome, both at Armorica itself and in Montreal.

Better than the club or its owners, however, is protecting Isabella, who is so open and gladsome and wonderful and who doesn't deserve any of what's happening to her. It makes me feel like I'm doing something good and worthwhile, even if I know that I'm not a good or worthwhile person. Even if I can't do good anywhere else anymore.

And maybe it makes me a stunted person, incapable of growth, but there's a deep kind of comfort in the simplicity of the directive, just like there was with Mark in those early days. Protect Isabella while she's outside the club, work in shifts to protect her while she's inside it. Sleep in the spare room in her apartment in case someone tries to terrorize her again.

There are no secret engagements, no power-hungry cardinals, no shadowy organizations hoping to profit off war. No husband and wife watching me like insouciant hawks watching a rabbit hop obliviously in the grass.

I take my assignment here as seriously as I take everything—but the honesty in Hugo's world is a goddamn relief.

Isabella looks down at my hand. At the gold wedding ring there. "Is this to drive away interested suitors, or is it real?" she says, maybe trying to bring the moment back to some sort of casual levity. "If it works to keep the suitors at bay, I should demand that Hugo give me a ring too. Although we'd have to make it clear to Edouard that it'd be more like a collar than anything else."

Isabella, first and foremost, is Hugo's submissive, but she is only that. Unlike Mark, who can't seem to love someone without also wanting to give them rug burn, Hugo is much more flexible when it comes to kink and romance. He's happily married to a monogamous, vanilla solicitor, and Hugo has his vanilla solicitor's permission to use Isabella to meet Hugo's other, more unique needs.

Edouard has Hugo's heart; Isabella gets his bruises.

The arrangement seems to work well for everybody—including Isabella, whose appetite for kink and attention is much like her appetite for shopping and who would probably wear out even an experienced Dom like Hugo if she wasn't frequently getting topped elsewhere.

"It's real," I say, and then after a minute, "but it's not mine. It was…exchanged."

"Does the ring have to do with her? With Isolde?"

"It's the one she gave Mark on their wedding day."

Isabella pulls off a leather glove and then lifts my hand to examine the ring more closely. The nitrile-covered tip of her finger is satin-like as it grazes the skin around the ring. It's warm as her hand would be underneath.

"I hate that she's made you like this," Isabella says. There's an edge in her voice that I haven't heard before, and I turn to study her face.

"Like what?" I ask warily.

"Melancholy. Lost. I can see you thinking about her sometimes, and it's like watching all the petals getting torn off a flower. Like even just thinking of her rips something apart inside you."

I look away. I don't like being that transparent. Professionally or personally.

"I was like this before I came to work for Mark," I say, and it's the truth, even if there are several other truths now sutured along its edges. "And Mark... Mark was the first, you know. I fell in love with him before I ever met Isolde. You know what he's like. How it feels."

I shouldn't be telling her this. It's about as professional as my unhappy disassociations when I think no one is watching, and Isabella has enough to worry about on her own. She doesn't need my failed ménage à trois laid in her lap. But after ten days of being her shadow, I know so much about *her*—I know she does her puzzles with the inside pieces first and what brand enema she uses—and perhaps it gives me the illusion of intimacy.

And it's nice, actually, to be able to talk someone about this. Someone who knows Mark too. Who's felt his shadow over their skin.

She runs her finger over my ring a final time and then offers me a small, sad smile. "Yes. I know how it feels."

eighteen

TRISTAN

I'm off the next night, a different member of Armorica's security trailing Isabella's footsteps, so I plan on eating a light dinner and reading a book. I open a kitchen cabinet and find the stock of things some staff member helpfully thought I'd enjoy as the resident American, pushing aside peanut butter and sugary cereal and then stopping when I see a box of Pop-Tarts. The s'mores flavor, Aaron Sims's favorite.

I pull out the box and stare at it. I don't need to open it to remember the shiny silver wrappers or pull one out to remember the sound of it crinkling. Sims would carry a package of Pop-Tarts with him into the strangest places and long past when you'd think his self-control would last. We'd be on a twenty-four-hour patrol or wedged in the back of a combat outpost or hunched inside of a stalled Humvee, and then you'd hear the rustle of plastic or see the shine and flash of the package, and he'd be happily munching away while we trudged or shivered or dozed in the heat.

It's a string of happy memories, of funny ones, of

good-natured insults flung back and forth, of shared crumbles of dry pastry. Of Sims making everyone smile even when we were pissy or itchy or exhausted.

I want to hold on to those memories, I don't want any other memories to crowd in, and I squeeze my eyes closed like it will help. Like I can block out what Sims looked like with a forest behind him and fog clinging damply to his uniform pants. Like I can block out how his hand shook as he trained his pistol on the new prime minister, as he planned to kill her husband and two kids.

Like I can block out what it looked like when I shot him through the throat before he could.

I put the box of Pop-Tarts back into the cabinet and decide to go down to the club before my own thoughts eat me alive.

Hugo and Kayden are sharing a table in the heart of the building, a lushly appointed lounge with floor-to-ceiling windows sunk into the dark blue walls. The upholstery and leather, the large fireplace and sumptuously stocked bar, could be in any exclusive hotel, but the windows themselves show the truth of Armorica: they open up to playrooms, some only barely lit, with shadows moving mysteriously inside. But some...some glow into the lounge, their happenings on vivid display. In the same field of vision right now, I can see an ornately framed painting of something impressionist and outdoorsy and then a woman pegging a man while he claws helplessly at the floor.

Heat seeps down into my groin, and I turn away, making sure to take a chair at Hugo's table facing the opposite direction. At Morois, Isolde had confessed that she wanted to do that to me, that she wanted to see if she could make me come hard enough that I cried, and it's now one of my go-to fantasies when I'm alone.

I don't need the visual reminder in front of my new boss.

"Tristan," Hugo greets warmly. He has a faint accent, the relic of a Breton childhood.

"Sir," I say and then smile up at the server who's appeared immediately and silently. I order a beer and then say hello to Kayden, who's ignoring a tablet next to him—open to a dense spreadsheet—in favor of a whiskey-looking drink with a cherry at the bottom.

"I didn't think we'd see you tonight," he greets with an easy smile. "You're hard to lure out when you're not working."

"He's still just settling in," Hugo says in my defense. "Not everyone needs to be the life of the party, darling."

"More room at the party for me then," Kayden parries, throwing me a wink.

I'm not sure how Hugo and Kayden met or how they went into business together. Hugo founded Armorica, I know, and has ten or fifteen years on his now co-owner, but I'm not sure if they met as kinksters or in the real world. However they met—and despite the differences in their personalities—their partnership is collegiate and frictionless, fed by Hugo's elegance and Kayden's good-natured honesty. They aren't partners romantically or sexually, but intellectually and socially, they are a bonded pair.

"I was restless upstairs," I say and thank the server after he sets the beer on my table. "I needed a change of scenery."

Hugo, who, like the rest of the world, knows Isolde's uncle is a cardinal, asks, "Did you see the news about the conclave?"

"I did," I say, and I hope I sound like a man whose biggest torment is being reminded of the woman he loves and not like a man who is desperately afraid that woman's family might try to kill her while he's gone.

Hugo settles back into his chair, shaking his head. "A sea of red capes and yet not a single drop of red blood between them."

"Hugo isn't a fan of the Church," Kayden says apologetically.

Hugo shrugs. He's wearing a buttery-yellow suit with a white shirt and cradling a glass of wine in one hand. He has deep brown skin, burnished tonight with a little highlighter on his cheekbones, and a short beard that betrays the few speckles of silver that his shaved head hides. He has dark eyes set behind rimless glasses, and whenever he smiles, his left eyebrow arches a little, as if in mild inquiry.

Kayden is also dressed well, but more like a former soldier's version of *dressed well* in a black suit without a tie and a white shirt underneath that's only been buttoned to his sternum. His brown hair is tousled, his jaw is covered in something more like scruff than a beard, and a tattoo peeks out from his chest, the black outline of pointed leaves. There would be a cluster of bright red berries if he unbuttoned his shirt any farther. The fine wrinkles spreading from his bright green eyes match his winter-paling suntan—he seems like a hard person to keep indoors when the sun is out.

Kayden taps on the tablet to turn it on again, sighs at the spreadsheet, and then pushes it away. "I can't," he says mournfully. "I can't think about math any longer."

"Any longer?" laughs Hugo. "You never started. Ah, belle! Here you are."

Isabella has approached the table from behind me and sinks to her knees next to Hugo, bowing her head.

He strokes it fondly, then finds her chin so he can look into her face. "Busy tonight?" he asks.

"Only one session, sir," she says. "An easy one. The Good MP."

"Is there a Bad MP?" I ask.

Kayden snorts. "You have no idea."

"You look ravishing," appraises Hugo, his entire attention on Isabella. She blooms under it, her cheeks going pink and her lips parting in a smile.

165

"Sir," she says happily.

"Did you have one of your old colleagues make this?" Kayden reaches over to poke teasingly at Isabella's bodice, a sheer corset with complicated boning and emerald dragons stitched onto the cups. With her black pencil skirt and heels, she looks like an office fantasy come to life. "Looks like the designer needed a drafting table just to sketch it."

"Isabella was a structural engineer before she began working at Armorica full-time," Hugo explains to me, smiling as Isabella swats Kayden's hand away. "Which means she's better at math than you, Kayden. Maybe you should look over the spreadsheets with her."

Kayden nudges Isabella again, dodges a revenge poke, and then leans back to take a drink. "I tried that, remember? This summer? She tried to make me use something called formulas. It was *awful*."

"My genius is wasted here." She pouts up at Hugo.

He smiles again, that eyebrow-arching smile, like it's clear to him what she's doing but also like he doesn't care. He's too charmed.

"You're right, belle," he purrs and leans down to drop a kiss onto her lips. His hand slips inside the dragon-embroidered fabric of her bodice to pluck at a nipple. "I'll have to find a way to make it up to you."

She's easy, *so easy*, to make happy, because a small twist of her nipple has her panting and staring up at Hugo like he's the god of her universe. No wonder she's so in demand—she's a Dominant's dream. A little attention, a little pain, and she'll make you feel like she's fallen in love with you, right then and there.

It's very close to my own sickness, my own quick tumbles into obsession—but not quite. Partly because Isabella has already confided in me that she doesn't think she's ever been in love, not even with Hugo, since their fondness for each other is something other than romantic. But mostly it's because Isabella's tendency to fall into swift and sudden worship seems to make her happy. It makes the people around her happy.

That can never be said of me and my worship. It's only ever made things worse.

"Well, apart from the spreadsheets, not a lot else of Isabella is wasted here," Kayden remarks, nudging at her knee with his toe. She's still squirming with Hugo's fingers in her bodice, but she does manage to flip Kayden off with one nitrile-gloved hand, which earns her a slap on the other breast from Hugo for her insolence and then a tender kiss on the mouth because he can't seem to help himself.

"You should go to your appointment, belle," Hugo says, releasing her and sitting back. "When you're done, I'll play with you some more. I know the Good MP never goes quite hard enough."

"He doesn't," she breathes. "So I'd like that, sir."

"Go on then."

Isabella gets to her feet with the help of Hugo and my knee as well—the pencil skirt complicating her balance—and then departs after a kiss to Hugo's cheek and sticking out her tongue at Kayden.

Hugo watches her with warm interest, looking like he wishes he could follow.

"Her engineering team was brought in to stabilize a bridge that had partially collapsed," Kayden says to me after she's passed through the doorway to the playrooms. His voice has grown quiet, uncommonly serious. "They had to get there immediately to make sure the rescue and recovery teams could do their job safely. There were twenty-seven bodies in the end. She stayed at her firm two more years, long enough to finalize the plans for the replacement bridge and see ground broken. And then she left."

"That was just about a year ago now," murmurs Hugo. "I think that she didn't want to walk away without making sure a tragedy like that could never happen again. But it broke her faith in something. I'm not sure what. She hasn't been able to get it back."

I take a long drink of my beer, chest tight with empathy. I hate that she had to see something that horrific; I hate even more that it broke her sense of purpose.

But I understand it. God, how I understand it.

I have another beer, talking with Kayden about his time in the armed forces while Hugo chimes in with observations from his past life in international law. And then I remember that I'd meant to grab a second security team member for Isabella's doctor's appointment tomorrow. I'll need to check the schedule to see who'll be on and if the club can spare them for an hour or two.

I explain myself to the owners, who tell me to take anyone I need, as the club will be quiet during the day anyway, and even if it weren't, they still want Isabella to have the extra protection. And I go to the office just off the marble-floored lobby, behind the wooden concierge desk.

There's no one at the desk, which I haven't seen happen once in my time here, and then also no one inside the office.

I don't like this—at Lyonesse, there's always someone at the desk or security office—but I'm still new here, and I don't entirely know Armorica's staffing rhythms and quirks. I pull up the schedule on the computer, half my mind cataloging possibilities for where the concierge could be—dealing with an unhappy member or chatting with the doorman in his little heated vestibule outside or even just using the restroom—and then pause.

The club's schedule is comprehensive, covering all

the staff down to the third shift dishwashers. Armorica's Dominants and submissives are on here too with their client bookings, which means I can see Isabella's schedule.

Only one session, she said.

But there are two on here.

I recognize the first name as belonging to the Good MP, but the second name is *Kayden Howell*. Kayden who is still ignoring his spreadsheets in the lounge with Hugo. Kayden who sees Isabella more as a sister in kink than a play partner. Kayden who wouldn't need to schedule a session with Isabella anyway.

I'm on my feet the minute I find the room number, darting back toward the playrooms and looking for the security team member who should be posted outside her door. He's not there.

I knock on the door and try to open it, knocking again when I find it locked.

"Ms. Beroul?" I call in. "It's Tristan."

Nothing.

I don't wait. I don't run back to the office for the master key that opens all the playrooms. I don't try to get help. I aim for the spot just next to the knob, and I kick the fucking door open.

The millisecond it breaks and flies inward, I'm charging into the room with my sidearm drawn. Adrenaline stretches the moment into infinity; years of combat bring absolute certainty to every breath.

I see him in person for the first time, someone I've only seen in pictures. Jovian Nantes, absolutely unremarkable in every way—dull pink-beige skin, dull brown hair, designer clothes that still manage to look dull on his average-size frame. He's got Isabella pinned to the floor with her face in the imported rug, and one of his knees digs into the back of her soft thigh. Red bondage rope is unspooled everywhere, a mess of it, but he's managed to tie her wrists behind her back, and he has a hand wrapped around the mangled knot between her wrists, like he's about to stand up and drag her up to her feet.

A hunting knife, serrated and mean, protrudes from his other hand.

He's frozen by my entrance, which gives me time to make sure there's no blood, that Isabella's ribs are moving, that there is a good twelve inches between the tip of his knife and her skin. She's completely naked, with only one white glove half on a hand.

"I'm taking her," Jovian says. His face is an ugly thing right now—angry and petulant and afraid. "I'm *taking* her."

"She's staying here," I say, too amped up to sound as calm as I should right now. I am bad at this part, the talking, the convincing, and I have the memory of Sims bleeding from the throat to prove it. I take a deep breath and try again. "Put the knife down, and we can talk about this."

"I'm not putting it down. Are you fucking crazy?" His fingers have tightened around the rope, and Isabella's hands are blanching white and bloodless. "You're letting me take her right now. She should be with me. I want her with me."

Isabella lets out a low, muffled sob underneath him, and he flinches like I've just fired off a round.

Interesting. I don't think he likes being reminded that he's the villain here.

On the way to the airport, Goran had given me a short biography of Jovian, as relayed by Hugo's security team. The feckless failson of some real estate baron out west, an "entrepreneur" with a string of stupid ideas and bankrupted ventures behind him, Jovian has had a lifetime of being cushioned from consequences. Until now, that's mostly been unlimited money and some substance issues being swept under the rug, but that changed when he met

Isabella. The boy who'd never been told *no* grew into a man who could only hear *yes*. He wanted Isabella, and he'd gotten everything he'd ever wanted, so when he told her in a scene that she should quit Armorica and move in with him and be only his forever, he must have expected that she would give him what he asked for, especially when he was asking so very nicely.

That she didn't, that she found his invitation frightening instead of wonderful…that Hugo had the nerve to strip him of his membership and tell him that he no longer belonged… It might have been the first real *no* that Jovian had ever heard.

It seems to have cut the last link he had to reality.

"Jovian," I say, steadying my voice. "You don't want to do this. You're a good guy, I know that. And a good guy wouldn't want to scare Isabella right now."

I think I sound convincing. Maybe I've finally learned how to lie?

But it doesn't matter. The tip of Jovian's knife drops a little, closer to Isabella's waist. His voice is nervy. Quavering. "It didn't have to be like this. You should have let me keep seeing her at least. I didn't want this to be hard. You assholes in this stupid fucking club were the ones who made it hard!"

"We can make it real easy right now," I say soothingly. As soothing as I can be while I'm standing in a modified Weaver stance with both hands on my gun and my finger on the trigger. "Just set down the knife, and everyone gets to walk away."

"I thought about making her less pretty," says Jovian, and underneath the quaking words slithers a chilling soullessness. "I could cut up her face. No one else would want her then, but I would. Then she'd have to go with me. Be grateful that I'd still take her."

Isabella is trying so hard not to make any noise, not

171

to move, but she can't help the guttural moan of fear that leaves her.

I could kill him for that alone. For rending that noise out of someone who does her puzzles from the inside out, who made herself build one last good bridge before she left a job that traumatized her, who is kind and open with everyone. It's like terrorizing a baby rabbit or a daisy.

"I should have done that from the start," says Jovian slowly. He lets go of the rope around Isabella's wrist to grab her hair and turn her face toward the wall.

I shift forward, my pulse thumping in hard, steady beats. "Put the knife down."

"It'll hurt, but only for a while."

"Jovian—"

"I'll leave one eye. I don't want her blind—"

A sob from Isabella.

Another flinch from her attacker, and then an expression of frustrated rage, like how dare she not want this—

"*Jovian*—"

The knife jerks sideways.

I squeeze my trigger finger as I move forward. I squeeze again, and then a third time.

Pop pop pop—heavy, loud, final.

There's an obnoxious whine in my ears as I drop to a knee and shove Jovian's limp body off Isabella, grabbing the knife and using it to saw at the rope binding her wrists.

When I finally get her free and sitting up, she's crying so hard that I can't make sense of what she's saying. It isn't until I see her bare hand that I understand it has something to do with her missing glove. That her hand being exposed is somehow the last thing she can bear right now.

I sit back against the wall and pull her into my chest, taking her naked hand and deliberately trapping it between us, gloving it with our bodies. And then I crush her against me, shushing and soothing, staring at Jovian's unlikable, unmemorable face as it starts taking on that masklike quality that comes after death.

I wait for the rotten fruit feeling to come, the one that came after I killed those two men in the basement of Lyonesse, the one that followed the realization that leaving the army hadn't meant leaving death behind. But it doesn't come.

I don't feel conflicted. I would do it again.

I can't stand the things I can stand to do, Mark told me in that closet, and I know what he meant now, because I can stand to do this, I can stand it easily, and that's more upsetting than the fresh corpse by the cane rack. I don't want to be someone who finds killing easy to do. Maybe I'm more like Mark and Isolde than I thought.

When what feels like the entire club—frantically searching for the source of the gunshots—finds us, Hugo sinks to his knees next to me and pulls me and Isabella both into a desperate, clutching embrace, his own tears coming fast and unashamed.

Kayden takes immediate control of the room, his friendliness hardening into the certainty of a soldier as he checks Jovian's neck for a pulse, notes the time on his watch, and starts delegating calls to emergency services and to other staff members so they can start shutting down the club.

Inside the shared ring of my arms and Hugo's, Isabella clutches at my shirt, quaking so hard that I'm worried about shock, whispering the same two words over and over again.

Don't leave. Don't leave. Don't leave.

nineteen

MARK

My footsteps echo on the wooden floor in a quiet corner of the Smithsonian American Art Museum as I wait for Tristan to pick up the phone. I'm doing my best to look casual, like any other besuited asshole who thinks a museum is just another place to do business, but I'm not feeling casual at all. I'm feeling like I want to drive to the airport and fly to Montreal and handcuff Tristan's wrist to mine.

"Hello?" comes Tristan's voice, and it's tired, so fucking tired, and I just want to hug him. I want to bring him home and feed him and then make him lie down in bed and sleep until he can't sleep anymore.

"Tristan, it's me. Hugo just called. I'm so sorry that I didn't call you earlier. I didn't know what had happened, and if I'd known, I would have—"

A short breath from Tristan, like a huff. "You would have what, Mr. Trevena? Come up here? Brought me back to Lyonesse as soon as the police were done questioning me?"

It doesn't bother me to be called *Mr. Trevena* rather than

Mark—I enjoy Tristan's little formalities—but it does bother me in that tone of voice.

A reminder of the distance between us. The distance I *made* between us.

"I don't know what I would have done," I admit. "But at the very least I would have checked on you faster. Are you okay? Are you hurt? Hugo said you weren't, but I know how proud you are."

"Oh, I'm proud? Remember when you tore your stitches open after Drobny's attack because you were too proud to ask for help moving things around? It's not right to throw stones, sir."

I remember tearing my stitches open. Vividly. Although it wasn't for pride.

"Please, Tristan. At least assuage my fears. I promise Hugo isn't going to think less of you for a sprained ankle or a fractured rib."

A pause. "I'm not hurt."

I rub at my forehead as I pace in the empty room. The relief is honey-thick and sweet. "Good. Good. And Isabella, she's okay? Hugo said her attacker got as far as tying her up."

"He wasn't in there long, we think," answers Tristan wearily. "Maybe ten minutes at the most. I think almost everyone at Armorica is loyal to a fault, but there was a new doorman… Jovian was able to get to him, pay him enough to make the fake session and then create a distraction outside. Of course, the concierge and Isabella's guard thought they were making the club safer by running out to check. Jovian slipped in during the chaos and attacked Isabella while she cleaned up after her last client."

I don't reply right away, and Tristan snorts.

"You're very loud with the things you don't say."

"That's not true."

"But you think Hugo and Kayden are too trusting."

"It's an ailment common to trustworthy people that they assume everyone else is trustworthy too. Maybe you can help them peel those assumptions out of their procedures going forward."

"Maybe. I can't be accused of assuming the people around me are trustworthy these days," says Tristan, and I hate the way he sounds right now. Cynical and alone.

My fault. I did that to him.

"Are you sure you're okay?" I ask.

"I'm unhappy with how okay I am, but yes, I'm okay. I don't—" He swallows. "It was easier than it was at Lyonesse. And I don't think it should be. I don't know."

He's too tender for this. It's a stupid and foolish world that will take a prom king and send him to war. A hard and inflexible father who will drive his dragon-novel-reading son to R-Day at West Point and probably not even use the full ninety seconds to say goodbye.

In any fair and sensible universe, someone like Tristan would have become an artist or a teacher or a farmer. He would never have needed a taxonomy for killing—fair, unfair, in self-defense, in the defense of someone else. He would have never met me.

In that universe right now, he would be singing to baby lambs and a passel of kids and probably to the hills and trees around him, because if anyone would be happy singing to some trees, it would be Tristan Thomas. If anyone was ever born to the plowshare and not to the sword...

But it never mattered. There is nothing fair or sensible about our universe, and he spent four years being crushed into the shape of a fighter and the next eight in the mud and smoke of war.

"You don't need me to tell you that you couldn't have done anything differently, but let me also say this: goodness is not a stable currency. It's exchanged on an open market with many others. It's negotiated, it's bartered, it's sold. And if you have to sell a little bit of your goodness to make sure that an innocent woman keeps her eye or that a fellow soldier doesn't assassinate an elected leader and her children, then I think it's better to be on the market than to hoard your goodness like a talent buried in the earth."

Tristan doesn't reply.

I wish I could see his face, but I'm calling from a cheap phone I bought outside a Metro station right now, and even a call to Canada has it practically spitting sparks in my hand.

And then the man I'm waiting for strolls into the room anyway.

"I need to go," I tell Tristan, and the regret is a pinch in my throat. "I—I just wanted to make sure you were okay."

"Thank you," he says woodenly. "Send my regards to Mrs. Trevena."

A click before I can say anything else. Like *I love you.*

Like *I made a mistake.*

Although there's not much point to a lie like that. Do I feel guilty separating him and Isolde? Do I hate every minute he's so far away from me? Yes and yes again, but would I do anything differently?

Of course not.

I put the phone in my coat pocket and walk over to my father-in-law, who's standing in front of a three-piece wooden etching of Joan of Arc. He's wearing a three-piece suit, as he usually does, with a long wool coat and scarf, but despite his clothes being as crisp and unwrinkled as a shop mannequin's on Savile Row, there's an undeniable jitteriness to him.

"Mr. Trevena," he says quickly and then looks behind us, as if to check that we're alone.

I nod. "Mr. Laurence."

"Thank you for meeting me," he says. His eyes are

darting around, lingering on the empty doorways into the room. "I know you're busy, but it couldn't wait."

He'd said as much on the phone this morning when he'd told me that he'd booked a flight to London for the express purpose of discreetly laying over in DC. "Oh?"

"It's not—it's not ordinary business," he explains. His face—always a severe one—is carved with lines when he turns back to me. "I think I'm being followed. And I think Cashel has something to do with it."

This does arouse my interest, but I don't give an outward show of it. I have been extremely careful to keep my father-in-law ignorant of my motivations and the depth of my knowledge, especially as pertains to Isolde and Mortimer Cashel. And while Geoffrey Laurence has the distinction of being the person I hate the most whom I don't also plan on killing, I think learning that your child murders people at the behest of an evil churchman should come from a father-daughter chat and not from a morally dubious son-in-law.

I'm old-fashioned like that, I guess.

"When Isolde's mother died, the entirety of the Cashel family's wealth and property were rolled into the family trust, with Isolde as the trust's sole beneficiary," Laurence continues. "Mortimer had renounced all claim to the family's money years ago when he took his vows, but he assumed the role of trustee. I obviously insisted on becoming a co-trustee after Inis's death, since I wanted to make sure things were done right. I mean, what would Mortimer know about stewarding a trust? He took his vow of poverty so seriously that Inis had to shove new socks in his bag whenever he'd visit."

That sounds like Cashel. His singular fusion of austerity and power. If his piscatory ring were made out of spent bullets rather than gold, he'd find it just as beautiful.

"He's never shown a lick of interest in the trust, so I—well, I haven't personally checked on it much in the last few years," Laurence says, a ruddiness coming into his pale cheeks. "It was delegated to someone below me. I glanced over the annual reports, made sure things were heading in the right direction, and moved on."

"And now you've found something."

He twists his hands together once. "Money has been siphoned off, little by little. Very carefully done, the way a banker would do it."

"The way the person to whom you delegated the management of the trust did it?"

A jerky nod, and the flush in his cheeks is growing darker and splotchier now. "I'm not proud of this, Trevena. That it happened at my bank at all could be catastrophic, but that it happened to my own family is a…a violation."

"How much money?" I ask. "Can you see where it went?"

"Millions over the last seven years. Less than ten, more than eight. The amounts were deducted as transaction fees or management fees and then promptly slid right out of Laurence Bank into a shell company. Which went into another shell company. And so on and so on until they eventually got to Armenia or Tajikistan or the Caymans and melted away. There were only two that our investigators were able to trace to their final destinations. One payment went to the tuition department at Stanford. The other went to a woman named Regina Springer." He digs in his pocket and hands me a folded piece of paper.

I tuck it away in my own pocket to look at later. "So you'd like me to look into it," I say, not really asking, because I already know. This was the nature of our agreement four years ago. His daughter as surety for our continued services to each other. "But why do you think that Cashel has something to do with it?"

"Inis adored her brother, you know," Laurence murmurs. "Said that his faith was a faith of peace and that's what the

179

Church needed in these times. She thought all the glad-handing and reconnaissance and mediating was just simple diplomacy, but I knew better. I knew he wanted to be the pope."

Laurence's eyes drift to Joan of Arc. Etched knights kneel adoringly around the saint as her eyes are cast heavenward, and angels are arrayed around her like the rays of a sun. She has a sword held in one hand, a distaff in the other, and a dazzling golden halo. Beneath her levitating feet are the words "Mes derniers voeux, ma dernière pensée, sont pour mon dieu, ma patrie, et mon roi."

My last wishes, my last thought, are for my god, my country, and my king.

It makes me think of Isolde. Of Tristan. Children asked to hold swords for lies that would make martyrs of them in a heartbeat.

My father-in-law glances at me and then says suddenly, "I know you've never liked me."

I look back at him, this man who sold his daughter into marriage to a known murderer. Who'd dictated that we consummate the engagement so her Catholic guilt would keep her from backing out of it.

That Isolde had been working for her uncle all along, that she'd wanted to consummate things—it makes very little difference in my mind. Geoffrey didn't know any of that, and he demanded it all anyway.

"You're correct," I agree. "I've never liked you."

He's too distracted for the confirmation to bother him, I think. "And I know I haven't been the kind of father my wife would have wanted me to be to Isolde. When Inis died, I felt like…like all the best parts of me went too. Like she was the trustee of them, like she was the trust itself, and without her…"

He looks back at Joan of Arc, his thin mouth pressing tightly together. "I know you don't think much of me, but I hope you can trust this: I would never let someone steal from Isolde. Her future and the future of the bank are everything I've worked to build. Even my very worst choices have been for that." He glances at my pocket. "We couldn't find anything on Regina Springer except for that address. But the child at Stanford was easier—her name was on the payment record. She's the daughter of a single mother, both of whom are quite active on social media. Both of whom seem to visit Rome quite a bit. Coincidentally, there is a prelate there who used to be the bishop of the mother's diocese. She worked in the diocesan offices with him in fact. Around twenty years ago."

"And the prelate…"

"Is a cardinal. Voting in the papal conclave as we speak."

Ah, of course. While money is being funneled from the Cashel trust to pay for the secret daughter's tuition.

Laurence smooths the ends of his scarf, a genteel gesture betrayed by the jerky, nervous movements of his hands. "If you were going to buy votes in the Sacred College, you could hardly be using Vatican money. It would have to come from elsewhere. And you would have to plan for it… You'd need to plan for years."

One of Cashel's strengths. "When did you start thinking that someone might be following you?" I ask.

"Yesterday," says Laurence. "Our investigator called the prelate's old diocese in the morning. By the evening, I noticed the same two men loitering outside the lobby doors of my building."

"If you saw them, that's a good thing," I say. "It means either they want you to know that they're there or that they haven't sent their best yet. With Cashel in the conclave, this is being overseen by someone underneath him." Like the Scales. "Have you done anything about the manager yet? The one who was actually moving the money around?"

"No," Laurence replies. "We'll certainly be pressing

charges, but it was agreed that we shouldn't alert him before we're ready to make our move."

Pressing charges, fuck me. Even now, watching over his shoulder, Isolde's father still has no idea what pit of hell he's tumbled into. For him, this is still all about money and politics and accounting and law.

"Don't do anything until I say to," I tell him in a low, urgent voice. "Call off the investigators for now, sit on the evidence, and let the manager continue to pull money out of the trust. You cannot let them know that you found anything of substance. It might be too late after the call to the diocese, but maybe not. If you play hard enough that you haven't found anything, pretend that it must have been some shoddy accounting and nothing more, you'll buy us all time."

Laurence's iron-colored brow lifts. "Some time until what? Mortimer is elected and he's taking his papal cues from the Borgias or Medicis?"

"You'll buy me time until I can make your daughter safe, Laurence. That's all I ask."

He studies me. "You care for her. Beyond our arrangement I mean."

"Not that you deserve to know it, but yes. I do care for her. I love her."

His shoulders fall, and he closes his eyes. "I'm glad. I'm glad that she—that I haven't taken that too. Does she love you?"

"Depends on the day," I reply honestly.

He opens his eyes and stares at the carved saint in front of us. "Inis was the same."

"I'll look into Regina Springer," I tell him, turning to leave. "Don't take any stupid risks in the meantime. However long you think Cashel has planned this, double it—triple it even. He's planned for everything, including you."

twenty

MARK

Once I get to Lyonesse, I call Lox, who is *NOT* happy to hear from me, especially when I have more things for her to do.

"I'm not Google," she carps at me. But I still hear her typing as I rattle off Regina Springer's address.

"I'll pay whatever you want," I say. "I know your little Alaskan commune of server farms and zip-tied redheads doesn't come cheap."

"Oh, fuck off." And then she hangs up.

A second later, I get a text message. Also I'm waiting on a call back, but I'm pretty sure I found Cara Sims. Once I hear more, I'll be in touch.

And then another one, right after. Okay, extra fuck off now.

I run my hand down my face. God, this day already feels a year long, and it's not even time for lunch.

I sit at my desk right as Dinah comes in. The two weeks between Saturnalia and New Year's Eve comprise our slowest season, and everyone save for Andrea and myself tends to dress more casually. So today Dinah is in an MIT sweatshirt and jeans instead of her usual latex and leather. The giant glasses perched on her nose and the reusable coffee cup in her hand are more *casual academia* than *in charge of Roman orgies*. Which makes sense, as I'd lured her away from a tenure-track career with the promises of more spanking and less grant application paperwork.

"There you are," she says, dropping into a chair in front of my desk. "I've been looking for you all morning."

"Impromptu meeting with Geoffrey Laurence," I say and then smile at the face she makes. "I know."

"I'm feeling grateful that my risk of having a father-in-law is quite low."

"Or you could end up with five at the same time."

Her laugh is bright and fast, followed by a *you got me there* smile. She's a bit of a tomcat. "It would take five to pin me down."

"Or just one if she's a certain princess…"

For that, I'm given a look that could score glass. Dinah doesn't like talking about the princess. "I didn't find you this morning to chat about my lack of fathers-in-law. I'm here because of Isolde."

I hear the disapprobation in her voice, and I turn serious. "What about her?"

"What about her? Mark, have you seen her?"

"Yes," I say and look down at the ring on my finger. No longer her ring, instead the black and silver one I'd given Tristan before he left for Ireland. It's fitting, I think, that he should have mine. It should have always been his, and the wedding should have been theirs, and they should be together right now, happy and untroubled by a living ghost like me. "I've seen her."

"I thought maybe it was just Saturnalia, that maybe once we weren't pretending we were senators and praetorians

184

hatching plots over wine, the whispers would die down," Dinah says. "But they haven't. Even after you spoke to Andrea."

The final night of Saturnalia, after I'd helped Isolde up from between my feet and walked her to the apartment, where she woodenly shut the door in my face, I found Andrea in the lobby of the club and told her to knock it the fuck off.

"I've never asked you to forgive Cashel for what he took from you, and I've never asked you to like Isolde," I told my treasurer. "But don't insult my empathy by humiliating my wife in public again."

Andrea had the grace to look slightly ashamed, but the defiance outlined in her jaw was just as unmistakable. "If she wants people to speak of her better, then maybe she should have behaved better. She—"

"Didn't want to marry me, doesn't want to be here, and can hardly be blamed for loving Tristan. Even I couldn't stop myself from doing that, you know."

Andrea looked back at me with an unhappy gaze. "She's not a victim, Mark. She's a saint with enough blood on her hands to paint over the inside of the Sistine Chapel and have plenty left over. She is the *enemy*."

"She is *mine*," I said sharply, and even though it was no longer true, probably wouldn't be legally true for much longer, it felt so good to say that I said it again. "She's mine. And I've welcomed her back here, so I'll ask you not to betray my hospitality."

Andrea hadn't asked *and if I did betray it?* even though it was all over her face. But she swallowed it down, forced it back. "You and I have been partners for all these years, and I'm grateful for it, because I couldn't have gotten this close without you. But that girl will be the death of you if you're not careful."

"My plans are extremely careful. That's all that matters."

Andrea had nodded then, and since that night, she'd stopped her own whispers and stares in the hall. She instead pretended Isolde didn't exist, which was an improvement at least.

But the rest of the club still whispers at night. Every night.

"Tell her she doesn't need to come into the hall," Dinah is saying now. "There's no point. It's only been two weeks since she's been back, and she already looks like a vampire has been feeding on her for years."

Dinah doesn't know about Ys or even about the saints, so I must be careful explaining things. "I've mentioned before that this marriage was arranged—"

"Yes, and that Isolde and Tristan left because they found out it was more arranged than they'd thought." Dinah had given me hell the morning I'd been found tied to my chair, firm in her belief that whatever had happened to me, I'd thoroughly deserved. I liked her more for it, for her steadfast protectiveness toward Isolde when it feels like everyone else at Lyonesse is determined to hate her.

"The reasons for the arrangement still stand. Are still rather pressing. It's important that Isolde and I appear... connected."

Dinah's watch lights up on her wrist, and she sighs when she looks at it. She gets to her feet. "Well, it's not going to help any of these pressing reasons if Isolde looks like she's being yellow-wallpapered while she's kneeling at your feet." Dinah scrunches at the curls hanging over one side of her face, looking troubled. "She asked me about the trial by iron, Mark. Last night."

I stare at her. It is so far outside what I would have thought possible that I don't even know how to react right now. "She *what*?"

"She heard Andrea mention it, someone else too. She wanted to know what it was."

"And what did you tell her?"

Dinah levels a steady gaze at me through her glasses. "That she should forget she ever heard those words."

I exhale. "Good."

"I don't know what's happening between you two, and I don't need to know. But whatever's happening is going to break her apart if you don't fix it. So, you know. Fix it."

"I will. And, Dinah?"

"Yes?"

"Let's pull aside the members who like her and make sure that they're countering anything they're hearing that we're not. Anguish and Christopher will help too."

"Consider it done."

I stay at my desk for a moment after Dinah leaves. My thumb goes to the inside of the black and silver ring, toying with it idly. Thinking of the tracker inside, of the other ring currently on Tristan's finger, which doesn't have anything untoward inside it at all—something I know for a fact, having had it discreetly checked after my wedding. In my pocket, I feel the hard, cool presence of crystal shaped into a chess piece. A queen. I touch it once and then get to my feet to find my wife.

twenty-one

MARK

Outside the hall, I've been avoiding her, but it hasn't been because I haven't wanted to see her. Quite the opposite. Just like that night on her father's desk, just like on Samhain, I sense myself at a precipice, willing to throw away years of literal blood, sweat, and tears simply to keep her close to me.

She deserves better than that. She deserves as little of me in her life as I can contrive to make possible.

So. Just the hall at night.

But Dinah was correct to point out that even the hall is extracting a cost from Isolde that I'm not sure she can pay. Every night, I see less and less of my vicious and conniving chess opponent; my arching, gasping wife who once nearly fainted just from crawling across a floor; my shadows and glass girl who can smell the same smoke on the air that I can, who knows what will and won't wash away when the rain comes.

Every night, she is stiller, quieter, paler.

Of everything I'd planned for, I hadn't planned for this one ridiculous thing: that the petty, grasping boredoms of my club would coalesce into this…this *miasma* of whatever the fuck is happening.

As if there's not enough going wrong right now, as if there aren't dead priests and rigged conclaves and smuggled weapons right there on the news. And I can't even sort out my own household in peace?

Goddammit.

Isolde isn't in the apartment. I see that the bed is rumpled—on my side. She's been sleeping on my side, which hurts in a way I can't find the words for.

I pull open the refrigerator doors and see it full of untouched food. The only dish in the sink is a glass still half filled with water. There's a small bunch of bananas hanging from a hook below a shelf, and when I flip open the trash lid, I see three banana peels and a half-eaten sleeve of crackers.

Worry slides into my chest like so much cold mud as I leave the apartment and go to her office on the floor below. She isn't inside, and judging from the fine layer of dust on the surface of her desk, it's been a while since she has been. Maybe since before she ran away to Morois.

I go downstairs to find a similar fate for her studio. Dust on the rubber knives, a staleness to the air. I rub at the edge of the black and silver ring with my thumb and then look at the door to the garden outside.

The walls block the wind, but the garden remains a basin of miserable chill, and my ears and fingers are pinched with cold by the time I get to the back of the garden, where a dormant cherry tree zigs and zags and droops next to a fountain with a layer of ice at the bottom. Gas heaters have been installed at convenient intervals throughout the outdoor space in case we decide to use it for our guests, but only one has been turned on today, burning by the fountain like a lonely torch.

Isolde is nearby—not perched on the fountain or nearby

bench but kneeling on the hard ground under the tree. She's not praying. Her eyes are fixed on nothing in particular; her hands are loose and empty at her sides. Her face, when she looks over at me, is empty of everything save for hopelessness.

I walk over to her and kneel. I take her hands in mine. Despite the heater nearby, they're frigid. "How long have you been out here?" I ask.

Her lashes lift as she stares at me. She's wearing a coat but no scarf or hat or gloves, and she's only in leggings and a T-shirt underneath.

"Isolde," I say.

White vapor curls between us as we breathe. "You'll ruin your suit," she finally says, eyes drifting to my knees on the iron earth.

"I don't care." I press her hand to my jaw—impossibly cold. Her lips are pale. "We're going inside now. Come on. Yes, that's it." I'm standing and pulling her to her feet. She sinks a little, like she might not be able to stand, and I catch her before she falls, pulling her into my arms.

The fact that she lets me is proof enough that something is very wrong.

I carry her up to the apartment, and when we get inside, I sit her down on the kitchen table. She lets me tug off her coat and hand her a glass of water.

"When's the last time you've eaten?" I ask.

She shrugs. Doesn't drink.

I press my forehead to hers, close my eyes for a brief moment. I've been in combat, covert action; I have been shot, stabbed, beaten, and strangled.

And the fear I feel now, swirling around this blank-eyed woman who won't drink some water, is more powerful than any fear I've ever felt, because I'm more helpless than I've ever been. More worthless.

Famous kinkster Mark Trevena, and here's his wife, cold

and dehydrated and hungry, as dull and inert as one of her dusty practice knives downstairs, and he doesn't even know where to begin to make her better.

God. All that work keeping her safe, only to lose her like this.

I kiss her forehead. "Drink, sweetheart. Just a little, if that's all you can do."

She lifts the glass to her lips and drinks a little. Not much, but some. I take the glass, set it on the table, and then pick her up and carry her into the bathroom, where I set her on the counter next to the sink.

"I'd like you to take a shower so you can warm up. I can leave now while you do so, or I can help you undress and then leave. Or I can help with all of it."

She looks at me, not offering anything, and I dip a little so I can meet her gaze more completely.

"I need you to tell me what you want," I clarify. "Do you want me to leave? Do you want me to stay?"

She reaches out and grabs my wrist. "Stay," she says. Her voice is barely there, only an outline of itself.

"For the shower too?"

She nods.

I strip her out of her clothes carefully but quickly, pausing only briefly to look at the florid smears under her knees. Very, very fresh bruises. How long had she been kneeling out there? Was today the first day? I could walk into the Potomac right now for how stupid I've been, how fucking certain I was that the best thing for her was for me to stay away.

The woman in the navy dress from two weeks ago, spitting nails in my office, felt so indelible and inviolable, as sharp and certain as a sword—and now here she is clammy and rusted, like something dug out of a long-ago grave.

Have the whispers of the club done this much? Truly?

I undress myself too, but I leave my underwear on, not

wanting to signal any ulterior motive on my part, and then turn on the shower. It hits the stone tiles with a hiss, and I check the temperature before I go back to help Isolde off the counter and into the spray.

And I can't help it. I know silence is what's warranted right now, but I'm shaken and floundering and so pissed at myself that I can't stand it, so I'm muttering to her as I guide her into the shower.

"No gloves, coat unzipped—there's supposed to be freezing rain this afternoon. You would have been encased in ice like a jewel under glass. You were top of your class at Columbia. Surely you can think of smarter ways to punish me. Close your eyes and dip your head back, good girl. And you're barely eating. At this point, why even hide from the other saints and Ys? If you're planning on stopping your own heart, but of course not before you leave some bruises all over your pretty knees first. *My* pretty knees, by the way, and my heart, the one you want to stop."

For the first time, a little life comes into her face. She opens her eyes to look at me.

I shouldn't be saying any of this, for fuck's sake. I'd decided when Tristan and Isolde came back that I was renouncing my claim to her, that everything would be as it was supposed to be in the beginning: a play on the stage, and no matter how well acted it was, it would always have a curtain drawn at the end. I'd let myself foolishly reach for what I wanted—*them*—even though I knew, I've always known, that the curtain would never drop on love, not for me.

But I'm foolish and weak right now, because I don't care about plans or endings or what a good man like Maxen or Tristan would do in my place. I care about *her*, and I love her, and this love flays me open, leaves nothing hidden, however bloody and primal.

I move behind her and start shampooing her hair; I

find her scalp and massage, applying firm pressure with my fingertips, going gentle around her temples and behind her ears and then pressing more deeply into the muscles at the nape of her neck. I rinse the suds until the water runs clear down her back; I get the conditioner and speak in low tones while I work it into her long, silvery hair.

"You are Isolde Laurence, Isolde *Trevena*, and you are not allowed to slip through your own fingers, much less mine. I won't have it, sweetheart. You are too dear, and you must know by now that I am too mercenary and too mean to let someone else take what's dear to me, even you."

She turns her head to the side, her face in profile. Her nose and cheekbones glisten, and water runs off the tip of her jaw. I'm gratified to see that the apples of her cheeks are growing flushed, that her lips are their usual shell-pink hue.

She seems like she's about to speak, but then she stops herself. Looks away.

I don't press.

I rinse her hair once again, and then I soap her limbs, softly but decorously, not lingering over her breasts or the exquisite dimples at the small of her back that I could watch glisten forever. But the webs between her fingers, the elegant fluting of her spine between her shoulder blades, the rounded slopes of her calves… I can't resist tarrying for a moment or two.

I've washed her and Tristan both like this before, but I could never get sick of it. How could you get sick of looking at your entire life, bound up in shower flushes and water-laced eyelashes, standing sweetly right in front of you?

We finish, and I have Isolde wait in the shower while I get a towel, not wanting to risk her slipping while her feet are wet. I dry her off, starting with her face and ending with her hair, and after I fold her into one of my robes, I catch her looking at me with eyes now slightly clearer than before.

Hope is a corrosive pest, but I still allow it to eat its way inside my chest.

"I'd like you to drink more water now," I tell her, and she breathes in and nods. It's the clearest communication I've gotten from her yet. "Will you go into the kitchen and do that for me?"

She hesitates, but she goes eventually. I peel off my wet underwear, towel off, and then pull on sweatpants and a long-sleeved T-shirt.

When I pad barefoot into the kitchen, she's holding the now-empty glass of water.

"Very good," I praise, and then I have her sit on the counter while I make a very quick meal for her. Toast with butter, apricot jam, and sea salt and then some apple slices with peanut butter.

I watch her eat slowly and then more quickly as her body remembers how it's done, until she's licking jam and sea salt off her fingertips. I catch her hand just as she reaches her ring finger and lick it myself, curling my tongue around the pad of her finger and then pulling it between my lips.

I pull back, our gazes meeting, and there is no question what either of us are thinking of right now.

The freezing rain has finally come amid all this, and the sky has gone dark.

"An early bedtime, I think," I say, and while it's a little delayed, surprise tugs at her mouth.

"We're not going to the hall tonight?" she asks, and the hope in her voice breaks my heart.

"I think we've earned a night off."

"And you'll…you'll stay here tonight? So I don't have to sleep alone?"

I think of the rumples on my side of the bed. Of the nightmares she might have been suffering through alone. My throat aches; I have to clear it before I speak. "Yes,

Isolde. I'll stay. Let me clean up here, and then we can get ready for bed."

She chews on her lip and then slides off the counter and goes to get ready for bed under her own steam. After I finish with the dishes, I follow, brushing my teeth with a spare toothbrush and then finding an unfamiliar charging cable to plug in my phone.

Two weeks ago, I lived here, and now it feels like a hotel. It's unpleasant.

Isolde is already in bed, on her side, and when I slide under the covers, she stays where she's at, even though I can feel the loneliness rolling off her like fog on ice.

"What's your safeword?" I ask her.

"Hyssop," she answers, confused.

"Great." Without any other discussion, I grab her and pull her over to my side of the bed, manhandling her until she's tucked against me and half draped over my chest.

And then...then I can't stop petting her. Stroking her. Shaping my palms against the curves of her shoulder or the subtle muscles of her back.

Fuck, I've missed this. Just this. Touching her. Holding her. It's how priests and monks and other holy people must feel when they're allowed to handle their reliquaries, all those beautifully wrought vessels made to carry sparks of God. I could *pray* right now, this very minute, that's how good it feels to have her in my arms.

"Why were you in the garden?" I ask, staring up at the ceiling. There's no water in the rooftop pool right now, so the ceiling is a glass canopy of darkness, limned in blue at the edges. At the windows, winter presses in with biting rain and the occasional spit of sleet. Below us, the club will be in the full thrum of evening, with music and guests and some suspension experts on the stage.

Isolde takes a minute to answer. She's been silent all this

time, but she's warm and fed, and she's been tracing the ink on my arm. The soft exhales on my chest have been steady and not labored.

"Why did you come looking for me in the garden?" she asks rather than answering.

I find a strand of silken hair and twist it around my finger. "I couldn't find you. I was worried."

"You haven't tried to find me before." Her finger still moves along my forearm, tracing the curved beak of the tattooed bird. A Cornish chough, which mates for life. She finds a long, raised ridge in its wing, a few raised scars nearby.

"It's important to find a reputable tattoo artist," I remark when she rubs at the ridge inquiringly.

But she doesn't let me change the subject. "It feels like you've been avoiding me."

There's no point in lying. "That's because I have been. I thought it better. For you."

A dull laugh. "Yes. So much better."

"You didn't run away on Samhain because you wanted to keep sharing a life with me," I state. "And you didn't come back because you missed me. You ran because I lied to you and because you couldn't bring yourself to kill me, and now you're here again because it's the best chance you've got at holding your uncle at bay. An uneasy alliance isn't the same as trust, and I didn't imagine we'd go back to blow jobs after breakfast just because your uncle has done us the favor of threatening you directly now." *And I don't want you to hate me when this is done. I want you to know that I at least tried not to take more than I needed.*

I don't tell her those last parts though. They're selfish thoughts, even for me.

"But that's not all of it, is it?" she asks. "You hate us for leaving you, even if you still love us too. You want to punish me, and if Tristan were here, you'd want to punish him too."

I acknowledge this. "Yes."

"So I'm not supposed to believe that you're staying away to hurt me?"

I sigh. "Give my mercenary nature a little credit, Isolde. Why would I choose a punishment that wounded *myself*? I can't be plainer about this than I've been: if I were the god of my own little world, I would have you and Tristan at my fingertips, and I would spend my days and nights afflicting you with my attention. Like a pillar of cloud and flame, I'd be with you always. So no, I haven't been staying away to hurt you. I've been staying away because the conscientious course of action also happened to be the most strategic way forward, and believe me when I say that almost never happens in my line of work."

She shifts and turns so that she's propped up on one elbow and looking down at me. "And today you decided that, what, it wasn't conscientious to ignore me anymore?"

The light from outside filters in through the windows and the ceiling, a little mottled from the ice and rain, and paints her in shades of indigo and Alice blue. I find a new skein of hair and wrap it in a blue-silver curl around my finger. "You've been fading since Saturnalia. I thought maybe—I suppose I thought it was a protective measure, that you were only trying to give the club as little to work with as possible, that you were simply missing Tristan and your freedom and resenting me for taking both of those things from your life. I didn't realize how much everything was affecting you, and I should have. I shouldn't have been so far away." I let out a tired sigh. "Forgive me, Isolde."

She studies my face. "I don't know that I should forgive you, but that's the problem, isn't it? It would be absurd to trust you ever again, and yet you *know that* and you *agree*. You're not courting my trust or my forgiveness, and that itself makes me want to trust you more. And then when we are stacking lie for lie, sin for sin, broken vow for broken bow—our sums aren't so far apart in the ledger, are they?"

"I'm ahead," I say. "By my reckoning."

"Yes, you are still the bigger monster," she says and lies down again, putting her head on my shoulder. "But I'm not far behind. And perhaps I'm worse, because I don't even know why I am what I am anymore. You've at least scratched your sins into the ledger yourself. The things I've done… I think I've done them for something that isn't real at all. For something that's never been real."

I hear it in that last sentence, the same desolation I saw in her face in the garden. The pointless stains on her knees from kneeling on frozen tree roots.

Opera music curls in my mind—handfuls of magnolia petals flutter down to a coffin lid gleaming in a hole.

There's a faint trembling under my hands and against my side now. The shallow stutter of a breath accidentally catching in a cinched throat.

"You took the boxes with you, so you know that Eliot died in a friendly fire incident in Košice," I say, stroking her shoulder. "But did you know that I was the one to drag his body into the dark and bring him home?"

"No," she says a little shakily. The sobs are close, which is okay. I'm not frightened of her tears. "I didn't know that."

"I watched as he was shot by American soldiers—soldiers who'd been lied to, but God, *so easily lied to*—and I listened to a soldier render aid to one of his own. One of *our* own. And instead of asking for help, instead of helping *them*, I had to creep up to my husband's dead body and tug him over wet cobbles and muddy grass and pray that no one heard me. His shoe came off—he was always so vain about his shoes, would never wear something practical—"

I stop short, having forgotten that small ostentation of his. The memory lances clean through me.

Clearing my throat, I start again. "Whatever the informant was about to tell him, we never found out, so three people died that night for absolutely nothing at all. I remember watching them load his body on a commercial cargo flight, no flag, no airmen to escort him to Dover, and thinking that we'd agreed to this, he and I. We'd joined the agency knowing that we could die doing something the world would never know about, that our songs might go unsung and all that bullshit, but what I'd never considered is that we might die for nothing. And then I thought…if we could be dying for *nothing*, maybe we could be killing for nothing too."

She's somehow shivering and utterly still at the same time. A barely anchored boat on choppy water.

"The year I left college for the army, I was happy to go to war," I continue. "I guess you could say that I'd felt called to it. You've been to Morois. You've seen the Trevena family chapel and the little cemetery. The Trevenas and cousins of Trevenas and neighbors of the cousins of Trevenas—the men who went across the Channel were the small gods of our woods. My grandfather wore a poppy pin every time he left the house. Maybe I had a different flag sewn to my jacket, but I felt like my destiny had finally come, like I was doing what I was made for. That my country needed me and our allies needed us, and that if any virtue was synonymous with holiness in our day and age, it would be patriotism. Courage painted in bright colors—red, white, and blue. I believed in that then like you believe in God now."

She moves a little against me but doesn't speak.

"It was different in the Rangers, but only by degree. If the missions were more complicated morally, the fervor and belief in our cause were tenfold. We couldn't be doing the wrong thing, because we were the right people. It was easy to squash out those little flares of curiosity, of concern, the rare unsavory moment." I sigh. "And then came the agency. Their invitation. They'd already gotten Melody. They'd already noticed that I was more like my MI6 grandfather than my heroic soldier ancestors. They knew that my conscience was…different. I was a man with muffled morals who'd made a god out of his country, so they offered me an altar to sacrifice on. I said yes, because I believed that every threat, theft, murder, and criminal damage to property was a step toward an endpoint we'd all agreed on. It made sense to me, my grandfather's grandson, that you had to fight darkness with darkness, and better me than some sweet recruit who just wanted to study Pashtun or Korean for the linguistic thrill, because it wouldn't hurt me to do the things that couldn't be written down in the reports. I didn't lose sleep at night over them."

"Until Eliot," she says.

"I know it makes me trite and solipsistic, but yes, the alley Eliot died in was my road to Damascus, the scales falling from my eyes, et cetera, et cetera, because they put my husband on a plane without a single honor and all for a mistake, a lapse in communication, for an empty and hollow *nothing*. And if that nothing was there then, maybe it had been there before. Maybe it had always been there. And I don't mean in every single skirmish or firefight, and I don't even necessarily think it pervaded the whole war, but it was a slither along the edges of it the entire time. A whisper on the pillows after the lights went out. And then—" I pull in a tight breath. "And then it was worse than everything being for nothing. The dying and the killing, it *was* for something. It was for John Lackland and for Ys. For money and for business done half a world away over artistically plated scallops and wine bought by the bottle. I think I would have rather had all the horrors of my life stem from primates fighting for hilltops than know it was all to make the same handful of people marginally wealthier, bit by bit. I would rather have Eliot's death mean nothing than know that it was for sale to the highest bidder in an auction none of us knew we were in."

I stare up at the ceiling, where the rain has almost completely turned to sleet, slowly blocking out the light.

"You say my sins are at least my own, but that isn't true, Isolde. They were stolen from me. My own actions were stolen from me. My life was a lie in the most fundamental sense because I didn't even know I was lying. I've been where you are, and I can't make this easier for you, but I can tell you that there is a tiny seed cupped in your palm right now, and that seed is *from this moment on, no more.* And like the mustard seed in the Bible, you can use it to move mountains."

For a moment, all is quiet save for the sleet pecking at the glass. And then Isolde shifts and sits up. I sit up too, but I don't touch her right away. I merely watch the shadows ripple across her back as she breathes.

"It's not enough," she says to the cold air and not to me. "I'd have to move mountains for the rest of my life if even one of the people my uncle had me kill didn't deserve it."

"I know about many of the people you've killed, and the world certainly isn't worse off for them being dead. Maybe you'll only have to move hills instead." I think for a moment and then say carefully, "You asked Dinah about the trial by iron."

"I don't even know what it is, and yet when I asked Dinah about it, she looked at me like I was asking to harvest an organ on stage."

"It's a sadistic display—and I mean *sadistic* literally—as that used to happen at a club here in DC. I put the club out of business after I opened Lyonesse and poached many of its members, and I intentionally did not incorporate the old club's customs into ours. I don't want to hear any more about a trial by iron from anyone, and I especially don't want you thinking about it while you're digesting what unholy things you've done in the name of holiness. And then getting some very Catholic ideas about punishment and forgiveness."

She turns in profile, a dent at the corner of her mouth. "You think you know me so well."

I run my fingers down the valley of her spine. "Not well enough. Never well enough."

My phone rings from across the room, and with a displeased exhale, I stop touching my wife and leave the bed to answer it.

It's Melody.

"Blanche just called," my twin says. "Tristan's father is dead."

twenty-two

MARK

Two days after Christmas, Isolde and I stand next to each other on the frost-crisped grass at Arlington National Cemetery, watching the officer in charge kneel in front of Ricker Thomas's widow—Blanche, my older sister and Tristan's stepmother of only a year—to hand her a folded flag.

Tristan sits next to Blanche, a study in geometry—straight back, square shoulders, arms perfectly in parallel. His hair has been cut back into regulation for the occasion, and the tightly locked muscles of his neck are etched with a chisel's precision.

I've never been one to be sentimental about something like hair—it was frequently a casualty of necessity in both the military and the agency—but I mourn his now. The way it had begun to curl against his neck and around his ears, the almost immoral sumptuousness of it. The world is such a hard and cruel place. Why must we also be denied Tristan's hair?

Blanche is crying, softly and prettily, as the OIC talks to

her in low, murmuring tones. Melody lets out a measured exhale next to me, and we are matched in our restlessness. We'd like to flank our sister like castling rooks and glower at everyone who approaches, friendly or otherwise, just so they're appropriately polite and deferential by the time they get to her. But Ricker Thomas was a general, and his funeral is crowded with military types from every branch—not to mention three Joint Chiefs of Staff, the SecDef, and Vice President Morgan Leffey (whom I know quite well and always enjoy seeing). So given the composition of the mourners, Melody and I had politely offered to stand behind the chairs reserved for us as Blanche's family to make room for the older guests, and for the vice president. We guessed that her Secret Service detail would want to surround her from every angle.

(We guessed correctly. Her agents are currently shifting and swiveling and tilting their heads to study every flicker of movement like suspicious, earpiece-wearing crows, and given how Maxen Colchester's presidency ended, I can't blame them.)

So anyway, Melody and I aren't near Blanche, even though we'd like to be, but it cheers me a little to see Tristan offer her his hand to hold. It's kind of him when he barely knows Blanche, when she'd only been a part of his father's life for a brief time…and when he might have every reason to resent her for the crime of being related to me.

"The coroner's report says it was a stroke," murmurs Melody as we watch the Arlington Lady bend down to speak with Blanche.

"Do you believe that?" I ask, keeping my voice as quiet as hers. With anyone else, I'd be very aware that I sounded highly paranoid, but Melody and I have chosen a life where paranoia is a virtue.

"You know, it's strange, but I think I do," Melody says.

"Blanche told me they'd been quibbling about some hypertension diagnosis—he was convinced he could tackle his blood pressure 'naturally,' whatever that means. But he was up against decades of smoking, and you know how soldiers in his generation smoked. It's remarkable that his health was that good for as long as it was actually."

I consider this, that someone could simply just *die*, and die for reasons that had nothing to do with arms smuggling or government interests or malevolent princes of the Church. That they could die because they were too proud to buy a pill organizer. Because they were in the army thirty-odd years ago, and the only way you got to take a break was if you pulled out a pack of cigarettes. Smoke 'em if you got 'em.

"Interesting," I say, and Melody lets out a delicate snort.

"I know, it's novel, someone dying of natural causes, but I'll be grateful if it means Blanche isn't a target."

I nod. I'll take a tobacco-wreathed tragedy over Cashel attacking me through Blanche any day.

The wind stirs enough to tug at the ends of various wool coats and the bottom of Isolde's dress. I tuck her into my side to shield her from the worst of the chill as the chaplain now speaks quietly to Blanche and Tristan, the last official condolences of the day. Isolde presses into me but otherwise remains the picture of self-collected decorum, with her eyes ahead and her gloved hands folded together.

Standing on the other side of my wife are Hugo Budic, Kayden Howell, and Isabella Beroul, all of whom came down for the funeral, which I think is uncommonly kind of them. What happened at Armorica with Isabella and her attacker seems to have forged a bond between them and Tristan, and the best part of myself is pleased that Tristan has such good friends at his new post.

The worst part of myself would like to steal him back.

"I'll see you at Blanche's," my twin says to me after the

service is concluded and people begin getting to their feet. She walks away without another word and goes to greet a senator from the intelligence committee before they can escape.

Tristan is now standing mostly alone under the canopy, looking lost as he takes in the uncompromising shape of his father's coffin, and my hand gives an involuntary twitch at my side as I watch him. Because I remember doing this very same thing at my own father's funeral; I remember understanding that *I was an orphan now*, realizing that a forgotten childhood fear had suddenly crawled out from under my bed, but instead of terror, I only felt a peculiar, muffled sort of bewilderment. Like I'd been cast in the role of orphan but no one had given me a script to follow or lines to say, so I was left to improvise the part as much—or as little—as I wanted.

I want to go to Tristan, and I want to go to Blanche, and I am very tired of being so far away from them both when all these people who barely know my sister *or* my bodyguard get to swarm around them and ply them with their awkward, hollow sentiments.

I shift forward at the same moment Isolde does, and then we both stop at the same time, seeing Tristan now snared in conversation with three men in the old blue service uniforms.

"We'll see him tonight," I say to myself as much as to her. I've offered Lyonesse's hospitality to Tristan and the trio from Armorica, and starting tonight, they'll be staying with us. It's a gamble to have Tristan back, even for a short time, but I'm throwing the goddamn dice. With Hugo, Kayden, and Isabella—with the club still quiet for the holidays and the papal conclave still in session—I'm hoping there's enough smoke to cover the fire of the truth: the idea of my puppy staying at some soulless hotel when he could be under my roof is absolutely unacceptable.

He needs to be home.

Incidentally, we're not the only ones who've tried to move closer to Tristan. I glance over and see Isabella Beroul—quite fetching today in an ivory coat and red lipstick—standing closer to the graveside canopy, like she was about to walk over there. But Kayden has caught her around the waist in a fraternal sort of tug and seems to be telling her something akin to what I just told my wife.

The same wife who is currently staring at Isabella with a look she might give an overvalued altar triptych with flaking paint and mold damage.

"Careful, darling," I murmur and gently steer her by the elbow to where Jago is waiting for us in the car. "People might start to think you're jealous."

———

Blanche's pale blue town house is teeming with people, but thanks to Melody's wife, Sophie—who skipped the service so that she could coordinate all the minutiae of such a gathering—the Capitol Hill residence is a smooth and gentle churn of nibbles and conversation and not the miserable crush of immiscible coteries and coats slung awkwardly over arms it could be.

Isolde, who was raised for moments such as these, steps in to help as soon as we get there, and she and Sophie begin discreetly collecting information for thank-you cards and facilitating introductions so that Tristan and Blanche aren't unduly in demand by the guests.

Melody and I ourselves take turns with our older sister, showing too many teeth when we smile, making sure that no one leaves the town house without remembering that Blanche is a Trevena and therefore not to be fucked with by anyone hoping to leverage something out of a general's widow. When Melody joins Blanche and me again after making some rounds, I go to get another drink. Just water since I'd like to stay sharp this afternoon—but I drink it from a rocks glass so I can maintain my useful reputation as an inept sybarite.

I treat myself to a moment of quiet in the conservatory off the kitchen. Blanche has rows of potted plants along her tall windows, and the plants are all neatly pruned, with perfectly damp and loamy soil, so very *Blanche* in the evidence of their consistent and attentive care.

I reach out to thumb the florid pink petal of a potted foxglove. I remember the poisonous plants Isolde and I had at Lyonesse during our wedding ceremony, how darkly luxurious they'd been. Foxglove just like this had bloomed everywhere, along with monkshood and nightshade and oleander and the occasional white spray of hemlock. Not too much hemlock, of course, just enough to pervade the gaps and clefts of the arrangement.

Filler is what I think florists call it.

"No uniform today?" a mild voice asks, and I turn to see Lady Anguish—or Nimue Moore-Rhys, as she's known outside Lyonesse—as she steps into the conservatory with a glass of wine.

"Not today," I say, a smidge dryly. "Where's Merlin?"

"With the little one," she replies. "He's had enough funerals for a lifetime or two."

I could stand a few more funerals personally, but it wouldn't be polite to say so.

Anguish joins me at the plants and then asks while looking over her shoulder, "Do you see that couple there, by Morgan?"

I follow Anguish's gaze over to a man and a woman near the fireplace. They are both tall, immaculately dressed fifty-somethings with the flaxen hair, white teeth, and glowing skin of people who *take the boat out on weekends*.

"Those are the Hesses," Anguish informs me. "Their

house borders the Thomas farmhouse, so they've been friends of Ricker's for a very long time. Their son disappeared in England a little while ago, right after he left the priesthood. It was very tragic."

"The priesthood." I can't say the Hesses strike me as the type to have a clergyman for a son, given the casual wealth glinting from their wrists and hanging subtly in the bespoke tailoring of their clothes.

"Oh yes, the Hesses are very Catholic. They even have a cardinal for a family friend. He arranged some things so their son could get the posting he wanted in England, near a place called Thornchapel."

Thornchapel. My mind helpfully offers up the memory of Father Minch's bible, of the titles and corresponding libraries written there.

"Stunning library," says Anguish offhandedly. "I might be able to connect you to the owner if you'd like. Or the Hesses could if you want to make their acquaintance."

"One of these days, I'd like to know how you do it," I tell her, watching her face closely now.

"Do what?"

"Know everything."

She waves the hand not holding her wine. "Oh, I don't know everything. Just the bits of debris that reach my shore. But I think you would be interested in knowing who their holy and eminent family friend is."

"I suppose I won't have to try hard to guess."

"The Hesses are very connected with the family that owns Thornchapel and have been since Ingram Hess went to school with Ralph Guest, whose son owns the manor now. If I had to guess, I would presume Cashel didn't strike up the connection to the Hesses randomly. I think he was interested in access to that library. Just as you are."

I'm still staring at her. "Have you talked to Lox at all?"

"No."

"Snooped around my office?"

"It's technically my office now, I'll remind you, but no, I have better things to do with my time."

Yeah, things like stuff a sock into her husband's mouth and make him jerk off on her feet. "So how do you know that *I* know about the Thornchapel library?"

She shrugs and sips her wine with a smile. "A hunch."

"You have a lot of those," I say, turning back to the flowers.

"That I do. I also have a hunch that Isolde is doing better than she was at Saturnalia."

I allow that she is, even though Anguish doesn't need her intuition for that. It's plain to see with her own eyes.

The lingering sadness and delicacy though… Those are also plain to see.

"And has Isolde finally forgiven you this small matter of manipulating her entire life?" asks Anguish with far, far too neutral a tone for her not to be privately amused right now.

I take a drink of the water that I dearly wish were gin right now. "She has not. And you're lucky I like you, you know."

The truth is that I doubt forgiveness will be forthcoming from either of us—much less trust and still less happiness—but we are made of shadows and glass, her and me, and in our dark and broken hearts, there is a part of us that enjoys the breathless bloodshed of what we do to each other. There is a part of us that will always find the glitter of moonlight on ice lovelier than a pink sunrise and that will always hope teeth come before a kiss.

We cannot help it, and we have tried. To the point of knives against throats and fleeing across oceans, we have tried.

"We are working toward rapprochement." And I add, to

clarify, "I don't think I'll be left tied to any chairs anytime soon, if that's what you're wondering"

Rapprochement might be a little strong, but there's not really a word for what Isolde and I are doing right now. We haven't had sex, we haven't even kissed, and I am still using a spare toothbrush in my own apartment. But I've skipped the hall every night since I found her in the garden, and instead, I make her dinner. I sit her on the counter while I wash and chop because I like her being close enough to touch whenever I like. After we eat, we sit by the fire and read, pressed together on the couch at first, and then slowly, inevitably, she ends up on the floor by my feet, her head resting against my knee. I'll stroke her hair with one hand while I turn my pages with the other until she starts falling asleep, and after that, we go to bed. And if I don't hold on to her tightly enough from the beginning, she drapes herself over top of me like a purificator over a chalice, sleeping like that until morning.

No nightmares when I'm there. I like to think that I scare them away.

For two days, the club was completely empty, silent and dim, as the doors were locked for Christmas Eve and Christmas. On Christmas morning, Isolde woke up to piles of presents by the fireplace, an embarrassing amount really, a window into how often she's been on my mind. Presents I'd been hoarding from before our marriage, all the typical things you buy a lover you want to impress—strands of South Sea pearls and antique rings of enameled gold and dainty bracelets set with diamonds and emeralds for her birth month—even though I already knew Isolde wouldn't be impressed. She's not very materially minded, my little angel of vengeance. She'd rather chase after treasures in heaven.

So I also bought her blankets and soft nightgowns and leather-bound editions of St. Thomas Aquinas or Thérèse of Lisieux and slippers to wear down to her studio and a cushion to bring out into the garden when she wants to sit out under the tree. I gave her a tea mug large enough to hold the actual amount of tea she drinks if she thinks no one's watching and peppermint candies strong enough to make her nose sting, just how she likes them.

All the luxury in her life has either been the marble-floored opulence of Laurence Bank or the baroque and punishing extravagance of the Church. All her spare time was bent to forging herself into a weapon, a weapon for someone else, and all the expensive things in her life have only ever been in service of that one singular goal. She was given designer coats to wear in public, but no one's ever given her a plush blanket and permission to spend the day by the fire, forgetting the world outside exists.

She was shocked at the amount of presents and then doubly shocked I'd wrapped them myself.

"I just can't imagine you getting tape stuck on your fingers, measuring out ribbons," she said, and when she looked at me with the morning glow caught on her eyelashes and on the tip of her nose—a faint hint of a smile at the corners of her eyes—a very strange thing happened.

I blushed.

"Well," I said, going to the espresso machine in the kitchen in a cowardly attempt to escape that look of hers. "I wanted to make sure it was done well."

I didn't need to tell her that I bought a pair of Ernest Wright scissors, scoured the city for exactly the right kinds of wrapping paper, and wandered the garden like a harvester of souls, shearing off holly and juniper to tie onto the boxes. It was worth it, every paper cut and discreetly taped seam, just to see her pleasure as she unwrapped them all.

She came up to me where I'd stood in the kitchen sipping my coffee, and she took the coffee cup from my hands and set it down on the counter. And then she stepped into my arms.

It felt so good to hold her in broad daylight, without the plausible deniability of the shadows around us, and I breathed her in, the sweet scent of her hair, the faint mineral scent of my own soap, which she'd been using since she came back.

"I wasn't trying to buy your forgiveness," I told her.

"I know. It wouldn't have worked if you had been. But thank you. You—" She pulled back enough to look at me. "You make a perfectly innocent Christmas morning feel depraved, you know."

I raised an eyebrow. "I do?"

"Every mug or blanket or book—I know what you were imagining when you got them."

"Is that so? Tell me how well you know my thoughts, Isolde. I'm curious now."

Her soft lips pull together. "I think you bought me that mug hoping you could sit me on the counter while you got the kettle going and then be the one to put the drink in my hands. I think you got me those blankets because you imagined me curled up next to you on the couch until I accidentally fell asleep. I think you got me those diabolically strong peppermint candies because you know I crave those little jolts of pain, and you like giving me what I crave as much as you enjoy watching the pain itself."

"Hmm." She was right, but I grumpily didn't want to give her the satisfaction of admitting it.

Unfortunately, she could read this thought of mine as well, and the ensuing smile reminded me of how she'd stood over Tristan in Morois, rolling her foot over his cock. Arrogant and assured, too lovely to do anything other than surrender to.

Unless you were me, of course. Then you'd only see all that self-assurance as a challenge.

That smile… I wanted to taste it so badly.

"I can't repay you in kind," she said, her smile fading. "I don't have any gifts for you."

"Play a game of chess with me," I bargained. "And then we'll call it even." And I'd still feel like I was coming out ahead.

"Okay," she said, and her lips twitched once more. She pushed a little closer to me, and instinct had me dipping my head, and—

A chime from my phone, signaling the only good reason to be interrupted while trying to kiss my wife. "I have to go downstairs for your last present," I said.

And I went down to meet a smiling Sophie and an impatient Melody, on their way to Sophie's parents' house after they made the handoff, and then I returned to Isolde with an armful of wriggling silver fur, alarmingly big paws, and an eternally wagging tail.

The look on Isolde's face... I wanted it commissioned in marble and frescoed on my walls. How often had I seen it prior to this? Maybe the night I took her virginity on her father's desk and maybe on Samhain? A look of terrified joy, of hope, of *happiness*.

"Mark," she whispered. "What..."

"An Irish wolfhound," I said and carefully handed over the squirming puppy. She started licking Isolde's face, and Isolde laughed—*she laughed*—and I could be the king of the world and not have been happier than I was in that moment. "Melody and Blanche found her at the farmhouse when they went back to look for some of Ricker's things for the funeral," I said. "She was under the porch and cold and seemed to be hungry, so they took her with them when they went back to the town house. They can't find an owner or where she came from, and the vet thinks she's been on her own for a little while at least. And I thought..."

I stopped. It felt grim to say on Christmas morning, too

grim to say while Isolde was giggling with a puppy in her arms. But that was our lives, wasn't it? Pleasure in darkness and dolor in the sunlight.

"I thought you might feel less alone," I said.

When our eyes met, I couldn't tell if it was happiness or sorrow or both arcing between us.

————

In the here and now, at the funeral reception with Lady Anguish, I say, "Tristan will be staying at Lyonesse until New Year's, along with Hugo and Kayden and Isabella. I hope— well, I hope it will cheer both of them up."

"It's a dangerous game you're playing," Anguish says. She nods toward the house, where we can see straight through the conservatory windows to the kitchen and the living room. "If you want the club to believe that you *don't* have an affair being carried out under your nose, you'll need to stage-manage the two of them very carefully. Just look at them now."

Yes, I can see it. Isolde ostensibly in conversation with a congresswoman who knows Isolde's father, Tristan nodding at a three-star general with his hands behind his back. And yet it doesn't matter that they're across the room from each other, that they're in completely separate conversations. Their eyes keep finding each other's, and their bodies uncon- sciously shift toward an invisible shared point of gravity between them.

It's like watching two very pretty magnets do their best not to collide.

"Don't stare too long," advises Anguish. "You're doing a very good job hiding your feelings, but it won't matter how aloof you appear if you can't stop watching them."

I rip my eyes away, down toward my drink. This jealousy… It's worse than being shot, worse than being stabbed. Except why then do I enjoy stabbing myself with it?

"I knew you were screwed the moment I saw Tristan," says my companion. "He looks far, far too much like Maxen. Prettier, maybe, and sweeter and sadder. But a green-eyed hero nonetheless, except a submissive this time."

"And also not hopelessly in love with his vice president," I mumble.

Anguish pats my shoulder. "I promise not to hold your little crush on Maxen Colchester against you forever."

"I'd appreciate that."

A thoughtful pause. "But you're not the only one who likes a green-eyed hero. Isabella Beroul seems quite taken with Tristan, doesn't she?"

"You've heard what happened at Armorica, I'm guessing. I think a little hero worship is probably inevitable. I'm sure he was gallant and kind from the moment he arrived in Montreal, and then he went and saved her life. All while having the nerve to look like an illustration from a book of fairy tales. It's very unfair of him."

"Isolde has noticed Isabella."

I snort and take a drink. "Yes, I'd say so."

"So you are jealous of Tristan and Isolde. Isolde is jealous of Isabella. Isabella is probably jealous of you and Isolde, and Tristan is presumably too preoccupied with grief to realize he's snared in a web crawling with three different spiders. But at any rate, it might be useful."

"Ah. Isabella's feelings, you mean." I consider this. "It would be messy to put her infatuation on display."

"If Isabella and Tristan are going to be at the club, it might be on display anyway. Why not at least use it to your advantage?"

And with that, she lifts her wineglass and leaves. My phone buzzes in my pocket, and I answer it while staring at the messy love triangle unfolding in my sister's living room. A love triangle that is absolutely pointless because two of those triangle points belong to *me*.

"Trevena," I answer.

"I've got a location for Cara Sims," replies Lox. "I'm texting you the link to my report now. As for this Regina Springer, I can't find anything that points to a connection with Cashel or any other cardinal. She's unmarried, no kids, owns a mechanic's shop in Albany. She's sick—lung cancer—but they've been able to keep it at bay for five or six years. The only potential wrinkle I can see is that her sister ran away from home when they were teenagers, and it was long enough ago that I can't find anything else about her. The sister probably landed somewhere and started over with a new name. The seventies were a simpler time."

"Indeed," I say. "So no connection with the Vatican? Or anyone higher up in the Church?"

"Nothing that I can see. Regina seems to be wholly uninterested in any organized religion at all and spends every Sunday in her shop. I couldn't even find baptismal records for her or for anyone in her family."

I scratch at my forehead with the thumb of the hand holding my drink. "Okay. Any progress with the *Revelata Scientia* images I sent over?"

"Since I don't know what I'm looking for, I don't know how you'd define 'progress,' but we found a handful of scanned versions online, so that should help us get to a workable translation at least. You've brought me weird shit before, but this is the first time I've ever felt like you've brought me homework."

"Thanks, Lox."

"I could say *anytime*, but I wouldn't mean it. Bye now."

She hangs up, and I lower my phone to tap on the link she sent over.

A moment later, I'm calling Goran at the club. "Are you busy? What about Nat? I have a small job for you two…"

twenty-three

TRISTAN

THE NIGHT AFTER MY FATHER'S FUNERAL, KAYDEN AND I SET Isabella's suitcases down in her and Hugo's room at Lyonesse and close the door. I point the way forward for Kayden, who's never been back to the residential section of the club, and steer us to the elevator at the end of the corridor.

It's disorienting to be back, and this time with my world tilted on its axis. We walk past my apartment door, and I remember moving in last spring, dreading the interrogative calls from my father. I'd dreaded them right up until the moment he died, dreaded them enough that I'd dodged them until I moved into Armorica, and even then we'd still only talked twice.

I can recognize that something is missing from my grief—or maybe too many things are added onto it—so it's a grief that's too unwieldy and too light at the same time. It's a badly balanced stack of cardboard boxes, and it feels like even if they tumbled and fell, nothing serious would be broken.

And yet I almost wish something *would* be broken, because it's wrong how not-wrong I feel right now.

How do you grieve someone who made your life harder? Who barely knew you? Who put his duty above fatherhood and offloaded fatherhood the minute he could to the faculty at West Point? How do you carry your actual grief at the same time you carry your grief for the person they could have been?

"So," Kayden starts with the casual ease I've grown used to from him. "Isolde Trevena. She's...." He shakes his head. "If I'd ever wondered who could make Mark Trevena settle down, she answers my question."

I don't answer. My affair with Isolde is common knowledge, and while I know Kayden isn't fishing for a reaction, I'm not sure what I could say right now that wouldn't betray more than I'd like.

"I know the two of you had a thing that caused some drama," Kayden goes on, again with a sort of oblivious warmth that smooths over any potential awkwardness. "But do you know if she ever plays with anyone other than Mark?"

"In a less affair-y way, you mean?" I ask a little dryly, and Kayden gives a delighted laugh.

"I love it when you tell jokes, Tristan. It's like getting to peek through the cracked door of a bank vault. And yes, that is what I mean, as it happens. I'd love to play with her if they're open to it."

The flare of jealous anger comes as pure combustion—scorching and then gone.

"I think they're both open to it, but it hasn't happened yet. Mr. Trevena is..." I search for the right word to convey all that he is. Something stronger than *possessive*, something hungrier than *ravenous*. But at the same time, sex is not as precious to him as attention, as devotion,.as claiming. I think he'd be more irritated by Isolde playing chess with Kayden than by Kayden shoving his cock down her throat—so long as Mark got to watch. "He is a little more complicated than Hugo when it comes to sharing."

"Ah, yes, well. We can't all be Hugo and Isabella. Perfectly matched sexually, completely happy with their emotional autonomy from each other. It gets them hot to play their sharing games, but there's never a real risk of Hugo's feelings being hurt."

We get to the elevator, and I press the button for the speakeasy-style bar on the second highest floor, where the others are waiting for us.

"Isabella is quite taken with you, by the way," Kayden tells me as the doors close. "I wouldn't be surprised if Hugo asks you about it."

"Asks me about it?" My voice is a little wary, and Kayden claps me on the shoulder.

"No, no, my reluctant lothario, I promise you're only a home-wrecker at Lyonesse. He won't be upset. He'll only want to know if you'd like him to share Isabella with you, make sure there's full consent on your side as well."

I must be making a face because he laughs again.

"Stop pouting at me. Is this about the home-wrecker remark? Come on. Who hasn't troubled a marriage or two in their time?"

"This seems like a very Kayden perspective."

"If that's the case, then you are looking at proof that everything will be fine! And you don't have to stop living so you can atone for one tiny, messy situation that anyone who's seen Isolde would understand."

Of course Kayden would equate *living* with *fucking*. "Well, you've seen Mr. Trevena too, so maybe you can understand exactly how messy it was."

His eyebrows lift to the shock of chestnut hair hanging over his forehead. "Oh, it was like that, was it?"

"Yes," I answer grimly.

"My point still stands though. How long are you planning on living like a priest?"

"It hasn't even been three weeks since I left Lyonesse, and my dad has been dead for one of them. I'm not worried about my sex life right now."

The doors open and we step out, Kayden still pestering me. "But you like Isabella, right? I mean, if everything is over between you and Mark and Isolde and you like Isabella, then why not enjoy yourself? Who would it hurt?"

Me, I want to say. *It would hurt me.* Because I'm still in love with Isolde and I'm still in love with Mark, and I don't think I can surrender the hope that somehow this is all temporary. That there's something waiting beyond Mark's retribution for us.

"I do like Isabella," I say, and it's the absolute truth. She's smart and open and kind, and in another life, maybe. Or if I knew with certainty that I'd never see Mark or Isolde again... "And she's beautiful too."

"She *is* beautiful," Kayden says with a friend's ferocious pride, and then it makes sense to me, his pressure, his insistence. He wants Isabella to be happy, and he thinks I would make her happy. Which, sadly, couldn't be further from the truth.

"She only thinks she likes me because of what happened at Armorica," I try to explain. "We're not a good fit, and I'm sure she'll realize that soon."

"How are you not a good fit?" demands Kayden.

"We're too alike." I lower my voice as we walk into the bar. The club as a whole is still very quiet after the holidays, but there are a few members here, murmuring in corners and hatching schemes for the new year. Mark, Isolde, Hugo, and Isabella are in the far corner of the bar. "I'm not...like you and Hugo. In bed."

"I assumed that was the case—but that's nothing if you truly want her! Just keep an open mind, Tristan, please."

Kayden is awfully close to wheedling, and it's so irresistible coming from a spank-happy playboy that I accede. "I will," I promise—and it's only a half lie, because sure, I can keep an open mind. Why not?

We get to the table, and then a streak of silver fur explodes from underneath, a bright red leash trailing from the neck of the creature. I lower myself and grab the leash just in time, snaring the puppy before she runs off. The scattered applause of five people breaks out as I scoop her up and turn to face them.

"Have a seat, Tristan," Mark invites. "If you put one end of the leash around your chair leg, you can keep both hands free while she gambols around."

I do as he says, make sure that her little chew toy is within attacking range, and then sit down. She also sits down, rolling on her butt until she falls over, and then starts licking my shoe. I'm in love right away.

"I'm surprised it's taking this long, honestly," Hugo is saying to Mark, presumably resuming whatever conversation they were having before Kayden and I arrived. Hugo sits on one side of the table, his arm slung across the back of Isabella's chair, and then Mark and Isolde sit on the other side, not touching. Kayden sits at the head of the table, and I sit across from him, between Isabella and Mark.

Isolde's eyes flick over to me, a bare instant of connection and yet an ocean of feeling anyway. It's been like this all day, solace and suffering all in one, the reminder that in her elegant, deadly body still beats a heart that misses mine, and yet there is no world where our hearts can beat together. Especially tonight, especially at the club, because I'm exceedingly and painfully aware that the few people who *are* here are watching our table with great interest. Watching to see how Mark deals with his wife's ex-lover under his roof once again.

Mark, for his part, is the picture of a powerful man unbothered by suspicion or betrayal. He leans back a little in his chair, long legs sprawled, a large hand curled around a clear drink that I now know is probably nonalcoholic. He's still in his black suit from the funeral, the tie knotted but the jacket unbuttoned. Isolde has changed out of her dark blue dress into a pair of winter-white trousers and a soft sweater in a mint color that pulls the green from her eyes. Her hair is down around her shoulders, the loose waves gleaming like silk. She's wearing a set of pearls I've never seen before.

"The Holy Father's death was quite unexpected," says Mark, reminding me of the topic at hand. "It could be that my dear wife's uncle didn't shore up enough votes ahead of time."

"You really think that Mortimer Cashel is angling for the job?" asks Hugo, doubt etched in every syllable. I remember how siloed Mark has kept his confidences; Hugo knows that Mortimer is Isolde's uncle but not about Ys. Not about the very likely hand Mortimer had in the pope's death. "I've heard he was charming, but he's been buried in the Curia his whole career. Hardly a man of the people."

"Working in the Curia is precisely why he has a chance at the job," says Isolde. Her voice is as polite and crisp as always, but there's a bit of fry around the edges of her words, a whiff of exhaustion or strain. "And I think he's been trying to court votes for some time, but as Mark said, it's possible he didn't get enough before the conclave began. Or perhaps he did, but there *were* also rumors of some kind of anonymous accusation right before the conclave started. Something to discredit him."

"Well, it's working," observes Hugo. "Two weeks of black smoke…very melodramatic."

"This is the puppy your stepmother found?" Isabella asks me, clearly uninterested in papal politics. She bends down to stroke the creature's velvet ears, and the dog begins wriggling toward her. Isabella and I both laugh at that, and then I look up to see Mark and Isolde both staring at us.

"Melody—my twin sister," Mark adds for Isabella's edification, "felt that she was a rather lachrymose dog and so has been calling her Crybaby. Unfortunately, and this is often the effect of my sister, her opinion has shaped reality, and now the dog responds only to that name."

"That is unfortunate," agrees Hugo gravely. "A dog should have a romantic name—a name befitting its noble bearing and innate ability to love."

"A French name, I suppose?" asks Mark after taking a drink.

"Naturellement. How about Petitcrieu?"

"Poor Petitcrieu," Isabella purrs at the puppy, who immediately gets to her feet and then props her forepaws on Isabella's knee, trying to get closer to the source of sympathy and ear scratches. "Oh, she likes it!"

"What sort of things do you have planned for New Year's Eve?" asks Kayden, oblivious to the nominative destiny of the dog. "I've never been at Lyonesse for New Year's, but I've heard legends."

Mark considers his drink. "With things being as they are at present, I think a more restrained evening would be in order, and I have my head of security doing a favor for me in Manhattan anyway—"

"I'm trying to convince Mark to host a trial by iron," Isolde cuts in. She looks so composed and elegant right now, with one leg crossed and her hands laced over her knee—just a wife discussing party plans with her husband, just a blond container of affluence and enviable manners. But the way the other men at the table react, she might as well have suggested we kick off the new year with a spot of necromancy.

"A trial by iron?" Kayden asks, worry carving his high forehead into segments. "Truly?"

Mark's reply is clipped. "It won't happen."

Isolde tucks her hair behind her ear. "I think we should

consider it. What better way to assure the club of my loyalty while also giving them a spectacle worth talking about?"

"I'm sorry," Hugo interjects, "am I understanding that *you* would do the trial by iron?"

Isabella and I look at each other, and I realize she's just as lost as I am.

"Could someone explain the trial by iron to me?" I ask. "I don't think I've ever heard of it before."

"You wouldn't have." Mark takes another drink and then looks down at his glass with a wounded expression, betrayed by his drink's refusal to be anything other than gin-flavored water.

"It's no longer done," Hugo explains, looking at me and Isabella. "The club that Mark ran out of business when he came to DC—it was one of their specialties. When Mark started Lyonesse, he refused to continue the practice, along with several unsavory others: unregulated edge play, same-day background checks for visitors, that sort of thing."

Kayden is appraising Isolde anew, his forehead still creased with worry but a subtle glint of curiosity in his eyes too. "The trial by iron is a public scene designed to test a person's limits. As far as I know, it was always a submissive, and the trial was tailored to them. The idea is that you take a hard limit or a deeply felt fear, and then you build an entire scene around exploiting it. So if a hard limit is something like being gagged, then you can assume the trial will feature all sorts of gags, the worst ones their scene partner can find. If you're afraid of fire, then there would be fire play. If you're claustrophobic, perhaps a vacuum bed. That sort of thing."

"And I'm afraid this is underselling it," Hugo says. "Because it's one thing to talk about someone else's limits or fears, ones you might not share and not understand the psychological torture involved. The trial I saw was for a male submissive who was terrified of medical procedures. They brought in a real examination table, a real nurse to hook him up to an IV, strapped him down and told him they were going to crack his chest open then and there. His dominant fucked him while he was sobbing through a panic attack."

"Jesus," Isabella whispers, and I have to agree.

"It's barbaric," states Mark. "Even if we overlooked the violation of boundaries and the deliberate perversion of consent—there's no elegance to it. No beauty and no gratification beyond a crude kind of bloodlust. And *bloodlust* wasn't always a metaphor either."

"I'd still have a safeword," Isolde points out. Calmly. Like they're discussing a new shade of paint for their bathroom.

Mark waves an impatient hand, the black and silver of my ring catching the oblique light of the speakeasy. "The point of the trial is to test a submissive's 'devotion.' The pressure for the submissive not to use their safeword is immense, and I just want to reiterate here, that pressure would absolutely discredit and destabilize the foundation of Lyonesse. It may be a home for sinners, but I won't have consent burned on the altar for the sake of a good show. If I break my own rules, even once, lawlessness will start filling the club like smoke, impossible to get rid of once it's there. It's not about the safeword, Isolde."

"I think together we could make it elegant," she says, again with that poised calm. "Not only in form but in function—an elegant way to put the suspicions to rest once and for all, my renewed loyalty on display for everyone to taste and see."

If she's embarrassed referencing our affair in front of the others, she doesn't show it. And Mark doesn't seem embarrassed either.

I am though. Ashamed that I've helped make any kind of world where Isolde thinks she has to do this.

"You know," Kayden says slowly. "There's no reason it

has to be quite as traumatic as it used to be. And if there was ever a time—having Hugo and I here to witness it might give the moment some 'egitimacy."

Mark's handsome mouth is taut at the corners. "Just as the moment illegitimatizes me, both maritally and morally. And before you can sermonize about how I have no legitimate morality left, just know that the pretense of it still serves me at Lyonesse."

Isolde puts her hand over his. That small action seems to carry with it the power of an electric shock—he only barely manages to stop the jolt that shudders briefly through him.

"Please," she says softly. "I want to do this."

He looks down at her hand, a muscle jumping once in his jaw as he does. "I know. That's what worries me."

"Will you at least think about it?" she asks. "For the next day or two?"

There's a hesitation in his movements as he lifts his other hand and then rests it slowly on top of hers. I abruptly feel that I'm intruding on something private, even as envy begins eating at my guts like a worm. I don't care that the jagged gap between them is so palpable that it might as well be outlined in yellow surveying tape; the way they look at each other says it all.

They are obsessed with each other.

"I'll think about it," concedes Mark with no small amount of bitterness. But the way he holds Isolde's hand the rest of the night makes me think that he very well might consider selling his soul for only that, only the slotting of her fingers into his and the occasional stroke of his knuckles with her thumb.

twenty-four

ISOLDE

I HATE BEING AFRAID, AND I'VE ALWAYS HATED IT BECAUSE there's no lonelier feeling than fear. No one can ever be truly afraid with you, never in exactly the same way—and even if by some miracle they could, then that would mean they can't protect you. They can't take the fear away. How could they if they are as weak as you are?

I'm afraid the first night I go back to the hall. Afraid of my own weakness, of how easily I can hate myself if invited to do so. Afraid of the loneliness leaching outward from some hidden well inside me, a ragged hole in my heart that I must have had since birth, afraid of how it freezes my bones and chills my breath.

I don't want to end up in the garden again, blue-lipped and empty, not even trying to pray, my mind drifting from horror to horror done by my own hands. All for a God whom I now think might be sick to see what I've done in His name.

"We don't have to go tonight," my husband murmurs, coming up behind me. He runs his hands up my arms to my shoulders, and they are so warm, so certain. How can a man so cold have such warm hands? And be so warm everywhere else? Sleeping in his arms at night is like sleeping tucked under a dragon's wing.

A cinch of desire low in my belly pulls even tighter, reminding me that *all* Mark and I have done is sleep. I wake up in the morning with stiff nipples and a needy cunt, and the willpower it takes to refuse to beg for his long fingers or his wicked mouth or the mouthwatering erection between his hips is almost beyond what I can spare.

I've never stopped wanting him. I've never stopped loving him; even hating him is not without its own erotic thrill. And I know all the very persuasive reasons why it would be stupid to return to how we were before Samhain: we don't trust each other; we've hurt and lied to each other; we have a broken marriage to perform; I'm only just now creeping away from a ledge in my own mind that I still don't fully understand.

But my God, do I want him. Even having him lift me onto the counter and bid me to stay there while he cooks, even reading at his feet, even having his long, strong fingers massaging my scalp as he washes my hair… He must understand that it's all subtle, seductive obscenity for me. That he only has to hold up a berry for me to obediently open my mouth, that every time I let him dry my hair and wrap me in a robe, I'm nearly shaking by the end. Pain I have craved since I was a girl, but here is the debossed side of it: I am as fragile as spun sugar, ready to offer him the air out of my throat, when his power over me is painted in strokes of homecooked food and the slow turn of pages at his feet.

I don't think I'll ever not crave pain, but I'll never forget how to crave this either.

I meet Mark's eyes in the mirror.

"It makes no sense," I say, "that you feel like the only person who sees me, all of me, I mean. Even the parts of me that don't feel quite real, even the parts I hide from myself. And yet of anyone I've ever known, you are the one person who can hurt me the most."

His fingers trace up to my neck, linger along the shell of my ear.

"I think," he says quietly, "that makes the most sense of anything in the entire world." His fingers move downward and gently circle the place just above where my neck and shoulder would meet. Where my collar would go.

My voice is a whisper when I tilt my head to grant him better access, and the word itself is a reflex, as honest as it is unplanned. "Sir."

A spasm—a quaking of his fingertips against my throat—and then he steps back, the touch at my throat vanishing as swiftly as the moment does.

In the mirror, I can see him looking down and to the side, his ribs moving hard enough to strain the seams of his shirt. A standing version of the Dying Gaul, a fighter panting in the corner of the ring.

"I meant it," I aver. "I—I don't know what to do with everything else between us, the future or the past, Tristan and my uncle and every lie we've told. But I do know that I mean it when I call you *sir*. I remember my safeword. I don't think I'll ever stop wanting you."

"That doesn't make it a good idea," says Mark, still not looking at me.

"Someone told me once that I was a terrible idea. That didn't stop him then, so why should it now?"

He shakes his head, and the light catches in the immaculately styled gold strands of his hair. "Would you call this last week *stopping*? When I'm washing your hair and wrapping myself around you like a constrictor under the blankets?"

"I can tell that it's all you'll let yourself have. And it's been exactly what I've needed, and I love it, and I feel just as—" My hand lifts to my throat in substitute of the word I'm searching for. "I feel just as much when you're cuddling me as when you're cuffing me. But I'm feeling better than I have been since the garden…and I…I want you to know that I still know my safeword. That's all."

He meets my stare in the reflection once more. "You may not be feeling better once we go to the hall tonight, and let me say it again: we don't have to go. Hugo, Kayden, and Isabella will entertain themselves thoroughly whether or not we join them, and Tristan is still going through his father's things at the farmhouse, as you know."

I turn and extend my hand. As I guessed, he's not able to resist this small invitation, and when our hands meet, his lashes dip and his throat moves.

It's all that he'll let himself have…the god of the underworld satisfying himself with touching his lips to the rim of his bride's goblet and nothing more.

"We've relied on the conclave occupying my uncle for too long," I say. "We need to start up the show once more."

"How far are you willing to go for it? I won't stand for finding you half-frozen again. I won't watch you unlock the door for death and then wait for him to come calling. And I don't know if I can survive knowing that you want to hurt yourself in a way that has nothing to do with God or with kink and that you haven't told me." He uses the hold on my hand to pull us closer together, his head bent toward mine. His scarred, rugged face, his eyes in impossible shades of blue. "You can be a shattered reliquary or an empty tabernacle, and you will be no less mine, but you must tell me. I can't—I have used you enough, and I will use you still even more. I can't leave you hollowed out after."

"I can go very far if I'm not alone," I say, and the fresh admission of my biggest weakness is painful, stinging my lips as I speak. For as long as I can remember, I have hidden

231

my vulnerabilities and lied about my defects. I've kept all my suffering as a secret, unseen crown of thorns, because who could I tell? My father, who only wanted me for his bank? My uncle, who would tell me all my suffering was meant to be laid at God's feet anyway? Bryn, who didn't know that I was a thief, an arsonist, and a murderer? Or Tristan, who hates the part of himself that can kill so easily, who always puts himself last, who is chivalrous and kind and good?

But Mark…Mark knows. He knows what I've done and how I've done it. He's seen me selfish and broken and foolish. He's seen my sins and, more embarrassingly, my mistakes. He's seen me sharp and dull, in the shadows and in the light.

He's looked down at his own hands and seen stains that will never wash clean.

"If I feel like I'm not alone," I repeat, "when it's just the two of us, then I can withstand a lot. I'll be honest with you, use my safeword, tell you how I'm feeling, any of it, so long as you'll stay."

He lifts my hand to his mouth and kisses the spot over my wedding ring. "Then let's go down to the hall."

———

I don't see Tristan as much as I'd feared or hoped when Mark told me he'd invited the Armorica contingent to stay here; in fact, I see him hardly at all. He's either at the town house or the farmhouse, helping Blanche go through clothes and documents and also sorting through the lingering artifacts of his mother's to either donate or put in storage. The farmhouse will be sold, which seems to me a sad thing, but it's the most practical, and despite Tristan's romantic soul, he also has a soldier's capacity for efficiency. For deciding what resources are essential and what ones only serve to make your pack heavier at the end of the day.

I do see the visitors from Armorica quite a bit. Since

Mark has temporarily relinquished Tristan's apartment back to Tristan and is staying in ours, he entertains them with lunch or coffee at our kitchen table. Kayden comes into my office to play with Petitcrieu while I reacquaint myself with my fake job and email dishonest apologies to my coworkers, and he tells me charming stories about his time in the army and all the different dogs he's met and befriended. Hugo and Isabella are very popular in the hall, playing onstage or inviting people back to playrooms.

Mark keeps his distance whenever we're outside our apartment. I kneel at his feet or sit next to him, ignored while Hugo knots Isabella into a bound work of art or paddles her until she sobs. By the evening before New Year's Eve, however, Mark's progressed to occasionally stroking my hair or idly tugging on the collar I've started wearing again.

In our apartment, Mark still won't do anything more than feed me and wash me, take Petitcrieu outside with me, and hold me at night while the puppy flops from one spot to the other on the bed.

"She'll be too big for your bed one day," said Mark with some amusement when I coaxed her closer so I could stroke her as we fell asleep.

"Then we'll get a bigger bed," I replied, failing to see the problem.

He gave an amused exhale but didn't argue.

For the most part, I like Hugo, Kayden, and Isabella. Hugo is all elegance, and Kayden is flirtatious and friendly. And Isabella is sweet, truly sweet. I try to remind myself that it's ridiculous to let *sweetness* of all things get under my skin, that she's also intelligent and resilient and kind and that she's been through too much to deserve my aversion. She's easygoing and convivial with me, even if I do sometimes see her watching me when she thinks I'm not aware. And even though it would be convenient to use her to advertise our still-recovering marriage to the guests, Mark doesn't play with her, pet her, or otherwise touch her…though I know he was eight inches deep inside her not even a year ago.

It's only that she is sweet and I'm not. She's luscious and tractable, and I'm as tense as piano wire. It's only that she's everything Mark could want in a submissive and everything that I'd imagine for Tristan in any other life.

Cheerful and accommodating and not a murderer.

The night before New Year's Eve, Tristan does manage to make it to the hall, just for the last hour. We're not in Mark's usual nook but down on the floor crowded around a temporary wrestling ring, watching a match between Christopher, the erstwhile princeps of Saturnalia, and a dominatrix. Christopher is happily losing.

Tristan comes up next to us, and even though I don't look directly at him, I feel him there next to me, my skin tingling, my molecules changing polarity, my sin-smudged soul stirring to be so close to his good one.

"Did I miss anything, sir?" he asks Mark.

But it's Kayden who answers first. "Not much, man. Just Mark allowing Isolde to do the trial by iron."

twenty-five

ISOLDE

"I DON'T LIKE IT," TRISTAN SAYS THE NEXT NIGHT AS HE RAKES his hands through his now-short hair. "The perception of the club isn't worth this."

"Then we are in agreement," Mark says calmly. "Nevertheless, here we are."

It's only the three of us in the wings of the stage, Mark and I sitting on stools facing each other while Tristan paces behind me. Mark is holding my hands in his, his grip anchoring and certain. I think of how we sparred with knives the first time we met, how easily he held on to his blade even as we wrestled and fought.

"It's okay," I say, trying to steady my voice. The nerves are coming through against my will. "It's going to be okay. It's just an hour on the stage. I can do anything for an hour, and anyway, Mark won't test me beyond what I can bear."

"Even God reneges on that promise," warns Mark softly. "Don't trust me with such things."

"I shouldn't trust you at all," I say as I look down at our

hands. "But we don't require trust from each other, not in the normal way."

"No, not in the normal way," Mark agrees. "We have something different."

Something primitive and beyond language. Something dark and old. The shared hunt of the wolves, the ruthless but eternal mating of corvids.

"I'll say my safeword if I need to," I say after a minute. "This isn't the hardest thing I've done, and it won't be the most fucked up, not by a long shot. This isn't like walking into a battle—something you've both done, by the way."

"It's different," protests Tristan. He comes to kneel beside me, and his eyes lift to mine in a flare of imploring green. "This is designed to test you, and more importantly, it's designed to humiliate you. And for what? The approval of people you don't care about?"

"We *need* their approval." I know my impatience is part defensiveness, that I'm revealing how uncomfortably prescient his question is, but also the three of us have known this math for half a month at least. It hasn't changed. "If the club doesn't trust me, they won't trust Mark. If they don't believe in my marriage, my uncle won't believe in me. The opinion of the club might be the difference between life and death for many people, myself included."

"I don't care," Tristan protests, his voice growing a little louder. "I don't care if you going out there is a literal stay of execution! There has to be another way!"

"Did I hear stay of execution?" Dinah cheerfully inquires as she clicks her way toward us in thigh-high vinyl boots and a zip-up bodysuit. She's dyed her hair back to a shocking purple and wears a purple matte lipstick to match. "You know that's how these trials used to be, back in the mists of time. They loved doing shit like this whenever they thought someone was guilty of witchcraft or infidelity or treason. And if an adulterer was a queen, infidelity *was* treason, since you were potentially bastardizing the line of succession and also showcasing the king's weakness. If he can't even control the body of his wife, how can he control a kingdom? You might as well hang a sign on him that says *usurp me now.* Therefore: unlawful queen fucking is punishable by death. *Everybody's* death, including the queen's. So in a trial by ordeal—any trial where innocence was decided by some public suffering or physical feat—the stakes were always life and death."

We stare at her.

She runs a finger under the vinyl hem shining against her thigh and then looks up to see us staring. "I took medieval lit at MIT. I remembered some things."

A trial by ordeal. Yes, that's what it feels like, like I'm being flung into a pond or made to walk across hot coals, my purity made manifest in front of a sea of hostile eyes. If I can bear whatever Mark has devised for me, if my loyalty survives the test, then maybe something like absolution will come after. Not proof of my innocence—rather difficult for anyone to claim that after literally running away with another man—but proof of my very real devotion.

"It's almost time," Dinah tells us. "The grand drape is still down, Mark, if you'd like to check everything."

Mark lets go of my hands and stands to follow Dinah onto the curtained stage. His finger trails over the back of my neck as he walks behind me, fleeting but no less possessive for how quickly the warmth disappears.

"Please don't do this," whispers Tristan, who is still kneeling next to me. "We can find another way to fix your reputation here at the club. With enough time—"

I stop him right there. "Time is the one thing we don't have, Tristan. The conclave will finish any day now, and my uncle will be occupied with his inauguration and initial

Curia maneuvers for only so long before his eye turns back to Lyonesse. I have to play my part here carefully. Too little progress and he might decide I'm more of a liability than an asset. Too much progress and he will wonder where his information is. Mark might feed me some expendable secrets to string him along, but it'll only work for a little while. Uncle Mortimer isn't easily deceived."

Tristan's beautiful mouth pulls into a scowl. "I can't stand this," he hisses suddenly. "I want to scoop you up and whisk you away somewhere safe, somewhere no one can hurt you ever again."

I brush my fingertips over his temple, the hair there tragically short, and smile sadly at him. "We already tried that, remember?"

He closes his eyes. His lashes are long and inky on his cheeks. I hate that this is the most time we've had together since he's come back, that any time we have had has been under scrutiny, around other people.

I hate that time itself has become this nonrenewable resource, scarce as blue garnets, rare as rhodium.

"How are you doing?" I whisper.

He doesn't open his eyes. "I should be asking you that question."

"I didn't have to bury a father this week."

I'm still running my fingers over his face—cheek, jaw, chin—and I feel the aborted words tensing his tongue. Finally, he says, "I think I could have buried my father a long time ago, and it would have felt about the same. It's not the same as when my mom died. And I don't think that makes me a very good son."

"Nothing will be the same as when my mother died either. Does that make me a bad daughter?"

Tristan's eyes open. His lips part, and I quickly shush him with a finger.

"Don't say I can't be a bad anything," I laugh. "We both know it's not true."

He shakes his head, his firm lips moving against my finger. Tickling. Tickling. "You're different than good," he says. "You're like the angels in the Bible, absolutely terrifying and yet completely holy too."

I used to think that about myself too, that I was God's will on earth, that I was practically glowing with his blessing to cleanse the Church of evil. And on balance, I think most of the people I killed were monsters in human skin. But how do you kill monsters without becoming one? And who gets to decide when death is the only currency left to spend?

"I think I'm more like the saints we have no business venerating, like St. Olga or St. Stephen of Hungary," I sigh and drop my finger. I think again of Isabella, sweet and honest and probably closer to an angel than I'll ever be, and I wonder if all the times I've been asking myself *When can I be with Tristan again?* I've been asking myself the wrong question.

Should I be with Tristan again? might be the question an actual saint would ask themselves.

"We're ready," says Dinah from the edge of the stage.

I look over to see Mark standing by a table covered with a sheet. Anything could be under it, and yet I see no St. Andrew's cross, no spanking bench, no medical tables or dog crates or sex swings. There's only a large mat on the floor.

I get to my feet, and Tristan catches my hand, his straight brows notched together in worry. "What did you tell him your limit was?"

"I didn't," I reply softly and pull myself free to join Dinah in the wings. I can hear the music and chattering outside, a casual furor that reminds me of nothing more than the noise in a theater before a play begins.

Mark and I will be the show tonight, the main attraction,

and then afterward, the hall will fling itself into drinking and dancing and general depravity to usher in the new year. And as always, the playrooms will be open to everyone who's under the drinking limit, with club Dominants and submissives waiting to serve the guests in the market for extra companionship.

"Are you ready?" Dinah asks. If she thinks any part of this is ridiculous or pitiable, she doesn't show it. Her expression is one of translucent kindness.

"I am," I say, and I do mean it, even if my hands are trembling at my sides and I can't stop the goose bumps crawling up my legs. I'm wearing a short red slip with nothing underneath—the opposite of what I wore the last time I was at Lyonesse for New Year's Eve, which was also a silk slip but in bridal white. If I'm going to do this, then I want to do it fully. No more dressing like I'm donning armor, giving them nothing to work with. I'll look the part of the treasonous queen if it'll season my suffering and wrench a deeper catharsis out of us all.

"Then we'll begin," Dinah says and gestures to the stage manager on the other side of the wings.

Soon the grand drape is coming up to wild applause, revealing the covered table and the devil himself, wearing a black three-piece suit with a white shirt and no tie. His hair gleams gold and his shoes gleam black.

His eyes are chatoyant under the stage's lights. Otherworldly and feline.

Dinah waits until the applause dies down before she sweeps onto the stage. I wait in the wings like we've discussed and try not to think about Tristan behind me—several steps back so he can't be seen from the audience—or Andrea or Sedge or Hugo or Isabella or anyone else whose opinion I might care about. My focus has to be on myself, on getting through what's to come, whatever it is.

Dinah is stirring up the crowd now, telling a grand and chilling history of the trial by iron, about how Mark forbade such a thing from ever happening here, why it's happening tonight. She is tactful when she talks about my absence from the club, but she doesn't need to be. Everybody here knows what happened. Everybody here knows I ran away with the same bodyguard that's here in the club at this very moment.

"And now, our lost little queen has returned to the fold," finishes Dinah. "She seeks the comfort of her owner once again. She seeks his approval and his love, and she's determined to earn it. She's asked to undergo this lurid and unmentionable trial to test her loyalty and her faith in him, and he's consented with great reluctance."

It's quite adept, the way she sets the scene. Me the penitent and Mark's feelings a cipher, a mystery that they'll be hungry to solve. Will he be angry? Hurt? Coldly inscrutable?

Will they witness a sliver of forgiveness, and if they do, will they judge it merciful or foolish?

"Come here, sweet queen," cajoles Dinah, and I step out onto the stage. The crowd is silent, and without the music, without chatter or applause, the hall's gravity feels like it's tripled. Inhaling and exhaling now take three times the effort.

Dinah takes my hand, and in an upside-down nod to our wedding, she puts my hand into Mark's, like I'm a bride she's giving away.

"This is designed to test your limits and exploit your fears," says Dinah. "But we are not demons. You can safe out at any time, just like any other scene."

But unlike any other scene, this isn't designed with foreknowledge and consent, for our mutual benefit and with my needs in mind. A trial by ordeal is what Dinah called it, and *ordeal* is exactly what's on the menu.

"What you are about to see is a violation," Dinah declares

to the hall, "and suffering. This is the first time this has ever happened, and it will be the last. We hope it's to your liking."

She steps to the side but she doesn't leave the stage, standing in wait like a Greek chorus. I look over to the table and swallow, then up to Mark, who is staring down at me with an opaque expression.

"You told me you already know my greatest fear and my hardest limit," I whisper. "What is it?"

"You'll see soon enough." He yanks me into him so that we're pressed together, and then he bends his head down to my ear and speaks in a low voice. "The two times I've had you up here before now have been simulations. Tonight is real. If you want this to work, then it must be real."

"And you? Will this be real for you?"

His lips find the sensitive skin below my ear; he nips at me, and I'm so nervous that I jerk in his hold. "It's always real for me."

Then his fingers are on the straps of my slip, underneath them. He slides the straps down my shoulders, and the silk kisses its way down my body to make a red puddle at my feet. He deliberately steps back and examines my naked form. It's a critical look—there's nothing of approval in it at all—but his hand twitches briefly at his side.

"Over there," he orders coolly, and he inclines his head at the mat.

I go to stand in the middle, shivering, trying not to look directly at the crowd. They loved me once—cheered for me, accepted me. Took my pain and pleasure as their own. Now I'm naked in front of them, and I feel like I'm being pressed into wine.

It's always real for me.

I look over at my husband, who is currently stripping off his suit jacket and then rolling up his sleeves. His vest is tailored to his torso without leaving a single gap or pucker;

the snow-white fabric of his sleeves against his muscled forearms is a museum-worthy display of arrogance and strength.

I would be wine for him. He told me it needed to be real, and it is, realer than I let him believe while I convinced him it was all for the club, all for my reputation and therefore my safety. That part is still true, but it's also true that I do want to prove something to him. That I want to show him that I'm still his, that I can be strong, that I'm ready to fight.

If that requires being crushed with shame and torment, so be it.

Without glancing over at me, Mark reaches out and flicks the sheet off the table with the panache of a magician. I'm just as eager as the guests to see what's on it—even if my eagerness is limned in dread. But the crowd hums in something like disappointment when they see Mark's tools for the night—not canes and crops and Wartenberg wheels, not the stuff of nightmares—but headphones and a length of silk and lots of synthetic rope. The orange-handled rope shears are the only thing on the table that look even remotely alarming, and they're only there as a precaution.

I remember the mat under my feet and then look up to see two rings high above me. I look back to Mark, a little confused. Suspension isn't something we've done, but it's not one of my limits, hard or soft, and Mark has bound me with rope plenty of times.

Mark meets my questioning gaze with a detached one of his own as Dinah addresses the crowd once more. "How to give an ordeal to a little pain slut like our Isolde?" she asks. "Mark could cane her until she screams, gag her until she chokes, but it would feel right to her, wouldn't it? To someone who feels clean after they hurt? No, that wouldn't work at all."

Mark approaches me with a length of red rope in his

hand and, walking around the front of me, smoothly and methodically begins wrapping the rope around my chest into a harness. How can this be it for the trial? Are we lying to the club right now? Pretending that I'm afraid of bondage or suspension?

"I thought you said this needed to be real," I murmur.

He pauses his work, and there's pity in his expression when he says, "It will be."

I don't know what to make of this. I've enjoyed it every time Mark's tied me up, run happy fingers over the lingering rope marks, been enthralled anytime we've had an expert in the club show off the poses and transitions of suspension bondage. Mark is even doing one of my favorite things right now, using the rope to frame my breasts in an elaborate pattern, something that makes them more sensitive even without any squeezing or compression. And the process is hypnotic, the warm brush of knuckles and fingers, the strangely supportive web of pressure, the soft hiss of the synthetic fibers against themselves.

My nerves are singing with apprehension; I still don't know what's going on. But there's a drugging, slurring kind of thrill tickling into my thoughts now, something that's a cousin to desire and dreaminess both.

Soon, I'm wrapped neatly from collarbones to ribs, my arms free because Mark is fussy about arms, wrists, and hands. *People don't care enough about radial neuropathy*, he'd grumbled to me now and again, and while no one needs nerve damage, I'm only just now appreciating that Mark took extra care with my hands because he knew how I used them. Because he used his own the same way. Very hard to cut the throats of your enemies if your hands are numb because a bad top didn't notice them turning purple.

He gets more rope, red as fresh blood, and returns to me, kneeling down to wrap my hips and thighs. It would be better if I kept my face toward the audience, if they could see the scraps of trepidation and shame, but I can't do anything other than watch Mark as he lines up the rope and begins wrapping it around my hips with an intoxicating mix of precision and ease. His experience doesn't lessen his attention for an instant; he is focused entirely on the red lengths belting my hips and framing my cunt. He is studying and checking his work as if there is nothing else in the world at all, no one else in the room, no days after today. Only the rope on my skin in parallel wraps and loops, only the gentle shush of the fibers as he pulls one length through the rest.

The stage lights catch in his hair as he bends his head to curve the rope where my backside meets my thighs, his hands sure and patient as they pull the rope back through the opening between my legs, the occasional brush of his fingers against my exposed sex almost too much to endure with dignity. The muscles of his back and shoulders shift under his shirt and vest, and his forearms flex against his rolled shirtsleeves as he pulls the rope through a final time and uses the excess to tie a garter onto one thigh.

It's purely decorative, I know, just a nice way to use the extra rope, but as he traces the line of it once with his thumb before standing, I get the feeling it's a decoration he likes very much.

My ankles are wrapped individually, and then finally Mark moves to my arms. Cuffs made of rope are knotted at each wrist, and then my arms are raised one at a time and bent at the elbow with my wrists resting at the back of my neck. The rope secures my arms like this, like wings around my head, and then Mark walks behind me and checks every single hitch and tuck with the scrutiny of a forensic auditor.

"No pins or needles?" he asks, sliding his fingers under the rope and then tugging here and there. "You can feel it when I pinch your pinkie? Your thumb? Can you feel my fingernail on your forearm now? And this one? Good."

I'm a little dazed from the steady, efficient eroticism of the act, and it takes me a moment to realize that Hugo has joined us onstage, striding on to the approval of the crowd and giving them a polished, royal sort of wave as he walks up to us.

I don't know what he's doing here, but there's a small bloom of certainty in my belly that I'd be more than okay with him staying up here, being part of the scene. Sharing is something that we haven't done—something complicated by the very nonconsensual sharing I did with Tristan in Belgrade and in Lyonesse's own garden—but Mark knows it's on the list of things I'll do…even on the list of things I'd *like* to do, provided Mark is there with me when it happens. And maybe that's the punishment, the trial—have the unfaithful wife act out her sins in front of an audience. Maybe Kayden would come up too. Maybe even Tristan…

But Hugo only gives me a Gallic buss on the cheek and then starts walking around me, checking ropes and knots, kneeling to check the harness around my hips and cunt and the ropes around my ankles. He asks me the same questions as Mark—gives me stern instructions to let Mark know the moment I feel any pins and needles, any at all, and then goes to stand next to Dinah at the edge of the stage.

I haven't forgotten that Mark is a master of the spectacle, that he knows how to stir and soothe the crowd according to his purposes, but it's still fascinating to see it again as he slowly stalks around me, his hand finding my waist, my hip, and then finally my hair. He wraps it around his fist as he comes to stand in front of me, his eyes veiled and his expression scornful.

The guests, lulled into something like a reverie by the rhythmic and beautiful decoration of my body with the ropes, lean forward, recognizing the moment as a threshold into the next act.

Mark, the showman, whose skills weren't honed on a stage but in the field with fake passports and a seductive smile, lets the moment germinate and unfold. Allows the tender shoot of it to find the light of their curiosity and impatience.

And then he says, loud enough for them to hear, "Would you like to say anything before we begin?"

I take a breath, impeded slightly by the position of my arms, and say, "Only that I love you, sir."

A tremble across his mouth, so subtle that I think I'm the only one who can see it. "Yes, of course. Only that," he says.

He takes hold of me by the chest harness and by the harness around my hips and, with barely a shift of his weight, lifts me from my feet. I'm suddenly facing up toward the ceiling, and before I can panic, I'm laid flat on my back on the mat.

"Stay," he says, like I'm a bad dog, like I'm Petitcrieu trying to run into the shower with us, and he goes over to the table and gets the silk and the headphones.

I think about this, about how so far there's been nothing of a trial at all, about how I'll need to give the guests *something* to believe that I've actually atoned—and if that means I'll need to fake some kind of agony, I suppose I'll need to start soon. But the expression on Mark's face gives me pause as he comes closer, as he kneels on the mat next to me. He's only bringing over headphones and a blindfold, but he looks like he's about to brand me with a cherry-red iron, that's how sober his expression is now.

"Your safeword," he says, the headphones by his knee, the blindfold in his hands.

"Hyssop," I say for the benefit of the crowd.

"I'm sorry for this," he says, his shadow falling over me like a vampire's. And then the silk is over my eyes.

The crowd is murmuring now—they've picked up on Mark's intensity, the grave look on his face—but I'm not being flogged or made to lick whiskey off the floor. I'm only bound and blindfolded, so what could the devil possibly reveal to his fiends that would warrant that expression? This whole production?

Mark is careful of my hair as he ties the blindfold, going so far as to lift my head so he can create a horizontal part and run the silk through my hair rather than over it. The silk is thick, utterly opaque, and when I try to open my eyes against it, I see absolutely nothing. Not even a crack of light at the bottom. The darkness is as complete as if I were standing at the bottom of the sea.

"So my sweet ones," I hear Dinah purr, the controlled, dramatic crack of her boots on the stage underscoring the sultry and sinister pitch of her voice. "We have a penitent here who isn't afraid of pain, who doesn't have a phobia of dentists or snakes, who hasn't given us a nice and juicy limit like pet play or crotch torture. What to do? What trial to put her through?"

Mark shifts—a barely perceptible dip in the mat—and then my skin is prickling with the awareness of him. I can smell him too, rain and stone and ionic charge, a storm of a man.

"But our Mark knows his beloved, doesn't he? He knows what can break her apart without anyone having to break a sweat. He knows that she can't bear—"

What I can't bear, I don't find out, because the headphones clamp over my ears at that exact moment, closing out all sound as if sound itself had never existed in the first place. All I hear is a perfectly calibrated *nothing*—the headphones are noise-canceling. I can't even hear the muffled impressions of Dinah's speech; I can't hear if Mark responds, if he's speaking too. But I do feel his hands come to either side of my bound arms, the drop of warm lips on a furled nipple.

I arch, the awakening need so sudden I can barely even think, but the lips are gone. A nose in my hair—and I can't even nuzzle into it because of the way my arms are bound—and then he's gone altogether. His lips, his nose, his hands by my head. The petrichor scent...

Gone.

Okay, I think. *This isn't so bad.* I've never done sensory deprivation before, but I've seen it done, seen the women with their headphones on while gleeful partners wield wand vibrators between their quaking legs. Whatever happens next, I can endure it, and if a wand vibrator is involved, I can probably endure it quite happily.

Except...nothing does happen.

Nothing at all.

I'm tensed at first, waiting. Counting each inhale like a notch carved on the inside of my skull, releasing every exhale like it'll be cut in two by some unexpected pain. Readiness poises my muscles and fascia, goose bumps stipple my sensitive skin, and I'm like a runner at the starting line, my ears straining for a gunshot I won't even be able to hear.

The longer it goes on—the nothing—the tighter my muscles get. It'll be any moment, the something, the interruption, the beginning of Mark's torture. But without my sight or my hearing, I can't strain for a signal, any signal at all, and the first drip of panic slides down my spine, a sizzle of nerve endings and a jettison of chemicals into my blood, all without my permission.

I need to calm down. What am I enduring right now that warrants panic? Darkness and quiet? Unending stillness? All the conditions for a good night's sleep?

Even the ropes, as expertly rigged as they are, are quite

comfortable. Not too tight but snug enough that I can feel every inch of them, where they wrap and fold and hitch. Where they delimit the most intimate parts of my body.

It's pathetic that I'm on the verge of a panic attack—especially because Dinah and Mark and Hugo are here onstage, and Tristan is in the wings watching. I'm not alone. Of course I'm not alone.

But the adrenaline and cortisol are doing their jobs too well, and the world inside my input-deprived mind becomes impossibly, unsurvivably sharp. The noise-canceling headphones are now deafening in their manufactured silence. The darkness is no longer dark but instead composed of pooling, contorting splotches of color, garish and unending. The cool air on my skin abruptly feels like a thousand Wartenberg wheels, unbearable in its vacancy, and the ropes around my arms and wrists mean that I can only move my legs and feet, which I do now as subtly as I can, desperate for any sort of stimulation.

It barely helps.

It is rare—rare on the order of a verified miracle—that my safeword comes to me during a scene and absurd that it should come to me when the scene itself is barely anything at all, and yet I can't stop thinking the word. *Hyssop hyssop hyssop.*

Cleanse me with hyssop, and I will be clean.

I move my feet a little more, my bare soles rubbing against the mat, and struggle in vain to regulate my breathing.

A tug on my chest and then one on my hips, pulling right from the middle of the harness. I'm...I'm being strung up, I think. The lines fed through the rings above. But no hands touch me or caress me; no lips find my shoulder. There are only the tugs, the pauses for inspection or locking a line, and then there is the first tide of cool air under my back and thighs.

Smoothly, with only a single pause, I'm suspended for the first time in my life. I'm face up, my head supported by my bound hands at the back of my neck, my feet suspended in the air with me, and all of me so well rigged and secure that there's no slipping, no creeping numbness, only a soft, gentle whisper of pain where the ropes press into my skin. My hair is hanging straight down, as unbound as my body is not, and for a moment—just one—I feel almost other-worldly, a spirit rising from the deep on a cloud of the sweetest, silkiest torment.

The panic hits like a meteor strike.

The tugging is gone; I've been tied off. I can no longer move my legs—only my feet—and the empty air beneath me feels like a pit, an endless one, without even plumes of sulfur or lakes of fire to interrupt the nothingness. If I fell, I would fall forever.

The silence is a roar and the shapes behind my eyes are malevolent, and worse, *worst*, is the air around me, all over me, because I no longer even have the floor to define myself against.

And there is nothing else—no sight, no sound, no scent nor touch—there is nothing else except for me.

I'm the only one here, and I'm alone.

I try to talk over the shriek of fear. I try to remember that Mark and the others are close by and that this is only going to last an hour. But I have no idea how much time has passed, and maybe it's only been five minutes since the headphones were put on, maybe only a minute since I was hoisted up in the air.

I might only be at the beginning... I might have an eternity left to go. An eternity alone.

This is hell, I think suddenly, with an accompanying inhale so jagged that it sends lines of fresh pain along the ropes of my chest harness. This is hell, to be alone, with only your own mind and your own memories, knowing that most of them hold horrors incompatible with sanity.

And that's what loneliness really, *really* is. It's being alone inside yourself, alone even from yourself, because if your own mind is haunted even for you, how will anyone else ever join you there? How could you ever trust them to understand? How could you ever even try? Mark had carefully tugged me to shore after he found me in the garden, but it's still there, that dark and endless sea, and I'm helpless to fight the tide.

My shredded inhales and half-choked exhales strain the harness, and each one sends pain—deep and also bright, pushing and also sparkling—burning along the lines of the ropes pressing into my back and shoulders. It's as if the ropes are soaked in gasoline and every breath is a match brought to the dripping end. It's fire and it's also a bruising crush, the kiss of gravity as the ropes dig into my skin, and it's fear, and it's the endless sea all around me and inside me where no one can ever get to me and no one wants to anyway.

I don't realize I'm crying until the tears start sliding free and catching in the blindfold where it lays against my temples. The silk grows wet within the span of only a handful of breaths, making it sticky and cold and unbearable, and I can't rip it off. I can't wipe my face. I can't *do anything*. I can't, I can't, I can't.

There's no way I'm not making noises now. There's no way that the sawn-off breaths can't be mistaken for anything other than sobs. I'm so nerve-scrapingly conscious of the soaked blindfold and the ugly, quivering shapes of my chin. Of how I must look like an insect caught in a web, helpless and wriggling and pathetic.

But don't they know the truth too? Don't they know that no one can come, no one can drive the shadows back, there's no escape from it?

It's truly getting hard to breathe now through the tears,

and I'm shaking so hard that I've started to sway a little, with a queasy rhythm that makes the open air around me seem even more vacant.

All those people I killed…all those bodies I left cooling in alleys or floating down rivers or burning in structure fires…Mark wasn't wrong when he said that the world was better off without most of them, but that's not actually the point, is it? Because who gets to decide what *better off* means and for whom? The Church? The CIA? My husband, driven as he is by a years-long quest for a revenge that only he understands?

Me, who was willing to follow a lie all the way to the end, all the way to a grave I wouldn't have seen coming?

I sinned against sinners and somehow sinned against myself too, and now I have nothing to hold on to. My belief in my own righteousness has turned out to be a child's fantasy; my capacity for love has been spiked all the way through by my gift of annihilation. I cannot claim to be good. I cannot claim to be faithful. I have nothing left.

But—

But something's different from the last time I felt this. From the last night of Saturnalia or the garden. Because the loneliness isn't just an idea, not just a vacancy slowly stealing all light and warmth from my mind.

It has a shape tonight; it has a presence. It's segmented into unforgiving lengths of red rope. It's clinging to my face as wet silk. It's the chilly void of unoccupied air around me.

It's the crawl of dizziness as I dangle, the silence, the silk. It's real, and it's here, and it's touching me, interacting with me. Holding me even, cradling me as I weep in front of hundreds of people who think the worst thing I've ever done is run away with a bodyguard.

Mark has shaped a vessel for the loneliness tonight. He wove it out of rope and covered it in silk and washed it in cool air. He gave it a shape and a feeling, knots and tucks, counterpressure and pain to answer the numb indifference.

How lonely am I? Just look at my skin, at the impressions left behind by the twisted fibers. You can measure it in inches. You can trace it from my feet all the way up to my heart.

You are not allowed to slip through your own fingers, much less mine.

I won't have it, sweetheart.

How lonely am I? Only as lonely as the person who tied these knots will let me be.

How can I be alone when someone will make the shape of loneliness itself for me, twist and hitch it so that I can put my fingers in its wounds and know that it is real, know that its effects can be felt, know that if it has shape and form, then those shapes and forms can be changed? Diminished? Destroyed?

An answering flood of turbulent but indelible joy.

You are not allowed.

I won't have it.

It's that easy. Because somehow Mark has found me in the dark and endless sea. He's swam from his own and survived. He knows my sins and he knows what those sins feel like to carry, and he still believes in a mustard seed nestled safely under curled fingers.

From this moment on, no more.

I take my first real breath in seven weeks of years, a shock of oxygen to my tormented system, and then somehow manage to take another. And then—a tug. A movement that's not the micro oscillation of suspension but something more, something deliberate.

Warm hands bend my leg back so that my heel touches my backside, and they are Mark's hands; I'd know them anywhere. Long-fingered and lightly calloused, nimble and certain and arrogant. I pull in a shuddering breath at his touch, so desperate to see and to hear him, and that very same deprivation makes the sensation of his touch almost dire in its intensity.

Quick movements of wraps and knots bind my calf to my thigh, frog-like, and then the same thing happens to my other leg, my weight shifting and moving as the lines are rerun through the hooks.

He threads rope under the place where the harness stretches from hip to hip. One more adjustment to my chest, and then I become aware that the slow tilt to the side I've been feeling has indeed left me sideways in the air. Pain blooms anew along one side of my ribs and one hip, and endorphins quickly follow, adding to the sparkles, the dizziness.

A hand slides to my waist and holds me as his other finds my breast.

I'm still crying, if more gently now, but the tears don't stop the arousal rippling out from his touch. My nipple stiffens, and the soft, private place between my legs—now open to the full view of the club—begins to ache. I whimper helplessly when I feel him step between my legs, aching to get closer to him and utterly unable to do so.

Hands move to my knees and slide up my thighs, then the same from my waist to my shoulders. He's running his palms all over me, everywhere that there's rope, as if enjoying his handiwork, and after an eon without touch, the sudden glut of it is intoxicating. I think I might be making noises worse than whimpering—I might be mewling like a kitten—and I dazedly wonder if he's teasing me for it in that wicked voice of his while I can't hear anything. I wonder if he's talking to the crowd, showing them the mess of miserable, tearful lust I've become.

When I feel his thumbs trace the rope running along the crease of my thigh, following the path it makes along the curve of my ass and along the outside of my labia, I'm almost certain he's talking to the hall. That he's showing them the pink haven outlined in red rope, asking them if they can see how slick it is.

He presses a thumb to the swollen point at the top of my cunt, and pleasure zips everywhere, moving as easily through my body as a current through water. I keen.

He tests me with a cursory finger, checking to see if I'm wet enough to take him. There's some movement; he's stripping off his vest and shirt, maybe, unfastening his pants. And then at long last, a big hand curls around the harness at my hip and something blunt and hot presses at my waiting hole.

Without sight or sound, I have no warning—and then he plunges straight into me like he's got an appointment to keep.

The invasion spreads me open and stretches me wide, intent on stealing the precious breath right out of my lungs. The tendrils of an impending orgasm snake up from my sex to my belly...already, this soon, with nothing more than two thick strokes. I must be the perfect height for Mark to fuck, because he grabs the harness around my hips with each hand and begins to pull me into him, meeting me with a searing thrust every time our bodies collide with hard, sparking smacks. I can't hear it, but I can *feel* it: the strength of his arms as he yanks me onto his cock, the glittering slap of his body against my clit.

It's as if he's adding his own body to the chalice of loneliness he's built with rope and silk. Caging the loneliness in, containing it. There on my clitoris—the hands curled over my hips—there inside me—both driving back the loneliness and also saying *it's real, it's real, you didn't make it up, I see it too, we'll see it together.*

My breathing is matched to the movements of his hands and hips; every slide into my body is more delicious than the

256

last until I wonder how I've gone so long without this, why I didn't walk into Lyonesse three weeks ago, crawl right onto his lap, and help myself.

His fingers find my clitoris again, and he works it with an expert, bossy touch until I'm on the precipice, until every muscle is quivering and every bright line of pain is fused around this one single ache. Until the entire bruised, slick, trembling, and lonely sum of my existence is a single spark quivering under the demanding strokes of his fingers.

And then right as I'm poised to fall, he reaches up to push off my headphones, which tumble with a clatter below, and he unknots my blindfold.

Without it, I am truly blind under the stage lights for a moment or two, so it's the sounds that announce themselves first—my own low whimpers, the slippery, smacking noise of penetration, and the cheers and yells of the crowd. My sight returns in slices of impression, glazed with tears: ocean eyes, golden hair. A face like a king's as he cuts down the last of a retreating army on a smoking battlefield—determination, cruelty, triumph.

"I want it, sweetheart." His bare chest and throat are misted with sweat, and his pants are low around his hips. The black and silver ring flashes on his hand over and over as he pulls me into him. "I want to feel it. Show me that you're ready to be my little wife once more."

Oh, the crowd loves that, and I do too, and I can tell myself it's because I'm dazed and drunk on endorphins and possibly barely conscious, but I know I'd love it wide awake and sober too, and he slams into me just *that* much harder, caresses my clit just *that* much faster, and I cease to exist.

The release tears me into pieces and sends me flying in every imaginable direction, racing outward at the speed of light to some unknown destiny. I can hear screaming, as high and pure as a choir's, and then I feel unconsciousness swooping down on me with dazzling scintillas and tingling lips and everything but the soul-destroying pleasure of this release disappearing from the world. My cunt contracts around him, my belly seizing in fierce clenches of ecstasy, and Mark groans too, impaling me with a viciousness that draws my climax on and on, even as my tears spatter on the mat below like rain.

He throws his head back, throat working, shoulders tense, and with a sudden, jerking pulse, he ejaculates, using the harness to keep himself buried as he gives me everything, days and weeks of it, in heavy surges. It keeps coming, his body still unloading, and the crowd is roaring and the world is shimmering and I'm completely limp save for the aftershocks of my orgasm and then…

His mouth on mine, but barely—

His erection still hard and slick as he fastens his pants—

The shush of the ropes as I'm lowered gently—

Mark's hands patiently unraveling the rope. Dinah speaking to the guests, asking them if they liked it, if they approve, if I was indeed found worthy. The din of approbation, the cheers as Dinah slyly asks them what they thought of Mark, the thrum of music and the shifting of the lights as the hall begins to dissolve into hedonism as we all whirl closer to the new year.

The curtains close as Mark slides the last of the rope from my limbs. He massages my wrists and arms, helps me straighten my legs. Methodically checks my fingers and toes for feeling. I murmur that I can feel everything and then close my eyes for just a moment, just for the next breath or two…

When I open them, we're in a playroom, one of the ones on the top floor with an interior window overlooking the hall. We're in an armchair, and I'm curled in Mark's arms. A soft, soft blanket is tucked around me. Mark's lips are in my hair.

"You did so well, Mrs. Trevena," he's murmuring. His hands echo his praise, soothing my shoulders and back and legs. "You were so brave, so good. Such a sweet little penitent."

There's a knock, Mark saying *come in*, and then hesitant footsteps as the door swings shut again.

"You shouldn't be up here," my husband says calmly.

"I couldn't stay away," Tristan replies.

Mark's arms tighten around me as he draws a quivering, gut-deep breath. "Good."

twenty-six

TRISTAN

THE ONLY ILLUMINATION IN THE ROOM COMES FROM THE club itself, glowing and flashing through the interior window, and then from a tall lamp in the corner, its light subtle and golden. I approach the chair, reminded strangely of the thrones on Samhain, and stop just in front of it.

I want to commit this to memory, this very sight: Mark's wide shoulders and bare feet, Isolde's large eyes and tousled hair as she's curled up in Mark's lap. She's a whorl of platinum hair and fuzzy blanket, but anything adorable or domestic about the scene is belied by the presence of a single exposed ankle, rope-kissed and delicate.

And perhaps the thin, scarlet line on Mark's throat. The closest Mark might ever come to wearing a collar.

"I asked Dinah to smuggle me up here," I say. My heart hurts, being alone with them, and it already ached watching Isolde tremble and suffer onstage. It throbbed as Mark fucked her, brutally and wonderfully, and I coveted everything about it. The tears soaking her blindfold, the ropes biting into her skin, the hard, slapping claiming after. I wanted to be her and to be him and just be *with them*, and there is nothing worse than loving a married couple, nothing more pathetic, because it's a love destined for the edges, for stolen moments and snatched time. It's a forever voyeurism that only gets sung about when it's time to sing something sad.

But if this is a pathetic life, then I'll live pathetically, and if this is love on the edges, I don't know that I can endure love in its glowing, fulsome center. I'm named for sadness after all, and maybe I could never have loved happily, never been inside one of those fairy tales where the ending is as simple as a kiss. If I ever thought I could rescue the damsel, I know much better now. Of the three of us, *I* am the damsel. And if I could, I'd lock myself into the tower of my two villains and throw away the key.

Mark's fingers are tangling gently in Isolde's hair, sifting and playing. "You sure you weren't seen?" he asks. "Backstage is one thing, but coming alone to a playroom is much harder to explain away."

"I'm sure." I can't stop watching his fingers in her hair. It's mesmerizing. Erotic beyond belief. "Dinah brought me up through the staff hallways. And I won't be missed. Hugo gave me the night off, and I told everyone I was going to bed early."

"That means we have you all night?" asks Mark silkily.

"Do you want me all night, sir?" I sink to my knees, already knocked sideways with prostrating desire. I'm between his planted feet, bracketed by his knees. Isolde is close enough that I could rest my forehead on her thigh. "You can have it. You can have anything you want."

His chest lifts once sharply, and his eyes glitter from above Isolde's head. "You think I don't want you for as long as I can have you? Tristan."

"I won't pretend that I've earned your forgiveness. That you don't still hate me for…everything."

"Isolde and I have decided to set ideas of forgiveness aside for now," he says. "It seemed easier."

"How long is *for now?*"

"Am I being interrogated?" asks Mark, amused. "If so, we need to work on your technique."

"What would you work on?"

"Firstly"—a professorial eyebrow—"you shouldn't pose your questions so broadly. Stay specific. Ask 'Does *for now* last until morning?' Or 'Will *for now* last until I go back to Montreal?' Don't give me room to wander too far away from your question, and don't give me room to build a little palace of hedges and half-truths, because I will if given the chance."

"Is there a *secondly?*"

The lights from the hall flash on white teeth. He's smiling.

"Secondly, don't ask questions with such a tragic pout. It lets your interrogee know what answers you're afraid of."

"And I suppose you know then?" It might have come out grouchily, but before I can finish speaking, he's reached out to run a light finger along the bow of my lower lip. He could have his hand down my pants right now for how lewd that feels.

"*Puppy,*" he says, half scolding. Behind my zipper, my erection surges. "Don't pretend that you didn't come in here with all sorts of thorny hopes clutched in a bleeding fist. Don't pretend you weren't watching from the wings tonight and having to strain all those pretty muscles of yours to keep from charging out onto the stage."

His smile widens, and I realize that I must have pouted even more.

"It's not fair that I'm such an open book to you, and yet I never know what you're thinking."

He presses down on my lip enough to see my tongue and then lets go. "No one is really an open book, Tristan. And I can tell you exactly what I'm thinking right now: that I'd like to see how sweaty I can make you in the next two hours."

I take a sharp breath.

"And even if I didn't want to fuck you tonight, which I very much do, my wife does, and after what she went through, I'm rather inclined to give her whatever she wants."

I look at Isolde, who is awake and staring at me with subspace-glazed eyes. She reaches for me, the blanket sliding down to reveal marked arms and shoulders, and I take her hand with mine and kiss her fingers.

"Let's not waste the night," she whispers.

"Are you sure you can?" I ask. She's still slumped against Mark's chest, her expression made up of equal parts lingering euphoria and post-scene languor.

"This might be our only chance." She falters a little as she speaks, and I know why. Because she doesn't just mean our only chance while I'm here at Lyonesse but our only chance at all. Our *last* chance.

I look up from her face to Mark's. His smile has faded, but his expression is otherwise neutral.

"I don't want you to think me miserly, Tristan," he says. "I'll share my toys. Why don't you slide a hand under the blanket and feel what I got to enjoy in front of the entire club tonight?"

When I catch Isolde's eyes, she's already nodding, shifting under the blanket to spread her thighs in Mark's lap and finding my hand once again. But when she tries to pull me straight to where I've been ordered to go, I rebel a little. I pull my hand free and drop it onto Mark's knee, warm and anchored with heavy muscle, and then slide it under the blanket to find her foot.

It's been too long not to savor this. Not to feel every part of her.

I pull the blanket aside so I can watch as I graze over

the incline of her foot to her ankle and then from her ankle to the curves of her calves, which are shockingly firm. The three of us watch as I make it to her knee and then replace my fingers with my lips, kissing the tender spot right where her thigh begins. I nuzzle the soft skin just above it.

Her legs are parted enough for a wandering hand but not for more, and Mark arranges her so that she's got her back against his chest and her legs draped and hooked along the outside of his knees.

Mark slides a hand down her stomach to her pussy and pushes two fingers in with no preamble at all. She's still wet from earlier, both her own arousal and his satisfaction, and when he pulls his fingers free, they glisten with pearly ejaculate.

He doesn't ask and he doesn't have to. I part my lips and accept his fingers like a sinner awaiting communion and then shudder at the taste. Sweet and a little bitter, the two of them together, something I've only tasted a few times, and yet a taste I'd recognize until my dying day. It tastes like the only thing I could ever want. It tastes like true love.

"You want to clean her up?" Mark asks softly, and I nod, dip my head immediately to her cunt. I can't breathe when he lets me do things like this. When he lets me play breeding games.

At the first trace of my tongue, Isolde gasps, squirms until Mark finds her rope-bitten hips and holds her firmly in place. I appreciate it because I want my own hands free. I press my thumbs to the soft outer labia and spread until the pulsing lights outline the slick hole and the small pink berry at the top, nestled under its hood. I lower my mouth again and kiss her cunt like I have seduction in mind, unabashedly making love to it. I can taste Mark inside her; I'm greedy for it, and I swirl my tongue to find more of it. I use my thumb to plug her opening while I service her clitoris and then suck my thumb when I pull it free.

I want to fuck where Mark has been. I want it so badly. I want to go bare inside her and pump her so full that she's dripping. I want Mark to go bare inside me... I want him to breed me like he paid for me.

"Tristan," Isolde breathes. "*Please*."

"If you make her come, you can fuck her," Mark says, magnanimous and casual.

I flick my eyes up to Isolde's, and she manages an assenting smile through her whimpers. I waste no time and return to my work—not that there's much left to do. I use my tongue to caress the tender pearl of her clitoris, I fill her with my fingers, turning them so I can gently press upward, and she starts quivering almost immediately.

Her hands find my head and press me closer; with my hair trimmed this short, I can feel each and every fingertip, the warmth of her palms. She's holding my mouth against her pussy, trying to buck against Mark's iron hold, and the noises she's making are the noises of unutterable agony, of torment beyond reckoning.

I'm so hungry for more of her taste, for more of those noises, that I don't stop as she shudders and bucks even harder, even more jerkily, my name on her lips between her broken groans. I grab the insides of her thighs and suck harder, lick faster, feeling her on my chin and my nose, wishing I could get closer, taste deeper, be part of her.

When she finally goes still, her hands loosening on my head, I force myself to stop. I rest my head against her thigh, my mouth still brushing against her flushed, wet cunt, and close my eyes as I breathe her in. She's slumped back against Mark's chest, panting, and I hear Mark crooning something to her, sounding pleased.

We stay like that a moment, me kneeling between both

of their thighs, Isolde enduring the aftershocks with small hitches of her breath. And then Mark says, "I think the table will serve your purposes quite nicely."

I know which table he's talking about, a padded leather one in the middle of the room. There's also a bed, neatly made with satin sheets and outfitted with hooks and cuffs, but the table is closer. If Mark means to watch from his chair, then the table would afford him the best view. And judging by the way he settles back and crosses an ankle atop his knee as I stand and lift Isolde into my arms, he's planning to watch from right where he is.

Isolde rests her head against my shoulder as I carry her, and even if I don't have Mark's appetite for pain or control, I still feel the thrill of gratified ego when she's like this. Isolde Trevena, a saint of the Church, the tightly wound murderess who never unclenches her fist around her rigid, rich girl poise, is now sweet and pliant in my arms. It makes me feel like I've done something right, like I've given her a gift maybe.

I lay her on the table and don't bother with any of the assorted accessories, toys, and restraints in the discreetly joined cabinets nearby. I work on unbuckling my pants, my hands shaking, and then pause when I hear Mark's voice behind me.

"Shirt, socks, and shoes too, Tristan. We're not heathens. It's only polite to be as naked as she is."

He certainly wasn't worried about being polite when he fucked her on the stage tonight, with his pants still hanging off his hips, but I'm pretty sure politeness isn't actually the point; getting to look at me without clothes on is the point. My breathing speeds up as I unbutton my shirt and toe off my shoes. I bend down to work off my socks, and when I straighten, I see that he's propped his head against his hand and is staring at me like I'm the provided entertainment for the evening.

A flush burns from inside my skin, along my chest and cheeks and throat, and I don't know what to do when he looks at me like that. I've never known what to do.

I'm physically incapable of denying him anything he wants when he looks at me like that.

I have to look away as I shuck off my pants and underwear, his attention is that unbearable. I fold my things neatly and set them atop my shoes and climb onto the table. The leather upholstery—soft enough to accommodate knees and elbows, firm enough that a face could be pressed into it and not incur any respiratory risk—makes a subtle noise as I crawl over Isolde, noises I feel more than hear.

Her eyes are dark as she looks up at me, and the rest of her is bathed in shadows that are only briefly burned away by the blue and purple lights from the hall, each pulse of light etching the rope's impressions into sharp relief. I sink down onto my elbows, and we gasp as our lower halves make contact.

I give a testing thrust—not inside—just sliding against the soft, wet valley of her. Her lips part, and I need to kiss her even more than I need to fuck her, so I slide my hands under her head, cradling it through that silky mass of ivory and gold hair, and bring my mouth to hers. Below, I still work my hips, getting her slick all over me, rubbing her clit with my erection as I do.

"Let's be real in the dark," she murmurs into my mouth, the words tickling my lips and tongue.

"I'll give you anything you want," I answer as I slot my lips to hers. "Anything at all, it's yours the moment you ask."

I kiss her with as much patience as I can stand—not much—until I give in and start dipping my tongue into her mouth. She receives it eagerly, her arms coming up to loop around my neck, and I keep kissing her as I reach down and take hold of myself, rubbing the tip up and down a few times to get myself all the way wet. My passage eased, I press into her entrance until I'm in up to the crest of the head. And then I freeze, choking off a breath as a sudden wave of euphoria seizes me, deep in my pelvis, curling insidiously in my balls, yanking at the base of my spine. I'm going to come *already*, and I can't stop it—it's been too long, and I'm too fucking turned on and—

"Do I have to do everything? If I'm going to be the cuckold, I'd like to at least enjoy a few minutes in the cuck chair," Mark says dryly from above us. Before I can process that he both understood exactly what was happening and managed to move over to the table without me noticing, he's reached between my legs, wrapped an unforgiving hand around the base of my testicles, and pulled down.

I hiss, my orgasm stalling and tripping over its own feet, and I drop my head down next to Isolde.

Fuck. It's like being harpooned in the stomach, except the harpoon is made of quivering, glorious agony.

Mark leans down to kiss his wife on the cheek. "Doing okay, sweetheart?"

Instead of answering, she turns to kiss him, and I have to listen to the sound of them kissing while I'm dying on top of her, the tip of my penis squeezed inside her slippery heat.

"You're doing so well," he's murmuring now. "My good wife. My pretty wife. It's not your fault that your pussy feels so good. No one can last long while inside you, darling."

I bite my own forearm to keep his words from driving me over the edge—an edge I probably couldn't go over if I tried, given the evil hand between my legs.

After what has to be hours, Mark finally relents and lets go. I stay as I am for a moment, too terrified to move. The climax has receded, but she still feels so good—

Mark runs a hand up my naked thigh and ass, giving the tensed muscles an appreciative squeeze. "I love watching you fuck," he informs me in a conversational tone. "I love watching all that goodness perish at the hands of base, atavistic lust. Where is America's hero now? Fucking another man's wife with absolute, mindless abandon. Getting ready to unload inside her hot cunt because he just can't help himself, honor be damned."

With that, he pushes against the curve of my backside, pushing me deeper inside Isolde. She arches underneath me and tries to spread her thighs even wider to take me.

"That's it," Mark says, a dark pleasure smoking around the edges of his words. "Go deeper. I want you all the way in, until you can't get in any more than you are. Oh, you like that? It feels good, doesn't it? It's so tight, it's really not fair to the rest of us. Pull out to the tip now, almost all the way out—good—God, you're so wet with her, I can see it shining all over you—back in. Harder, my little knight, *harder*. She's begging for it, aren't you, sweetling? Yes, I thought so."

I can't survive this, not the silken sheath I'm currently fucking, not the slender, sweat-gleamed woman underneath me. Not Isolde's closed eyes and arching throat, not Mark's indecent commentary, as poisonous as it is beguiling.

And still he goads me, slapping a wide hand on my haunch like I'm an animal at work.

"Is that as hard as you can go?" he asks a little scornfully. "As good as you can fuck? I don't loan out my bride lightly, Tristan. I expect a nonpareil performance. I expect peerlessness."

Shame tugs at my heels, but lightly, because Mark has always known how to season humiliation with enough proof of his secret approval—and his plain desire—that I am assured my humiliation is making him happy, that I'm pleasing him. And so too now, because even as he's telling me I'm not fucking his wife well enough for his taste, he's walking around the table, finding the back of my head, and pressing my face against his groin. The erection inside his trousers could be made of iron, that's how unyielding it is against my lips.

Peerless performance or not, he is alchemically hard: metal out of flesh, desire out of disloyalty. A husband ready to go after watching another man on top of his wife.

Isolde lifts her head too, and together we are kissing over his clothed cock, open mouths, wetting tongues. He doesn't rock against us, although I feel the trembling restraint in the hand on my head, but he does grunt when we try to take more of him in our mouths. A low, haughty noise, like this is only his due.

My lips meet Isolde's over Mark's zipper, and we kiss deeply. I find a breast with one hand and palm it as I toil in the cradle of her hips. Her cunt fits me like a glove, snug and narrow and so needy that it clings to me when I pull out. The wet caress of it sends hot, tickling pleasure down my shaft and into my groin; my balls are pulling tight again, and every muscle in my stomach and back and legs is quaking.

"Oh God," I breathe, pulling back to look at Isolde. Her face is so open right now, so unusually open, and I wish I could draw or sculpt or paint or that I could capture the ephemeral on film the way Mark's dead husband did—anything to look at her like this again, whenever I wanted. To see the real Isolde, without her armor and her secrets and her cool insistence that no one get too close, even as you know that she wants nothing more than someone to be close enough to feel her tender, lonely heart.

"I love you," she exhales, and I bend my head into her neck.

"I love you too," I say, the excruciating pleasure clawing at my body, and then, at last, tearing me all the way open. I spill into her with a series of wrenching, jerking spurts, slicking my way even more and making everything immediately wetter and filthier. I feel like a beast fucking into her while she's already turning her head to kiss Mark's erection, but I can't stop. I don't think I can ever stop.

But stop I eventually do, gasping on top of Isolde while she kisses her husband's groin and he strokes her hair.

"Was it good, darling?" he asks her.

"Very good," she mumbles.

"Let's see how much he gave you. Get to your knees, Tristan."

I shakingly manage to obey, my sides heaving and the cool air immediately assailing my wet dick.

Mark shifts to run a thoughtful hand between his wife's legs. Opaline cum gathers immediately on his fingers, and he looks impressed.

"This is so much, puppy. You've been saving up."

I shudder. He knows what this does to me, and he's enjoying it, enjoying the way my half-lidded eyes can't move from his fingers toying with Isolde's cunt. Every flash of light from the window shows more ejaculate spilling and pooling out, coating his finger as he probes deep into her channel. She squirms, sensitive there, but then goes still and breathless as he adds a second finger and enough pressure to counteract the ticklishness.

"You'd think he's never come before," Mark says and shakes his head as if in pity. "We sent him away to a kink club, and he comes back nearly bursting with seed. What should we make of it?"

"I haven't," I whisper. Two sets of blue eyes—one drugged, the other dangerous—find me. "I haven't been with anyone at Armorica."

Isolde blinks. "Not even Isabella?"

"I've only been gone a few weeks," I say with a huff of laughter. "Give me some credit."

"I won't credit you where there would be no debt," Mark

says. "Isolde and I are here together. You are alone. I wouldn't blame you for needing relief."

A small scowl flits over Isolde's lips, but they're so full that the effect is only to make me even more aware of how much I enjoy looking at her mouth.

Mark looks down and laughs. "I see my jealous wife and I are not of the same mind about this."

His fingers are still inside her, and he must do something that I can't see, because she moans.

"I am jealous," she admits. "I want Tristan to ourselves."

"But surely you are jealous of me? Because I enjoy taking my relief inside Tristan very much, and you've seen what it does to him."

"You know very well that's a different kind of jealousy," she protests—and then gives another humming moan as he adds a thumb to her clitoris.

My hard-on, which had never fully abated after pulling out, is kicking back to life. Quickly.

"Yes, yes, because we all love each other. Or hate each other. Or whatever it is that we do. But it doesn't arouse you at least a little to think about him getting so desperate and so full of cum that he just *has* to fuck? That jerking off thinking of you isn't enough anymore, and he can't even think straight until he gets inside someplace warm and tight?"

Isolde's lips are parted, and her eyes have hooded so far that I can only see a glimmer of her stare from under her lashes.

"He might even be thinking of you while he fucks someone else. Wouldn't that be awful and perverse? Closing his eyes and imagining his Isolde underneath him while he strokes into Isabella's lovely pussy? It's a good one, Isolde. I've had it before, although yours is my favorite. Which might make me a predictable sort of husband, I suppose."

"You are the furthest thing from predictable," she

mumbles, hips chasing the wicked touch between her thighs. "Oh *God*."

"I've already told you that *sir* will do. And anyway, God isn't listening right now. He can't hear how you're getting wet all over again from thinking about Tristan fucking someone else. About how he'll be in so much need that he can't help himself, but he'll bitterly regret every drop of cum that goes into someone who isn't you."

"Sir," I grind out, pleading and furious. My hands are gripping my thighs, and my dick is now pointing straight up at the ceiling, fresh arousal pooling at the slit.

"But isn't that right, Tristan? Isn't that what would happen if you used sweet, accommodating Isabella for your private needs? You'd come so hard because you'd need it so badly, but all you'd be able to think about is this cunt right here, about how perfect it looks when it's dripping. This cunt, your seed: worth the wrath of heaven itself. And even if you can't help needing a substitute, you'll be so, *so* miserably aware that it's not enough, it's never enough until you're right...back...here."

With each of his words, he taps two wet fingers against Isolde's clit, wringing three pathetic whimpers from her.

A bead of precum spills over the crested tip of my organ and down over the sensitive frenulum. I pant like I'm being flogged.

"Of course," Mark says, with a clarion sort of malice in his gaze, which immediately terrifies me, "we could make him pine for so much more. Couldn't we, Isolde? He's already besotted, but I think we could make him shame himself with it. Would you like to do that, my queen? Send Tristan away so thoroughly possessed by you that you never have to worry about him fucking anyone else without you foremost in his feverish, obsessed mind?"

Fuck, his words—*his words*. I am panting again, and I haven't even touched myself. I haven't even moved.

Isolde nods frantically. Her feet slide against the table as she twists in abject, wretched lust. "Yes, sir," she says on an exhale that could be a sob.

The *sir* from her slices a small aperture in Mark's sangfroid—he mutters *Jesus Christ* under his breath and scoops her up so quickly that her hair swings below her as he carries her back to the chair.

"Are you going to kneel there dripping onto the table all night?" Mark asks over his shoulder. "Come on then."

I scramble off the table, and then Mark instructs me, with the same offhanded voice he'd use back when I'd serve him after his injury, to take off his trousers.

I do, almost dizzy with déjà vu as I kneel to unbutton his waistband and then tug the zipper all the way open. But of course when I did it before, there was no inflamed wife in his arms, kissing heatedly at his jaw and neck and throat, no blond hair tickling my hands as I carefully worked the trousers down around his hips.

When I stand up, he's fighting off a smile as Isolde attacks him with hard, sucking kisses. "I think she likes this little fantasy I've conjured," he says sotto voce and then says, "Don't worry, dearest. We'll take care of that cunt again. We're going to send Tristan right to St. Peter, and then I'm going to make you scream. How does that sound?"

"It sounds like you're making a sales pitch instead of making good on your promises," she accuses, and that earns one of his rare, true laughs, all the way from his stomach.

"You've got me, pet. I want you nice and amorous before I ask if a certain act is still within your limits."

Isolde lifts a brow into a perfect arch. "My limits are the same."

"So being penetrated anally is still something you're interested in?"

She and I both freeze.

Mark continues. "And being penetrated by two people at the same time? That's still acceptable?"

Isolde looks over at me. I know I'm looking back, but my mind isn't registering any other information right now. All I can think of is Mark's dick nestled tightly in her ass. The feeling of him moving inside her while I'm there too.

"Yes," she says. "Fuck. Yes. I want—that's still acceptable. Sir." The words come out in short stutters. I'm barely upright.

In the next scatter of light from the window, I can clearly see the dark flush on Mark's cheeks.

"Wonderful," he says. The word comes out like it's been dragged over gravel. "Then let me make good on my promises."

He sits in the chair with Isolde in his arms and arranges her so that she's facing him. With the precision of a seasoned assassin, he angles himself with one hand, grips her hip with another, and with a quick movement, she's impaled. Her hands flex on his chest like the paws of a cat caught by a sudden landing; she shivers and her head drops forward.

Mark meets my confused gaze and nods at the small side table next to the chair without breaking eye contact. "Everything you'll need is in there."

"Aren't you...I thought..."

"You thought I was that poor a host? To set the table for a rare delicacy and then make you watch as I took it all for myself?" How he manages to look so disdainful when he's peering *up* at me, I have no idea. It's a skill I've only ever seen displayed by tailors and drill sergeants. "Now, to that drawer. The lube is what we're concerned with at the moment."

With shaking hands, I open the drawer to find lube and a rechargeable wand vibrator. Mark talks me through the next part with the indifferent voice of a bored professor, but I can perceive all the subtle little frayings of his self-control.

The rasp in his voice, the swallow of his throat, the way his hips press ever so slightly up into Isolde as he watches me slick my fingers with lube and step behind Isolde.

"Okay?" I ask her in a murmur, and she looks back at me over her shoulder. Her hair hangs down her back, and it swishes as she looks. Mark—without really meaning to, it seems—reaches up and catches a lock between his fingers.

"Yes," Isolde says. "Just—slowly."

I nod. "Slowly," I promise.

I press a fingertip to the thin skin between her cheeks, painting over the pleated ring with the lubricant, swirling until I find the center, the place where the tight muscles can be made pliant and ready. I drop my head to kiss her shoulder and—standing between Mark's planted feet once again—invade her with tender patience.

She straightens, her head falling forward again, her hips moving a little to accommodate the unfamiliar pressure. She's had her ass played with before, with me and with Mark, but as far as I know, it's only been a finger or two and some slender toys. This is the first time she's gone further, taken something wider and longer, and I want to make sure she's as comfortable as possible.

It's probably a good thing to take my time anyway, because simply the squeeze of her around my finger has me dragging in long, heavy breaths, my hard organ bobbing and seeking.

I slide my finger out to the last knuckle and gently knead at the opening, using my free hand to stroke her arm and shoulder. Mark sweeps her hair over one shoulder so that it hangs in front, giving me the length of her back to caress at my pleasure.

Her breathing is a little jagged as I continue, with every atom of patience my body can muster, to gradually massage the tension away, to make the intrusion feel natural and welcome, to accustom her to the fullness and pressure. And slowly I can feel it, the forgiveness, the tractability. It's easier and easier to move my finger.

Mark, inhumanly observant, cradles Isolde's head in his hands. "That was three easy breaths in a row. Ready for two fingers now?"

She nods at him, and he keeps his hands around her face as I carefully introduce the second finger, taking time to tease and push at the nerve-ridden circlet before sliding a little deeper and crooking there.

A short hiss comes from Mark, and with a frisson of erotic surprise, I realize he can feel the work of my fingers, that I can wring a reaction out of him as well as Isolde. I slide deeper in, to the point where Isolde's body is no longer an airless squeeze but hotter than hellfire and softer than an angel's wings.

I stroke through the silk and feel the implacable column of her husband there. I stroke harder, a small masturbation through his own wife's body.

Mark jerks and then gives me an offended look, like I've just pulled a dirty trick on a playground.

It's Isolde who speaks then, with a quaver of a voice. "Tristan, go easy on him."

Mark briefly licks the bottom of his top teeth, a wicked, satisfied gesture that Isolde misses. I suddenly feel as if I've been scolded by the teacher while the actual instigator stands smugly behind them, unnoticed and unpunished. "Yes, Tristan, go easy on me. I'm an old man, and I can only withstand so much, you know. It would be cruel to taunt me over it."

I shake my head, unable to help the small bubble of happiness in my chest. *This* Mark, this Mark above all others, makes me feel like I've stumbled into a fairy realm and decided to drink the fairy wine and eat the fairy food.

This is the roguish king who could cajole innocent knights into dancing under his hill for centuries, his caprice lined with equal parts playfulness and icy violence.

He can just be so goddamn *charming* sometimes. It's not fair.

"I would never taunt, sir," I say.

"You don't even mean to and you taunt, like a jewel glinting in a case or a spring day outside an office window. Lube yourself up now, more than you think you need. And don't be shy about making a mess. No one's coming to inspect the room and make you run a mile for every unrolled pair of socks."

Isolde turns to watch as I follow Mark's instructions and drizzle lube along the top of my penis, listening to his advice about using more than I think I'd need. God knows I've been on the business end of a lubed-up rod enough times to know that more is always better.

Her lower lip catches between her teeth as her eyes follow the rhythmic shuttle of my hand up and down, up and down. She squirms, fucking herself wantonly on Mark's cock, and he drops his hands to grab her hips.

"A reprieve, sweet one," he says evenly. "I am either going to come right this instant or I am going to forget the entire point of this exercise and attack both of you like a fox around a pair of bold little bunnies, and either way, my plans will be quite disrupted."

She goes still but paws helplessly at his bare chest, fingers twisting in the golden hair there. I can tell it hurts, but it's a fast and vicious smile that passes over his face and not reprobation at all. He slaps her backside hard as I step behind her.

"If you want to spar again, I'm more than willing," he says and nuzzles her throat, inhaling with transparent pleasure. "I like your claws as much as the rest of you, kitten."

She reaches up to slide her hands into his hair, tousling it, tugging on it. "You are all claws and teeth, so it's only fair."

"I wish it were any other way, Isolde. I can swear that to you with my hand on a Bible and a sword at my neck. May God strike me down if it's not true."

I think of the supply closet before I left.

I don't want to be spoken of in whispers.

"I'm happy to be the sword at your neck," she says and runs her hands through his hair again. I know how silky it is, spun gossamer and sunlight. "But you don't have to swear. I wouldn't have you any other way."

"You hate me," he points out. Only curious, not defensive.

"I love hating you and I hate loving you. We are the first day of creation, darkness and waters, a welter and waste."

"I suppose that makes Tristan the light," Mark says, looking past Isolde to me. "Well, don't just observe the vagaries of marriage, sunshine. Let's see what illumination you bring."

There is one thing about loving a married couple that I didn't think of earlier, and that's how it feels to be folded into their dragon's nest, welcomed in from the cold. An open door glowing with light and beckoning the weary traveler inside.

Listening to their combative courting of each other feels like I'm in the courtship too in a strange way. Let into the archives of a museum or the light-controlled cells of a rare books room. It's privileged information, the way the two of them are when they're alone, and I'm being given the honor of learning it.

I drop another kiss on Isolde's shoulder, and then I have to bend my knees a little to get lined up.

"How precious," Mark says, and there's a shift now in the tenor of his corruption. From impish to remorseless.

"Reach back and pull your cheeks apart for Tristan. Yes, just like that, so he can see your hole. Show him what he's about to get, how tight it is. How obscene."

A flurry of lights from the window show me exactly what he's promised—a shining, wet hole, promising suffocation. Vulgar release.

Whenever the lights flash, I can see exactly what I need to see, and I step even closer as I fist my dick, pressing the wide, crude head against the delicate eyelet calling me home.

Just this small amount of contact is enough to grip me by the spine and shake me until my teeth rattle, and I know it must show on my face, because Mark observes, a little coolly, "It's a little early to disgrace yourself, don't you think? At least get inside first."

I would love to snap back, to remind him that just a minute ago, he had to force Isolde to stay still so he wouldn't spend too early either, but my concentration is wholly bent on clenching every muscle in my body, in somehow managing to slowly push forward without howling at the ceiling like a wolf.

"Breathe out," I tell Isolde in a low voice, and she exhales. I slip forward to the second ring of muscle with a grunt, and she lets out a gasp of discomfort.

Mark rubs her thighs. "I know, gorgeous, I know. Want me to help so you can hold on to me instead? Here, here." He replaces her hands with his own, large enough that his splayed fingers nearly reach all the way to where I'm breaching her. She does as he suggests and grabs uselessly at his shoulders and neck and hair, all a fuss. And then my tip pops all the way through the cinch, and the three of us share a single, shattered inhale.

"It's so hot," I mumble. "Fuck. Sir. *How.*"

I don't even know what I'm saying, but Mark seems to understand. "Now you know why I can't get enough when it comes to you," he agrees, the gentle tone he'd just used already melting back into something unearthly and malign. "There's nothing else like it. Tight enough to choke your cock, and then all that smooth heat beyond. Go in deeper. Feel it for yourself."

I slide in another inch or two with some clench-jawed effort, and then I begin to feel him, not just as lack of room but *him*, the unrelenting shape of his desire in her pussy.

"Oh," she breathes, still palming and grasping at him. "I feel both—*oh*."

Mark's hands do their cruel work and part her even more, to the point where every detail is neatly exposed when I look down. The wet pink hole stretched thin around my intrusion. The vein running along the top of my dick. The heavy erection spreading her cunt open below me.

I run soothing hands up her back and down to her waist. I drop clumsy kisses on her shoulder and the nape of her neck. "I'm going to go all the way now," I say. I sound like I'm being strangled.

She nods, and then I press and press and press until I'm fully seated and the three of us are a chorus of cleaved inhales and tormented exhales. Isolde is making a moaning kind of hum, somewhere between pleasure and pain.

"Does it hurt or does it feel good?" asks her husband.

"Yes," she answers weakly. "*Yes*."

I'm still doing my utmost to caress her and lavish her with touch, but time has elongated into one urgent, eternal shiver, and it's exactly as Mark said, an indecent squeeze followed by a velvet cloud made of heat and illicit pleasure, and when I pull out and feel myself dragging along his erection, my knees nearly give out.

"Fuck, oh my God, fuck," I pant. This would already be too much on its own, but with him inside her too, it's fucking deadly, it's the end of me, it's slaughter by fuck, because I don't think I can take another stroke and survive.

But between us, Isolde is shifting, testing, moving in the tiniest ways, her inner muscles clutching and flexing and sliding. There's a mist of sweat along Mark's throat and collarbone now, and the muscles of his chest and stomach are quivering, and I am much the same.

"I'm afraid if movement is what's needed, then it must be you," Mark advises me. His jaw is clenched hard enough that a muscle leaps along the side. "Slow at first. I can help with my hands."

I close my eyes, suck in a breath. I'm going to come, and I'm going to come so quickly that there will be no doubt what fucking Isolde does to me, what it does to me to fuck her at the same time as Mark, to *feel* him, and perhaps that was the point after all. If the flight across the Atlantic, the declarations of love, the nights spent chasing away nightmares, and weathering the storm of Mark's attention—if those aren't sufficient enough on their own to prove that Isolde and Mark are the only obsessions of my sick and besotted heart, then here's this physical proof. I'm undone just from being *inside* her.

But fate has spoken, and I must answer the call. I pull out at a slow, bone-humming pace, savoring the clench of her asshole and the swelter around my tip, the rub of Mark against me, and then push back in. Heat rushes up my thighs, and I have to put a hand briefly to Mark's knee to catch my balance, because consciousness is becoming harder and harder to hold on to.

"I can feel you trying to rub your clit on me, dearest," Mark says to Isolde, still holding her wide open for me to stroke into. "Does it feel good? Do you want more?"

"Yes, more," she hums and leans forward onto his chest. The change in angle makes us both groan. "Breed me there, Tristan. I want to feel it."

Darkness swarms over my vision as the blood rushes from my head and up from my feet, my entire body converted into a damp, trembling clutch of need.

"You heard her," says Mark softly. "Give her more. It's the least you can do with what I'm giving you."

Even inhaling too deeply will make me come at this point, but I'm as unable to resist as I would be if he had me on marionette strings. I clench my stomach and pull out almost to the crown, looking down to see the sight of my erection sliding out of her perfect asshole, and then I push back in again, the ring of pink around my length only visible when the club lights flash the brightest. Mark's hands frame the lewd view, and I can see how each thrust has me rubbing against him, our balls nearly touching whenever I'm all the way seated.

Isolde has begun pressing back against me, meeting my thrusts, and the roll of her ass, the arrogant hands helping her, the taut, muscled cincture that I'm piercing with my own thick need…

That's it, it's over, and somehow Mark knows, because somehow Mark always knows.

"Look at me," he says in a low voice. "Thank me."

I look up and meet his dark, glittering stare. Wordless pleasure, filthy pleasure, the primal sensation of fucking a slick hole—I'm being overridden by my body, overwritten by this blistering, phoenix-like ecstasy.

But his eyes are constant, they're standard candles, fixed points of navigation, and whatever is left of Tristan Thomas in this moment must obey.

"Thank you," I choke out.

"For what?"

"For letting me fuck your wife. For letting me breed her. For letting me fuck her ass. For letting me feel your dick inside her, sir. It feels so good against mine."

A satisfied smile overtakes his features. "You're welcome, puppy."

It was too late before that, but it's the *puppy* hanging in the air that I surrender to, the cataclysm that is his smile and Isolde's low moans and all the slick squeezing and scorching of this intimate place of hers. I buckle as my cock swells and pulses, hard and fast, desperate to breed even as I have to list forward and support myself on Mark's shoulders, my dick jerking in her hole and giving her everything I have left to give.

Mark lets go of Isolde and reaches up to touch my face as I stare helplessly at him, the eruption spurting on and on, unending, dizzying.

I reach up to catch Mark's hand so I can keep it pressed against my jaw. The wedding ring on my ring finger—the ring from a wedding that wasn't mine—flashes. He stares at it a moment, all sorts of emotions moving through his face, and then he brings my hand to his mouth and kisses it.

"You make me so proud, baby," he murmurs. "I'm so pleased with you."

With a grunt, I pulse out the last of my cum, and then I slide free of Isolde and stagger backward into a wall. I want to trap Mark's words in a jar like fireflies.

You make me so proud, baby.

I'm so pleased with you.

Mark eyes me where I'm barely holding myself upright, even with the wall. He stands up with Isolde in his arms, his glistening length pulling free as he carries her over to the table. He deposits her there limply and turns to me.

"Your turn in the cuck chair," he says, tone brooking no disagreement. "Before you collapse."

Somehow I manage to make it over there, and I drop into it like I've run a hundred miles. My heart is pounding, my skin is hot and ruddy, and stinging twitches of pleasure are still coursing through me. A scrim of sparks and gray has been pulled over my vision.

I watch as Mark comes over to the side table and helps himself to the lube and the vibrator. With a few strong, sure movements, he has Isolde at the edge of the table, the wand turned on and buzzing on her clit, and has once again speared himself into her flushed, ardent cunt.

It takes almost no time at all. Her back bows, her limbs thrash, her head tosses on the table. Mark's control is almost gone, I think, entirely threadbare, because he fucks like a lost man brought in from the cold. Her entire body twists and seizes as she calls out his name—*Mark, Sir, Mark*—and Mark lets out an unholy groan as she comes on his dick, going motionless and lifting the wand as if to savor her crude undulations in their purest form.

She gives a long, broken moan, still arching and trying to fuck herself against Mark, and then after a long moment, she finally uncurls and goes quiescent.

Mark slides free and drops a kiss right between her breasts. "Stay," he tells her, like she can do anything else, and then comes to kneel in front of my chair. He presses two fingers to my pulse, studies my face and respiration.

"Can you stand?" he asks.

"Not for long," I say. I sound like I've just been wrenched from a deep and dreamless nap.

He regards me for a moment. The lights from the window paint his golden hair in shades of blue and purple and pink. "What's the difference between a dragon and a wyvern?" he finally asks.

Bemused, I slowly reply, "Dragons have four legs. Wyverns have two."

"What's twenty-three percent of two hundred?"

"Forty-six."

"Dulce et decorum est…"

I inhale deeply, the cool air clearing my head. "…pro patria mori," I finish faintly. It's from one of his favorite poems.

His hand flexes around my wrist. "Good enough," he says, standing up. "And what do you say to stop me?"

I exhale shakily. "Hazel."

He takes my hands and helps me to my feet. I'm as good as my word—I can walk over to the table, but I'm grateful for the support as soon as he bends me over the edge.

"Can I fuck you?" he asks.

Yes. The answer is always yes. Even if I'm wrung out from fucking harder than I've ever fucked before. Even if I'm so sensitive that merely the air on my skin feels vaguely sadistic.

"Always, sir. Forever."

"We can dream, can't we?" he asks wistfully. And then my legs are kicked apart, and my asshole kissed and licked once, fondly. The click of the lube bottle echoes in the room.

As Mark readies himself, I turn and look at Isolde, who is staring at me with a look of soft, open affection. Staring at me like the Isolde she might have been if she'd had a mother who'd never died, a father who really loved her, or an uncle who saw her as something more than a tool.

"You're so beautiful," she murmurs. "Like a painting."

For some reason, that makes my chest ache. She thinks I'm beautiful like a painting; she says it like she'll never have another chance to say it.

Cool, slick fingers work me open as I rest my cheek on the leather table, facing her. I brush the hair away from her temples as Mark pushes a finger all the way inside, and then a second.

She's on her back and I'm on my stomach, and we're close enough to touch each other's lips and eyelids with wonder like Adam and Eve discovering each other in Eden, and it occurs to me as Mark presses the head of his cock against my opening that this is very nearly the same position we were in on the roof in Belgrade. The night our god announced how he'd punish us for tasting the fruit of the forbidden tree. Isolde is wrung out and supine rather than sitting up, and we're not surrounded by rolling fruit and splinters of glass, but it's still very close. There's still that same jealousy, clinging like a winter mist, and there are still secrets strung between our words like pearls on a necklace, and our love is still a tessellation of obsession and misery. But something is different tonight. Perhaps it's that we know that the tessellation *does* add up to love.

Or perhaps it's that we know the correlating and bleak truth: love isn't enough.

Not for us.

But it's still a moment of bliss and peace when Mark brings himself inside me as I stare into Isolde's eyes. When Mark leans forward with one arm sliding under my torso and the other gathering Isolde close. The kind of peace that the Church promises, that I used to think was waiting for me at the end of a storied career in the army. The kind of peace that no one can ever, ever hold on to, no matter how hard they try.

The lingering discomfort of Mark's entry is barely legible to my body as anything unpleasant, I'm that relaxed and dosed with every kind of endorphin—and with Isolde's face so close to mine, with Mark kissing my temple while he squeezes my hip, with the dazzle of lights from the club making everything dreamy and unreal—the coarse pressure of him can only feel beautiful and godlike.

And the pleasure comes as it always does, a questioning curl in my belly, a sidelong graze along my thoughts, tensely braced muscles transmuted to quivering eagerness. Then pleasure is all I am, and peace—and maybe this can be enough. Maybe if the three of us can find our way back to each other, if we can find a way to hold on to each other through the fire and the hail, then peace will be waiting at the end. Not peace like *stillness*, like calm—never that with Mark—but peace like a cold and lustral sea crashing against the rocks, peace like rain at Morois, thunder probing between the trees and rolling over the moors.

"If I could contain what I feel for the two of you," breathes Mark, "if I could even express it, if I could even *shape* it to myself...my God. You have unmade in months what took years to create, and fool that I am, I am letting you."

His grip grows tighter, and the delicious violence of his sex grows erratic and desperate. Raw, urgent sensations overtake me, a brutal euphoria with every thrust, a looming orgasm knotted so viciously around my prostate that I'm surprised I'm not mortally wounded by it.

"Dreamed of this so much when you were gone." The words are a series of serrated grunts. He's fucking the air right out of my lungs and maybe his own lungs too. "Having you bent over just like this. Isolde watching. Breeding—fuck—I—*fuck*."

I think I've already started jetting seed onto the floor—everything below my chest is one vindictive snarl of pleasure, of gorgeously agonizing release—but if I hadn't already, I would merely by listening to Mark chase down his orgasm like a mortal enemy. The table jolts across the floor; he growls and bruises; his cock is splitting me in half, and I want to worship him for it.

With a series of thrusts that would earn him damnation even without the rest of his ledger available to heaven, he swells and then begins pumping me full. Bare and wet and shameless, so fucking shameless, and my mouth is open, my face pressed into the table, and he makes sure to use me all the way through it, pinning me down as he strokes a few times more to milk the last of it into my ass. Pinning me down as if I'd ever voluntarily leave.

And at last, it's finished. The lights scatter over us, and Isolde traces my mouth. Mark is still inside me, draped over me, crushing his wife close.

I can almost hear the sea.

I can almost count the spaces between the waves.

Mark eventually pulls free, furnishes warmed wipes from somewhere, and we're cleaned as carefully and lovingly as the family silver. He helps us upright and checks us over. Aside from the suspension for Isolde, the night hasn't involved anything more kinky than what our bodies can do on their own, but that's never mattered for Mark. Both Isolde and I are as wrecked as we would be after paddles or binder clips or whatever other torments he could conjure.

He finishes and steps back to eye the both of us. Somehow Isolde and I have ended up holding hands. I'm not sure how.

"Bed, I think," he says after a minute. "Let's fight the clock a little longer yet."

So we nestle in bed, the three of us, Isolde in the middle, her head on Mark's chest and my head on her chest. Under the heated blanket, I draw sleepy circles on her abdomen.

For as long as we're there, we don't sleep and we don't speak. What is there to speak about? What can there be to say? Nothing's changed from this morning to tonight—Isolde is still safer at Lyonesse than anywhere else, and she's still safer when I'm away. We can't trust Mark, and he can't trust us, and there are many minutes in the day when I'm not sure if I can trust Isolde either.

But the thing that stitches us together is older and deeper than trust...older than love itself, maybe. I used to believe in fate, in destiny. It was easy to believe when I was the basketball star, the prom king, the favored son of West

Point. Easy to believe when your life is made of trophies and roses blooming on the side of a sturdy white farmhouse, when you wake up to the bleating of lambs in the spring but you're only three stoplights away from a brand-new coffee shop, when you're good at singing and school and push-ups and making people smile. It was only watching McKenzie Reed's heart drain its freshly oxygenated blood right into a puddle that I realized what I'd been calling fate had been a brightly painted backdrop—a lie. A lie that almost grew hilarious when people tried to repeat it to me.

You were meant to be there, someone told me with complete certainty after I shot Sims. *The universe made sure you were.*

But the universe didn't shoot Sims in the throat last year. I did. And it wasn't fate or destiny that killed McKenzie on our first deployment—it was body armor that was designed with a male chest in mind. It was McKenzie's quick reflexes that had her returning fire before the rest of us. It was hasty intel or bad intel or incomplete intel from someone in an office somewhere half a world away from that wet alley in Kraków.

But right now…right now I can almost believe in it. Not the fate of fairy tales but the fate of myth. Inhuman and unyielding. Impossible to deny.

Even through the thick window glass, we hear the hall counting down to midnight, the numbers dropping into the single digits.

"I'd like a kiss," says Mark after the crowd cries *three!* And what argument could there be to that?

Who would want to make it?

We meet at Isolde's mouth, a kiss that's one kiss and three kisses all at once, and there's something so softly awkward and earnest about it that it could be a first kiss, a first kiss for all three of us, fumbling and heartfelt and spontaneous.

We linger there for a breath, for another breath more, as the din from the hall fills the room. The lights outside are frenetic and dazzling, like we're suspended inside lightning itself. Here there's only eternity, sweet and quiet and golden.

It doesn't make fate any less cruel that the three of us can taste eternity on each other, but it does make it so much harder to fight.

When the kiss ends, Isolde says quietly, "Will you promise us something, Mark?"

He looks at her, blue eyes veiled. "Maybe."

"No more lies," she says. "No more secrets. Please. Just… the truth, and all of it, no matter how ugly, because I can endure ugliness, but I don't think I can endure being made apart from you, even if the divide between us is only a few whispered words."

He doesn't hesitate. "No more lies," he says. "I promise." And then he kisses us to seal his vow.

As the kiss breaks, I close my eyes and try to pretend what's coming isn't coming—but even fate can't stop time. When I open my eyes, I see Mark staring at my hands curled between the three of us, like my hands hold the secrets of the universe.

"Isolde and I should go back to the hall," says Mark, though he doesn't sound happy about it. "At least for a few minutes."

Isolde and I don't argue—we both know it's what should happen—and the three of us reluctantly get out of bed and find our clothes. I'm sore inside and out; Isolde's body is still engraved with the memory of the ropes. Mark keeps watching us with a look that would make any rational person feel hunted to extinction.

It's a kind of sin, dressing, leaving each other, but we commit it together, tugging on clothes and running fingers through hair, making our way to the door and pressing the button indicating that this room was recently in use and needs cleaned before the next guest comes in. Mark and Isolde leave first, together, Isolde with one last quick kiss and Mark with a hand around my neck and his forehead pressed to mine. Three hard breaths, and then he lets go.

And then they are gone.

I wait a few minutes and open the door. There is a cloud of people at the far end of the hallway, laughing and chatting around the open door to a playroom, but it's too late; it would be more suspicious to slam the door closed and hide at this point. I send up a flimsy sinner's prayer that they won't notice and slip out of the room. I use the staff elevator to descend a level and then walk down a long hallway to my apartment, suddenly so tired I can barely keep myself moving.

I make it to my door with a pained, pitiful relief, fantasies of falling face-first into bed occupying my mind, which is possibly why it takes me a second longer to notice her than it should.

Isabella Beroul, standing by my window in a gold lingerie set. She's partly turned away, her gloved hands at her sides, and she doesn't look in my direction as I close the door.

"Ms. Beroul," I say quietly, coming to stand a few paces away. "Everything okay?"

"Your door was unlocked," she says to the window.

"It usually is." Lyonesse is generally only accessible to its members, and even if a member broke in here, they wouldn't find anything I'd care about being stolen. Some books, some clothes, a service cross from my first deployment that might as well be a miniature headstone for McKenzie Reed. A thief would be welcome to all of it. "Is there something I can help with, Ms. Beroul?"

She turns a little to face me, her eyes red but dry. Goose bumps pepper her arms and curvy thighs, like she's been standing by the window for a long, long time.

"Hugo's husband has carved out New Year's kisses as one of his privileges," she says with a rueful sort of smile. "And you left early, and I thought maybe you'd need someone to kiss at midnight like me. So I came to find you, where you said you'd be."

"And I wasn't here," I say, understanding.

"Were you with them?" she asks.

I don't want to lie, and she's not whom we need to convince of our lies anyway, but there's something curled in the way she asks, something trying to protect its soft belly. Like an affirmative answer would gut her. And she's been through so fucking much, I can't stand the idea of being the one to hurt her again.

It doesn't matter. My hesitation is all the answer she needs. Pain darts through those wide brown eyes before she gets a chance to duck them down, and she starts to leave.

"Isabella," I say, breaking my own protocol. "I…"

She reaches me and then lifts up on her toes to kiss my cheek.

"It's okay," she says. "I don't know why I let myself hope anyway."

It's after the door closes that my phone buzzes in my pocket—it's Mark, and it's nothing but a picture.

A plume of white smoke under the canopy of a dark Roman sky.

The conclave is over. They've elected the new pope.

twenty-seven

MARK

I WATCH CASHEL ON MY PHONE, COMING TO THE BALCONY overlooking St. Peter's Square and breaking tradition by smiling at them with his vulpine smile, showing off the rakish gap in his teeth and the friendly dimple marked into his cheeks. He waves, he prays. Once, after he speaks, his hand jerks upward, as if to touch the side of his jaw, but he catches himself and drops it back down.

I tap a response to the text I received just an hour ago from the clockmaker in Manhattan. I have a repaired mantel clock waiting for me to pick it up from the shop, according to the message.

"I need to go to the penthouse for a couple days," I tell the table during a late breakfast in the speakeasy the next morning. "I have some business in New York."

"I'll come with you," says Isolde in a polite but firm sort of way that's difficult to quibble with in front of our guests.

"Here might be more comfortable, and it will only be for a short time." Translation: *You'll be safer here, and I'll be back as soon as I can.*

My wife meets my eyes with hers, large and blue-green and unmovable. "I'll be comfortable wherever you are," she says calmly.

"Gosh, I've been wanting to shop in the city for a while," Isabella comments dreamily.

Hugo turns to her and strokes her hand fondly. "There's no reason you couldn't, pet. You don't have appointments at Armorica for another week. I'm sure Tristan wouldn't mind staying with you?"

"I'd be honored to," Tristan affirms.

"I can stay too," offers Kayden. "I know Hugo is eager to get back to Edouard, and since Hugo will be at Armorica anyway, I'm sure he won't mind sparing me for a few days."

"Are you also dreaming of Madison Avenue and ribbon-handled shopping bags?" inquires Hugo, amused.

Kayden gives a handsome pout. "Obviously."

I incline my head, as if I think it's *fabulous* that four extra people are coming to Manhattan when I need to accomplish something incredibly sensitive and tenuous and secret. "There's a hotel next to my building," I tell them. "I'll make the arrangements, and we can leave this afternoon."

_____

The others are settled in their respective hotel rooms, and Isolde and I walk into the penthouse with flurries caught in our hair and Petitcrieu jumping at our heels. We unhook her leash, watching as she tears through the new space, sniffing and sniffing and sniffing, like the leg of every chair and the base of every cabinet hold the sum total of the world's knowledge.

I take Isolde's coat and enjoy the warmth of her through her cashmere sweater dress as my fingers brush against her. A faint blush tinges her cheeks, and I wonder if she's remembering the first night she came here. She'd been armored in every way possible—with clothes, with quiet resistance—and it hadn't mattered. She'd crawled a few feet and tumbled into subspace faster than a stone flung into a pond.

She's still standing in the foyer when I return from hanging her coat in the closet, and I drag the back of my knuckles up her neck.

"I want you to take me upstairs," she says quietly.

"To the loft?"

"Yes."

I nuzzle the spot behind her ear. She smells like heaven—honey and flowers and earth. "Are you sure?"

There are plenty of reasons not to: everything unresolved between us, all the secrets I told her I wasn't keeping anymore. She won't thank me later when she discovers the truth, and my secrets aside, we'll both be missing the shape of Tristan between us. Dispirited from the strange twin to infidelity that is the two of us without him.

But there is one very good reason to take her up to the loft, and that is the lovely curve of her shoulder as framed by the city lights through the window.

I stare at it as she replies, "I'm sure, sir."

Ah, that *sir*. Rarer and rarer but sweeter and sweeter, because I know she means it when she says it.

I am only a man. I take her up to the loft.

———

Two hours later, Isolde is face down in bed with her head pillowed on her arms, her shoulder blades striated in thin, crimson ridges, and her breathing as deep and even as I've ever heard it. I'm sitting on the edge of the mattress and running my fingers over those ridges, trying to bargain with myself.

It can't be wrong if it makes her feel better. It won't matter once I'm gone. What would a little more hurt? et cetera, et cetera—the predictable haggles of a sinner against his sins. But it doesn't matter now. The entire affair will be drawing to a close very soon. Cashel will have his inauguration within the week, and once his pallium and ring are in place, he'll have a week more of audiences, interviews, and administrative undertakings before he turns his eye to his niece or to me. And then the final gambits will start.

I have the florilegium, my great work, but my trust in its usefulness is layered with doubt. Its success would rely on the earnest actions of politicians—some of whom are in the pockets of Ys—and it would depend on a curious and vigorous press. The same press that cheered for me and my fellow soldiers as we boarded planes for Carpathia, that waved away concerns about the instability there, about the infeasibility of us simply popping in, mowing down some baddies, and leaving with a jaunty wave to the tossed flowers and blown kisses of the Carpathians.

I know what I need for my final play, and I know what I have. I need Brittany Hill, and all I *have* is a scribbled list of old books and an address for someone named Regina Springer.

An address and, of course, my new houseguest.

I take Petitcrieu for a quick and chilly walk in the rooftop pet area, deposit her back in bed with Isolde, where she coils neatly in the hollow shaped by Isolde's waist, and then return to the elevator, which I take one floor down after keying in the code.

The elevator doors open to Goran at a kitchen table with a scatter of cards between him and a woman in her early thirties, who is sitting with one leg drawn up to her chest and a vape pen dangling from her hand. Nat is fast asleep on the couch, an arm flung over her eyes and her hoodie rucked up enough to show a knife sheathed at the waist of her utility pants.

"Fuck," concedes Goran with typical military grace. "You fucking got me again." He tosses down his hand, and Cara Sims wastes no time in scraping the bottle caps piled in the middle toward her side.

"Sorry I'm late," I say by way of greeting.

Cara twists to look at me, the *Architectural Digest*–featured chandelier over the table casting every faint line around her eyes and every crease in her lips into unflattering relief. Dark roots have grown into her bottle-red hair, her fingernails are brittle and bitten, and there is a hunted look in the shadows of her cheekbones and under her eyes.

That said, her eyes are feline and quick and sharply lucid. The lackeys of Ys were fools to underestimate her. I know CIA officers who wouldn't have lasted a day with the kind of tail she had, but she'd lasted nearly a year after her brother's failed attempt to kill the Carpathian prime minister elect. And it wasn't even Aaron Sims's botched, blackmail-driven assassination that put Cara in the crosshairs of Ys—it was that he'd made the mistake of *telling* Cara, presumably on a line that Ys was listening to.

I'd wondered why—when Ys seemed so interested in becoming a legend in certain circles—they cared if some dead soldier had told his sister about it. His unconnected, peripatetic sister whom no one would have believed anyway. Why go to the trouble of trying to harass her into silence? Why start chasing her?

It must be that Aaron knew something else, something more. Something beyond the blackmail and illegal weapons.

Or he knew someone who did.

"You must be Mark," Cara says. Her voice is wary, but it's possibly an inborn wariness and not one I've earned outright. I've done my best not to give her any reason to distrust me since Nat and Goran scooped her out of a bus stop near Grand Central Terminal. I made sure they explained thoroughly that we were friends of Tristan and that we knew she wasn't safe. Made sure that even as Goran and Nat kept her here in my apartment, below the one I actually use, she had all the amenities of a cherished guest.

But she would be foolish not to be wary. I applaud her for it.

I walk over and offer my hand. When she thinks it over for a moment and then takes my hand to shake it, I do only that. A firm, reassuring shake—no kiss on the knuckles, no winching myself closer, no knowing smile. She's not a mark or a potential agent or anyone other than the unlucky sister to an even unluckier brother.

"Can we speak for a minute?" I ask, inclining my head toward the loft area.

She glances over at Goran, who gives her a steady look, and then nods. "All right."

Goran makes a show of giving us privacy, clearing up the cards and turning on one of his true crime podcasts.

"Still enjoying your murder shows?" I ask him as Cara stands up and carries her glass into the kitchen.

"I'm waiting for them to cover those poisonings from last year," he says earnestly. "The ones in Tokyo, Vancouver, and DC. We talked about them during one of our meetings, remember?"

I remember.

"Poisoning was the only thing they had in common, Goran," I reply. "People are poisoned all the time, for all sorts of reasons. There was nothing else linking the murders together, not geography, not their jobs—not even the kind of poison."

"There's nothing linking them together *yet*," Goran says with the conviction of a podcast subscriber.

Cara returns from the sink, and I point the way to the stairs. "Let me know if they ever find anything," I tell the former Marine as I leave the kitchen—mostly out of polite interest but a little out of professional interest too. Sometimes an amateur investigator is able to find things authorities would never even think to look for.

Cara and I climb the stairs to the loft, and then I invite her to sit in one of the armchairs facing the night-sparkling city.

"I'm sorry for the ambush at the bus stop," I say as I take a seat myself. "I hope it wasn't too frightening after what you've been through."

She shakes her head. "I was scared at first, but Nat and Goran told me they knew Tristan, and I guess if there's anyone I trust to be a knight in shining armor, it's him. And," she says, glancing around the bookshelf-lined loft with its designer lamps and its multimillion-dollar view, "this is the first time I've ever lain low so high up in the air. It can't be all bad in a place this nice."

"Bad enough if you only have Goran to play cards with or Nat's cooking to eat," I say. "Now, can you tell me everything you know about Aaron's involvement with Ys?"

Cara puts her vape pen to her lips, her eyes downcast when she inhales. When she exhales, the vapor curls around her like steam from one of Tristan's wyverns. "Yes," she says tiredly, and she tells me everything she can.

It is as Tristan had explained in Rome, although in greater detail, and when she's finished, I ask her when she thinks her brother started working for Ys, how she thinks they might have communicated with him, and how much money he was able to send home and how frequently. There are few specifics in her answers but enough to confirm my suspicions that Aaron had fallen prey to Ys sometime the year before last. When I ask if she remembers anything hinting at direct Church involvement—using Church buildings as storehouses or charity missions as cover for moving supplies—she shakes her head.

It's a long shot, but I have to try. "Do the names Regina Springer or Brittany Hill sound familiar at all? Could Aaron have mentioned them to you before your final phone call?"

She takes a hit off her vape pen while she thinks. "I don't think so. Aaron never talked about new girls. It was always the same four or five from the town we grew up in. He was kind of stuck in the past that way. I would remember if he'd mentioned anyone new."

I'm about to thank her for talking to me when she adds, "He never talked about new girls, but there was a priest he talked quite a bit about around his third deployment, the one before his last."

I don't move, listening intently.

"You wanted to know if they were using churches and things for what Aaron was doing, and he never mentioned anything like that, but the deployment before this one, he was closer to the Polish border, and there was this priest there, like *with* them on base, God, what's that called—"

"A chaplain?"

"Right, right. A chaplain, Father Adam. Aaron talked about him kind of the way you'd talk about someone you had a crush on, you know? We're Catholic, but we're pretty laid-back, and Aaron was the laziest of all of us about it. He never wanted to go to church, and he hated dressing up. Wriggled out of everything he could after his confirmation. And then all of a sudden, he's into rosaries and chaplets, and he's wearing two different kinds of scapulars and telling me and Chloe to go to Mass and reconciliation and all this stuff? And you'd think that if his conversion was about mortality or killing people or whatever, it would have happened during his first deployment, but it didn't. It was after he met Father Adam."

"Did he share that deployment with Tristan? Could Tristan have met or seen this Father Adam? Maybe could recognize him now?"

"Tristan wasn't there—Aaron complained about that constantly. He was the kind of friend who needed his buddies around all the time"—a flickering smile—"but I think that's part of why he latched on to Father Adam so hard."

"Did he mention anything about Father Adam being younger...older...anything distinctive?"

Cara's fingers tap idly on the pen. "He mentioned that Father Adam did PT with them, so he probably wasn't older? I guess? But Father Adam was gone by the end of the year. Maybe his chaplain assignment ended, I don't know, and then Aaron abruptly stopped talking about him. Then the religious stuff kind of reversed itself too. He was very cynical at the end."

Arms smuggling will do that. "Do you think there was any relationship between his newfound faith—or the flagging of it—and when he started working for Ys?"

She looks tired all over again. "It's impossible to tell, isn't it? He never mentioned anything like that to me—that he felt compelled to send us extra money out of his newfound Christian duty or whatever—but maybe inside, he felt that way? I don't think it's out of the question, but Aaron was always obsessed with being the man of the family, with providing for us, so it could have been something he did all on his own. Organic Aaron," she adds a little wryly.

My questions exhausted and a new name cataloged—Father Adam—I get to my feet. "Thank you for talking to me. This has been immensely helpful, and you are safe here as long as you want to stay."

"This is the most sleep I've gotten in months. Even with Nat's cooking, this feels like paradise compared to some of the places I've been hiding in."

"Then you're welcome to it. I hope it won't be required for long."

She looks up at me. Dark lashes, sharp eyes. There's a

certain beauty to the hardness of her face. She reminds me a little of Andrea, actually. Flawless marble that's been used for crenelations and arrow slits instead of statues and fountains. "You're going after them, aren't you?" she asks. "Downstairs, they didn't know anything about Ys when I asked, but you know things like you've been trying to know things."

I pause for a moment, my thumb toying with the inside of Tristan's ring. "They killed my husband," I finally say. "Eight years ago. I knew the day I watched them spread dirt over his grave that I was going to make them pay."

Cara doesn't ask anything else. She just sucks on her vape and nods. "Kill the bastards. Kill them twice if you can."

twenty-eight

MARK

THE FOLLOWING EVENING, AFTER MY BODYGUARD HAS escorted Isabella through every glass-fronted temple to consumerism that exists on Fifth Avenue, he comes to the penthouse.

"Ah, Tristan," I say from the kitchen when the elevator doors open and Petitcrieu scrabbles across the hardwood in a flurry of flapping ears and noisy claws. "Thank you for coming. I know you had a long day."

Isolde, who is eating at the kitchen island, betrays nothing of her myriad feelings about Isabella Beroul save for the tiniest hesitation in the movement of her fork. Tristan, for his part, sighs as he shrugs off his wool coat and scarf.

My wool coat, I notice with some pleasure, the one from Morois. I like that he keeps wearing it. I like seeing it on him. I also like the idea of punishing him later for the casual theft of it.

"Is there any dinner left?" he asks as he comes into the kitchen, bending down every other step to pet the dog. He's wearing a black suit with a tie still knotted at his throat, and he starts tugging at it as he drifts to Isolde's side. Little magnets, the two of them. "I'm starving."

I fetch the plate I have warming for him in the oven— seared steak and rosemary-flecked potatoes, the first thing I ever made for him—and then I add some kale salad before setting it in front of him with a fork and knife.

"Are you not eating?" he asks as I go to pour him a glass of wine.

"I already ate," I say. And then I add softly, "It's nice to see you."

He looks up from where he's already started tucking in, a blush spilling from the apples of his cheeks to the neatly trimmed sides of his hair. "You just saw me," he says and looks back down.

"It's been a whole day. It feels like a lifetime." I watch him for a moment longer, the strong jaw, the straight nose, the dark eyebrows and lashes, the full, rosy mouth. My Pre-Raphaelite knight, wrenched into this ugly world. "Tomorrow night, you'll return to Montreal, and then who knows when I'll get to steal you back?"

"It won't be forever," he says with a certainty that I envy.

Isolde's eyes lift to mine and then dip back down. "That's right," she says, soothing in her own quiet way. "Just until this is over."

But I saw the understanding in her gaze. She might not know how I think things will end, what I've planned for, but she knows that there's something underneath the casual way I hedge around the future.

I clean up as Tristan and Isolde finish eating, enjoying this little domestic eye of the storm, even with the thunder that only I can hear rumbling at the edges. Petitcrieu has passed out under their feet, lulled into submission by the occasional rub from an affectionate foot. They murmur to each other between bites: Tristan telling her about his day,

Isolde asking questions about Armorica. Tristan's shucked his suit jacket, and Isolde is barefoot in loose lounge pants and a sweatshirt that hangs off one shoulder. An old Army one of mine that she must have found in the bottom of a drawer somewhere.

Maybe while she was snooping, which is a charming thought. My pretty little spy.

When they're done, I coax Petitcrieu into her crate, clear away their plates and wineglasses, and ask lightly, "Does anyone want to join me upstairs?"

They look at each other and then at me.

"Yes," answers Tristan.

Isolde nods.

They go together, hands linked, Isolde only coming to Tristan's shoulder—though the businesslike muscles of her exposed shoulder keep her from looking like a prototypical damsel.

I do feel like a villain following them, however, chasing them up to my wicked bower and feeling absolutely no shame about it. If this is the last time I get to trap my knight before the world unravels, then I plan on enjoying every last second of it.

Plus I worry about them, my darling playthings. I worry that Tristan is too good and that Isolde is too used to thinking of herself as the hand of God to act on her own. That simply won't do, and I've always known that would be the case, but as with everything else, I thought I had more time.

Tristan and Isolde mount the last step to the loft—I treat myself to a final glance at both their backsides, works of art even beneath trousers and lounge pants—and then I follow them into the open space, which is separated from the penthouse with a glass railing. The rest of the loft is lined with cleverly fitted cabinets and spotted with debauched furnishings: a low leather sofa clearly designed with sex in mind, a leather-upholstered table with a hole in the middle, and a St. Andrew's cross.

I turn on a lamp in the corner and then pad over to one of the cabinets. "Isolde, you'll want to take off your pants. Tristan, why don't you roll up your sleeves?"

I am already quite ready for the evening since I've been planning for it all day, so I'm already barefoot and wearing nothing but sweatpants. I'm not shy when it comes to my many scars, but I am deliberate about when I show them. Tonight, I want to show as much of myself as possible. The skinny ridge and uneven scars under the ink on my forearm, the snarl of scar tissue on my shoulder. The now-healed scratch marks on my chest from an angry cat in Morocco.

I gather the things I need and turn to see Isolde rolling up Tristan's sleeves for him. She's already obeyed my request and stripped from the waist down, but she still wears my sweatshirt, and the overall look is so adorably sexy that it's easy to forget that she left four men bloody and lifeless in a Serbian nightclub only a few months ago.

She finishes with the sleeves as I set everything down, and they both watch me as I approach. I come up behind Isolde and slide her hair away from her shoulder so I can kiss it. Her skin is like silk under my lips.

"Safeword?" I murmur.

"Hyssop," she says, my wife who constantly seeks atonement and who, like King David, probably needs it.

"Hazel," adds Tristan.

And then for the hell of it, I say mine. "Honeysuckle." They look at me, surprised, and I shrug. "It's good for Dominants to have a safeword too."

"You've never used it before," Isolde points out.

"How often am I good?" To illustrate my point, I slide a hand down over Isolde's luscious backside and squeeze until

307

she shivers. "Now, Tristan, you should sit down. Yes, there on the sofa. And, Isolde, allow me to help you onto his lap."

Tristan looks up at me with confusion all over his lovely face. "Um. On *my* lap?"

"Yes, yes, look alive now. There you go, Isolde, exactly there. Good girl." Once Isolde is where I intend, she looks up at me too, a question in her face. I kneel on the floor next to the sofa, where she's braced up on her elbows. "Do you trust me?"

She narrows her eyes. "I think you know the answer to that."

"Do you trust me for the next twenty minutes?"

Her gaze remains doubtful, but a smile pulls at her mouth. "Maybe for the next fifteen."

I brush some hair away from her face, wishing I could etch her features into my memory, wishing there was some way I could promise myself that I'd never forget the sea-colored eyes, the narrow nose, the winged brows, and the delicate jaw.

That I'd never forget the perfectly imperfect parts of her: the slightly overlapping front tooth, the upper lip with no dip in the middle, the haughty cast to her chin. Like God was too excited by his own creation not to rush through the details.

"Do you remember the night after our wedding, at Lyonesse?" I ask, posing the question to Tristan rather than to Isolde. "Do you remember why she said she liked pain?"

Tristan has been stroking the backs of her thighs, completely entranced. His fingers are lingering over the crease behind a knee when he says, "Because she thinks she deserves it."

"You have to be careful with people who think they deserve pain," I say softly, still stroking the hair away from Isolde's face, still looking into her aquamarine eyes. "Because

308

sometimes they don't think they deserve for the pain to stop. Sometimes it feels too good to want to stop. Sometimes it feels so awful that even *wanting* to stop feels like proof that they're the weak and miserable creatures they thought they were. Sometimes they might think they deserve pain so unequivocally that they begin wanting to hurt themselves rather than having someone else do it. Isn't that right, Isolde?"

A pause, and then a small dip of her chin.

"And that's not kink anymore, is it?" I ask kindly.

She closes her eyes. "No," she whispers.

I press my lips to her temple. "No," I echo. And then I look up to Tristan, who's looking down at Isolde with a troubled expression. "When you love someone who feels better with pain, you have to be careful, especially with someone like Isolde, who can handle rather a lot of it. Her body won't lie—you'll be watching her skin, checking her pulse, her responsiveness—and there are ways to make the same amount of pain feel like so much more."

"Like with the trial by iron," comments Tristan quietly.

"Yes," I say, kissing Isolde's temple again before I stand up. I'd rather not talk about the trial by iron. Agony is one thing, but *agony on display* is another—and in front of a callow and vicious audience that doesn't deserve anything like what Isolde gave them that night. "You're going to spank her until her ass is red—not pink but red. You'll hit this spot here too," I add, indicating the crease where her thighs meet her cheeks. "That'll be enough for light bruising. If you really want things to hurt, you'll have her on her feet but bent over clutching her ankles. It'll tense the muscles and give each strike less cushion. Feel free to hold her legs down if she gets too kicky."

Tristan's flush has spilled down his cheeks to his neck, and his lower lip shines from licking it. "I—I don't know. It's not something I've ever imagined doing." He places a wide hand on the small of Isolde's back, right over the twin dimples there. "I know I've hurt you a little before, when you're close to coming, but..."

Isolde twists to look back at him. "It's okay," she says gently. "I want you to."

I don't know that I've ever seen someone as conflicted and also as superhumanly aroused as Tristan Thomas in this moment. His green eyes have gone black, and his shoes are shifting restlessly on the floor.

But his frown and the protective hand on her back speak volumes.

"You can still make her come," I coax. "That's the point of this—her release. And you'll have given her something she needs, given it safely and responsibly. You like taking care of her, right? Serving her? This is just another way to serve."

He runs a hand thoughtfully over the curve of her backside and then gives it an experimental slap. Hard enough to move the flesh, gently enough that I'd consider it more flirting than spanking.

"I just lectured you about safety so you would know there's a difference between being safe and being a fucking gentleman about it. You've seen me with her. You've sparred with her. Give her what she can take."

He pauses, chest moving hard, and then brings his hand down on the other cheek with an air-splitting *crack*.

Isolde makes an involuntary noise, erotic enough that I briefly forget what I'm doing. Tristan is staring at the back of her head in wonder.

"Again, puppy. Harder." My voice is a little rough at the edges now. "You want her red by the end."

He spanks her again and then another time, enthralled by the way her bottom moves with each strike, and then the next time, when Isolde starts wriggling in his lap, he looks up at me with a helpless expression that I could

310

commission a hundred oil paintings of and never get tired of looking at.

"I could have told you there were advantages to not being a gentleman if you'd only asked," I say with some amusement. "Get the spot at the top of her thighs a few times, and then give her a little reward. Your choice."

"A reward," Tristan says, mostly to himself, and I can tell he likes the idea. He would. He's not a natural sadist any more than I'm an angel, and pain will always make the most sense to him with pleasure wrapped around it. It's not a bad thing. It gives me hope that he'll take care with her, rather than a demon like me, who will always be drawn to the furthest edge of a person's soul.

He delivers four quick smacks to the sensitive creases below her ass, and while she's still squirming in his lap, he reaches between her legs and cups all the needy flesh there. She squirms even harder but with a goal in mind, chasing the friction. He lets her go at it for a moment or two, and then with excellent instincts, he pulls his hand free just as she gets a little too keen. She goes motionless, save for a shiver of frustration that she can't seem to suppress.

"Well done," I tell Tristan, and he tucks his lower lip under his teeth and nods, like he doesn't trust himself to speak.

He repeats this pattern a few times—hard swats, followed by caresses between her thighs that have her wriggling in an entirely different way—and then seeing the effects of his labor, he warms to his task admirably, varying the depth and power of his strikes, soothing over the red splotches he's made and running pleased fingers under her sweatshirt to stroke her waist and spine. I watch from above, idly rolling my palm against the front of my sweatpants, enjoying both the power of Tristan's arm and the glimpses of needy cunt that appear every time Isolde squirms. I watch his hands a moment more, hands that are so lovely and yet have done such violence. It is a small corruption in my soul that I can adore them as much as I do.

She's crying out with every swat now, her legs starting to kick up reflexively. "Don't let her kick," I advise. "Use your leg if you can't use an arm—good, yes, exactly."

Tristan has hooked one leg over both of hers now so that she's pinned behind her knees but still bent over his other leg, and then he delivers a flurry of spanks that would have any seasoned spanko beaming with joy. I take in the shade of red on her skin—bright, not yet magenta—and then squat down so I can see her face.

When I push the hair away and tuck it behind her ear, I see tears caught in her eyelashes like dew. They haven't fallen yet, so they're new, but the rest of her is a mess. Hair is caught in her mouth, the tip of her nose is as red as her ass, and there's a little glisten of drool on the leather cushion where she's been rolling her face.

Perfect.

I narrate this to Tristan and tell him to give her two or three more as a nice little coda. They have the effect of spanking the tears right out of her; they drop fatly onto the sofa, as audible as raindrops.

The last spank earns us a guttural moan, and Tristan and I make eye contact. His sides are heaving, sweat gleaming in the notch below his throat, an outrageous erection tenting his trousers. I reach into the waistband of my sweatpants and give my own dick a few quick jerks as I watch Isolde panting with her red backside up in the air. Her loose sweatshirt has worked its way up enough that I can see the curve of her left breast.

"Such a good girl, wouldn't you agree, Tristan?" I let go of myself so I can use both hands to cradle her sweaty, tear-stained face.

"Yes," answers Tristan hoarsely.

"I think we should give her a real reward now."

Tristan groans and then moves his leg so that hers are free again. She doesn't take advantage of her new freedom, just lying limp across his lap until he starts toying with her pussy. I can't see what he's doing, but I can hear it, how wet everything is, and I can see the effect on Isolde. With slow, dazed shudders, her body starts chasing his touch.

"Show me how wet she is," I demand, and Tristan complies immediately, holding up two glossy fingers. "Taste her," I add, and he closes his eyes with pleasure as he licks his fingers clean. I pull in as deep a breath as I can manage, searching for some shred of control.

It's not about me—*yet*. I want to give them this.

"Her clit now." I go back to looking at Isolde, nuzzling my nose against hers. "It'll be easier if you slide your hand underneath her hip. Yes, like that. And then you can use the fingers of your left hand to give her something to come around."

Her breath stutters and falls out of her like she's never exhaled before in her life, and when Tristan starts fingering her in earnest, she turns into a beautiful spread of quivering muscle and poppy-red skin.

"Will you come for him?" I ask her in a murmur. "Will you show him that he was such a good boy for spanking you?"

She nods frantically, her mouth parted in a desperate kind of need, and I can see a sliver of pink past the white line of her teeth. What I wouldn't give to stand up and push my erection past those flushed lips, to rub against her soft, slick tongue.

Just a little longer. Them first, them first.

Tristan, sweetheart that he is, seems unbearably close to losing it in his pants while Isolde soaks his hand and shame-lessly tries to fuck herself on his fingers.

"You're making us so hard, darling," I tell Isolde, pressing

313

my forehead to hers. "You're so good. Tristan can't stand it, how good you are. Can you let Tristan give this to you? Can you show him how grateful you are?"

She nods against me, gasping, and her lashes flutter to her cheeks as a soundless scream freezes her chest. Then several deep, pulsing quivers ripple through her body, down to the soles of her feet and out to the ends of her twitching fingers. When she finally finds her voice, it's with a sharp wail, a swear word, Tristan's name.

Tristan watches with a rapt and hungry expression, his eyes fixed to where his fingers are still wedging her open, his legs more and more restless under her body. As she goes limp once again, I kiss her warm, damp mouth and then her temple.

"Beautiful girl. You should see Tristan now. He's not even lucid after watching that. Take a deep breath. There. And another."

Tristan is licking his fingers clean, still staring at her cunt.

I move my mouth to her ear. "I think you could return the favor if you wanted, you know."

She has her head on her arms now. "With a spanking?" she asks in a mumble.

"I do think he'd like that, but I have something else in mind. Do you remember when you first came to the penthouse, years ago, and I told you what the hole in that table was for?"

Her eyes slide open, suddenly much more awake. "You want him to…"

I nip at her ear. "I want you to do it to him. I'll show you how. Don't worry."

She inhales at the pressure on her abused bottom when I help her sit up. Tristan shifts, as if in a sweetly ironic protest at her feeling any kind of pain, but I shake my head.

314

"We'll spoil her in a minute. But right now, you need to get undressed."

He glances between Isolde's flushed face and mine before he reaches down to unlace his shoes and pull off his socks. He stands, and his hands are shaking as they move to unbutton his shirt, so I step in and help, enjoying immensely the uneven movements of his chest, the sweat on his throat, the rapid flick of his bright green eyes. Like he senses danger but can't tell which direction it's coming from.

Astute of him, because as I unbutton his shirt, Isolde presses herself against his back and starts unfastening his trousers so that he's now pinned in place by people intent on stripping him naked. She struggles a little to tug the zipper pull all the way open, and I tut as I watch her struggle.

"That's so embarrassing for you, puppy. You're so hard she can't even get your zipper down. What are we going to do about that?"

Tristan's head falls backward when I reach into his pants to trap his erection flat to his stomach so Isolde can finish. I go back to his shirt, working open the final three buttons until I can slide the entire thing off his shoulders and tug it free with Isolde's help.

His chest and shoulders are beautiful, muscled and smooth, and his stomach is sleek and firm. The dark hair on his chest—and the hair leading from his navel down—could be painted on, it's that graceful and pleasing. I have a rueful moment where I think of my own body, scarred and marked, and compare it to his unblemished form. Clearly God couldn't bear to mar one of his loveliest creations, even through a literal war, an armed incursion into our club, and a love affair with the same assassin who once sliced her ambivalence into my neck.

After we have his clothes off, I find Isolde's hand and wrap it around the stiff organ currently bobbing between

Tristan's hips. "Lead him over to the table," I tell her. "You can probably guess how we want him once he gets there."

Tristan may need some coaching when it comes to spanking, but Isolde needs almost no guidance when it comes to topping. I can see the momentary hesitation—a mere instant's worth—once I step back and she realizes she's meant to pull our bodyguard over to the table by his cock. But Tristan in his hyperoxygenated haze certainly doesn't notice, and she quickly converts her always regal bearing into something lofty and heartless, so that by the time she's pulling him forward, she looks like she's made a storied career of leading people around by their dicks.

It creeps up on me, almost sinister in its obviousness, how much I enjoy watching the two of them together. How much I enjoy the distance of it even, getting to take in the entire picture of her slender hand wrapped around his ruddy flesh, the dramatic difference in their heights, how Tristan stares down at Isolde with an unsteady expression, eyes lost, lips parted. A man who's just realized he'll let someone lead him straight into a pit of fire and he won't do anything to stop it.

I am jealous still, eternally fighting off the itch of anger under my skin when I think about this torch they've been carrying since the yacht. But it's also something profoundly erotic to see them together, to see both these restless, radiant spirits try to sate their restlessness with each other.

It's inarguable: I love watching them love each other. A small gift, and one I didn't plan on, but I'm grateful for it anyway…even if tonight might be the last time I get to enjoy it.

Tristan mounts the table—I'm teased with a flashing view of the eyelet between the curved muscles of his backside—and Isolde manages with casual grace to keep hold of his cock the entire time, guiding it right through the hole in the middle until she has to let go. She looks over at me, and I silently tilt my head at the cuffs dangling from the corners of the bed. Scarlet blooms anew on her chest as she starts cuffing Tristan's ankles, and I wonder if she's thinking of the time that I cuffed her to this very table, years ago. I know I'm thinking of it. It had strained every ounce of my control to have her bound in front of me, a flogger in my hand, and to keep things purely instructive. To explain the difference between suede and oiled leather when all I wanted to do was crawl on top of her and coax her lips open and taste her. Make out until we were both panting. Bite her pretty breasts until she begged for mercy.

Isolde cuffs Tristan's wrists now, and I amuse myself by bracing an arm on the table and then ducking my head underneath to watch his cock bob uselessly through the hole. A gossamer string of precum leaks from his tip and drops to the floor when his erection gives a sudden jerk. I reach out and give him a light tug, enjoying very much the pained groan from above the table.

"Come down here, Isolde," I call.

Isolde drops lightly to her knees and crawls under the table, a wicked gleam in her eyes as she beholds the genius of the milking table, the humiliation of it and the specificity of its torture. Tristan can't pull away as Isolde gives the under-side of his erection a pensive flick; he can't thrust into her hand as she grips the head. His shameful need is on indis-putable display—the twisting blue veins, the flushed skin stretched tight, the vulgar fluid beading at the crown. The table has reduced all his desire, all his vitality and strength and attention, to the swollen penis jerking pitifully through the table's hole.

Isolde is enthralled. She needs no coaxing from me when it comes to caressing and stroking and then stopping the moment he gets too close; she makes me laugh when she

317

finds her own little mean streak and flicks him again, when she runs her nails down his length, lightly but certainly *memorably*.

There is one thing I do want to see though. "Use your mouth. See how needy you can make him with it."

Tristan moans—it's unclear if it's a moan of *yes* or *no*. This sparks a grin from Isolde, and she meets my gaze under the table, both of us partners in cruel crime. "He's so wet," she murmurs as she scooches closer, angling just underneath the thick organ and touching her tongue to the end.

Tristan jolts, the table shaking, a heart-stopping shock via soft, pink tongue.

"I know," I murmur. She's swirling her tongue around Tristan's slippery crown now, lapping at the slit, and I am very close to having her crawl over here and service me as well. "He always gets wet like that. He's such a little slut. Aren't you, Tristan?"

I straighten up so I can thread my fingers through his hair and tug. His head is turned to the side and facing me, so he can't lift it much, but I do get to see the mindless expression on his face when he says, "Yes, sir."

"*Yes, sir* what?"

"I am a little slut," he confesses breathlessly. "I love being slutty for you. I—*oh shit*—" He groans as Isolde does something unseen, and I take mercy on him and let go of his hair so he can rest his head on the table.

I stroke down his bunched arms and tensed shoulders, follow the valley of his spine to the muscled cleft and then down below that to his scrotum, tightly bunched and ready to unload. But Isolde isn't letting him get any closer than the edge—she'll jack him hard and fast or suck on the tip of him like a lollipop, but the instant his grunts shift into moans, she lets go, pulls back, and leaves him to writhe as much as he possibly can face down on the table. Which isn't much.

After caressing Tristan's thighs for a few minutes, I join Isolde under the table, sitting, since I'm too tall on my knees.

"Take more of him into your mouth. Let him feel your throat."

She does it right away, her pink lips stretching around him, the top of her throat flexing.

"Swallow," I say softly, and she does, the movement compressing her throat around him. Limbs flail above us, and I hear bitten-off curses. Isolde pulls off just in time to arrest his climax, and we both watch as his erection swells and judders and leaks. And then, once the swearing stops above us, I nudge Isolde aside and take him in my own mouth.

The skin of his organ is thin and silky and scorching, and I taste the salt of his precum as I give him a long slide all the way into my throat. I do it again and again, several torturously paced movements, swallowing against him every time, until I feel him reach the final, angry swelling just before release.

Then I back off and laugh when I hear more twisting and scrabbling on the table above. Isolde laughs too, and I pull her into a quick, happy kiss, open-mouthed and smiling. I guide our kiss closer to Tristan, break away from her mouth so I can lick at him and then kiss her and then kiss her with the tip of his cock between our open mouths.

He's begging from above us now, truly begging, his sanity clearly on the line, and finally, I decide on mercy.

"Let's drain him dry, darling," I say, kissing Isolde's cheek, and she sets herself to the task with ruthless delight, wrapping both hands around him one above the other and then jerking him hard and fast. It's brutally efficient, and the onset of the orgasm must be overwhelming, because Tristan has begun grunting and pulling at his cuffs, like he's trying to escape or like he's trying to press himself through the table, maybe both at the same time.

I crawl out from under the table and stand up so that I can play with him. I palm his flexed ass and lean down by his ear. "Can you come for us now? Can you show Isolde how much you can give? Because you like doing that, don't you, showing off how much that big cock can leave inside someone? How good you'd be if only someone would let you inside—"

He shudders, groans, and then his entire body is a quivering, rolling, seeking mess. I hear a pleased noise and lower my head to watch as Isolde works rope after rope of cum onto the floor. His cock pulses in her hands, jolting with each spurt, and there's enough fluid that we can hear when his ejaculate hits the hardwood.

It goes on and on, Isolde milking him with admirable relentlessness, an alabaster puddle growing underneath him, the cuffs clicking and clanking as the orgasm tears him limb from limb.

Finally, the spurts grow further apart, smaller, until they're just a few drops, and then after a dry aftershock or two, he's finished.

I straighten up and kiss behind his ear. "Good boy," I croon, licking where I just kissed. "You gave up so much. You like being milked, don't you? You like showing off for us like a stud at a show. I'll tell her to put something inside you next time. Then you'll give us even more, so much that you'll be empty for days and days."

Isolde crawls out from under the table while I'm working on the cuffs around his wrists, and she starts on his ankles. Once he's free, I check his circulation and then help him roll over so I can check his cock and balls for any discoloration or loss of sensation. He curls up like a shrimp when I test the feeling in his dick by running my fingertips along the underside.

"*Ahhhh,*" whimpers our brave, decorated hero.

Isolde, whose ass is still glowing bright red, doesn't look very impressed by his fortitude.

"Get him into bed, and then water for yourself and him," I direct. "I'll be right in."

She takes his hand to induce him off the table and into my bedroom, which is right off the loft. Once I hear water running from the bathroom, I get some cleaning supplies, take care of the cum puddle under the table, and wipe down the leather.

By the time I join them, they're both tucked in, Isolde's head pillowed on Tristan's chest and her hair spilled everywhere, on his shoulder and across his throat and all over my pillow. I don't climb into bed with them right away—I watch them a moment instead, and they watch me, the three of us caught in a quiet tide where nothing needs spoken, nothing needs saved or studied or solved.

They are so beautiful together, my two beloveds, one dark-haired, one fair, both with full mouths and doll-lashed eyes. They look so *right* holding each other, as if they were sculpted this way and only chiseled apart at the very last moment, and I try to take comfort in it, even as it scalds the inside of my mind with envy.

But I've always known I wasn't sculpted alongside anyone else, that I wasn't made to fit against anyone else—that I don't deserve something as gentle or noble as that.

I don't believe in fate, but this, I think, is ordained: I was meant to live alone. I'm meant to die alone.

But I'll have tonight, if nothing else.

I approach the bed, padding silently to the edge.

"More?" Isolde asks, watching me.

"I should think so, Mrs. Trevena," I reply. I pull the sweatpants off, leave them abandoned on the floor, and then go to my bedside table for lube and a small towel. They watch the bottle of lube with wary interest as I set it and the towel on the bed—and then their stares move to my naked body.

321

Tristan's tongue grazes his bottom lip, and my cock lifts in response. There was a time—unbearably short-lived from my perspective—when I had his mouth available for my use every moment of every day. Under my desk while I worked, at night while I relaxed in the shower, in the back seat of my car while I caught up on the news.

What the hell? It wasn't the plan, but just a minute won't hurt. I move onto the bed and kneel in front of my matched set of lovers. Isolde is between me and Tristan, but she's shifted so that her back is pressed against his chest and she can face me. She's moved down just a touch, enough that her ass is tucked against Tristan's lap and that I have access to Tristan's mouth.

"Keep his hands down," I tell Isolde and then delight in her mean genius as she presses one of Tristan's hands against her breast and guides the other between her legs. His hands curl possessively over the soft flesh on offer.

I couldn't have restrained him better with a neoprene sleep sack.

His lips are already parted for me, and I guide the end of my dick into his mouth, sighing at the first exploratory flick of his tongue.

Fuck. That's more like it.

I reach for his head, his short hair tickling my palm as I hold it in place, and I flex my hips to push in deeper, deep enough that his lips are stretched and the full velvet length of his tongue is pressed against the side of my erection. "God, you're so good," I say, rocking a little deeper, just so that I nudge the very back of him. The angle is a mess; I'm sideways and at my widest like this, and there's no way for him to use any real skill right now, no way for him to work his tongue or open his throat, but I think I love it all the more for that reason. It's just raw biology now: hard cock, willing mouth, and some things don't need the seasoning of experience, truly. Some things are perfect just as they are.

I move in and out a few more times, going as deep as the position will allow and feeling his hot throat close defensively around me. I want to hang on to this until I can't hang on to anything else: his too-short hair, his eager tongue, the tiny muscles fluttering along the delicate depression of his temple. When I pull out and he looks up at me with a mindless need all while his hips pump restlessly against Isolde—that moment I memorize too.

I grab the lube bottle and then find Isolde's hand, tugging her away from Tristan. "I need your help," I implore with a smile.

Confusion draws a neat little line between her eyebrows as I hand her the lube.

I clarify: "Put him on his back, and slick up that lovely cock for me. I'm going to put it to good use."

Isolde does as she's asked, pushing a hesitant Tristan on his back and dispensing lube into her palm.

Tristan lifts his head as if to ask a question but then drops it back onto the pillow the moment Isolde's slippery hand makes contact. His toes curl, a little at first, and then all the way to his soles as she makes a fist around him. She's good at this though, so good at reading his pleasure, at backing off before it can fully take root. She has him slick and shining with just a few pumps of her fist, and when she's done, she lets go. His cock smacks wetly against his stomach and then lifts a little again, hard enough to go seeking sensation.

"Is it my turn, sir?" she asks, and it occurs to me that she assumes that she'll be taking Tristan's cock inside her next, that this will be a repeat of New Year's Eve.

"We're going to try something different," I say. I find the lube and squirt a liberal amount onto her fingertips. "It's my turn, actually."

323

She doesn't move, as if she doesn't believe me, her eyes narrowed ever so slightly.

"It's not a trick, I promise." I take her hand and guide it between my thighs, making sure to spread my knees farther apart so that she can reach where I want her. I press my fingers against hers, sliding them just...*there*...and pushing one of her fingers against my rim. I exhale as she breaches me, and Tristan exhales too, his eyes avid on where her hand disappears between my legs. "That's it," I tell her as she works more lubricant inside. I make eye contact with Tristan when I say, "Make it so he can glide right in."

No one needs to be touching him for his toes to curl this time.

I smile with one of the slow smiles that I know he finds particularly bewitching and watch as his arousal bobs into the air again. "Would you like that, puppy?" I croon. "To fuck me? For me to ride you until I come?"

For her part, Isolde seems unbearably turned on while she fingers me, her nipples furled tight and her breathing fast as she plays with the muscled opening and explores inside. My erection flexes between us, very interested in what's happening, and I drop my head backward when she adds a second finger, my stomach shuddering right above her curious touch. It's been so long, since Eliot, and I've forgotten how it feels, vulnerable and honest and obscene. I've forgotten the immediate fever of it, the goose bumps, the clammy sweat. The heat and gravity of a newborn star cradled deep in my pelvis.

"That's enough," I grunt. "Hold him up for me."

Tristan's eyes are pressed shut, like watching will kill him, and even Isolde looks like I could knock her over with a feather when I swing a leg over his hips and reach down to wrap my hand around hers. Together, we hold him straight while I lower myself. Until I feel the hot, plush tip of him at the gates.

Fuck, it's a lot, and I know it'll be a long slide down to the bottom. Even lubed up and teased open, I can feel the resistance, the bracing against it, and the deep tongues of pain licking from where we're pressed together.

But even though it's been eight years, it would take a lifetime to forget my best party trick. I take a deep breath, embrace the sweet bite of anguish, and bear down. My hole opens, and I impale myself with one swift, slick glide.

Tristan sounds like he's been shot underneath me, and my own ragged breathing isn't much better. I'm straddling his hips, my hands flexing instinctively at his stomach as I shiver my way through the shock of having that massive thing tunneling into me, and air is hard to come by, impossible to draw all the way into my lungs. The aching organ resting against his abdomen is now tumescent to the point of pain. I can feel my heartbeat in the shiny, flared tip resting above his navel.

"Sir," Tristan breathes, eyes still closed. "I can't last. Please, I can't do it. I'm going to come."

I drag my hands up his quivering stomach and chest, back down again. I reach behind me to feel the hard, trembling muscles of his thighs. "You'll last," I say. The words are taut, strung as tight as I am. "You'll last for me. Won't you? Long enough for me to take what I need?"

He nods miserably, twisting his head on the pillow. I can see every cord of his neck, every vein near his temple.

"Good, baby. Now your job is to stay still and let me use that nice dick of yours."

Isolde is kneeling next to us, the crumpled hand towel by one delicate foot, her mussed hair covering her breasts and her hands in knotted fists on the tops of her thighs, like not touching us right now is taking all her strength.

I take pity. "You can touch him if you'd like. If you think he can stand it."

325

She wastes no time, moving right next to Tristan and passing her hands over his chest and shoulders and arms. It's not for him, this touching. It's for her, for her pleasure, and who can blame her? He's irresistible, an intoxicating combination of primal human power and hopeless acquiescence, particularly tempting to monsters like Isolde and me.

(I don't blame myself either, in case you were wondering.)

I lift a little experimentally and sink back down again, shifting, leaning and tilting, bracing my hands on his stomach until I find the angle I want. It only takes a few seconds for that long-forgotten shock of bliss to arc through me. I shudder and fuck myself back on Tristan to feel it again.

"God, puppy," I mumble. "That's so good. You feel so good right there."

Letting him inside my body seems to be some kind of torture beyond anything held inside Lyonesse's armory, because Tristan is barely breathing now, the skin around his lips white with strain and every sinew beneath me stretched as if he's on a medieval rack. Isolde is captivated by this, her hands tracing over his tight tendons and bulging veins, her lower lip pulled into her mouth. Her eyes stray to where we're joined, over and over again, and I move a hand between her thighs to see if her clit is swollen again.

It is, a firm pearl, needing only a graze of my fingertip to wring a whimper from her lips.

Ah, why not? Why not indulge every depraved fantasy I've had since I hired Tristan? I grab Isolde by the waist and lift her—the added weight driving me down hard onto Tristan and making us both grunt—and then set her down on Tristan's stomach and push her back. Her legs fall open on either side of ours, and her back is pressed to Tristan's chest, her head next to his on the pillow.

I look down and run my thumbs along the soft crease between her sex and her thighs. When I press my thumbs into the middle, she glistens. As pretty as morning dew on a flower.

She parts her legs even more, trying to lift her hips and mostly failing since the surface she's lying on is comprised of strained-and-panting Tristan. I smack her clit once, not in admonishment but just because I like watching the pain sparkle and dance all over her skin. I like seeing that haunted look in her eyes, the one that says *how did you know?* And then I anchor her with a hand on her hip, while my other hand lines everything up, the indecent length of me with the hole I dream of at night.

That first press of hot flesh on flesh is enough to make my control waver. With my bodyguard wedged against my prostate and my wife spread out like an unspoiled feast in front of me, I don't know that I'll make it any further.

I want this though, enough to fight off the fevered need shivering up my cock and stabbing deep into my belly, and I push myself in so that the entire head is squeezed tight in her channel.

The small movements of Tristan breathing underneath her are enough to make me rock in and out of her, only by the barest degrees but enough for me to appreciate the shine she leaves on my dick every time it slides farther out.

I gather some of that shine onto the pad of my thumb, press it against the sensitive knot above her pussy, and rub until she's squirming, until she's inadvertently taking more and more as she seeks the pressure of my touch. Finally, my self-control ends. I'm halfway into her cunt, a dark and ruinous rapture is building around where I'm speared on Tristan's body, and I'm so very aware of the glittering night slipping away from us, of the entire world pressing in at the glass walls of my home. Of Tristan's plane ticket to Montreal and of Cashel's new ring.

Now is all we have.

I take Isolde by the hips and drag her down, all the way down, so that I spread her open, so that her thighs are draped over mine. The wet welcome of her pussy is worth fighting wars over, absolute proof that the story of Troy and Helen makes complete sense. I would raze cities and defy gods to feel this again.

I rock into her—I can't manage a real thrust, not like this—and it makes Tristan rub along the inside of me, a euphoric slide both inside and out. I move again, resting the palm of my hand over her sternum, essentially pinning them both in place while I use them to make myself come.

"I'm obsessed with your cunt," I mutter to my wife, moving harder now, my dick fisted almost entirely by her tight, velvet channel as I rock between her and Tristan. "I think about it all the time. How wet it is. How tight. How hot it feels on the inside." I lean forward, just a little, just enough that every time I go deeper, her clit is massaged by my body. "I can't blame Tristan for wanting it. I want it too. Even if it belonged to someone else, I would still be consumed by it. How many times have I made you ride my lap at Lyonesse because it's the only thing on my mind? Not managing the club or wooing new members, no, it's that soft, tight opening between your legs, under your little dresses, always so available in the hall, right there for me to see and touch. You can't begin to understand how I missed it when you were gone. I missed looking at it, kissing it, eating it. Filling it with my cum."

At the last part, Tristan makes a broken, whimpering noise.

"It's okay," I soothe him. "It's okay. I knew you were taking care of it for me, weren't you? Petting it and pleasing it. Making sure it was dripping with seed every day."

Tristan gasps and finally opens his eyes, a man determined to see his murderer's face before he takes his last breath. Isolde turns her head to his, not quite able to kiss him but something like it, and he makes a pathetic noise.

"I can't hold on. It feels too good, please, sir—"

"Shh. We have this pretty cunt to fill up first, don't we? You can last a little bit longer, can't you, Tristan? For me?"

I move my hand to cup his face, and his lashes flutter a little, although his eyes stay open this time. He watches me with terror and worship both, a look that sinks right to the fucked-up core of me, twisting ecstasy around all the pleasure I'm already taking.

"I thought so," I say softly. "You know, I've said that touching is earned... Would you both like to touch me now? I think you've earned it. I think you're earning it by being so very good for me tonight."

My wife reaches for me right away, grazes her fingertips over the tattooed words on my hip and the scars flecking my stomach and chest. But for his part, Tristan is a man spellbound, slowly lifting his hands to slide up my thighs.

I suck in a breath, watching their movements, reminding myself that he's touched me before, inadvertently, casually, while he helped me dress or shower after I was stabbed. This shouldn't feel like getting stabbed all over again. This shouldn't feel so fucking wonderful that I want to hate myself forever.

And yet it does—and it's this tender and wondering petting that breaks me.

Yes, the beautiful cock splitting me open, and yes, that wet cunt gripping my dick, but their hands on me, their curiosity and their love and their lust spilling over in even the lightest brushes of their palms—it's an entirely new kink, an undiscovered shore. My head falls forward, a few locks of hair falling free, my heart pounding beyond what I think it can medically bear. They pet me and I fuck with urgent, snapping rolls of my hips. I circle Isolde's clitoris with my thumb, and I am so hard inside my wife, harder than I've ever been, and when Isolde's hands go still on my stomach and her eyes catch mine, I know she's tumbling over, and I know she's going to take me with her.

Her cry has Tristan and I both coming undone, and I start fucking her cunt as hard as I can right as her orgasm has her inner muscles rippling delicately along my length. She doesn't look away, and neither do I, and Tristan is looking up at me too, a desperate, apologetic look in his eyes.

"I'm sorry, sir," he mutters, and I think he's apologizing because he's about to come, but then his hips move underneath me, a jerky, half-involuntary thrust, and I realize he's apologizing because he can't stay still any longer. He has to fuck.

And I should scold him for it, I should punish him somehow, but his face is so exquisite like this, with the incessant, biological drive to rut and breed, and his need to be good for me. And each desperate thrust has him stroking my prostate with a pressure and a rhythm that would have even a seasoned hedonist giving it up within minutes.

I pant, I grab Isolde's hips, I breathe both their names—*Tristan, Isolde*—and then it's yanking at me, rushing up from nowhere, a cruel and gnawing ecstasy that I won't survive. It's a surging crest of heaven, inevitable and elemental and profane, and when it finally breaks, I go plunging under, tumbled and wrenched by the sheer force of my release. Tristan keeps going, like he's truly unable to stop, and each thrust of his has me sliding deeper into my wife, and I'm pumping her full, spilling with heavy pulses, each contraction harder and better than the last, and I don't remember the last time that I managed to drag in a real breath. Sparks fly at the edges of my vision as my body gives the two of them every last bit of me there is.

I'm still ejaculating—weakly, irregularly now—and

I grab Tristan's hand to guide him to where I'm spending inside Isolde, so that when I pull free, he can see the milky fluid overflowing and running down my still-wet cock. I press his fingers to Isolde's cunt and watch him slowly apprehend that he's feeling my cum inside her.

"Oh God," he says. It's a prayer and a lament at the same time. "*Oh my God.*"

I'm sensitive everywhere—every nerve ending somehow multiplied by seven—but I'm grateful for it, because I can *feel* Tristan swell inside me. I can feel every single jerk and throb, the new heat, the fresh slickness. I know exactly what surges and shudders match which gasp, which dip of his eyelashes, which frantic squeeze of his hand on my thigh.

Isolde has shifted so she can kiss his neck and jaw and suck little spots along his neck, and semen has started dripping from her snatch and pooling in his navel. When his orgasm gradually uncurls its claws from him, he lifts an unsteady hand to touch his stomach. He moans when he lifts his fingers and sees what they're wet with. His eyes close.

"Fuck," he whispers.

I let myself have ten more seconds. Ten more seconds of his hips digging into my thighs, of his strong body stretched out underneath me. Of Isolde's arms now around Tristan's neck but her eyes on me. Ten more seconds of slick, fast-cooling seed and goose bumps peppering skin and breathing slowly returning to normal.

Ten more seconds, and then the world outside the window can strip us and sell us for parts if it wants.

I bend down and kiss both of them in turn.

twenty-nine

MARK

Hours later, when the aftercare is finished and a long shower taken—and the inevitable sex enjoyed afterward—I gently disentangle myself from a sleeping Tristan and slide out of bed. Petitcrieu has decanted herself into a pool of gray fuzz and too-big paws between Tristan's knees and doesn't even prick her ears when I draw the covers back up. I slip on some pants, brush some hair back from Isolde's face, and then leave the room.

Downstairs, I go straight for the low wooden bar behind the sofa, pouring myself a finger of scotch…and then adding another finger before stoppering the bottle again. It's still dark and will be for a while yet, and even the city has gone still, streetlights changing colors for empty intersections, sporadic headlights moving over empty sidewalks.

I only know she's coming because she wants me to know. She doesn't bother hiding her reflection in the glass, and the blanket she has wrapped around herself hisses on the floor as she walks. But her feet make no noise, and I've watched her long enough to know that she'd be able to stick to the darkness, choose a perfectly oblique angle for her approach if she didn't want to alert me. I might sense her a split second before she wanted me to, but only barely.

I don't speak as she comes to my side, but I do offer her a drink from my glass, which she takes. I watch the smooth slide of her throat as she swallows. The play of city lights over her skin.

She hands me the glass. "I know what you're doing."

I find this idea rather amusing. Even *I* barely know what I'm doing, least of all when I'm with her. "Oh?"

"I just wish I knew why." She tucks the blanket more tightly around her. It's a thin one that's normally folded at the bottom of my bed, and it's not really warm enough for January, not in a glass cavern like my penthouse. She's all goose bumps now, and the glow from the window limns the fine gold hairs of her arms, all raised in a futile effort to keep her warm.

Impatiently, I take her hand, tug her to the sofa, and make her sit on my lap once we get there. I set my scotch down and fuss at the edges of the blanket, grumping under my breath about misplaced masochism and how it won't matter how much work I've put into keeping her alive if she insists on dying of hypothermia instead.

I hate it when she's cold. So many nights in the hall when the plan was to have her kneeling on the floor and then she'd wind up in my lap instead because I'd look down and see the goose bumps on her thighs.

She's staring at me as I finish tucking the blanket around her feet.

"You love me," she says, like it's a statement of fact, which it is.

"Yes."

"And you love Tristan."

Another fact. Inconvenient but incontestable. "Yes."

"So why are you acting like you're about to disappear?"

This surprises me. "What makes you think that?"

She doesn't roll her eyes, but there's a pointed flick of her gaze that must be the etiquette-friendly equivalent. "The loft. The *here's how to hurt her, here's how to top him.* You wouldn't go to the trouble if you knew you'd be there to do it for us."

I don't respond, mostly because any easy response would be a lie, and any difficult one would be mostly incomplete anyway.

"You said no more lies. You said no more secrets. Remember? On New Year's Eve? You promised."

I kiss her forehead. Because I want to and because I need to interrupt her study of my face. She's too perceptive. I'm adept at giving nothing away, but she's getting very good at taking what isn't being given instead.

This is the problem with baby cutthroats, of course. Baby heroes are so much easier to manage.

On the other hand, she'll understand better than our baby hero in the end why I had no intention of keeping my promises about secrets and lies. She'll hate me for it, she'll build elaborate fantasies about throttling me, but she'll understand.

"I don't know what's going to happen next or who will make the first move." I speak the words against her temple, moving my lips to her soft, moonlight-colored hair. "But I do know that you have to take care of Tristan. We know he's strong, we know he's brave, and we know he would die protecting you. But he'll never think to protect himself. He's not wary enough or watchful enough. He's not made for this."

"And we are." The words are leached of all feeling, but I hear the desolation underneath them.

I'll lie about a lot of things, but I won't lie about this. "Yes. We are."

"Even if I don't want to be."

This time, I do let her see my face. I take her chin between my thumb and forefinger so that she has no choice but to meet my eyes.

"This again?" I ask softly.

A bitter twist to her lips. "Why not?"

"I cannot tell you to forgive yourself for what you've done as a saint. But I can tell you that if what you are keeps yourself and Tristan alive, then you are the best and holiest thing I can imagine."

Her lashes drop to her cheeks, nothing but silver in the city's artificial burn. "I am so far from holy."

I debate telling her what I say next, but I'm keeping so much else hidden that it feels like I should share this at least. "That first night of ours, on your father's desk—I don't think I ever fully explained why I left."

Her eyes snap to mine. "You said it was because you realized you had feelings for me. That you were scared of what they could change."

"That's true, but I didn't understand how much those feelings might change my plans until I found that gift from your uncle in your room. The holy card."

"Julian the Hospitaller," she says slowly.

"The patron saint of murderers. And written on the back, *Tu me superbus*."

Her voice is hollow when she translates the Latin. "*You make me proud*."

"I'd known your uncle was preparing you for sainthood— that little dojo of yours has churned out more than a few saints in its time. But I'd hoped he'd keep you in waiting a little while longer, allow you the rest of your college years at least. I'd hoped you'd get longer than I did after I joined the army, that your hands would stay clean long enough for your heart to finish growing. But he didn't. He made you into a killer at the age of nineteen, and I knew that if he'd dip your hands in blood, then he wouldn't hesitate to use you against me the moment he was able. If we were close, clearly in love, clearly intimate, then the pressure would have begun right away. I wasn't ready for that, and more importantly, Lyonesse wasn't ready."

I drop my hand, freeing her to look away, which she does.

"I wanted to stay that night with you more than anything," I say tiredly, "but the game had already begun. Your uncle had made the first move. It was either my obsession with you or everything I'd built my life around since Eliot died, so I chose revenge. Not that it mattered. I thought of you constantly, wanted you incessantly. Every time I saw you after that, I knew I was only a sigh or a smile away from checkmate."

Sadness haunts the shape of her mouth now. I run my thumb over the seam of her lips as if I could rub all the unhappiness away.

"At nineteen, you had the power to terrify me. *Me*. I don't want to boast, but in any other circumstance, the idea of Mark Trevena being terrified of a nineteen-year-old heiress would be ridiculous. But I knew with a marrow-deep certainty that if you wanted, even if you only *half* wanted, you could knock me over as easily as a chess piece. Don't waste a gift that rare on someone else's idea of holiness, Isolde. Maybe you don't think you're good, but you're able to protect good people, and if that isn't its own kind of virtue, then I don't know what is."

She doesn't speak, not to agree and not to argue, but she's allowed me to caress away her pout, and when her eyes drift to the window, she seems pensive rather than miserable. I can't resist. I tug her chin back toward me and press my mouth against hers.

336

She makes a noise in her throat and wraps her arms around my neck, fingertips swirling in my hair as I cajole her lips apart and stroke my tongue against hers.

"Clearly, I can still touch you," she murmurs, and a hand drops from my head to the waistband of the lounge pants I pulled on. She reaches inside, circles the stiff flesh she finds there, and then I circle her hand with my own. Together, we work my erection into a flushed, weeping state, until all thought of logic and prudence has left my mind, and all my thoughts are of tight openings and arched throats.

"Bed," I growl, standing up and lifting my wife in my arms as I do. And I carry her upstairs to bed and to Tristan, who is more than happy to be kissed awake for all the wicked little plots we have in mind.

thirty

MARK

Morning finally finds Manhattan, and a cool gray light slants over their limp, snoozing forms as I get up and quietly get dressed. I've never needed much sleep, but war and life as a covert operative cured me of whatever need I'd had left, so a few hours feels like plenty as I lace up my shoes and then step back into my closet and shut the door.

There's a narrow opening hidden behind the full-length mirror, leading to a small room with a built-in desk and an array of monitors. But I don't bother with any of that this morning. I climb onto the stool so I can reach the paneled ceiling, and I press up until I hear a click. A section of paneling drops open with hydraulic-assisted leisure to reveal a ladder, which I pull down and climb. I have fond memories of my father doing something like this every Christmas, of how privileged and mature I'd felt when he'd finally let me go into the attic with him to get the tree.

Needless to say, we have very different attics.

The building I live in is a pretentious rod of glass and steel that has no business being as high as it is. I find its architecture distasteful for the same reason I built Lyonesse in a similar style—it conveys wealth and influence and nothing else. No beauty or meaning or innovation, only a callow flaunting of capital.

I much prefer Morois and its warped windowpanes and flagstone floors.

However, if you must live in Manhattan and if you are in a line of work that requires discretion, there is a distinct advantage to living in a pencil-thin *fuck you* of a building. Every structure of this height requires mechanical voids every ten or twelve stories, and while mechanical voids are crammed full of boilers and AC units and ducting, they also make a great place to store things. Like guns.

Or hired Slovakian muscle, as I once had to do before my wedding.

There is a section of ductwork that branches off from the rest, and I use a screwdriver hung neatly nearby to loosen the screw tacking the salient section of duct in place. Once I have my small armory exposed, I do a quick survey of what I have, select a compact sidearm and shoulder harness along with an extra magazine, and, on a whim, grab a knife harness too.

I'm fighting shivers by the time I finish replacing the ductwork—there are no walls or windows in the voids, just the steel supports and the equipment, and January is making itself known. I walk past the chair where I kept Drobny's man tied down while I had a few words with him and past my small cache of fruit snacks and sports drinks (a few of my guests up here have stayed for longer than a day) and then climb back into my little security nook and replace the ceiling panel. There is another way into the void—a service elevator accessed from the basement—but I prefer only to use that when it would be impractical to use the ladder. I pay off the building's security team quite handsomely, but there's no need to provoke fate more often than necessary.

Tristan and Isolde are still asleep, both of them laid out like someone fucked them into next week—which I did—but Petitcrieu watches me with curious amber eyes as I buckle on my shoulder harness, slot the gun in the holster, and then pull a jacket over it all.

"Come on," I whisper, and she jumps off the bed and races down the stairs and straight for her food bowl. I feed her, and while she eats, I write a short letter to Tristan.

I have an errand that can't wait, and I might miss you before you return to Montreal. If that's the case, I wanted to say what I should have said when we exchanged rings at Lyonesse.

I love you.

You are the best man I've ever known, and I have known many good men. When I first saw you at your father's wedding—a green-eyed hero complete with regulation hair and valor devices—I thought of Maxen Colchester, another good man. But you are something else, something beautiful and apart, because you have kept your heart in your hands through it all. I don't know if you realize how rare that is. Even Colchester couldn't do that, not as nakedly or sweetly as you have done.

I don't know how to say it other than this: I will always want to bury the embers at dawn, but you make me hope for the sunrise after, however unlikely it might be.

Stay safe. Love Isolde.

I don't believe in fate, but if ever fate meant for two people to love each other, it was the two of you.

- Mark

PS: Cara Sims is in the apartment downstairs. I've left the code at the bottom of this letter. I think she'd be glad to see you.

I take Petitcrieu for a quick walk, return her to the penthouse where she promptly whines to be helped back up between the two warm and sleeping bodies in bed, and then I leave before I can talk myself into delaying any longer.

No one smart keeps a clockmaker waiting for long.

———

The Manhattan clockmaker is located in the East Village, tucked between a laundromat and a vape shop. There's graffiti and some litter outside, but signs of post-hipster gentrification are everywhere. I wonder if they'll need to move soon—there's only so long that a barely trafficked clock shop will escape notice in a hot property market.

Jago drops me off and then idles double-parked outside as I go in. It's early, only just after eight, and the feeble sunlight hasn't yet filtered down to the street. The shop is all shadows and ticking hands when I step inside.

The clockmaker, a young man with sienna-brown skin and twists tied up in a bun, comes to the counter after I ring the bell.

"May I help you?" he asks in a British accent.

"I have a mantel clock that's waiting for me. Mark Trevena."

"I'll see if I can find the slip for it."

My phone buzzes as he goes into the back, and I glance down. Lox. I silence the call, planning to call her back once I'm finished here.

"Here's the slip, sir," the clockmaker says and extends a piece of paper to me. "I know we quoted you the full repair,

341

but unfortunately, we couldn't find the parts. We'll of course extend a discount for this."

I open the folded paper.

Brittany Hill
- no birth certificate
- no taxpayer identification number
- no known address
- no employment history or travel records

And then below that, I see the name and address for a dentist's office in Nemi, Italy, along with a date from ten years ago.

I look up from the paper to find the clockmaker watching me. I know the shop is empty, but the clockmaker rules are so inviolate that I find myself nearly speechless when the clockmaker adds, "I am sorry we weren't able to find more," in plain English rather than timepiece metaphors.

"It's quite all right," I say. "I've been struggling with this one myself."

"We've been working on it for six months and still can't find anything more than what you've got in your hand." There's a distinct note of professional irritation in his voice. "A dental appointment ten years ago. It's a disgrace, actually."

"Nothing like that at all. It's more than I've found so far." I hand the paper back to him; I have the address memorized already.

"Still, you have my apologies for this. We pride ourselves on being able to offer more."

At the prices they charge, I appreciate the regret, but I am polite enough not to say so.

"Is there anything else I can help you with before you go?" he asks, and he does sound like he wants me to say yes, to smooth over the lack of Brittany Hill in the world.

"There is, as it happens," I say. I pull a postcard from my suit pocket and set it on the counter. A Victorian illustration of foxgloves with an address written on the back but nothing else. "Do you think you could get this to its destination in the next day or two?"

The clockmaker bends over the card, studying the address, and then nods.

"And do you have something I can write with?" I ask. I'm handed a marker that looks like it's meant for labeling boxes, and I write a single word on the back in neat, clear letters. *Nemi.* I cap the marker, set it on the counter, and then adjust the black and silver ring on my finger. "Actually, I have one more thing. If you don't mind."

thirty-one

MARK

I CALL SEDGE AFTER I SLIDE BACK INTO THE CAR, AND JAGO starts maneuvering us north.

"Can we freeze the rest of my day?" I ask. "I'm taking a little field trip upstate, and I might not be able to take any last-minute calls."

"Of course, sir." A tactful pause. "I'm sure Dinah will be able to handle a club emergency, but it would help to know how available you'll be if anything comes up?"

"I'll be…Albany amounts of available."

"Albany." Dryly.

"Yes, it's for a personal project of mine. I should be back in Manhattan by evening, and then Isolde and I will return tomorrow."

"From your personal project in Albany. Yes, sir." It's spoken in the sober tone of an assistant taking notes, but Sedge is talented in the art of implying a reaction he's not evidentially giving. In this case, a reaction of complete disbelief.

"Will you do me a favor, Sedge? Will you let Andrea

know I'll be back tomorrow, but Goran and Nat will be out for a while longer?"

"Are they going to Albany too, sir?"

"No, no, nothing like that." But I don't clarify any further. I haven't told anyone aside from Tristan about Cara Sims…and therefore, I haven't told anyone where Goran and Nat have gone. It seems easier to keep everything contained until we know more about what Cara's future looks like.

"Yes, sir," says Sedge when it becomes clear that I have nothing I'm willing to add. "Have a safe journey."

"I've got Jago with me," I say, catching my driver's eye in the rearview mirror. "No one will dare touch me while I've got a giant, brooding Cornishman by my side."

Jago just shakes his head and looks back at the road. But he's smiling. He likes me, I know he does, because he once saved my foot from getting run over by a supply truck during a joint CIA and Royal Marines operation in Armenia. (With Jago, such a thing is essentially a proposal of marriage.) I poached him from the bootnecks the moment he was free, and he's been silently squiring me around ever since.

I say goodbye to Sedge and then raise the barrier between me and Jago and attempt to return Lox's call. She sends me straight to voicemail, which is the most Lox outcome I can think of, and then I occupy myself by pulling up the address of Regina Springer's auto shop and examining the outside, the nearby buildings, the layout of the streets.

The city starts to breathe around us, the buildings getting lower, the trees pressing harder against the road. Soon we're moving at speed, and I lift my eyes from my phone to watch the trees fly by, stark and skeletal, wetly reaching up for the gray clouds. I think of Morois in winter, of the sodden leaves and stubborn moss, the snowdrops and hawthorn that defy the cold and the axial tilt of the earth to bloom anyway. I think of Tristan gathering wood in the snow, of Isolde's collarbone gilded by the light of the fire.

I once stepped into Isolde's dojo curious about the girl who seemed like such a convenient answer to all my problems—as leverage against Cashel, as a potential asset who could be flipped, and in those early, dark days, as a vessel for retribution, a treasured body to pay Cashel back for the treasured body he once gave me in a dark alley. But I left that day with something more than curiosity, something deeper. The more I watched her, the more fascinated I became. They took her for gold when she was titanium; they admired her polish when she was nothing but swirling smoke underneath it all. And the first time she crawled to me, bowled over by a few seconds on her hands and knees, I considered that my plans would have to change.

I hired Tristan already knowing of him, of his heroism, his haunted beauty, his provocative hands. I invited him to apply for the job not because he was going to be Blanche's stepson but because I already knew I could count on him to do the right thing even when it was hard, because I knew that he could protect Isolde—even from me if necessary.

Because I'd read the interview years before when a reporter asked why he was single, and he said it was because he was ready to fall in love at a moment's notice. He said it like it was a liability, and *oh, Tristan, puppy, you were right. It's such a liability.*

If only I hadn't been liable as well.

The phone rings as we're getting off the highway—Albany is hunched and grim under a depressing sky—and I see Lox's name on the screen.

"My dear hacker," I say. "Any news for me today?"

"No? Yes? I don't know. We finished building the *Revelata Scientia* translation from the scans online and found our old

346

friends in there, mentioned as a group of princes undertaking the study of alchemy."

"Ys?"

"The same."

"So that's why Minch had it in his Bible."

"That's what we thought too, but also he was very specific about it being the version at that library, right? So we converted the images you sent into text and compared the text to the other versions we'd collected, just to see if there was anything different about Minch's edition than the rest."

"And there was?"

"There was. Because in Minch's edition, there's no mention of Ys at all *or* of a secret group of princes. Only the study of alchemy among nobility."

I toy with the inside of my ring, considering this. "Why index a book that *doesn't* mention Ys?"

"I don't know, but Nimue connected me to the owner of Thornchapel, who let me look at the original scans of the book he has there, *A Treatise of Politicks Large and Small*. The scans in their online archive have a sentence about Ys after discussing the Hanseatic League, but their *original* scans don't. I've got someone hunting through metadata to see if they can figure out when the deviation for this one occurred and possibly who introduced it while I hunt down the rest of the originals on the list."

Jago rolls us to a stop in front of the auto shop. I tap my thumb once against my ring and then unbuckle my seat belt.

"Thank you for telling me," I say as Jago opens my door. "And keep me updated on whatever else you find. I'm visiting Regina Springer today, and I'll let you know what I find here, if anything."

"An ephemeral money trail leading to a garage in Albany? You're saying you don't have much hope that's going to be worth your time?"

"Have fun with the old books, Lox," I say with good cheer and then hang up. Jago comes to stand next to me, looking up at the broken plastic sign mounted to the front of the garage. The windows at the front look like they've never been cleaned.

I scan the area—there's a church across the street, strikingly Gothic but also undeniably abandoned, some shabby houses clad in rotting clapboard with air-conditioning units tilting precariously from upper windows, and plenty of empty brick buildings with temporary fencing along the outside.

"I'm looking for someone, and I don't want to scare her off if she's easily rattled," I tell Jago, going over to the cloudy, yellow window of the shop's lobby and trying to peer inside. No lights. The old TV set mounted to the wall is dark. "Do you mind finding a discreet place to wait for me?"

Jago makes sure to give the derelict street a pointed look before nodding with the expression of someone who thinks their boss is a dumbass.

"You worry too much. And I'll call when I need you!" I add, waving him off and then trying the shop door. It opens, sleigh bells attached to the back jangling as it does, and I step onto the chipping linoleum.

A wiry man with warm beige skin and gray hair emerges from a far doorway, wiping grease off his hands with a bandana possibly older than I am. "Can I help you?" he asks, the words friendly even if he couldn't look more surprised that someone is standing inside the shop.

"I was hoping to speak with Regina Springer," I say. "About an old friend."

A frown pulls at the deep grooves running from his nose to his mouth and etches horizontal lines across his forehead. "Regina died last week. The funeral was just two days ago. I'm sorry, I thought everyone knew." He doesn't sound accusatory, only awkward and maybe a little mournful.

I don't have to fake my unhappiness about this news. "That's tragic. I'm so sorry." I ask the next part in the delicate tones of a respectful acquaintance. "Was it the cancer?"

A shoulder lifts under the well-worn shop uniform. "Partly, they say. She was doing more chemotherapy, but then she got the flu. It was slow at first, then fast. She wasn't awake for the worst of it, which was a blessing."

I nod, face solemn. "It sounds like it was."

I'm already thinking through next steps—if I should try to filter through the shop records, if her house has been packed yet—when the mechanic says, "If you're still needing to ask about your friend, Regina's sister is probably at home. Just across the street, in the old rectory." He gestures with the bandana through the window, and I look out, seeing the red brick house on the far side of the abandoned church.

"I think I might pay her a visit, actually. Let her know how sorry I am to hear about Regina. Thank you so much."

He nods. "It's sad stuff. Everyone around here liked Regina, but she and her sister kept to themselves. Almost no one at the funeral. Not a good way to end."

No, it's not. But there are very few good ways to end a life, and even a good end isn't always an easy one.

I thank him again and leave, the sleigh bells rattling as the door slams shut behind me.

I cross the street and crunch across a gravel path through the graveyard to the rectory, head ducked against the piercing wind. Weariness seeks the corners and edges of me as I stoop down to swipe a fresh-looking bouquet from a grave, a prop to shore up my pretense as a visitor offering condolences. Fuck, I'm tired. And I don't want to be cold or carrying stolen remembrances. I don't want to be chasing leads. I don't want to be seeking answers only barely related to the questions I'm asking.

I want to be in bed, wrapped around Tristan while Isolde

curls against me from behind. I want to be at Morois playing chess with the set Isolde gave me as a wedding gift, genuinely concerned about losing to her while Tristan lies in front of the fire and reads. I want the rest of my life to be worshipping the very two hearts I once planned to blight and then destroy, and I want it enough right now that I almost consider turning back, calling Jago to pick me up. This was always going to be a dead end, even before I found out that Regina Springer was literally dead.

But I am my mother's child, my grandad's grandson, and the same part of me that refused to give up during one of our long outdoor games of hide-and-seek, even after the rain started or the dark came, can't actually fathom dropping the stolen flowers and going home.

If it's a dead end, I'm going to see its tomb with my own eyes.

I get to the rectory door and knock twice. The same creep of decay that hung over the auto shop is present here too: dry weeds feathering around a statue of the Virgin Mary, crumbling mortar between the bricks, a dead tree limb on the roof. But I do see curtains hung neatly inside and, through the curtains, a wedge of tidy kitchen. And at one point, the flowerpot by the door must have held flowers. Two sisters living alone, pulled under by the slow tide of cancer and age.

No one comes to the door. I knock again and watch the windows for movement, for shifts in light or reflection, and see nothing. I glance around to make sure only the trees and tombstones can bear witness and then check under the flowerpot for a key. There isn't one.

I don't have anything to pick a lock with, and breaking an old woman's window really is in bad taste, even if I want to rifle through her dead sister's things. I'm about to walk around to check on a potential back door when I notice the path of worn grass leading from the rectory to the church itself, to a narrow door set into the back of the stone nave. It's cracked, just slightly.

I keep the flowers in my hand as I stride through the graveyard to the door, planning on keeping my story simple enough to elaborate on if needed but specific enough that I can prompt Regina's sister for some clues about why Regina might have been receiving money from a cardinal. I push the door open—it's shockingly heavy—and step into a cavernous space of dark stone and stained glass.

The windows are intact in their pointed arches, and the heavy wooden pews remain, but the altar is gone and the air is damp and lonely. There is half-collapsed scaffolding in one corner, a pile of abandoned organ pipes in front of the dais, and amid the rafters, I am almost certain I see an altocumulus of leathery shadows—bats. The massive hammer beams supporting the roof are carved into the shape of angels.

They stare down with sightless eyes, their mouths rounded as if in song.

I see her immediately, a silver-haired woman perhaps in her late sixties, sitting in the second pew and smoking a cigarette. She's wearing an old leather coat and boots that show their age, and the cold has daubed her pale cheeks with red. She glances over at me with flat gray eyes, the wrinkles on her lips deepening as she brings her cigarette to her lips.

It's a strange fact of being what we are that we killers can recognize each other in the wild. I have never met or seen this woman before in my life, but I know we are the same. It's something in her eyes maybe—or maybe it's what *isn't* there. Kindness or humanity or remorse.

She blows out a wreath of smoke as I walk up to her pew and sit down. She ashes her cigarette onto the floor with an impatient tap and says, "Look me in the eye when you do it. That's all I ask."

thirty-two

MARK

I sit back in the pew, stretching my arm out along the back while I set the flowers to the side. We are far enough apart that either of us would have plenty of time to react if the other moves.

"I'm not here for you," I reassure her. "I actually came for your sister, because I had some questions for her. I'm sorry about your loss, by the way."

The woman watches me, the inborn wariness of a predator tempered by something else. Grief maybe. "Thank you. We only had each other, you know. It feels like an amputation." She turns her eyes toward the magnificent array of stained glass behind the dais where the altar used to be. I notice a pile of beads in her lap—a rosary made of some dark, dull metal. "What questions did you have for her? Maybe I can answer them."

I abandon my earlier plan and decide on the truth. "Your sister was getting money from a trust fund managed by a Catholic cardinal named Mortimer Cashel. I want to know why."

She laughs, a thick, wheezing noise that sounds like forty years of tobacco smoke. "Oh, I know why."

I wait patiently while she finishes laughing and then takes another drag on her cigarette.

"They were never payments to her," the woman says after she exhales. "They were payments to *me*."

"Ah," I say. "For…services rendered? Did your sister help?"

"Yes, services of a sort," she replies. She taps more ash onto the floor and then explains, "I've spent most of my life trying not to exist. No bank account, no work history, no taxes filed. So Regina collects the money for me." Then she corrects herself with a frown. "Collected."

"You've gotten paid recently," I remark. "Does this mean you're still active?"

She shakes her head. "I guess you could say that I get royalties on a few of my larger projects. Or more accurately that I'm paid to keep quiet. Murder for hire isn't exactly the kind of thing that helps a new pope's reputation."

"Given the Church's history, I'd say that's a pretty recent development. How long did you work for him?"

She pulls in a drag. "Started when I was nineteen. Last body was three years ago now."

"Nineteen," I repeat. I think of Isolde, brought to Rome to poison coffee and pierce flesh, not even to her second year of college.

"I ran away when I was sixteen. It was the seventies, you've got to understand. It was so easy for the city to swallow me up, help me chew myself into a pulp. There was a bad girlfriend, then some dope, then a boy I fell in love with. That last part ended with two black eyes and me working a crew spot on a cargo ship to Spain. I ended up in Ireland a couple years later, sleeping rough, living rougher, and that's when Father Cashel found me trying to sleep in the doorway of his parish church. He gave me dry clothes and something to eat and let me sleep in the office. Started giving me odd jobs. He never leered at me or put his hands on me or made me feel small. He listened and helped—the opposite of everyone I'd met since running away."

She looks down at her cigarette, which is now smoldering at the filter. She tosses it to the stone floor with a sigh and pulls the pack from her pocket.

"Cigarette?" she offers.

"I don't smoke."

"You young ones never do. What are you, private? Freelance? That's too nice a suit for government work."

I accept the compliment with a gracious nod. "I'm freelance, I suppose, but I only freelance for myself. I started in the agency though."

"Ah," she says, now digging for her lighter. "You do have a bit of an agency vibe."

"What would that be?" I ask, curious.

She sticks a cigarette between her lips. "Old school, you know?" She lights the cigarette and inhales until I hear her leather jacket creak. The rest of her thought comes with a cloud of smoke. "Chatty. Genteel. You've got manners."

"That's flattering."

She rolls her eyes. "Manners are a waste of time."

"It depends on the time," I say, crossing my legs and giving her a cordial smile. "This isn't a waste at all."

"You religious?" she asks suddenly.

"I dabble."

She points the cigarette at the stained glass making up the better part of the apse of the building. It's the crucifixion writ large: Christ in the middle with the three Marys near his feet and John the Beloved looking ardently up at him, then the two criminals on either side, each in their own window.

"Jesus loves even the worst of thieves and vilest of

sinners," she says. "Like us. At least that's how the story goes. Father Cashel made me feel like...like I could earn a fresh start. I worked around the church. I went to Mass. And I finally gathered up my courage to see him for confession. I told him everything."

"You'd killed people by then?"

"Two. The boy who gave me the black eyes and then a guy smuggling hash into Europe who thought I tried to screw him on a deal. But that wasn't the worst part of my confession. The worst part was that I didn't feel bad. Not even a little." She takes a thoughtful inhale and then looks at me. "You ever feel bad about them? The ones you've killed?"

"Some. Not very many." I think for a moment. "But the *some* weigh on me. They died for vain and petty reasons. That irritates me."

"Guessing that's why you went freelance."

I shrug. "I'd rather the vain and petty reasons be my own. So Cashel wasn't troubled by your lack of remorse?"

"He told me that it was okay, that it was a good thing actually, a gift from God. That he'd been looking for someone like me whose sins could help save God's kingdom. Gave me this." She hands me the rosary, and it's as heavy and cold as it looks. The crucifix is beveled and embellished, oddly baroque for being made of what looks an awful lot like gunmetal.

"This must have been before he was overseeing the saints," I say, twisting the beads around my fingers to hold up the crucifix to the light.

"Much, much before," the woman agrees. "Even after he became a cardinal and was in charge of the saints, he still had me do his more...extracurricular tasks. Things he didn't want the saints doing or even knowing about. Like knocking off his sister."

She says it so casually, one killer to another, as if she

hasn't made time slide sideways with just a handful of words.

"Pardon me?"

She glances over at me, and confusion gives way to something like pride. "You didn't know? So people still don't know. I've always thought I did a good job keeping that one clean. It's one of my 'royalties,' actually. He really doesn't want that one getting out."

"Inis Laurence died in a car accident," I say slowly. "Are you telling me that the car accident was staged?"

"The accident did happen," the woman says. "But it was *made* to happen. One of my best jobs, and it was also one of the easiest, because my dad owned the auto shop before Regina, and I grew up crawling over engine parts. I siphoned off some brake fluid, introduced a slow leak so the rest would drain on her drive home, and then I was there blocking the way to Cashel House on the coastal road when she came home that night. The brakes failed, and she swerved and went right over the ledge."

"I apologize—I'm still caught on the fact that Cashel wanted his own sister dead. That is…staggering to me."

Isolde's uncle killed her mother.

The death that turned her father into a living profit-and-loss sheet and brought Isolde into Cashel's influence was planned.

"It's pretty dark when you think about it," the woman agrees, like we're talking about some atrocity she had no part in. "They'd argued the night before. She'd learned something—I always thought she must have learned about me and what he'd had me do, but looking back, I think it must have been bigger than just me. I only ever killed people who needed it, people who would have been righteously killed in the Old Testament, you know? Creeps and killers and bad priests and a few of those sisters who ran Magdalene laundries. No one would have missed them. No one would have really been sad they were dead. Until his sister. She was the first one who—I guess I feel worse about her than the others is all. She had a little girl, I think."

I'm staring at the penitent thief rendered in stained glass, ordering the timeline in my head. So Cashel had people killed even back when he was a parish priest, long before he'd been promoted up to Rome. If Ys has existed for centuries, like the rumors say, then it's not impossible that he could have been working for Ys separately by then, climbing the ranks of the secret organization at the same time he climbed the ranks of the Church until he was at the top of both. "Does the name Ys mean anything to you?" I ask her.

A plume of smoke. "No. Should it?"

I turn to study her face, the deep lines, hard features, eyes like stones. I don't think she's lying. I don't think she'd even see the need to.

My phone rings, and the noise in the soaring stone vaults of the church is startlingly loud. A handful of pissed-off bats spring into a flapping nightmare, the noise of their wings echoing everywhere, almost as bad as the phone itself.

"So sorry," I tell the woman and the bats. "One moment, please."

I see Jago's name as I accept the call. "I'm sorry, sir," he says the minute I pick up. "I didn't notice them if they were following us before, and I only just now saw them as I was circling the block—"

As he's explaining something that makes absolutely no sense to me, the door to the back of the church opens, and I see the glimmer of pearl-colored hair, the outline of broad shoulders. "Thank you, Jago," I say tiredly as I get to my feet and step out into the aisle between pews. "You didn't do anything wrong."

I hang up as I meet Tristan and Isolde near the pile of organ pipes, Tristan looking around the church and Isolde assessing the woman who's still sitting and smoking like nothing's changed. Isolde's posture shifts subtly into something slightly more feline and aware. She also recognizes a fellow monster.

"Tristan, Isolde, this is..." I pause politely, and the woman correctly interprets the prompt.

"Barbara," she says. Finishes off her cigarette. "Pleasure to meet you both."

"Marvelous." I turn to my two troublemakers. "Now can I ask why you two are *here* and not in Manhattan doing any number of productive and pleasant things?"

"The doorman gave me this when I returned with Petitcrieu from a walk." Isolde hands me a piece of paper, thin but finely milled. I still have the gunmetal rosary twined through my fingers, and the beads clank as I unfold the note to see a typewritten address.

The address of the auto shop.

"It's from the Scales," says Isolde. "There was no good reason I could think of that the Scales would give me an address in Albany on the same day you told me you had an errand upstate. I was worried. So we left Petitcrieu with Goran and the others and came up here in a cab."

"Have we met before?" Barbara asks, staring at Isolde. "You look familiar."

As my wife shakes her head, my phone rings again, the bats lose their shit again, and I pick it up with an irritated sigh. "Yes?"

"We have a problem," says Andrea. "The FBI is here, and they have a warrant. Do you remember the congressman whose toothbrush you poisoned last year? The warrant says that you obstructed a congressional proceeding, committed wire fraud, and a whole lot of other shit. Anyway, the FBI is claiming that Lyonesse and everything in it are now forfeited assets, and they're trying to seize the club. That would mean the servers too."

Fuck.

This is Cashel's doing, I'm certain of it. I'm not sure how he learned about my date with the congressman's gastrointestinal biome, but there's only one entity that could topple my carefully balanced bulwark of local bribery and international sin peddling, and that's the Church and its saints. I might woo bodies, but Cashel deals in the seduction of souls, and the faithful are everywhere.

"Call Anguish," I say quickly. "She needs to come to the club right away. The assets are fully hers, not mine, so they can't be seized in connection with any of my alleged crimes."

"Fully hers? But—"

"Remember when I told you that I sold Anguish half the club?"

"Yes," says Andrea slowly. "I reviewed the contract before you signed it."

"Well, I'm sorry to say that you reviewed the version I wanted you to see. I sold Anguish the entire club in exchange for unlimited access to the data in perpetuity. But everything physical about Lyonesse is hers, including the servers. No one can touch the club, for now at least."

"They'll be able to take your work computer and any personal electronics here though…"

"I'm quite hygienic when it comes to information," I assure her. "Don't fight them on taking anything from my office or apartment. They won't get anything of value there."

Andrea blows out a long breath. "Why didn't you tell me that you sold all of Lyonesse to Anguish?"

"You hating it was fantastic cover," I explain without regret. "It made it look like I sold off part of the club as an inadvisable whim and not as a planned strategy. Now call Anguish, get Dinah, and tell the FBI that they can serve me the warrant in Manhattan."

"Are you really going to let them arrest you?" she asks disbelievingly.

"Andrea, even with Cashel's maneuvering, no one has the stomach for a headline with *president's aunt* and *sex club* anywhere near each other. And that's exactly what will happen when they arrest me. Amid the embarrassment and Embry Moore being very grumpy with everyone, my extremely well-paid lawyers will have me home and in my own bed in a matter of hours."

"As long as you're confident," she grumbles.

"*Call Anguish.* We'll talk soon."

I hang up and look at my audience.

"You're a busy man," remarks Barbara. And then to Isolde, "Are you sure we haven't met?"

"She's Cashel's niece," I say, not saying the implication aloud—that she's Inis Laurence's daughter, so Barbara should choose her next words with care. Isolde should know about how her mother really died, but I'd rather she learn when she has time to process something that fucked up, and apparently we're on the FBI's timetable now.

Fuck me, why did it have to be the FBI? Isn't it bad enough getting arrested without having to look at a suit purchased with Kohl's Cash?

When my phone rings for a third time, I seriously consider smashing it with the heel of my shoe. The bats fuck off for good, disappearing up the belfry at the far end of the church. "I'm a little busy—" I say as I pick it up, but I hear Jago's heavy breathing, and I stop talking immediately.

"Nine or ten, sir. Coming into the church now."

"Jago, don't risk yourself—"

The front doors of the church swing open. I strip off my

coat as I move toward Tristan and Isolde, tossing it on the floor, reaching into my suit jacket—

The air itself splits, snaps, cracks back into place, and Barbara falls to the side and then to the floor, part of her face missing. From the belfry, I hear the very faint fuss of the sleep-deprived bats.

Appropriately warned, I stop moving and slowly lift my hands as they surround us. The crucifix of the rosary swings and thumps against my palm.

They're not wearing any kind of uniform—just dark tactical clothing with no helmets, eye protection, or packs—but they move with a silent, sinuous grace that belies years of experience. Isolde stiffens when she sees one young woman step forward. She has burnished skin, a thick black braid slung over one shoulder, and a battered brown scapular over her vest—undeniably a saint. Someone Isolde has worked with before, if memory serves.

So the saints are here. Which means that I was being watched or that Cashel was watching Barbara. More important than either possibility is that the Scales moved so quickly to have Isolde sent here. Which means Isolde's uneasy reprieve under Cashel's trust has ended. Cashel can have only one outcome planned then, with only two variations likely.

The short way or the long way.

And as three saints break off to move behind each of us and press a gun to the backs of our necks, I have to imagine that the short way is very short indeed.

"The Holy Father would like to see you, Mr. Trevena," the leader of the group says with a level, almost courteous voice. I can tell which saints are newer, I think, because the more seasoned ones remind me of Isolde—contained and shuttered—while the others have a feverish glitter in their eyes. The soul-rusting reality of homicide hasn't yet dulled the shine of their zeal. "And you too, Isolde."

"Is your plan to drag the three of us to Rome?" I drawl. I discreetly scan the space as I speak, wondering if Jago has ignored my bitten-off warning. One brave bat has fluttered back to the rafters, determined to sleep in his own bed apparently. "Surely the Episcopus Romanus has better things to do with his time than come to Albany."

"The three of you? No." The leader looks at Tristan. "The Holy Father hasn't asked for this one. There's no need to bring him with us."

Not good. If they leave him here, they won't leave him alive.

I slouch back a little, loosening my posture into that of a well-dressed inebriate. "He should have asked for him," I volunteer. "He thwarted Cashel's plans in Carpathia last year, didn't you, Tristan? I'm sure the pontiff wouldn't mind a word or two with the hero who saved the Carpathian prime minister from a premature death?"

The muzzle at the back of my head is unwavering, the pressure consistent even as I sway and shift. I wouldn't expect less from a saint, but it does make me miss Filip Drobny's crowd. They were much sloppier and so, so easy to fool into making a mistake.

"What do you think, little wife?" I say, turning my head a little to see Isolde. She stares back at me with a completely blank expression, having gone into saint mode herself. Perfect. "Should we talk your uncle into meeting some military royalty? Maybe Tristan can walk him through how fucking flimsy the assassination plan was from start to finish?" I gesture a little to emphasize *start* and *finish*. Above Isolde's head, I see the blurred, drunken flap of more bats returning from the belfry.

"Enough," says the leader. Her voice is still utterly neutral. "We're not changing our plans."

Isolde's eyes are now on my left hand, where my thumb is in the middle of my palm. One of our signals.

Watch me.

Her gaze slides to mine. Her chin dips ever so slightly. She's watching.

Tristan for his part has gone completely still, his eyes roving from saint to saint, his breathing even. He might as well be back in the hills of Carpathia on a dangerous patrol.

I toy with the rosary in my right hand as I talk. "Was Barbara part of these plans? Did you know about her? It's a waste of time to lecture you all on holiness, obviously, but I would have thought some loyalty would be in order. But maybe you don't know exactly what she did for your fearless leader." The beads aren't looped around my fingers any longer. The crucifix makes a slow, dizzy pendulum in the air.

The margin for error is nothing, absolutely nothing. Three of us need to simultaneously move two or three inches of very important skull out of our warders' lines of fire—and two or three inches sounds like nothing, but with killers as well trained as the saints, it'll take all our considerable skill.

And more bats.

I have succeeded in irritating the leader with my sermonizing, and she steps forward, her jaw working to the side. "There's nowhere else to go, Mr. Trevena," she says. Wonderful, wonderful exasperation is evident in her voice. "Nothing else you can do. Your pet bodyguard will die here, and you will go to Rome, where you will also die. But if you're cooperative, I believe the Holy Father will show mercy. Normally, apostates die painfully, but as a consideration to you, he may give Isolde a clement death."

"And who will give you a clement death when it's your time, Veronica Ramos?" I ask softly. "Who will look after the mother in Quezon City? The little sister in California?"

She goes very still.

Control is like peeling off a sticker: you pick and pick

and pick at a corner until it's bruised and ruffled and split, and then it peels back all at once, faster than you think.

"You," she says in a trembling voice, "should stop talking."

Shadows move along the ceiling, but I'm careful not to look up. "I find a common problem with saints is that you spend too much time in your own realm, permanently baroque as it is, and you forget about the earthly kingdoms, the modern ones. You've come to take me. You know my name. Do you actually know who I am and what I do?"

More shadows in the rafters.

The crucifix swings wider and spins too, like a hypnotist's pendulum gone frantic.

"You're starting to see it now, that thing you tried so hard not to look at. How there are no old saints, how the saints are never allowed to trust each other. How far you've come from the little Veronica who wore a scapular because she loved the Virgin Mary more than anything else. You killed that little Veronica, didn't you? You killed her willingly because you thought you were keeping her safe, and now there's a part of you that knows, late at night, that when they turn on you, there will be nothing left to die."

Veronica, shaking, reaches for the gun at her hip right as I let the rosary fall. Right as I move my thumb from the middle of my palm to run across my fingertips, something that in Lyonesse means *good*, but here with our lives suspended under the slow decay of hammer beam ceilings and nesting bats, I'm hoping Isolde will realize means *now*.

She does.

And it happens all at once:

The rosary tumbles onto the pile of organ pipes and slides frenetically into the jumbled tubes, sending up a jangling, discordant cacophony that flushes at least a hundred bats from the rafters in an explosion of erratic flight, right down into the sanctuary. The three of us move, almost as one, as the unprepared saints flinch and duck—Tristan dropping to one knee and slicing an elbow upward as he turns, Isolde a blur of blond hair and agile hands, myself ducking, turning, trapping my would-be captor's arm and stealing the gun.

The other saints are recovering now, and a shot goes off, sending more bats panicking for the door. I shoot the saint closest to me in the head, make for Isolde and Tristan, and then I'm tackled from behind, the gun skittering out of my hands as my head hits the floor and the world becomes a queasy shimmer.

Fuck.

I bite back the stabbing pain in my head, and I roll and roll again as a bullet comes from somewhere and ricochets off stone. And then I find myself next to the organ pipes once more. I grab one the size of a metal baseball bat and come up swinging, catching a saint in the knee and then again in the chest. They stagger back as Tristan next to me finally wrests control of a gun, and more bullets pop off. Isolde hisses as a line of blood appears like magic on her upper arm—a graze.

I can't take the time to reach for the gun I'm wearing under my arm—I can't give this saint even an instant's reprieve to reach for his lost pistol. I come down again and again with the pipe, dodging the strikes that I can, enduring the ones I can't, hunting him relentlessly backward. The other saints are taking cover from Tristan's fire now while Isolde is fighting Veronica for her gun.

With a series of hard, thudding clangs, I knock the saint sideways and then down to one knee. I bring the pipe against his temple before he can find his balance, and the minute he topples over, I drop the pipe and go for his gun, right as Isolde wrests Veronica's away. Veronica, though, is quick and clever, and she darts behind the stone pulpit before Isolde can get her finger on the trigger.

But the three of us are armed now, and without communicating, we move closer and angle outward, shooting and moving as if we share the same mind, the same nervous system, the same pulse. Another saint falls, but there are still five or six of them left, with more ammunition than we have and the convenient cover of the pews on their side.

Like the bats, we need to make for the door and hope to God that Jago is out there somewhere, and the car is nearby.

I run out of bullets and pull my own gun from my holster and start shooting again. "The door," I shout to Tristan and Isolde, who both nod.

Which is when the front doors open again, and this time, I can't count the number of saints who pour through.

thirty-three

MARK

It's the easiest decision I've ever made.

I shove Tristan and Isolde both behind the pulpit—Veronica long gone—and press my gun into Tristan's free hand.

"Go," I say hoarsely.

"Absolutely the fuck not," Isolde hisses.

"Sir" is all Tristan says. Hearing that one word right now feels like having my chest bludgeoned in with an organ pipe. I can't stand it. I don't deserve it.

"I have help coming if they succeed in getting me to Rome," I say, which is technically true. "Cashel wants me alive. I have a chance. Tristan doesn't, and I won't risk you, Isolde. Please."

Stone chips spray as a bullet hits the side of the pulpit, and I feel my cheek open up. Hot blood trickles down.

I reach to the small of my back and pull the honeysuckle knife from the harness I took from my penthouse earlier this morning. I hand the knife hilt first to my wife.

"I need you to be my shadows and glass girl right now," I tell her. "Think of what I said last night by the window."

Her chest lifts once, hard, and her chin begins to quiver. She remembers.

He's not made for this.

And we are.

Yes. We are.

Only Isolde is built to make a choice like this, to save Tristan at the expense of saving me. And I love her so much for it that I could weep.

Tristan watches this silent exchange and then starts shaking his head violently, seeing the shift in Isolde. "No, no, whatever you're thinking—"

"He's right," she says. Her voice is throaty and thick, but I see the clarity in her eyes. "We can save two of us this way rather than no one. It's the only choice."

More stone chips fly, razor-edged confetti, but I ignore it to yank Isolde into a hard kiss.

"I love you," I say and bury my nose in her hair. Even amid the gun smoke and pulverized stone, I can smell honey and flowers. "I would marry you again every day if I could."

Tristan is staring at me like I'm asking him to shoot me in the throat, and when I kiss him, he clings to me.

"Don't make me do this," he begs. "Don't make me leave you."

I press my hand to his heart and then fold his hand over that. The black and silver ring presses into his palm. "Do you feel that?" I murmur. "I'm holding on to something good. You do the same for me." I move my eyes to Isolde so he understands. "Carry it carefully for me. Okay?"

Veronica has crept almost to the dais, and I have to let go of Tristan so I can return fire.

"Go!" I tell them both. "Find Jago. Get to Anguish— she'll be able to help you get somewhere safe, with Lox or back to Morois. But you have to go now."

Isolde does it. With tears in her eyes and a steely set to her mouth, she yanks Tristan toward the door. And he is forever the Ruth to her Naomi—where she goes, he will follow. A flash of silver daylight, a cascading shatter as a bullet hits one of the stained glass windows, and they're gone.

I pull back behind the pulpit again, on my knees in the shards of stone, and for the first time in a very long time, in the middle of a church being broken for the sake of my sins, I say a prayer.

Please let this fucking work.

I drop my gun, grab one of the sharp flakes of stone, and drag it against my forearm, over the wing of my tattoo. Right next to three other short, hastily made scars.

There's no time to pray again before the saints round the corner. Pain flashes from the back of my head, and the world goes black.

———

Plane engines thrum underneath me. The edge of Veronica's scapular catches the faint artificial light of the cabin.

An IV tube stretches up from my arm.

I think I prefer the darkness of unconsciousness to this, and that seems to suit the darkness just fine. It happily takes me back under before I see anything more.

———

I'm sitting in a chair.

It's my first thought, and it's a bad one. It's never good to wake up in a chair, as I learned at the hands of my own wife last autumn. It's especially not good to wake up when dried blood still crusts the side of your face and the hair of your forearm. One of my eyes is swollen enough to affect my vision—a gift from the saint I sent to heaven with an organ pipe—and the jagged wound on my forearm hurts so *fucking much* that I am certain I've accidentally severed a tendon or cut a nerve.

I'm naked or near to naked, wearing only my boxers, and I'm handcuffed with my hands behind the chair. They've taken my watch, which upsets me a great deal. My black and silver ring, they've left on my finger, which I remind myself to be grateful for.

"It's good to see you awake," says a soft Irish voice, and I look up to see the heterochromatic eyes of the man who ordered Eliot's death and the death of his own sister. The man who would kill Tristan and Isolde if he had the chance.

Tristan and Isolde. They made it out the door. Did they find Jago? Did they get out of Albany and to Anguish?

"Are you thinking of my niece and the bodyguard of yours? I regret to say that they made the journey with you. I also regret to say that your driver did not. Although he did die bravely, trying to defend them."

Jago. Fuck.

I force myself to breathe, to think, even though I'm still groggy from whatever they used to keep me under during the flight here. "You kept Tristan alive," I rasp.

"I decided he could be useful. As an incentive for you or perhaps Isolde. I'm sure you'll appreciate that there are one or two things I'd like from you before the inevitable happens."

"Lyonesse," I say.

Cashel sits on a stool in front of me, piscatory ring glinting under the exposed light bulbs that hang from extension cords slung over metal girders. The floor is concrete; I don't see any windows. A warehouse?

"It would be useful for me to know what *you* know about Ys, of course," Cashel is saying. "But the rest of your treasury will be put to work as well. How funny to think that you've built a temple of secrets, all for the sake of destroying me, and in doing so you've created a weapon beyond anything I could have made myself. Thank you for that, Mr. Trevena, truly."

Are Tristan and Isolde here too? Or at a different location?

I rub the inside of my injured forearm against the back of the chair and bite back a groan. Fuck, that hurts.

"I've always wondered though, and I hope you'll indulge me by answering," Cashel goes on, lifting a hand to press against his jaw once and then dropping it. "How did you connect *me* with Ys? I've worked hard to be careful, to keep a wall between the saints and Ys, making sure anything they did for Ys, they thought they were doing for the Church. That will change now, of course, no sense in wasting resources, but I like to think I've been careful."

Talking is good. I should do lots of that, buy myself as much time as possible. I grind my forearm against the chair again and pretend that the pain is heat and then pretend the heat is light.

Harmless, bright light. It helps a little.

"John Lackland," I push out. My voice is dry and strained with pain. "The deputy director of the NSA. Remember him?"

"I do. I remember also that you killed him last year. Very cleverly done."

"I try." *It's not pain in my arm. It's heat. It's not pain in my arm. It's heat.* "The NSA shouldn't have anything to do with CIA business in ordinary circumstances, so after Kraków, the fact that Lackland coordinated the meetup between Eliot and our asset struck me as strange. It also struck me as strange that the deconfliction protocols were so flagrantly ignored. The only variable I could see that tied everything together was Lackland's potential involvement with this group, this Ys that the asset had wanted to talk to Eliot about. Because if Lackland was implicated in something the asset knew about—if he risked exposure—then friendly fire in a troubled city was a neat way to tidy up both after the asset *and* anything that Eliot might piece together later and with a decent degree of plausible deniability besides."

Fresh blood is dripping down my forearm now, hot and slick on my skin. I have to press my arm harder and harder against the chair as I discreetly rub it back and forth.

"It would have been a decent degree of plausible deniability *if* an angry, grieving CIA officer hadn't been left alive after," says Cashel affably, ruefully. "No one accounted for you in their plans. Though I suppose that's what I get for trusting John Lackland. So how did you get from Lackland to me?"

"I went back to the arms dealers our asset was working for and worked my way inward over the years. I found myself happily torturing the brother-in-law of Filip Drobny's cousin's best friend one day, and he let something slip. Something about his boss's boss. He'd never seen the man, only heard him a single time on the phone, but the Irish accent stuck with him. It left me with only a shred of a suspicion, but it was enough to start poking at the edges."

"Or have your pet hacker Robin Loxley poke at the edges," Cashel adds pleasantly. "But this is a lovely cast of characters, at least. And most of them now dead at your hands."

The nice thing about the past twenty-four hours is that I don't feel like I need to hide the occasional wince or grunt as I continue to abuse my bloody forearm with the back of the chair.

"I don't think anyone will miss John Lackland," I say. I sound breathless. "And Drobny couldn't have been surprised after the attack on my club."

"One wonders why you allowed him and his lackeys into the club in the first place if you knew they were connected to Ys."

"Him, I wanted. His lackeys, not so much." Blood is dripping off the ends of my fingers now. "I didn't account for someone inside my club letting them in. A failure on my part, I freely admit."

"I presume you wanted him as a guest of your hospitality?" Cashel asks with a smile. There is no doubt as to what he means by *hospitality* in this instance, and he would be correct. I'd wanted Drobny contained and questioned, and *contained* would have involved duct tape and an IV.

"At the time. My plans changed after I found his people following Isolde."

"They were following her?" This seems to be news to him, which is interesting.

I flex my hands in the handcuffs, straining my fingers up, my forearm now so slick with blood that my fingertips slip right off my skin. "He used our wedding planner and at least one of his men, although I think there were probably more, to keep tabs on her. My theory was that he wanted some leverage against you—first as a threat, to send you pictures and the like to prove that they were following her, and second as more than a threat if needed. Which means two things: one, that Drobny didn't know you at all and didn't know that you'd sacrifice Isolde in a heartbeat if it threatened you, and two, that there was trouble in Ys paradise. And where there's one unhappy arms dealer, there's more, I'm sure."

Cashel crosses his legs, his red leather shoes stark against his white cassock. "That's a keen insight, Mr. Trevena, thank you. Oh, hello," he says to a tall man striding into my line of sight. He bends down to whisper in Cashel's ear while Cashel idly presses his fingers to his jaw again.

I use the opportunity to duck my head, clamping down on a scream as agony rips up my arm, panting hard for several long moments until I can think again. Luckily, Cashel is still listening to whatever his guard is saying and seems sufficiently agitated by it not to notice anything else.

"My apologies," he says tightly, inclining his head. "I'm afraid I need to discuss something of a sensitive nature." He gets up from his stool and sweeps off into the shadows with his foot soldier.

It's time to pray again, and pray I do.

Please let this fucking work.

I say it like a Hail Mary, like a liturgical recitation. I may be a sinner, but I think God would be interested in what I'll burn on his altar if he helps me out.

When Cashel returns with his usual serene expression restored to his face, my breathing is even and regular, and I'm feeling a lot better about things.

"Apparently, my old friend Barbara has not been as faithful to me as I have been to her." Cashel sounds genuinely saddened by this. As if his saints didn't shoot her in the head with no preamble or warning. "She's sent a packet of information to a reporter. After the anonymous email that went out before the conclave, the reporter is obviously intrigued."

"That's a shame."

Cashel doesn't sit this time, only regards me with a beatific expression of compassion and forgiveness. "I know you sent that email, Mr. Trevena. I felt it was a rather feeble stab at things, but even feeble stabs have a compound effect given enough time. That said, I had expected better from the infamous Sea Hound. The legend is larger than the man, perhaps?"

I approximate a shrug as best I can with my hands pinioned behind me. "Perhaps."

Cashel's foot soldier comes back in at a jog, whispering in rapid-fire Italian to Cashel, and Cashel's mask abruptly drops. The gap-toothed smile, the twinkling eyes, all of it extinguished in an instant. There is only a collection of features devoid of any humanity, bereft of all emotion, with empty, empty eyes.

Even I find it chilling, and I'm generally immune to such feelings.

Cashel slides those empty eyes to me. "Is this your big play then? Your ace in the hole? Freeing them now is pointless, and I need you to understand exactly how much, because you are still *here*, at my mercy, and I will find them again. And it will go worse for them because of what you have done. Make him suffer," he says to his underling and then leaves in a flutter of tassels and a flash of red shoes.

A metal door slams from somewhere I can't see while Cashel's man approaches me. He looks neither excited nor dismayed to be tasked with torturing me—something that endears him to me a little, because I've been in that situation more times than would be considered civilized.

It's too bad then that he has to witness my real ace in the hole.

"I could just break your nose and some fingers, and we could call it a night," he offers. His voice is the voice of someone who's hoping to clock out of work early.

"We could," I say back cheerfully. "Or I could kill you instead."

He laughs. I laugh. And then the handcuffs drop to the floor as I stand up.

His expression is almost worth the trauma and tribulation of working the pick out of my forearm, something that never seems to get easier anytime I do it. But I've never regretted having the plastic tool embedded under my skin—surgical grade for strength, plastic so as not to make a fuss around any security machines reactive to metal—because it's saved my life three times now, and I'm hoping to make it four.

I step toward him, nearly naked, sharp, bloody pick in hand.

"I'm ready to call it a night when you are," I tell him.

thirty-four

TRISTAN

OUR RESCUERS ARE POLITE TO THE POINT OF SADISM, TREAT-
ing Isolde and me with such deferential concern that I think
Isolde is ready to fling herself from the back of the delivery
van that's currently taking us to parts unknown.

"It's fine, truly," she says, her jaw tight as a rescuer probes
a blooming bruise at the corner of her mouth. She's already
been checked for a concussion, force-fed a sports drink and
a protein bar, and given a handful of anti-inflammatories.
The bullet wound streaking the outside of her arm has been
cleaned, glued, and wrapped. And if she had things her way,
she'd still be back in the dank Italian warehouse we'd been
brought to, personally murdering every single saint who'd
attacked us in the church.

Which would have been mostly unnecessary, as many of
them who'd accompanied us here to Rome were dead now,
thanks to the painfully courteous people in this van and the
three other vans following it.

"Thank you," I say again to the leader of the rescuers, a
man with deep olive skin, thick black hair, and wire-rimmed

glasses named Valter. He looks familiar to me, but the itch of memory gets worse the longer I look at him.

"Det var så lite," he says lightly, waving a hand.

I squint, unable to place the language.

"It's Swedish," says Isolde. And then: "He was at my wedding."

Shit. Right. That's where I know him from. He sat in the back row with the quiet demeanor of a distant cousin or an acquaintance from work, nothing noteworthy about him. That said, there was no one I watched more closely that day than Mark and Isolde, nothing I noted more than how easily they spoke their vows or how fiercely they kissed. It hadn't been my best day of work, observationally speaking.

"I was at your wedding," Valter says. "Mark and I are old friends. We came of age together, you could say, back when he was new at his agency and I was new at mine."

Ah. So he *is* an acquaintance from work. Just the kind of work that comes with several degrees of security clearance.

"Anyway, it was no problem," he says. "I owed Mark a small favor—there was some nasty business near Malmö last autumn, and I needed to take care of things…informally. It took us all the way to Östersund. Mark was happy to lend his expertise in exchange for a promise to stage an extraction later."

The remembered words drift across my thoughts:
Did you know it snows in October in Sweden?

So as far back as last year, he'd planned on having Valter rescue us. But—

"Mark was taken before us," I say, trying to understand. "How could you have known we'd need rescued? And where we'd need rescued from? And *who* we'd need rescued from?"

Valter lifts a hand, like *oh it was all so easy.* "As for whom, he'd told us about Cashel and the saints last year. As for where, he put us on alert two days ago, sometime in the afternoon, and we've been tracking you ever since. Once we saw you were in Rome…"

Two days ago, the afternoon… That would have been morning in America.

Mark asked for help before he ever drove to Albany.

I rub my hand down my battered face, considering what the world must look like from inside Mark's mind. Months ago, he earned this favor, knowing the circumstances he'd need it in, and two days ago, he'd decided those circumstances were looming near enough to send a message to Valter. The layers of his plans, the steps he's taken to weave himself a path to the middle of Cashel's web…

I can't keep up.

"I'm so sorry," Isolde says, her voice hard. "Did you say you've been tracking us?"

"Yes." Valter looks puzzled. "You're wearing trackers. Well, you are," he says to Isolde. "And Mark is wearing one as well."

Isolde is shaking her head as she palpates her black pants and close-fitting sweater, as she runs quick fingers along the hems and seams. She checks her boots—and it's as the van turns slowly onto a narrow street and a lonely street-light winks across the length of her honeysuckle ring that we realize.

She stops unlacing her boots and sits up, holding her hand in front of her face. The ruby sparkles darkly.

And then I remember how he found us at Morois and again in Rome. I remember how strange and beautiful I found his gift of the black and silver ring before I left for Ireland. A cruel reminder that I'd never wear any other kind of ring from him, a constant source of obsession, an unyielding reminder of his attention. A gift I treasured and never took off.

I remember him switching our rings in a closet at

Lyonesse, his fingers warm on mine as he gave me his wedding ring to wear, and he carefully slid his own gift onto his finger.

My eyes meet Isolde's.

"I'm going to kill him," she says.

Valter is greatly amused by all this. "This is a very Mark thing to do," he observes amiably. "But it did save your lives tonight, if that sparks any forgiveness. We wouldn't have been able to find you otherwise."

"He's not wrong," I tell Isolde.

Hot fury tightens her bruised mouth. "He told us there'd be no more secrets. No more lies."

But what would we have done if we'd known this particular secret? Taken off the rings? And then where would we be? Because there'd been no fighting off the heavy wave of saints that swarmed us and Jago as we tried to make it to the car. There'd been no resisting whatever they'd injected us with to make us abeyant for the journey to Rome. And we'd woken up tied to two steel pipes in a building with bloodstains on the concrete, so the options for helping ourselves then had been rather limited too.

"Sometimes Daddy does really know best," Valter says with a laugh. "And speaking of Daddy..."

The van has stopped in front of a house with a terracotta roof and flaking stucco. Graffiti covers the rusting gate. In the sweep of the headlights from the vans behind us, I see someone standing near the front door...someone with hair the color of beaten gold.

We get out, and Isolde makes it to him first. Whatever she was going to do, he's stopped her, catching her hand and then spinning her around. He puts his mouth near her ear, whispering.

"I don't care. You lied," I hear her seethe.

"I'm happy to see you too, sweetheart," he murmurs,

kissing her temple. "And surely, you'd guessed? You didn't guess? It's okay. You'll know better than to trust a pretty gift next time."

"Two saints escaped," says Valter to Mark, clearly enjoying this glimpse into Mark's love life. From the cage of Mark's arms, Isolde struggles in vain. "We were careful, but they'll be after you. I'd move quickly."

"As quickly as we can," says Mark. "Thank you, old friend, for coming on such short notice. I know you're far from home."

"I don't know that any favor is enough to repay what you did in Östersund," Valter says. "But you understand that it'll be hard for us to get away again, at least anytime soon. I'm already in enough trouble as it is." He's smiling but there's a serious note in his voice. I can only imagine the implications of Swedish intelligence operatives on Italian soil, doing something unsanctioned by either government to satisfy what seems to be a private debt.

Valter comes to clasp Mark's shoulder, Isolde temporarily going still between them. I can see by the way her hands shake that she's dogged by exhaustion and crashing adrenaline. I am too, although I'm standing in the dark, so I can hide it better.

Mark grips Valter's elbow in return. A short nod, the kind that comes from a well of shared history, and then Valter lets go and walks back toward the van.

"You're in good hands," Valter says to me as he passes by. "Even if it doesn't feel like it."

"Will it ever feel like it?" I mutter, and the spy laughs.

"Oh!" he adds, reaching into a long pocket on the side of his pants and pulling a bundle of burlap free. "We found this when we were doing our final sweep. I thought you might like to have it back."

I unwrap the burlap as Valter slips back into his van.

His people leave with the same brisk efficiency they rescued us with, rolling smoothly away and disappearing at the turn of the road, headlights sweeping and then vanishing with machinelike precision. I look down at the knife in my hands, its hilt inlaid with rubies and gold.

I turn back to Mark and Isolde to see that Mark is smiling, a real, happy smile. As I come closer, I can see the swollen eye and the trails of dried blood framing the side of his face, which streak down his neck and disappear into the collar of his shirt. He's still wearing the white button-down he had on under his suit jacket, but the rolled sleeves look irremediably stained, and a long tear in the side exposes freshly purpled ribs. One of his forearms looks like it's been dipped in dark paint and left to drip dry.

He looks like he's just climbed his way out of hell, and he has the nerve to smile down at Isolde like he's earned himself an angel.

He bends to kiss her forehead, her nose, her stubborn mouth. She refuses to kiss him back, but she doesn't resist him kissing *her*, settling for a glare when he pulls back to meet her eyes.

"Will you behave now?" he asks, affection plain in his tone. He finds her ferocity as endearing as he finds my obedience, I think.

"This isn't over," she sniffs, looking away. An offended cat who will sit by its owner but ignore them the entire time.

He kisses her temple, like he can't help but kiss her, and jealousy leaps through me.

"Scourge me all you'd like," he purrs. "I look forward to it. But be good for now so that I can kiss Tristan without fear of being executed for my little crime, hmm?"

The jealousy is still there, but when Isolde relents and Mark reaches for me, it transmutes from a baser metal into gold, shimmering and molten. I let Mark take my hand, my arm, yanking me into him so he can cup the back of my neck and kiss me.

He tastes like blood.

We breathe together a moment, Isolde tucked between us.

"Why didn't you tell us about the rings?" I ask as we break apart.

There's not enough light to track the subtleties of his expression, but I do see something wary and resigned there. Perhaps even guilty, though I'm not sure what guilt would look like on Mark's face.

"Some things aren't meant to be atoned for," he says finally. "They simply are as they are meant to be. And any devil worth his salt is happy to take the blame for them." And before we can interject, he says, "But there will be time to put me on trial later. For now, we need to move."

He takes my hand and then puts his other at the small of Isolde's back, guiding us toward a small car in front of the house. It's old but not too old, worn but not battered, forgettable in every way.

"Where are we going?" I ask. "Home?"

"We are going to the end," says Mark. "To Nemi."

thirty-five

TRISTAN

I'VE NEVER HEARD OF NEMI—A LAKESIDE TOWN LESS THAN an hour's drive southeast—but Isolde's expression when we get into the car is pensive. Finally, after Mark maneuvers us out of the half-abandoned neighborhood and toward larger and larger roads, she asks, with no inflection in her voice, "The summer palace?"

"Your uncle uses the palace as cover," says Mark, changing lanes and merging onto a highway denuded of traffic this late at night. "For visiting Nemi."

"Why Nemi?" she asks. "I've never known him to go there."

"He's got a bad tooth," answers Mark, but he doesn't elaborate any further, and Isolde doesn't press. In fact, within just a few minutes, she's fast asleep.

————

Dawn isn't far off when we arrive in Nemi, which is perched on a steep hill above a lake and thicketed with pines. As we pull into town, Mark informs me that Nemi is famous for a sacred grove—where a pagan priest would fight strangers to the death in an ancient custom that endured until the reign of Caligula—and also its strawberries. The town is quiet, full of cobbled streets and buildings sun-bleached into pale pastels. Streetlamps glow a soft orange; above us, the Alban Hills push broodingly into the sky.

Our destination is just above the town itself, a buff-colored house with walls around it and a new metal gate. A mounted sign outside advertises it as a short-term rental, but Mark pulls right up and presses a call button mounted outside the gate.

There's no greeting, but Mark doesn't seem to expect one. When the speaker clicks, he says, "It's Trevena."

"Took you long enough," a deep American voice says after a minute, and then the gates slide open. Mark rolls the car up the drive.

Isolde is awake by the time we park, and as we walk up to the front door—stiffly, sorely, slowly—I appreciate what a mess the three of us look like right now. In clothes at least two days old, covered in blood, beat to hell, haggard and weary. And when the door is opened for us and I see our host's reaction, I know we must look even worse than we feel.

"Holy shit," the man says. Then he looks us over again and shakes his head. "Well, you better come in, I guess."

There are showers—not shared, even though I'm sad about that less for sex reasons and more because I don't want to let either Mark or Isolde out of my sight—and fresh clothes. I'm given food, some Advil, and then pointed toward a bed, where I lie down and sleep for what feels like a million years.

———

It's morning when I wake up, a clear one with cool air coming through a cracked window and a soothing view over the lapis saucer of the lake. I'd had a nightmare, I think, judging by the rapid thud of my pulse when I sit up, but by the time I dress and use the en suite, with a new toothbrush and tooth-paste helpfully provided, I'm wooed into something like calm. The view, the air, the sound of a house bustling full of people—even though I know we're not safe, that we're only another misstep away from being chained to a warehouse pipe again, everything about the morning feels like safety. It's like the best parts of the farmhouse and an army base all rolled into one.

Downstairs, Mark is sitting at a table with a lanky man with dark brown skin and a short woman with pale, pinkish skin that looks easily sunburned. They're wearing tactical clothing, boots, and expressions of sly capability that make me think they're something more complicated than military.

The open-plan living room is crowded with another ten or eleven people, a few of them playing cards, two of them napping, and the rest gossiping like old men at a dough-nut shop. Black duffel bags and gun cases are stacked neatly against a wall.

I walk to the table, and Mark gestures at the empty chair next to him without looking at me.

"I think any day now," Mark is saying, and the lanky man nods.

"We had someone at the Mass he said yesterday, and it looks like the swelling has reached his jaw. Any longer and he's going to need a hospital, not a dentist."

"He'll schedule a visit to the museum of the summer palace under some pretense, and that's when he'll come here for treatment. I don't suppose there's any way to…"

"Look at the dentist's schedule? It's all done by paper and phone, alas."

Mark picks up his cappuccino and sips, and as he does, he puts his arm over the back of my chair. It's casually

385

possessive, flagrant even, with the way his fingers pluck at the shoulder of my shirt, and I flush, because we're in front of other people and he's married to someone else, and also because his claiming, affectionate touch makes me want to sink to my knees and press my face into his thigh. Even with everything that's happened…maybe even especially with everything that's happened.

I think of his hand pressing against my heart as bullets flew around us.

Do you feel that?

I'm holding on to something good.

It wasn't even a question for him, to risk himself in order to save us. Like it was preordained. Like no other option existed for him.

The people at the table don't seem surprised by Mark's fingers toying idly with my sleeve. They notice, because they are the kind of people whose job it is to notice, but it seems like an utterly neutral detail to them, and they carry on talking.

"I wonder how my clockmaker got that appointment record then," wonders Mark aloud, looking out the window.

"We checked on that. The office had a brief foray into online booking software, abandoned after only a few months." It's the woman speaking now. She nods at her colleague. "Palmer made friends with the former office manager of the dental practice. Seems like the system was dropped after a few high-profile patients raised concerns about safety, so they went back to a fully analog system. She was grumpy about it, even years later."

Palmer scrubs at his shaved head with his hands as if personally victimized by the paper schedule. "We've got someone listening on the phones here at the house. It's very Cold War, very old-fashioned."

"Palmer is a man of modernity," Mark informs me. He

turns his head when he speaks, and when I look back at him, the full weight of his gaze, the same color as the lake outside, nearly breaks me. It's never been fair that his attention can feel like this, that something as inconsequential as sharing a dry little comment can feel like he's chosen you above all the world to share his kingdom.

For his part, Palmer is shaking his head in vigorous denial. "I'm merely practical! *Ferguson* is the modern one. You should see her try to use a paper map. She was driving circles in Athens for half a day the last time we were there. Missed a rendezvous with an agent by three hours."

The woman—Ferguson—flips him off with an unbothered smile.

They talk a little bit longer, mostly about the location of the dentist's office and the layout, and then after Mark's finished his drink, he withdraws his arm from my chair and stands up. "I'm going to check on Mrs. Trevena," he tells the table and then tilts his head to indicate that he wants me to come with him.

I stand, make an awkward goodbye to Palmer and Ferguson, and then follow him up the stairs, where he leads me into a room with a king bed and a view of the glittering lake. The pillows on both sides are dented, and I guess I can't hide my envy, because he says with some amusement, "You were already asleep by the time I finished talking with Ferguson and Palmer, and I didn't want to move you. You can sleep here tonight if you'd like."

I would like, but it does make me wonder what it means. What any of the last two days—two weeks—this last year—means.

And does it matter? While Cashel is still hunting us? What future can there be when our present is filled with bullets and blood?

Isolde is sitting on the window seat, her back against the

wall and her legs drawn up to her chest. Her hair is wet, wet enough that it shines in the morning light and drops gather at the ends. She's wearing nothing but the blanket she has wrapped around her shoulders.

She looks at us as we approach, cerulean gaze wary and closed off. Mark isn't intimidated by this at all; he strolls over to the window and half sits on the deep ledge, facing his wife.

"Well?" he prompts as I trail behind him and come to a stop just in front of the ledge, able to look at them both. "I know you want to ask, Isolde. No need to hold back."

A minuscule shift of her eyebrow. "Okay then. Why are we really in Nemi?"

"To kill your uncle," answers Mark easily.

For her part, Isolde doesn't seem to react to this at all. Perhaps she already suspected this was the case—or perhaps she's already accepted that it's the only way forward. "And who are the people downstairs? Since you've exhausted the generosity of the Swedish intelligence service?"

Mark's fingers are playing with the edge of the blanket around Isolde's feet. "Some CIA officers we know can be trusted. They're, *ah*, let's say, an unofficial loan."

"From whom?"

"Embry Moore owes me a favor," he says offhandedly. His fingers have found their way under the blanket now, are stroking the top of one delicate foot.

Isolde stares at him. "The president of the United States owes you a favor," she states.

"You remember our ceremony at Lyonesse, darling? When I cuffed you to a bed and fucked you until you came so hard that you cried?"

Isolde and I both blush, but Mark continues speaking and stroking Isolde's foot, forever shameless.

"I'm sure you remember all the beautiful flowers we

388

had too, nightshade and hemlock and oleander, that sort of thing. Well, I know it's customary to send guests home with gifts, so I invited them to help themselves to anything they wanted before they left."

"You sent our guests home with poisonous plants," says Isolde in some disbelief, and then she and I come to the realization at the same time. "The poisonings last year...the artistic planning director in DC, the deaths in Vancouver and Tokyo... There was a connection between them all along."

Mark's caresses have moved up to Isolde's ankle now. "Hundreds of guests were there that night, all of them witnessing each other rifle through our wedding's little poison garden and select souvenirs for themselves, all of them now either complicit or indebted to me—or both."

Her eyes narrow. "You said poisoning wasn't your style."

He sighs, put-upon. "It's not *my* style, darling. I can't help what people want to do with hemlock and nightshade after they take such things home. But that part isn't important. The wedding gifts were merely the smoke after all. The fire was in the foxgloves."

We're both rapt right now, and he knows it. He smiles to himself, enjoying our attention a little too much.

"Do you remember Melwas Kocur?" he asks us. "I'm sure you do, but however much you remember him, I'll tell you that Embry Moore remembers him much, much better."

Given that all my deployments were directly or indirectly related to that narcissistic psychopath and his ability to radicalize people even while he was behind bars, I would say I remember him very well. But certainly President Moore and the First Lady would have cause to remember in a very different way, since Kocur kidnapped Greer Colchester-Moore, and both the captivity and subsequent rescue were a source of private and public pain for Greer, then-president Maxen Colchester, and then-vice president Embry Moore.

Mark has started running his knuckles up and down Isolde's leg, and she barely seems to notice, that's how much her attention is on his words right now.

"It's annoying to kill someone in a semiresponsible prison—and I promise it's not a habit of mine—but for the sake of my own interests and Carpathian peace, of course, Melwas Kocur was a problem I was interested in solving. His medication and food were carefully watched, so I knew I couldn't simply pay someone working at the prison to poison him. It would need to happen further upstream. Luckily for me, Kocur had one indulgence while locked up: tea. Custom-ordered from a place in France." Mark massages the muscles of Isolde's calf, propping her foot on his thigh. "Do you know how tedious it would be to check every single tea bag that gets pulled from the box? A sealed box exactly the same as all the other boxes that have come before? And anyway, who would think to look at the *tea* later, when foxglove's poisonous compounds are the very same compounds in Kocur's heart medication? And even if they did look at the tea, who would think to check receipts for some party flowers from half a year ago and half a world away?"

"So you supplied who knows how many people with the means for murder and had an imprisoned authoritarian killed, all so you could have the president owe you a favor." Isolde's voice gives nothing away, and her expression is reserved, but when Mark's fingers reach her knee, her thighs fall apart as if they'd never been pressed together at all.

"Dear one, when are you going to admit it?" asks Mark. He slides his hand past her knee and stops midthigh, his thumb tracing slow semicircles over the silky skin there. Isolde's lips have separated, her pulse pounding in her throat, but her eyes are still wary. They are fixed on her husband.

"Admit what?" she asks.

His hand moves, and I don't have to see his destination. I can hear it. The wet drag of his fingers through the perfect place between her thighs. The careful and deliberate insertion of a finger. She arches under the blanket, her head falling back against the wall.

"That you like it when I do bad things," he says, twisting his wrist. She inhales. "You like when I take a knife to the world and pare it like an apple."

She doesn't want to admit any such thing, but the evidence is undeniable. When Mark uses his other hand to push the blanket off her shoulders, the berry-pink tips of her breasts are erect and there's a telltale flush on her chest. I catch a glimpse of her slick and blushing cunt as the blanket starts to come undone around her legs.

"Do you want me to kill more war criminals to woo you into my bed?" he asks in a voice that's as sincere as it is seductive. He would do it, of course. He'd kill anyone it took to keep Isolde coming back to him.

Maybe he'd do it for me too, except all three of us know the truth—he doesn't have to. He doesn't have to do anything to keep me coming back.

Isolde's eyes are glittering from underneath her long lashes, crescents of defiant blue-green. "I guess you'll have to try it and find out."

He tuts, his hand moving between her legs. "Forced to seduce my own wife," he says sorrowfully. "What has become of me? Tristan, come here. Get on your knees and take pity on me in my derelict state."

Isolde watches as I step closer and sink to the ground; her hips lift and seek Mark's touch. For his part, Mark nods down at his pants, indicating that I should be the one to unfasten them and draw out the hot, veined length.

I do, nuzzling against it a moment, and I press my face against the gold hair surrounding his cock too, kissing and breathing and just allowing myself to enjoy this part of him that I love so much.

When I finally put him in my mouth, Isolde's breath stutters. She is a rustle of blanket and bare feet pushing against the window seat, and she is reaching for Mark's hand, his wrist, to try to get him deeper, to get his thumb against her clit pressing harder.

Mark inhales as I give his tip a slow and seeking swirl and then inhales again when I slide him as far back as he'll go. His hips flex a little, as much as they can while he's on the window seat, and he tries to fuck my mouth like that, an inch back and forth, just the barest amount into my throat and then back out of it.

"Doesn't he do such a good job, little wife?" he croons to Isolde, all while his merciless hand continues its work between her legs. "Doesn't he service me so well? Look at those pretty green eyes, the way he wraps his lips around me. Can you see his throat when it—just—*ah*, fuck, there, there, can you see it? That bulge? That's me. He's letting me fuck all the way in there. It feels so fucking good, baby. Yes, keep taking it. That's a good boy."

My eyes are watering, and I can feel every nerve ending between my navel and my knees, and Isolde is watching us like we're pornography just for her, and then she twists back against the wall, her entire body arching into one sinuous, shuddering curve as her pussy convulses around Mark's invasion. He doesn't stop fucking my face, but once she's finished, he pulls his wet hand free and sticks his first two fingers into his mouth, sucking the taste of his wife off his skin.

He comes almost immediately from tasting her, and it seems to be a mean and spiteful orgasm given how he suddenly fists my hair and keeps sucking on his fingers, like he's afraid someone will make him stop. His cock pulses thickly, jetting seed down my throat; the hand in my hair keeps my throat impaled the entire time. He curls over me a little, hips moving reflexively. Small, mindless thrusts, like I'm a toy meant for use and nothing more. I can feel the precum smearing across the head of my dick, because that's what being his toy does to me.

A final spurt and then he slides free, replacing his erection with the fingers that had been inside Isolde and then licked clean. I suck eagerly on them too, wanting to do anything for him, anything to show him what a good boy I can be.

He stares down at me, eyes all black, and then looks over at Isolde, who is panting against the wall with her thighs apart and her slick pink flesh exposed.

"Use it," he says to me after catching me looking between Isolde's legs. "Use it to make yourself come. I know you want to. I know you want to fill it up. It's so soft, puppy. It'll feel so soft and tight. Go, get up now. See how she's already reaching for you? She wants it too, don't you, Isolde? That's what I thought. Give him this, and I'll let you use him later. We'll tie him up and you can ride his mouth or his cock—or both. I think you'd like riding his mouth, wouldn't you? Especially if he came inside you first and you were making him lick you clean."

His words are a quiet, beautiful weapon, as poisonous as the flowers at their Lyonesse ceremony, as sharp as Isolde's knife, and I barely make it between Isolde's thighs before the climax starts burning its way up my legs and begins to yank dazzling, breath-stealing pleasure from the bloody, vital center of my being. Isolde is sitting on the edge of the window seat, and I'm standing in front of her with her legs locked around my waist, buried to the hilt inside the married love of my life, and it only takes two thrusts inside that tight glove of a cunt before the ripping, tearing pleasure is spilling into her and pumping her full.

I rut through it, using my own cum as lube, and everything is messy and so constricting that it still takes some strength to force my way in, over and over, despite how wet she is. I drive home with a final, bone-breaking thrust, holding myself all the way in for the last few pulses.

I should be embarrassed, but no one could have lasted longer in the circumstances—not with Isolde's velvet welcome or the absolute fucking obscenity Mark was murmuring to me. Jesus Christ.

Isolde's hands come to either side of my head, and she pulls me down for a kiss. A gentle one, a pure one, that doesn't at all match the heavy, sliding flesh between us.

"May I?" asks Mark, and then he's kissing us too, soft and slow, his hands on our backs and arms and heads. We are steered to the bed, but we don't undress any more than we already have, and we don't fuck. Isolde is wrapped in her blanket again, and Mark and I are zipped back up, and Mark just…kisses us and plays with our hair and twines his fingers with ours.

I don't know that I've ever seen him this *affectionate*. Not desperate, not feral or hungry. But more like he can't stop touching us. Like he wants to use up a lifetime quota of kisses before sunset. Like he wants the very whorls of his fingerprints to match ours.

"Are you very angry with me about the rings?" he asks us after an hour or two of this. The sun is lovely, a January memory of summer, and I am drunk on whatever neuropeptides come from having a monster aggressively pet and cuddle you. I never want it to end, and when I roll my head to look over at Isolde and the dazed way she's tracing the veins and tendons of his forearms, I think she feels the same.

"No," I say. "I should have known. But when you switched rings with me at Lyonesse, I thought—"

"You thought right. It was for us." His eyes are so much

lighter in the Italian sun, the kind of blue that makes you think of floating on your back while birds wheel overhead and happy voices call from nearby. "I would have done the same thing even if there wasn't a tracker inside the ring."

"I don't like not knowing," says Isolde after a moment, tracing carefully around the inflamed cut on Mark's bird tattoo. The cut has been cleaned and glued shut, but there's no doubt it will be an uglier scar than the ones underneath it.

I shudder when I think about the reason for the cut, for those scars, the mental fortitude it would take to birth salvation from your own arm, like a fucked-up facsimile of some Greek god. I shudder when I think of the kind of mind it would take to even dream up such a preparation.

Isolde moves on to Mark's hair now, combing through it, sanding over his scalp with her fingertips. His eyes fall closed. "If you really want me to be your wife, your honeysuckle queen, you have to treat me like it. Like a partner," she tells him quietly.

He doesn't reply to that, his eyes staying closed as she continues stroking that fine hair. But I see his hand twitch a little at her waist, an involuntary flex.

"And I want to go with you," she says. She says it with a tense, quavering tone, something she's been working up the courage to say. A request she's nervous will be denied.

"Go where, dear one?"

"To kill my uncle."

Mark opens his eyes. He searches her face, chewing momentarily on his bottom lip. It's such a boyish gesture on him, especially as he's looking up at her. Right now, he just looks…young. And uncertain. And in love.

There's a troubled set to his mouth and a new shadow in his eyes when he finally responds. "If you want to be there, I think it's your right to go. But I'm not making room for mercy, Isolde. Not for him. If you go, then you are attending his trial already knowing the verdict."

"I understand," she says.

"Truly?"

"I don't want mercy. Not—not after everything that's happened. But I feel like I should bear witness to it."

Mark turns his head to look at me. I'm lying next to him, our heads on the same pillow, and we are almost nose to nose now. "What about you?" he asks seriously. "Are you comfortable witnessing this?"

Comfortable watching a defenseless old man executed at his dental appointment? An old man who is supposed to speak with the authority of God here on earth?

"Yes," I say with no hesitation at all. I couldn't care less that he's tried to kill me—he has that in common with thousands of militants in Carpathia after all—but trying to kill *Isolde*? After years of exploiting her faith as a weapon for his own ends?

No, even if he vowed never to hurt Isolde again, never to even *think* about her, it still wouldn't be enough. The part of me that didn't feel conflicted in the least about killing Jovian Nantes, that only felt strange about *not* feeling strange, that part doesn't care about Mortimer's age or his papal election or anything other than Isolde living the rest of her life free from his malice.

I think Mark must see all this in my face, because a knowing smile flickers across his lips. "Good."

A knock sounds, and even though we aren't indecent by typical standards, something about the last couple of hours feels too intimate to share. We are all out of bed and put together when Mark answers the door and we hear Ferguson say, "The call finally came through. Tomorrow afternoon, the pope is coming to Nemi."

thirty-six

TRISTAN

THE REST OF THE DAY PASSES IN A BUSTLE AND BLUR OF PREP. The cards are put away, the gossip stops, and we watch digital walkthroughs of the dentist's office, discuss contingency plans, rehearse over and over again the infiltration and the sweep. At some point, Mark gets a phone call from Lox and paces in the cobbled courtyard for over an hour while they talk. Isolde leaves too, not because she gets a call but for her own unknowable reasons, and I find her eventually on the terraced roof of the house, staring out over the lake. It's still winter, but the sun makes the day gentle and kind, and our long sleeves are enough to keep us warm. I pull her back against my chest and wrap my arms around her anyway. Just because I want to.

"Mark still on the phone?" she asks. A breeze waves the sedate, eternal boughs of the pines between the sleeping oaks and beeches. The air is so clean up here, so new and fresh. It's not Morois, but after the damp air of the church in Albany and the fetid Roman warehouse, this smells like heaven.

"Yes," I say. "He's agitated by whatever it is. You should see the state of his hair right now."

She puffs a small laugh, which makes me swell a little with pride. She doesn't give those easily.

"Do the Armorica people know you're safe?"

"They do."

"What—what happens after this?" she asks. She asks it quietly, like she doesn't want to, like she's dreading the answer, like she resents her own weakness. "Will you still work at Armorica?"

"If your safety no longer depends on my distance, then I will be at your feet with my heart held aloft in my hands for you," I whisper into her ear. I feel her draw in a shivering breath, and I kiss her neck. "I love you, Isolde. I would only ever stay away to keep you safe."

She nods and turns into me. "I promise I won't always be this jealous of Isabella," she mumbles into my chest.

"I like it," I admit. "It makes me feel wanted." Matches the sickness inside myself, the one that loves too quickly, that loves too much. It's not healthy for us to feel and crave jealousy and possession like this, and yet…

It's hard to sleep that night, and something's shifted inside Mark since the countdown began. I don't entirely know what it is—when we fuck, he is as wicked and enticing as ever, luring us into fresh depravity as we both use Isolde's cunt at the same time, frotting slickly against each other while she shivers and pants between us—but there is a bruising yearning in his touch, something that feels like resignation, that feels…grim almost. Mark stares at both of us as he comes, eyes flicking between Isolde and me, and even his final grunt of pleasure has a bleak, bitten-off edge to it.

I fall asleep next to him with Isolde in my arms and a knot growing just under my rib cage, a knot that's there in my dreams and there the moment I wake with a stretch of cold bedding at my back.

He's already up.

It's already time to go.

I can see why Mark goes to such trouble to collect favors as our paramilitary friends stage themselves around the dentist's office and, with a quiet signal via our earpieces, begin to work their way into the building with oblique grace. They use the building next door to access the roof and the terraced street below to access the lowest level. They come in through the front door, Mark, Isolde, and myself with them.

Mortimer has security, as we knew he would, a layer of hired muscle and a handful of saints, but it's not nearly enough for a team of the agency's best plus the three of us. Within fifteen minutes, we have the building secured, the dentist, hygienist, and office manager escorted away. Bullet casings litter the floor, bodies are everywhere, and Isolde is flicking blood impatiently off the edge of her knife.

Palmer and Ferguson share a few quiet words with Mark, and then we take the stairs to the dentist's actual office, where Mortimer Cashel has been brought. He's sitting on a chair near a window overlooking the lake, blood spattering his white shirt and face. He's not wearing ecclesiastical clothing today, perhaps trying to blend in, but I notice he's still wearing the piscatory ring on his pinkie finger. His jaw does look a little swollen, and there's a red splotch of fever at the corner near his ear. He'd waited too long to take care of that infected tooth, it would seem.

"Thirty minutes," Palmer reminds us. The prearranged amount of time we have with Mortimer before we need to clear the scene. Murdering a pope and making it look like an accident is complicated business, even for a team like this, and they'll need to get started as quickly as possible.

Mark thanks him, and Palmer shuts the door. It's only the three of us and Mortimer now, and while the office is spacious, furnished with a slender minimalist desk and only two narrow armchairs, it abruptly feels like there's no room at all in here.

Mortimer looks serene. Isolde is pale, entirely shuttered.

And Mark…looks like Mark. Casual, predatory, his proprietary fusion of cold disdain and magnetic charm dripping from his handsome features.

"At last, I get to meet Brittany Hill," Mark greets, crossing his arms and leaning against the glass of the window. He has the sleeves of his black tactical shirt pushed up, and I can see the swollen red wound along his tattooed forearm.

Mortimer folds his hands in his lap, a busy gentleman being mildly inconvenienced. "I suppose I should ask how that name came across your desk."

Mark smiles. "*My desk*. I like that. In this case, my desk is a drafty spot in Manhattan where I occasionally interview new friends. You remember Filip Drobny, obviously, and how he had Isolde followed? I caught up with one of those followers the day of Isolde's dress fitting, and we had a nice conversation. He shared the name *Brittany Hill* with me. I did tell you my theory, about trouble in paradise?"

Mortimer nods benignly, gesturing for Mark to continue, which he does with good cheer.

"At first, I thought Brittany was the name of a mistress or a secret child. It didn't fit with anything I knew about you, but then maybe you were more ordinary than I'd grown to believe, with an ordinary man's flaws. But then I learned that you had a far more ordinary flaw than even a broken vow or two—bad teeth. Worse than bad teeth: bad luck. Bad luck that a tooth should give you trouble right before the conclave. Bad luck that a dentist's chair was destined to be one of the few times you'd be truly powerless—and worse luck still that if you used the Vatican's dentist, everyone from Rome to Reno would know when you'd be vulnerable to attack."

Isolde's uncle looks at his hands, sighs. "I hate admitting you were right, but perhaps I should have taken men like Drobny more seriously. Clearly, their discontentments had consequences. Trouble in paradise, as you say."

Mark smiles at him. It's not a nice smile. "It's funny, Cashel, all these years I've been trying to find a way to kill you—wooing, seducing, hacking, spying—and all it took was going back to my roots and hitting someone tied to a chair. I did scuff the bottom of my favorite shoes doing it though," he finishes and then adds, like it's a crucial detail: "They were Ferragamo."

"So you have found me, and now you plan to kill me," states Mortimer. "And you've brought my niece with you and your little shared pet. Who shouldn't even be here, really. He should be transitioning to civilian life and maybe meeting some nice elementary school teacher and settling down to dabble in raising chickens and growing tomatoes. And yet you've made sure he can never escape this small accident, this one understandable trespass, of killing your husband."

I'm irritated at being talked about like a pet—and irritated at my irritation, because I know that's the point, that Mortimer is trying to fuck with our heads—so it takes me a minute to process his mistake.

"I guess you don't know everything," I say with some scorn. I've come to stand in front of the long, low desk so I can see Mortimer's face better; Isolde has done the same thing but in front of the window near Mark. The sunlight makes their hair glow, haloes of violent angels. "Mark's husband died in Košice. I've never been to Košice."

Mortimer laughs, a real laugh, his eyebrows lifting and a dimple digging itself into his cheek. "Oh, you don't know at all! How unexpected."

My irritation has returned. "I saw the newspaper article about his death. Eliot died in Košice. In Slovakia. Tell him, sir."

Mark is staring at Mortimer, his face hard.

"Sir, tell him. Tell him he's wrong."

He doesn't look at me when he says, almost gently, "I cannot."

I can't trust my own memories, my own mind. I *saw* the clipping, I heard Mark talk about Eliot's death, I know I did. But the look on Mark's face…

"The CIA does that," says Mortimer in the wise and benevolent tones of a teacher sharing an important lesson with a favorite student. He's still smiling. "You believed what they wanted you—and the entire world—to believe. You understand, surely: it's extremely awkward when an American soldier shoots a fellow American, especially when said fellow American is meeting with a known arms dealer at the time."

This is a lie, a blatant fiction. I would *know* if I killed a CIA officer, much less one who was married to the man I now love.

But Mark isn't disagreeing with Mortimer. He isn't scoffing or smiling or treating it like some kind of verbal ploy. He's merely watching Mortimer like a man watching an opponent slide a piece across a chessboard.

Fear trickles down my spine.

"Sir…" I start. "That can't—that can't be right." I dredge up the memories, of McKenzie dead on the ground, the snapping of bullets back and forth. "We'd had a report of insurgent activity there, weapons drops. The intel came down straight from Stuttgart, and when we got there, it seemed exactly like the report said it would be—and no one called back that they were friendly—"

I try to remember exactly how it unfolded, all of it a messy, drizzled blur. We heard voices while on patrol, saw the two dimly outlined shapes at the end of the alley. We called out, announced ourselves, and a gunshot cracked through the air. McKenzie was the first to return fire, and then I got my weapon up just in time to see the flash of a silver wristwatch; I squeezed off three shots.

McKenzie had dropped to the wet ground, the other soldiers with us were hit—I didn't see the wristwatch again, but the bullets still came—and I had to keep firing. I had to call for help. I had to render aid after the shooting finally stopped. And when help came, there'd been no one in the alley—no bodies at all, only blood, like it hadn't even happened, except it *had* happened because McKenzie was dead.

I've always wondered how they'd managed to vanish like that, if they'd been hit but not killed, able to drag themselves away. I've wondered why I didn't hear anything else afterward, why I was lauded and praised and also not deemed worthy enough to know what the fuck McKenzie had died for, whether they had been insurgents or petty criminals or *what*. I'd wondered if any tiny, infinitesimal difference in the sequence of events would mean that McKenzie could still be here today—if we hadn't heard anything in the alley, if she hadn't been the first to return fire, if she'd been angled literally in any other direction when that fateful bullet struck.

I've wondered about so many things when it comes to that night, but I have never *ever* wondered about that silver wristwatch.

And I can't make myself believe it; right now, it is simply the most ridiculous fucking thing I can think of—that the wristwatch from that night is the same wristwatch I never saw Mark without, that the person I was trying to kill was the handsome grinning man from Mark's pictures. That Mark's grief, Mark's revenge, founding Lyonesse, marrying Isolde—every fucking thing that's happened for the last eight years—every bit of it was because I saw silver glinting in the dark once upon a time.

I stare at Mark, and finally, *finally*, he looks back at me.

And for a split second, his control is burned away. I see every last bit of what these eight years have done to him. Fury and anguish and heartbreak. Hatred and obsession.

Love.

For eight years, he's built an entire kingdom to destroy the crown of one man, and for eight years, he's done it knowing exactly who robbed him of the one thing he'd held close to his heart. Who pulled the trigger and how many times.

I think Mark loves me. But staring into his vast, turbulent, heartless eyes, I suddenly come to understand that he hated me long before that. That he might still.

Mark blinks and he's back to his cool composure, expression betraying nothing, and I am shaking; I can't make myself stand upright. I slump back against the desk.

"You hate opera music," I say in a broken mumble, scrubbing a hand down my face. It's only barely on the fringes of my memory, the soloist's tragic voice floating into the night air. Just one more way that McKenzie's death was too fucking absurd to exist inside the ordered and valor-laden coherence of the reality handed to me by my father and West Point.

"I hate opera music," Mark agrees.

Isolde can't hide her own shock—a rare thing for her—but there it is, in the splotches on her cheeks and her flicking gaze, as she stares at both of us.

"You said you hired me because you knew I'd do the right thing," I say. I say it like I'm pleading with him.

"And once, eight years ago," he says softly, "you did the wrong thing."

The third box in Mark's safe makes sense now, the articles and clippings and pictures going all the way back to the Distinguished Service Cross. So this was why he'd been following my career like a silent panther after its prey, watching as I became exactly what the army wanted me to be—a hero—and as being a hero shattered whatever was left of my will and my mind and my resolve.

You are the only candidate, he said when he interviewed me for the job.

And now I know why.

"How?" I ask Mark in a whisper. "How have you been able to keep that hidden all this time? How have you been able to look at me—kiss me—and at Morois—" Oh God, Morois. When he'd shut himself away with his grief, and I'd shamelessly wriggled my way in, offering him the relief of my body when I'd been the one to create the need for relief in the first place. When I'd begged him to let me help him mourn, and all along, I was the reason for mourning. He'd fucked me into the carpet knowing I'd killed his husband. He'd let Eliot's killer dress him and wash him and kiss his feet.

"It wasn't precisely *planned*," replies Mark, who's now looking at the lake. A muscle jumps in his jaw. "I wasn't supposed to care about you. I wasn't supposed to want you. I've been around handsome men before, Tristan—I can generally hold my own. And then you ruined it. You ruined everything by being so good and sweet, my own little Maxen Colchester but better, because you let me right into that tender heart with no fight at all. Years spent stalking the man who killed my husband, only to find that I loved him like I'd never loved anyone before. You see what a fucking mess that made, right?"

"I'm sure he's beginning to see it now," says Mortimer, interjecting with the silky, inveigling curl of incense smoke. "He's a smart boy. He's putting together that there would only be one reason to hunt him down, one reason to trap

405

him in your cage once he escaped the army's, and it wasn't for the pleasure of providing him with health insurance. You didn't stalk him for eight years only to offer him a job—you stalked him to kill. You stalked him to stop that tender heart from beating at all."

thirty-seven

ISOLDE

Tristan's cheeks and lips lose all color, going ashen as he stares at Mark with a hopeless, wounded confusion. My uncle smiles to himself, pleased to see his arrow strike true, and it's that pleased smile more than anything that begets a deep and toneless horror in my marrow. He's smiling because he's right.

He's smiling because it's true.

For a moment, we are simply a tableau of lies, the handsome knight, the wicked king, the holy man wielding the divine authority to drag what was done in the dark into the light. My heart is barely working right now, a cinch of tight muscle, and my fingers and toes flicker and spark as my circulation struggles to keep up.

Tristan looks like he's going to faint.

The moment ends, the tableau breaks. Mark sighs and pushes himself off the window, stepping toward my uncle with a disappointed expression.

"Is that *your* ace in the hole?" asks Mark mockingly. "You are predictable in every way I can imagine, Cashel, because the world is an orrery to you, a fixed, mechanical universe where nothing ever changes that can't be predicted, nothing ever moves that can't be measured. Change is beyond your mind's reach, and even your curiosity is dulled with the certainty that everyone, always and everywhere, is secretly hoping to be the worst version of themselves."

My husband lifts his eyes to Tristan. Dark, turbulent eyes, with the plundering strength of his body on full display against the glass.

"I wanted to kill you," he admits. "In the beginning. Isolde too. You, the person who pulled the trigger. Her, the only soft spot I could find in the man who'd made sure a trigger would be pulled."

My heart constricts to the point of pain, once again becoming a knot of bloodless muscle, and I squeeze my eyes shut. All this time—all the danger I felt rolling off him, all the trust I gave him anyway—I'd let this man tear me open and eat me whole, and he'd hated me through it all. He'd wanted to kill me all along.

I asked for you. I wanted you. He said that to me the night he gave me my engagement ring. And I've known since Samhain that he asked for me because of who my uncle was. But I hadn't followed the logic any further, any deeper.

That I was to be revenge in its purest, oldest form.

I'm going to be sick. *I'm going to be sick.*

"But," Mark goes on, starting to circle my uncle's chair now, "life is not an orrery where we must spin forever in circles after being flicked by a careless finger. Life isn't fixed. I fell in love with Isolde without meaning to. I became more obsessed with Tristan than I care to admit before I even met him. More importantly, I learned what the three of us had in common. Can you guess what that might be?"

He's come around to the front of the chair, nudging my uncle's black velvet loafer with his boot.

408

"No? No guesses? I suppose we all know well enough. Three years ago, I learned you'd smithed Isolde's faith and her fear into a knife made to fit your hand. Last year, Tristan had to shoot his friend in the throat because of the little hierocracy you're trying to build in Carpathia. The three of us have *you* in common, Your Holiness. We have your schemes and your crimes. How could I blame Isolde or Tristan when they were as much victims of your stupid fucking plans as I was? How could I punish them for what you'd done to me when you were doing it to them too? It doesn't matter what order love and clemency came in for them, because they did come. I did change. They changed me."

He moves his stare, a dark, uncomfortable blue, to me and then to Tristan.

"I might resent them for it some days," he finishes softly, a little bitterly, "but they are forever safe from me. And I am no longer safe from them."

Tristan's head dips, like he can't bear the weight of Mark's gaze. His profile, with his straight nose and full mouth, is a study in shell-shocked beauty.

I still can't breathe. I think I believe him. How can I afford to believe him?

"So I'm disappointed that this is all you've got. They might never forgive me, they might fear me, but I'd as soon harm them as I'd let you live. That is the difference between me and you, Most Holy Father: I'm not afraid to be known. I might steal and I might lie, and I'll always live in the falling slant of a shadow, but it's not because I'm frightened of the light. And I think you are. I think perhaps there was one person left whom you cared about, one person who you could bear to be seen by, and I think perhaps you thought you could have her see all of you. I think you thought she would hear about everything you've done and applaud your vision and your cleverness and your tenacity. You thought she'd agree with you that there was a new order waiting to be dredged from the slush of the old and that only you had the imagination and force of will to do so."

My valves open, my atria fill, and my ventricles release. Suddenly, blood is thrumming through me, hot and vital and laced with premonition.

"But she didn't react that way, did she? You told her about the saints, and then you told her about the careful, bloody foothold you made in Dublin as a priest. You told her about Ys. And instead of seeing how adroit and ingenuous you'd been, she saw tombstones. Land mines and burned crops and preventable diseases, and you skittering over it all like a spider. And unlike you, she had a conscience. She felt a need to stop you—in fact, she was going to do something rash unless she was stopped. So you stopped her."

For the first time, my uncle's eyes move to me. He's facing the window, which means the sunlight can perfectly illuminate all the uneven blue and green speckles, the heterochromatic eyes that run in the family.

My mother had them too.

"Barbara told me in Albany," explains Mark. "How you arranged for the death of your sister. That part is a certainty, but I'm guessing a little as to the why. Am I close?"

There's an expression on my uncle's face that I've never seen before. I think it's regret—although there's a flatness to it, a distance, that renders it almost unrecognizable as the kind of regret anyone else would feel in his shoes.

Which means it's real. Whatever he's feeling, it's not performed for anyone else, and however stunted and anemic, it's genuinely his.

Which means—which *means*—

"Oh God," I whisper, a jagged rift opening up in my chest. I am going to be sick. "How? *How*? How fucking could you?"

"She was going to the Holy Father, Isolde," my uncle says, the warped regret in his face deepening. "I couldn't let her destroy Ys or me simply because she couldn't see what I was trying to show her! I asked Barbara to make it as fast and as clean as she could, because I didn't want Inis to suffer." He adds this last part as if it were a charitable work, a show of deep and feeling humanity, that he wanted his sister's murder to be quick.

I'm shaking now. I can't even think. "I lost everything when she died," I breathe. "*Everything*. My father and myself, a normal future. Everything died with her."

"But it was better, Isolde, because I was there," my uncle says, shifting forward in his chair, all pretense of nonchalance gone as his expression changes into a nightmarish version of itself: his wide grin like a rictus of corruption, his sparkling eyes like the matte and muddy edge of water against weeds. "I was able to guide you and shelter you and help you *see*. You are so very like Inis, and it felt like a second chance, to take you and mold you and make you a part of the world I was building. I loved your mother, and I love you. Nothing I've done has been easy for me."

Tristan—still stunned from the revelations of the last few minutes—stirs. "Who fucking cares?" he asks, his melodic voice unusually harsh. "Are we supposed to care that it was *hard* for you to kill your sister? To plan for Isolde's kidnapping and execution?"

Mortimer twists to regard him with a raised eyebrow. "You've come to kill *me*, Mr. Thomas. Are you going to begrudge me my final confessions?"

I step closer to my uncle—not so close as to be in danger but close enough that I can see the short, reddish lines of his eyelashes. The rolling scars on his cheeks.

"Why?" I ask. It's a simple question, but it also doesn't feel simple at all as I ask it. As my voice shakes and my heart jolts erratically in my chest and my thoughts are filled with a laughing, loving woman who was *good*. "Why do all this? To my mother? To me? You can't think you have God on your side. You can't think you're doing something other people will thank you for."

My uncle turns back to face me. Like before, I think the expression on his face could be one of belief, but it's too strange and hollow to mimic belief as anyone else would recognize it.

"God has nothing to do with this. It's *me*," my uncle says. "I won't let him claim credit for my work. I'm the one ensuring the future of the Church. I'm the one toiling day and night to remake gravity so that the Church survives. And when I'm done, there will be something like what hasn't been seen in hundreds of years—a pope to be *feared*. A Church with earthly power once again."

Mark comes up beside me. Gorgeous Mark, with glinting hair and well-shaped lips and a bruise under a perceptive blue eye. Mark, who wanted to kill me at first. Mark, who lets me fuck the man who killed his husband.

"You are done now," says Mark almost kindly. "This is the end. There's no rescue coming, no persuading Tristan or Isolde to help you. There will be a car accident this afternoon, tragically ending in an eruption of fire and making you something of a martyr. You will be dead long before that though." He pulls out a knife from a harness, and I see it's *my* knife, my honeysuckle one, the one he gave me.

But he doesn't move toward Mortimer. Instead, he hands me the weapon hilt first, his expression serious.

I meet his eyes. They are still the eyes of the man who's lied to me over and over again, but the clarity in them right now is a gift.

I take the knife.

For the first time, real panic enters my uncle's voice. "You don't need to do this, Isolde. We can talk about Ys—come to a negotiation about your future. I was hasty, I admit, and eager for solutions that felt elegant at the time. Isolde—please, we can pray together—"

I think of my mother's smile. Of how soft her arm was when she let me climb into bed with her and use it as a pillow. Of how she smelled like sunshine, even in winter.

I think of how Mortimer took me under his wing after she died. How every year brought me more and more under his control until I ended up married to someone who wanted to kill me, until I ended up alone and disconsolate and bereft of the belief that had pulled me through the years. My uncle had taken the sun from my sky, and he'd taught me how to kill without asking questions instead.

The knife feels right in my hand. And when Tristan comes behind Mortimer and holds him down with two large hands, that feels right too.

"Do you remember what I told you the day we met?" asks Mark. "About the knives?"

"Standard grip is for a fair fight," I say. "Reverse grip is for when you mean it."

I shift the knife in my hand so that the blade is pointing down from the outside of my fist and step forward. And when I bring the knife down, I make sure I mean it.

thirty-eight

ISOLDE

MY UNCLE DIES SMILING, WITH BLOOD SMEARED ON HIS teeth, with his hands folded neatly over the wound in his chest as if in prayer.

Before his last breaths burbled out though, Mark leaned down and whispered something in his ear. My uncle, with a knife jammed between his ribs, couldn't truly laugh, but it was a reflex he couldn't seem to stop either. "Clever Minch," he mumbled. Bloody foam flecked his lips.

"It fooled me," Mark told him. "For years."

"Just as you've fooled them. Will you tell them?"

Mark didn't look up from my uncle, but I could tell by the care with which he stood up that my uncle had meant Tristan and me. *Will you tell them?*

God, what more could there be to tell?

My uncle didn't seem to expect an answer from Mark, and he didn't get one. He instead rolled his gaze up to my face. The knife was planted in his chest like a tree, and the rubies glittered like small, hard fruit.

"You are so like her," he choked between sucking, drawing gasps.

The words were only wet, airless suggestions of themselves. They were his last words, and his smile was the same smile I'd seen a thousand times before, gentle and wise, as if nothing had changed between us. But his eyes, before they dimmed, seemed to hold an entire host of malformed emotions—regret and anger and maybe even longing.

Or maybe—after Mark said *It's over, Your Holiness. You can stop at last*—maybe his eyes held a profound and exhausted relief.

I don't know if I'll ever entirely understand why he did any of it, but I've seen the effect of power on a person, stronger than any opiate, the burn of it more irresistible than liquor. I don't think it matters whether he started this nightmare out of misplaced faith or impatience with the system or ordinary ecclesiastical ambition—once the power came, there was no other answer, no other longing, no amount other than *more more more*.

There is no time to linger over his body and reflect, however. Mark yanks my knife free with one forceful pull, Tristan guides me away. Palmer and Ferguson come in, and we're shuffled down to the lowest level of the office, through a door to another building, out to a waiting car, which takes us to an airfield where a cargo plane is ready. We are shown to a run-down crew area with flat, hard beds, and I mean to stay awake, I mean to talk, but Mark makes both of us lie down, and then he sits in the chair nearby, watching us with a blue, inscrutable stare.

I fall asleep thinking about my uncle's mismatched eyes slowly filming over in death, and I don't dream.

———

Mark still has a warrant in the United States, so we land well

415

outside DC on a quiet airfield, and while manifests are being presented and import processes are begun, we're discreetly smuggled off the plane and taken to a car with the keys left inside.

There's a moment when Mark gets behind the wheel and pauses, and I know he's thinking of Jago. His hands tighten on the wheel once, and his long lashes dip and then lift again. He turns the key in the ignition, and the three of us are bound for Lyonesse.

It's not a terribly long drive, but the silence is centuries' worth of silence, eons of it, and yet no one moves to lift it. It's too heavy to lift, too laden with the truth, and where would we even start? When Mark hired Tristan? The alley in Kraków? The scream of rubber on an Irish road at the end of my mother's life?

It doesn't matter how much sleep I've had on the plane; it's not enough to bring any kind of clarity to the brittle snakeskin of secrets we've shed in the last twenty-four hours.

It's strange and heart-twisting to pull into Lyonesse's garage without Jago. I didn't see him die, but I did see him trying to give us suppressive fire as we ran toward the car, and I wish—I don't know. I wish I knew more about him. If he had a family, if he enjoyed working for Mark. If he knew that something as simple as driving a car for a kink club owner might end in his death.

Mark parks the car, turns it off; the interior lights come on with a bluish glow. He still has flecks of dried blood in his hair, and while the swelling has gone down around his eye, the bruise makes him look reckless and brutal. He looks like Hades himself right now in the otherworldly light.

"We have a guest," he says, nodding toward a spate of black SUVs parked at the front of the garage. A man in a dark suit and coat stands in front of one, his hands linked in front, an earpiece visible.

416

"Is that...the Beast?" Tristan asks hesitantly. "Like the president's car?"

Mark is already opening the door and climbing out. "Sure is."

"Is it a good thing or a bad thing that the president is waiting for you, sir?"

I'm getting out of the car myself and see when Mark waves a hand—the nails dark with whatever blood couldn't be washed off on the plane. "Probably a bad thing," he says, sounding deeply unbothered. "He'll lecture me about how he can't just be killing popes whenever I ask, I'll remind him of how much he enjoys Melwas being dead, and so on. The usual back-and-forth."

"You're really not afraid of the president being angry with you?" Tristan asks as we walk toward the doors leading to the club.

A scoff. Like Tristan had asked if Mark was afraid of his high school band leader. "I've seen that man go off in his pants while watching Maxen Colchester fish an ice cube from a glass. No, I'm not afraid of Embry Moore." Mark says all this as we pass by the Secret Service agent standing by the Beast, and the two exchange nods. Then he adds, "You should shower and change while I'm indulging the president's pique. Afterward, I'd like to speak with you both."

His voice has shifted from its unruffled, dismissive tone to something a little more closed off, something shrouded, and worry nips at my tired bones once again.

Will you tell them? my uncle had asked.

The club is always quiet during the day, but today it seems utterly empty, and when we reach the lobby, Ms. Lim meets us and quietly informs Mark as to why. Lady Anguish—Nimue—has opened the club for weekend hours only until Mark's warrant and asset seizure are completely put to bed, mostly to limit the guests' liability should the FBI come knocking, trying to interview people or squirrel themselves into other caches of information. But to counter the perception that the club is truly in danger, Kayden and Isabella have come back down from Montreal to help Anguish charm and schmooze the guests when the club is open, to reassure them that while Anguish is in charge, their privacy is safe and Lyonesse will persevere.

"They are waiting in the hall now," Ms. Lim finishes, gesturing up the stairs.

Mark nods and then waves Tristan and me to the elevators instead. "Shower," he commands. "We'll address everything else after that."

————

Tristan and I shower together, a dazed, tired affair that nevertheless ends with him wedged inside me, his mouth open against my neck. I think I might be too wrung out to come, but Tristan coaxes me there anyway, to a quiet climax that leaves me slumped against the shower wall while Tristan uses my pussy to finish.

We dress—Tristan borrowing Mark's clothes, me in trousers and a sweater—and we go down to the hall with skin free of dried blood and damp hair.

"How are you feeling?" Tristan asks in a gentle voice as we leave the elevator. "About what happened in Nemi?"

What happened in Nemi is too big a category to accord only one emotion. Right now, it's defined entirely by its lack of emotion: I feel almost nothing.

"I should feel more," I answer. "I should feel worse. I loved him more than I loved my father, and even after everything that happened this fall and I knew my uncle had started to see me as a liability, I never thought I'd—" I stop. It still doesn't feel real. The crunch of bone, the runnels of hot blood over the hilt. The wheeze of punctured lung and the blood-smeared smile.

Like something from another life, even though it was only yesterday.

Tristan doesn't say anything but finds my hand, holding it tight.

"But how can I feel more? How can I feel worse?" I ask, not really asking him or myself or anyone at all, just issuing an empty inquiry up to the sky. "Trying to kill me is one thing, but my mother? She was so good. Really good. I think not putting that knife into his chest would have been the greater sin, but I'm scared that I can't tell sin from sin anymore, much less sin from righteousness."

"I felt the same way after I killed Isabella's attacker," says Tristan. "I still feel that way. How many people have we killed in the last week, Isolde? How many people have been killed for the sake of our rescue or survival? They chose it, they chose to risk death in order to deal it to us, but I know I should feel something more, something like that slow rot I felt in the army, and I don't. Maybe because I know there was no other choice...but it still feels wrong not to feel wrong."

We are coming to the hall now, to the balcony where Mark is talking with President Moore and Lady Anguish. Isabella, Kayden, Dinah, Andrea, and Sedge are waiting near the entrance to the hall, and a handful of Secret Service agents are scattered between them and the three people conversing in Mark's usual nook.

"Ah, Isolde," Kayden says, coming forward to take my hand and kiss it. Next to me, Tristan doesn't physically react, but I can practically feel the air hum with jealousy. Fitting, because when Isabella gives Tristan an unhesitating hug—her glossy blond-red waves bouncing, her amber eyes large and limpid—I have the childish urge to yank him back.

The vagaries of jealousy are infinite, because the jealousy

I feel in regard to Isabella is immature and stifling, but when I think of Tristan and *Mark* together, the jealousy is like a cathedral. Capacious and holy. And yet on New Year's Eve when Mark poured all sorts of poisonous fantasies into my ear about Tristan fucking Isabella, I came hard enough for my muscles to ache the next day.

My husband waves us over as President Moore straightens up. Mark is slouched against the railing, blood-spattered and still wearing clothes that could be described as *need-to-know chic*. Lady Anguish is in a green pantsuit with a white silk blouse, a snowdrop brooch pinned to her jacket, and she smiles enigmatically at Tristan and me as we mumble quick apologies to the Armorica visitors and walk through the cloud of Sedge's and Andrea's disapproval to the nook.

"I have more to protect than just a presidency," President Moore is saying to Mark. He sounds a little grumpy but perhaps a little mollified too, like whatever Mark has been saying to him has sanded the edges of his irritation at being roped into a papal assassination.

"I know you do," says Mark affably. He could be the devil of Lyonesse on any other night, wooing a prospective member into unlocking coffers of the darkest, strangest things they know. "I have no intention of endangering your wife or your husband, Embry. You know I like them both."

Tristan and I both pause, our fingers twitching against each other's, the same question arcing through us.

Your wife or your husband? President Moore only has one spouse—the First Lady, Greer Colchester-Moore, née Galloway.

The president searches Mark's face for a moment. "I don't think I like you knowing as much as you do."

Lady Anguish trails a slender hand on the railing and says meaningfully, "Embry."

It's a little chiding, a little auntlike, because she *is* his aunt, the much younger sister of Governor Vivienne Moore of Washington. But it's not the weight of blood, her years in the political maelstroms of Olympia and DC, or her marriage to the political powerhouse Merlin Rhys that layers her voice with authority.

It's something deeper than any of those things, something older, and I think of the dream I had on my wedding night, of her standing in a forest with torches burning in a circle around her.

President Moore flicks a petulant look her way, but he does press his mouth together for a minute while he seems to master himself. He turns his head toward me and Tristan as we come to a stop, and his eyes, a blue I've only seen before on the petals of wildflowers, soften the tiniest bit as he looks at us.

"Don't make me regret helping you," he says finally to Mark. "You've been a good friend to us and to my aunt— and I haven't forgotten what you've done for my sister and her husband—but a disgraced war criminal is not the same as a newly elected pope. You owe me."

Mark bows his head. The gesture is courteous, completely conciliatory.

It doesn't seem to make the president any happier, but there's nothing else he can do, and he knows it. With an afflicted noise, he leaves, striding away on long legs and waving at the Secret Service agents who scuttle after him with flapping coats and gleaming shoes.

Lady Anguish smiles at us, a small, enigmatic smile. "My nephew can be skittish when it comes to protecting his family. The potential blowback from something like this isn't something to be taken lightly."

"They understand," says Mark, straightening up. "Just as they understand that Palmer and Ferguson are the best at

421

what they do. This won't be laid at anyone's feet at the end of the day, much less Embry's."

Anguish nods. "That's correct, it won't be. But he'll still worry in the meantime. He's never been as good at hiding his worry as Maxen. Or you."

Mark grunts.

"And on that note, I'll be in the lobby for the next hour or two, speaking with Ms. Lim. If anyone should need me." The last part she says with a delicate emphasis, her eyes shifting to mine. Her gaze is penetrating and clear.

I can't help the small shiver that races up my spine and then plucks with lingering fingers at the nape of my neck. It lasts even after Anguish has left the balcony and the hall altogether.

Mark watches her go and then looks down at his hands briefly, a war in his face, a man watching the enemy overrun his trench and choosing to stay anyway.

"Let's take a walk," he says.

thirty-nine

ISOLDE

"I don't expect forgiveness," Mark says. "I want to start there."

He's leading us to the end of the balcony's horseshoe, angling to one of the small bar areas closest to the door. When he gets there, he leans over the counter and starts digging around. After some clanking and cursing, he emerges with a bottle of scotch. He's drinking for real then. This feels ominous.

"And before I say anything else, it's important to understand that Ys isn't entirely finished just because your uncle is dead. There are the various war profiteers waiting in the wings and the diplomats and the captains of industry and whoever else still counting themselves as members."

"And the saints?" Tristan asks, forehead wrinkled. "Will they still count themselves as members?"

"I don't think so, but that's an educated guess more than anything else. The saints are the Church's, and Ys is a thing apart from the Church, even if churchmen have occasionally been recruited for its ranks. Cashel hadn't yet fully grafted the two together before he died, and that makes us lucky, because I don't think he invested much into the structure of Ys, knowing he'd eventually be using the Church's. This is the trouble with crime, actually: administration. You wind up needing secretaries and accountants and interns just the same as you do anywhere else, and this is doubly true if your chief interests lie in starting and sustaining wars. Evil takes a lot more emails than you think. In this respect, Ys has been a thin and wobbly thing, since your uncle was the chief fulcrum on which it turned, but that also makes it a convenient tool to scoop up and turn to your own uses if you have the vision and the access. And there is one person in the Church Cashel did trust enough to give the keys to the kingdom."

"The Scales," I realize.

Mark pauses at the railing to unstop the bottle. The hall is always empty during the day, but there is something about how empty Lyonesse is right now that unsettles me. I've grown used to the constancy of guests and staff, to never being truly alone even when I felt lonely.

"The Scales," confirms Mark. "A role indelible to the saints, and I think Cashel made the role indelible to Ys too toward the end. If the Scales is ambitious enough, then this is their chance to seize everything and finish what your uncle started. Fusing Ys and the Church together for good."

Mark starts walking again, taking a drink while he moves and pushing through the double doors that lead to a hallway of playrooms. Tristan and I follow after exchanging another quick glance, each of us verifying the other's uncertainty. I have no idea where Mark is going with this.

"Sir…" Tristan starts, but Mark just shakes his head.

"I know, this isn't really new information, but I just wanted to be clear before my confession that Ys is still dangerous while the Scales is alive. For a very long time, I planned on keeping things as they were until I knew for a fact that the Scales was dead—but after Nemi, my appetite for secrets seems to have vanished."

"Are there more secrets than me being the person to kill Eliot?" Tristan asks, and I'm surprised at the weariness in his voice, the defeat. He's been so steady today, so quick to offer a soft smile or an arm around the shoulders. But of course, he has to be as exhausted as I am, as twisted into knots by all this. "More than having once planned to kill us?"

We pass the vacant playrooms on our way to the elevator, all of them with doors propped open, the faint scent of leather cleaner filling the corridor.

"This is a small thing compared to those," says Mark. He glances once at Tristan's hands and then away again as he stabs at the elevator button. The doors open immediately and we step inside. "At least I thought so. I thought of all my secrets, it might be the easiest. I thought it was not so bad a thing for me to…borrow…the two of you for a while. Especially if I planned on leaving you alive at the end. What was the harm in a little detour of your lives? Lives that were already being detoured by unworthy masters like the army or Cashel?"

Mark pushes the button on the panel and turns to look at us while the doors close and we float up to our floor.

"It's Isolde's fault, this last secret. Because my plan for revenge, the one that seemed so clear in the beginning, started unraveling the first time Isolde crawled to me in the loft. Unraveled into looping piles during our first kiss, and the first time I made her come just from spanking her, and the night I found the holy card from her uncle. It became clearer and clearer that not only could I not kill her but that I needed to keep her shielded from the fallout. That I wanted her to have a future where she was safe, where she had someone to care for her with as much vigilance and affection as I would myself."

The elevator bobs to a stop, and the doors open. We step out, and rather than ask any questions or take his words apart for details, I wordlessly reach for the scotch, and Mark hands it to me.

We walk through Mark's office and into our home, the tall windows giving us a view of a silver sky outside and the huddled gray city underneath. I remember Lady Anguish's snowdrop brooch, though, and think about how spring is already stretching its arms underground, stirring and sighing into the smallest exhales of hope and warmth.

Mark takes the bottle back from me and wanders over to the window, next to a table holding a chess set missing its queen.

I suddenly miss Petitcrieu with a fierce, irrational ache, a child missing a favorite blanket or stuffed animal. I know it's for the best that Petitcrieu has been with Cara and Goran and Nat, but it just seems like playing with her giant paws would fix everything right now.

"It's funny," Mark murmurs, the words distant in the kind of way that makes me think he's talking to himself more than us. "That the remedy for one revenge was inside another."

I join Mark near the window, but I don't stand. I sit at the table with the chessboard. Tristan stops near the bookshelves, framed by war poetry and yellowing paperback mysteries as he watches us with vulnerable green eyes.

"Tristan once told an interviewer that he was ready to fall in love at a moment's notice." Mark turns to look at Tristan, who gives him an uncertain look in return. "The interviewer wrote that he was a romantic at heart. Something I didn't think about much when I first read the interview, other than to be annoyed by it. Who was this handsome baby murderer whose biggest problem was falling in love too fast? Why should anyone care when Eliot could never fall in love again?

But it mattered after I realized I couldn't bear to kill Isolde. It mattered after I realized that Isolde would need someone to keep her safe and well cared for after"—he gestures vaguely with the bottle—"me."

I am several steps behind his words now, my mind unable to put the pieces together. "Are you saying that you hired Tristan to take care of me?"

My husband turns those complicated eyes toward me. "I hired Tristan to fuck you," he says. "I thought I was making that obvious."

Tristan has frozen in place, only his chest moving now. "I'm sorry?"

Mark sighs at us, his stolid and unlettered students. "I never planned on living past destroying Ys, but I knew that even if I managed to survive, Isolde didn't deserve to be welded to me afterward. Even loving her as I did—*because* I loved her as I did—I knew it was better for her to be free after it was over, either by my death or by legal decree, and be watched over and loved by someone else. And then here was this soldier I'd been following for years, this soldier who was apparently an incurable romantic, who was infuriatingly, horribly *good*, a talented fighter and a kind friend and a certi-fied hero. Here was someone who could keep Isolde safe and doted on if she'd let him. And then the irony being once I met you, sweet Tristan, I realized she could keep you safe as well. But you were both so fucking stubborn in your own particular ways, and it wasn't as if I could sit you both down and rationally explain that I knew Isolde was a saint and that Tristan had killed my husband and also that there was a secret organization called Ys that might kill all three of us, or why it would be in your best interest to link together after I either died or granted Isolde a divorce, or that actually it would be better for everyone if you two went ahead and fell in love while you were at it. Yes, Isolde was safe from *me*, but

I still needed her to get closer to Cashel, and if I still needed her, then I wanted to make sure she could leave me—or my graveside—with someone who could keep her safe."

My nervous system is burned out over the last week—my adrenal reserves gone, my ability to respond to this with any semblance of dignity or pride gone. I simply stare at Mark with a dry throat and a heart that has no blood left to bleed for him.

"You *wanted* us to fall in love," I say dully.

He takes a drink and then sets the bottle on the table, wiping his mouth with the back of his hand. "I wouldn't use the word *wanted* with that much precision," he finally replies. "I wanted it like I wanted to cut out my own liver, but the alternative, leaving you alone after what I'd dragged you into... I wouldn't want to do that to anyone. Much less to a bride I treasured." His eyes meet mine, and his voice is quiet when he adds, "A bride I loved."

Some blood spills from my bloodless heart, wrung out with great force. I duck my head.

"I don't—" Tristan is struggling with this, I can hear it in his voice. "You didn't make me have sex with her. I did it all on my own. I felt fucking awful about it."

"Tristan," I whisper, looking back. This is all so long ago, and yet the bitter self-hatred in his voice is enough to pollute the room, it's still that strong.

Tristan ignores me, his eyes firm on Mark's. "I violated my own ethics, my professionalism, my sense of loyalty, my own feelings for you. *I* did that."

There's pity in Mark's face now. "But I knew you would, puppy. I set you up to fail in every way possible. I made sure you left for Ireland angry with me and hurt and betrayed too. I put you on a yacht for three weeks with a sad damsel full of secret sharp edges—catnip for my hero, my masoch-ist. I filled that yacht with your favorite books, with dresses for Isolde and translucent swimsuits too, with chapels and martial arts studios and basketball courts. I pampered you with ridiculous meals. I had you move rooms next to each other. I told you over the phone to woo Isolde in my place. I watched those cameras every day and night, you know, the ones on the yacht, needing to see my plan succeed. I was in agony when it finally did."

"But your shoulder," Tristan protests weakly. "You couldn't have *planned* to get stabbed… You couldn't have planned for the stitches to rip after."

But Tristan underestimates the resolve in Mark, the kind of resolve that can spend almost a decade with this kind of single-minded vengeance as its only animating force. I stared into those ocean eyes in that abandoned church, and I saw the unshakeable, burning determination there. The determination to fight for us, to die for us. If ever a man were to get stabbed on purpose, it would be Mark.

"You are correct," Mark allows. "I didn't plan on getting stabbed. I was going to manufacture some kind of business that would mean I couldn't go to Ireland, but when Drobny attacked the club, I saw a better chance, a stronger excuse. I took it."

Tristan closes his eyes. "I've known since Samhain that you've been pretending to be bad at fighting, but it still hadn't occurred to me…"

"That I would intentionally allow myself to be stabbed? It was one of my more adventurous ideas, I'll grant you, and I knew I'd have to be careful if I wanted use of that shoulder later. But it healed too quickly anyway." A heavy sigh.

"So you ripped open your own stitches." Tristan opens his eyes. He looks horrified. "We thought you were moving furniture, ignoring your doctor, but you tore them open yourself. Mark, Jesus Christ."

There's a flash of fondness in Mark's expression when

Tristan speaks his first name. "Thank you," Mark says, gratified, even though Tristan hadn't actually complimented him. "I do consider that moment to be a high-water mark for me, at least as far as commitment to a goal goes."

"I don't understand." My hands are on either side of the chessboard, my thumbs framing the bottom and my pointer fingers pressed against the sides. They shake enough to rattle the pieces ever so slightly. "You were so angry in Belgrade. You were *livid*, Mark, the kind of livid that can't be faked. You were *hurt*. How could you have been wounded when this was your miserable fucking plan all along?"

He doesn't answer for a long moment, his eyes on the fading sky outside. When he does speak, his voice is tattered and low. "I arranged for all this before I fell in love with Tristan. And it had been long enough since I'd seen you, Isolde, that I'd started to hope that I'd love you less this time. That maybe what I felt for you had been overblown in my memory, and you didn't really have such power over me."

A rueful smile.

"But then I did fall in love with Tristan. Then you came back, and it turned out what I felt for you before had only been a ghost of the real thing. Yes, this was my miserable fucking plan, for the two of you to fall in love, but I didn't count on loving you two quite so much, you understand. I have never, *ever* wanted two people to be so entirely mine, to the point that I sometimes can't think straight for how much I crave you both. I'd rather tear my own stitches open again than watch the two of you be together without me, and yet it's my own doing."

I stare, lips parted.

Mark looks down at the chessboard, at the spot that's still missing its queen. "And I guess I'd hoped," he says in a quiet voice, "that our vows would mean something somehow. Our promise to stay faithful to each other. That even though you and Tristan had fucked on the yacht, even though you pined for each other after our wedding, that you'd wait until our marriage had ended to take up with him again. It hurt when you didn't. I know that's childish of me, but it's the truth."

No one speaks then, with Mark's honesty burning the air, his deceptions and his obsessions crackling and searing the very atoms between us.

Even this, I think distantly, a little hysterically.

Even this.

Loving Tristan, something I'd thought was my very own sin, my very own miracle, had been manufactured. Like everything else in my life—my mother's death, my uncle's role as mentor, my sainthood, my marriage—all of it might as well have been chiseled in stone by fate itself.

Is nothing in my life my own? Not even my secrets and mistakes? Will there never be someone I can point to and say *They chose me. All on their own, they chose me, and I chose them back.*

Can I really say I'm not alone when the two men I love are only with me by design?

I'm reeling from this, floating several queasy miles above my feet, as Mark leaves the apartment and then returns with something in his hands. A folder, expensive-looking, the front cover made of a matte black and the back cover of a glossy white.

I think—dizzily, strangely—of the sails of Theseus's ship. Like my fate is folded between those two colors, and tragedy will follow if I pick the wrong one.

"You'll find everything in order," says Mark, handing me the folder.

I manage to let go of the chessboard and take it. When I flip it open, I see the words *Petition for Dissolution of Marriage* at the top.

I am really floating now. Uncomprehending. "Divorce papers," I say numbly.

"Per our prenuptial agreement, you are retaining all Laurence assets and taking half of my liquid assets that aren't tied to proprietary information owned by Lyonesse. Petitcrieu isn't in here, but she is yours. She was a gift."

Tristan steps forward. Stops. "Mr. Trevena…"

Mark looks at him. "I'm giving you both a choice, Tristan. What I should have given you a long time ago: the freedom to walk away and the freedom to survive me. Let's tally up my lies, shall we? I've hidden that Tristan killed Eliot, that I wanted to kill Cashel, that I knew Isolde was a saint, that I planned to kill you both. I knew and didn't say, for however short a time, that Cashel had killed Isolde's mother. I put the two of you together like dolls, the seeking one and the lonely one, and made you fall in love, and then I punished you both for it. In the last week, you've been shot at, attacked, kidnapped, and made to kill a pope." He nods down at the folder and papers in my hands. "Isolde, divorcing me is the only logical option. But as a counterargument, I will offer this: every word I've spoken today is the absolute truth. Loving the two of you is like tearing open my flesh, and I would pay any price to continue doing it for the rest of my life. I love you and want you to be my wife. I love Tristan and want him to belong to both of us. But because I love you, I'm telling you the rest of the truth, and it's that I'm sorry for what I've done. This is the plain black ink of my apology."

He leans down and presses his nose into my hair, and despite everything, my pulse leaps. Then he takes the folder out of my hands.

"I'm putting this on the desk of my office," he says. "Lady Anguish is downstairs, and she's been instructed to take you wherever you want to go if you want to leave. All you have to do is take the folder and walk out the front door."

I tilt my face up to his to see his expression better, and he drops a hard kiss on my lips. I taste scotch and dried blood.

"I love you," he confesses. "More than anything. But I'm sorry. I can't watch as you leave me a second time." He steps over to Tristan and cups his hand around the back of Tristan's neck. "Take care of her and yourself," Mark says. "I love you more than anything, baby."

Their kiss is softer than ours was but still intense, and Tristan is panting when Mark breaks it off and walks out to his office, presumably to leave the folder on his desk.

He doesn't return.

And for the first time since I met him at the age of seventeen, Mark Trevena is as good as his word.

For the first time since I met him, I am free to leave.

forty

MARK

A CLINICALLY STUPID AMOUNT OF SCOTCH IS THE NEXT ORDER of business, but I left the bottle in the apartment, and I don't plan on returning anytime soon, so back to the hall I go. I'm aware that I need a shower and clean clothes and above all to *sleep*, but sleep doesn't feel like enough to numb the end of my marriage, numb the end of whatever I have with Tristan, because he'll leave along with Isolde, of course he will, and—

And I remember one last thing I need to do before I can curl up somewhere and embrace my self-inflicted misery. I see my final chore alone in the hall, standing at the balcony with her hands braced on the railing and her head bent, the others gone.

I come and stand next to my old ally. When I put my own hands on the railing, I see blood streaking my ring on the hand closest to hers. Andrea catches it immediately.

"Is that his?" Her whisper is almost reverent.

"It is."

Her eyes linger over the dull rust of it, her lips parted. "Did you make him hurt?"

"I thought of every way I could flay him raw in the short window of time we had and all the ways I could keep him alive long enough to pluck out his right eye and cut off his right hand. I wondered if I could get creative and extremely literal with thirty pieces of silver." I stare down at my hands a moment, flex them on the railing. I would have enjoyed doing any of those things—or all of them—immensely. "I gave his death to Isolde in the end. Of the three of us, he wronged her first and he wronged her the most, because he stole her future right along with her mother's life."

"He stole all our futures," Andrea counters. "Anything we were, anything we were going to be, it all stopped that night in Kraków, and we couldn't do anything else but destroy him."

"*We* couldn't, maybe," I say, looking up at the hall itself, a cathedral of glass and concrete—a cathedral I built not for the glory of God but for the sweetness of revenge. "You and I aren't built to forgive and forget where others might have. Others might have had futures with regular jobs and mortgages and healthy marriages. But you were twenty-four when McKenzie and Eliot died, and I was twenty-eight—we were old enough to choose what we did next. Isolde was a child when Cashel took her under his wing, and a child already prone to thinking love and pain were the same. I know you don't like her, Andrea, but at least believe me when I say that I sincerely thought she had the greater claim to his life."

Andrea sighs and looks out at the hall.

Her way of conceding the argument.

"It feels better than I'd hoped," she says after a minute. "I see the news reports about the crash, the cardinals rushing back to Rome, all these obituaries, and I feel *so good*. I hated him so much, Mark. I hated him, I hated him, I hated him."

Her words lift into the air like an offering, like a liturgy.

I let them linger awhile before I speak. "All that's left now is the Scales." I'm a little surprised at the weariness I hear in my own voice. All I've wanted for eight years is to destroy Ys, and the hard part is done now. There is so little that remains, *and yet.*

Yet my appetite for revenge is changing. Shrinking. It's like being brought a heaping plate of food after you've already eaten your fill.

"Ys is in disarray. So is the Church. The Scales won't be hard to flush out." Her voice carries through the empty air around us, full of energy and will. Her appetite for revenge is undiminished.

I'm envious of it—I wish I had anything burning inside me, anything at all, to distract me from missing Tristan and Isolde.

"Did Lox call you? I asked her to while I was in Nemi."

"She did." Andrea looks over at me with sharp, assessing eyes. "I don't doubt her work, but it contradicts everything we'd thought about Ys. Everything we'd heard and from sources we trust too."

"Cashel admitted it when he was dying," I reply. "It's true."

She blows out a breath between thin but flawlessly painted lips. "It makes me feel a little gullible, actually."

"That's the genius of it. No one likes feeling gullible, so they don't question it. But everyone likes thinking they know something deep and secret, so they swallow it whole. Cashel knew how to play us all, friends and foes alike." I push back from the railing with an exhausted breath. I might have to skip the scotch and just go straight to sleep.

"And Isolde?" Andrea asks, not tentatively—she's never been tentative about Isolde—but a little carefully. Perhaps out of respect for our fellowship, which has been steadfast, if mostly pragmatic at its core.

"I gave her the papers," I say, and then I close my eyes against the sudden burn there.

Shit. I hate crying. Fuck.

"I'm sorry," Andrea says a little awkwardly, as if she has to remember how sympathy works.

"You don't have to pretend." I still have my eyes closed, but it's not helping. My throat has clamped shut, and I can't breathe right.

How long has it been since I cried? And I'm going to do it *here*, in front of *Andrea*? What the hell?

Andrea's words are deliberately chosen. "I know it's not her fault that she's Cashel's niece, just like I know it wasn't actually Tristan's fault that he couldn't save McKenzie's life. I try to…remember that. That they are only tied to my tragedy, not responsible for it." She pauses. "Will you be okay?"

I huff a laugh. It's short and strangled. "Does it matter? This was always the plan. Them together, me alone, whether I was still alive or not."

When I dare to open my eyes, I see Andrea's face turned back down to her hands on the railing. Her hair is gathered in a sleek ponytail, exposing her troubled profile, the sudden sparkle of tears on her lashes. The shift is so abrupt that I can't actually account for it, even after knowing her for eight years.

"I didn't mean to infect you with my romantic despair," I say as I swipe at my cheeks with the heel of my hand. I really have to get out of here. "I'll be fine, Andrea."

It's a lie. I don't think I'll ever be close to fine again, but it doesn't matter. She barely hears me.

"Sorry," she says thickly, turning her head away. "It just hit me that we've done it, we've killed him. And this is what's left. Finding the Scales. Being alone. They say revenge won't bring someone back, and I *knew* that, but maybe I didn't realize that I was filling the hole McKenzie left behind with punishing the people responsible. And I never liked Isolde or Tristan, but I did like seeing you happy. It made me think that maybe one day I could be—"

She doesn't finish her sentence. She doesn't have to.

I put my hand over hers on the railing. The dried blood on my ring stubbornly refuses to reflect any light, polluting the gleaming bands of silver on either side of the black. "Live now, Andrea," I say. "Don't let Cashel take any more of your future. If we wait on justice for happiness, we'll never smile again."

And then I leave her to her tears so that I can finally go spill my own.

———

I don't sleep, even though I should.

I go to the garden, to Isolde's favorite spot by the cherry tree, and I sit under its bare branches while the outdoor heaters glow nearby and stave off the worst of the chill.

I can't seem to stop crying—the kind of rib-jerking, breath-stealing crying that fizzes my vision with static, that makes thinking impossible—and there is a shaking deep in my body, like my bones are trying to wrench themselves free. Isolde is right to believe love is the same as pain, because this fucking *hurts*. It hurts like nothing has ever hurt—no injury, no other loss, not even walking away from Eliot's grave with only his watch on my wrist.

It hurts like a broken sternum with every shuddering breath; it hurts like blistered skin with every exchanged molecule of oxygen in my capillaries. My nerves are exposed to the open air, my organs are in a glistening pile at my feet, and my brain tears and rips at itself, gnawing on every memory of starlight hair and green eyes, of chess matches and hymns sung in a haunting tenor. If I could bury myself alive with my bare hands, I would, but what would it

438

fucking matter when *I already have*? I buried myself with my own fury, my own stubborn pain, and I might have carved a cancer from the world, I might have made it a safer and better place with Cashel's death, but I cut myself apart to do it. I cut other people apart. I took a saw to any chance of happiness and didn't stop even when I got to gristle and bone.

I always wanted to be the one burying the embers at dawn. I should have known that the last embers I buried would be my own.

I have no idea how much time has passed—have had no grasp on time since the saints took Eliot's watch off my wrist—when I hear footsteps on stone. Short strides, a softer footfall. My shredded heart jumps, barely, weakly, and my lungs refuse to inflate when I see the garden lights glint off golden hair.

Hope—it's a fire, a knife, it's soil in my mouth. The last red kiss of a funeral pyre in the dark.

But the glinting is more copper than gold—and of course, the footsteps I want most I would never actually hear. Isolde never makes noise unless she wants to.

It's Isabella Beroul coming toward me now, wrapped in a soft, camel-colored coat, her hair loose around her shoulders. She's wearing red gloves with the white line of nitrile just barely visible above each wrist.

I'm not enjoying this habit I'm making of crying in front of people whom I'm not particularly close to—my club treasurer and now Isabella—but I don't think I could disguise what I've been doing even if I tried.

My eyes are swollen, my chin dimpled. My ribs and throat are at odds with each other when it comes to pulling air into my lungs. Also I'm sitting outside in January, at night, leaning against my soon-to-be ex-wife's favorite tree and staring at a fountain that's been shut off for winter.

There is no chance of reclaiming my usual self-assurance, and I can't even bring myself to care. Let everyone see me like this: my friends, my enemies, the ghost of Mortimer Cashel himself.

Let them see that I did exactly what I set out to do and immolated myself in the process, that I used myself for kindling, my future as accelerant.

That I blew on the flames with air I should have been using to say *I love you. I'm so sorry.*

I love you.

Isabella doesn't hesitate when she sees me, and she doesn't hesitate to sit next to me either, even though I know a coat like that has no business touching the bare dirt. She sits partially on her hip, her legs curled next to her.

"People are looking for you," she remarks, tucking her coat around her knees.

"People."

"Sedge. Kayden. They're worried."

God, what I'd pay to hear two very different names right now. "Ah."

"I checked your office and then your apartment too and didn't see anyone there, so I thought I'd try here next. Seems like a private place."

Didn't see anyone there. I clear my throat, but the words come out sounding like they're made of ash anyway. "In my office—on my desk—did you see anything there? A folder, maybe?"

She shakes her head slowly. "There wasn't anything on your desk, sir. I walked around to the other side to look out the window, and I would have noticed if there was."

It's what I expected, what I've been grieving—apartment empty, divorce papers gone—but the confirmation of it is enough to make me wish for death. Just complete darkness and absence of being. Ending is the only way I can go on.

And still my flattened lungs pull in air. Still my mangled heart attempts to beat.

There is no folder on my desk, and my body stubbornly refuses to die.

"Andrea told Kayden," she says after a minute. "About the divorce. I'm so sorry, Mr. Trevena."

I lift a shoulder. The tears have mostly stopped now, just slow tracks of brine sliding to my jaw. I don't bother to wipe them away.

We sit there for a long time, hearing the breeze and the river. Distantly, sirens.

She breaks the silence with a soft question. "Did I ever tell you about how I started wearing the gloves?"

As far as I know, she hasn't told anyone, or if she has, they've guarded her secret with ironclad discretion.

"It was the bridge collapse," she says when I don't answer. "We got to the site so early—they needed to know how safe it was for the rescuers and if the bridge could bear the weight of ambulances and cranes and whatever else—and there were some people who were still alive—"

She stops a moment. Adjusts her outer gloves so the leather is pulled tighter around her fingers.

"We heard voices when we got there. Faint but alive. Calling for help. Their car was trapped between two others, and it was slipping into the water. By the time the rescue got the back window broken and their seat belts cut, it was too late for all of them. But we tried. We made a human chain and pulled the people out. The teenage daughter was last. She was still warm when I helped carry her up."

"Oh, Isabella." I take her gloved hand in mine.

Isabella lifts her sad gaze to mine. "She felt all wrong when I was carrying her, and the wrongness was my fault, or at least partially my fault, because I'd watched her die. I'd watched her *become* wrong as they tried to winch the car free.

And I got home later, and I couldn't unfeel how wrong she'd felt, and it was like everything I touched became wrong too. Like I'd taken the wrongness into my hands and now I was its spreader, a bringer of the plague. I could barely eat, because I had to touch the food before I put it into my body. I could barely dress myself, because even the clothes felt tainted after my hands had been on them. It took five days for me to think of gloves, and now it's been two years with my hands covered. Two years since I've truly touched anything."

I tighten my grip around her hand. I've seen her in countless positions of physical vulnerability—I've had her tied to the top of my desk—and this moment under the dormant cherry tree is the most intimate one we've ever shared.

"But you know what?" she says, the wavering that had ruffled the edges of her words now growing steady. "I wouldn't do anything differently. It cost me a piece of myself, cost me connection, the simple joy of a manicure or rubbing a puppy's ears or digging my hands into some grass on a summer's day. But the alternative is…what? Not trying to help when I could have? What use would digging my fingers into grass be if I knew I'd purchased it with cowardice?"

She leans forward, and with the hand I'm not holding, she flicks the tears off my jaw. The leather of her glove is smooth against my face.

"I don't know what happened between you and Isolde," she says softly, "but I know that whatever it was, you've done the right thing by giving her a choice. I know that even if doing the right thing leaves you broken after, it'll have been worth it."

I catch the gloved fingers still touching my face and kiss the back of them. "You are kind to share this with me. Thank you."

"You're welcome. And the coda to the story is that I made an appointment last week to see someone about getting screened for something like obsessive compulsive disorder, so maybe I'm not doomed to wear the gloves forever. Maybe you're not doomed to this either, sir."

I try to smile at her, but it's a faint and uncertain smile. What could she mean by *doomed to this*? Doomed to tears under the tree? The empty apartment upstairs? The empty life waiting beyond the next sunrise?

No, I've chosen my doom, because I've made it from scratch. I made it like a Swiss watch, designed to tick precisely and reliably to this one end: Cashel dead and Tristan and Isolde safe and happy.

And I executed it admirably, did I not? Did I not pick the two of them so well for each other? Did I not make them fall in love?

That's some comfort at least. If nothing else, I know how to build a watch.

More footsteps come in the dark, and when I look away from Isabella, I see what I shouldn't, and that's a pair of broad shoulders, dark hair that's slowly outgrowing a brutal haircut, a dolefully pretty face with a doll's eyelashes and a full mouth. Well-made hands that once ended my husband's life and that I can't help loving anyway.

"Tristan," I say as he comes to kneel next to me. I should feel ridiculous, like a painting of a dying king propped against a tree while his retainers comfort him, but the only thing I can feel is stunned, broken.

Hopeful.

"Sir," he says quietly. "Let's get you inside."

"Is she…"

"She went with Anguish," says Tristan, and hope is once again soil in my mouth, the taste of death itself as it's extinguished. "Nimue, I mean. Nimue is going to give her a place to stay for now, since Isolde doesn't want to go live with her father."

"Right," I say. "Of course. Nimue is a good friend."

Tristan's eyes have almost no color under the strung lights of the garden. When they search my face, they are all silver and black, just like the ring I gave him. "But I am staying," he says. "Here. With you."

I shake my head. "You should be with her. That's what I wanted. That was the plan—"

"Fuck your plan," he bites out. And then adds unconvincingly, "Sir."

"Tristan."

"We're going inside now," he says firmly. "And I'm staying. And this is hard enough without you arguing, so please just shut up and let me wash the blood out of your hair. Okay?"

I want to fight this. I want him to be with *her* so that they'll both be safer, so that they'll both be consoled, so that two of us can be fully happy at the very least.

But I'm exhausted and Tristan is beautiful, and I don't have the heart to fight him or anyone right now. I've been fighting since I was eighteen years old; half my life has been war. Out of pure fatigue, out of reflexive desperation for the peace of strong hands and green eyes, I whisper, "Okay."

forty-one

ISOLDE

"ARE YOU SURE YOU'LL BE OKAY?" ASKS THE FIRST LADY A week later. She and the president and their assortment of children are getting ready to leave their riverside enclave (whimsically named New Camelot) for the bustle of the capital, and I'll be left here alone.

Well, not quite alone.

"I'll take good care of her," comes a warm voice from next to me. It's a voice filled with the kind of certainty and assurance that makes the whole world feel sturdier and sweeter. A voice that could inspire an entire nation.

"You better," mutters Embry Moore as he expertly loops a scarf around the neck of a jumping, spinning toddler. "Or Mark will kill us. Divorce or no divorce."

Greer Colchester-Moore gives me a wincing smile over the tiny baby snoozing in her arms. "Embry means that we're all happy to take care of you."

Maxen Ashley Colchester—who is very much not dead—leans in to kiss his...*wife? Not-so-much-a-widow?* on the cheek and then gives the baby a loving nuzzle. "Embry means that Mark makes him nervous."

"The man made me help him *kill a pope*," the president says, exasperated. "I thought you were Catholic! Surely you see the gravity of this!"

"If it helps, I was the one to actually kill the pope," I volunteer, taking a stab at levity. It almost works. The others smile at least. Even if I feel the same dissociative jolt whenever I remember that I killed my uncle less than two weeks ago.

Embry grumbles something about pope killing still being a classic Mark Trevena idea, and Greer leans in to kiss my cheek goodbye. "Call me if you need anything at all," she says, a gracious hostess even when she's absent. "We'll be back soon. We never stay away long."

"Not enough spreader bars at the White House," whispers Embry.

Greer closes her eyes briefly in a put-upon expression and then opens them. "We are leaving now," she announces, and Embry flings open the front door while Maxen takes a discreet step backward so he can't be seen by the Secret Service agents outside.

I wave goodbye as the brood hustles through the cold February air to the waiting Beast.

Maxen watches them climb into the car and then roll down the drive with a pain that feels too private to witness.

When they're finally out of sight, I close the front door.

"There are few things worse than having happiness within sight but not within reach," the former president says and gives me a sad smile. His eyes are even greener than Tristan's. "But that's fate for you."

"I don't believe in fate," I say automatically.

Surprised amusement flickers in his eyes and pulls at the corners of his smile. "You don't? Not to be trite, Isolde," he says warmly, "but I think fate very much believes in you."

Maxen Colchester mostly keeps to himself while I'm here. He chops wood and tends to the horses and reads alone in his study. I don't bother him, partially because he's Maxen Colchester, and it would be like bothering St. Michael or St. George or some other holy warrior at rest, but also because I find the solitude almost...settling. So different from the solitude at Lyonesse after I returned. With the trees and the half-frozen river and the quiet, I find my thoughts tearfully, softly, achingly, coming to a kind of order.

In my room, a black-and-white folder sits at the bottom of a dresser drawer, along with a holy card and a small chip in a plastic bag. I still wear the honeysuckle ring on my finger.

At night, as I usually do without Mark or Tristan, I dream, although my nightmares have been replaced by something else, a half nightmare, a memory.

I'm standing in the lobby of Lyonesse, the divorce papers in one hand, a bag of clothes in the other.

Tristan stands in front of me, sorrow carving his features.

Stay, he pleads in my dream, just like he did in real life. *Don't give up on what we could be.*

We can't be anything, I say back, again just like in real life. *We were made up from the very beginning. Put together like dolls, like he said. This isn't real—we aren't real.*

He touches me then, a hand sliding into my hair and cupping my head. *We said we aren't real in the dark. But we always were, Isolde.*

And then in the dream, something happens that didn't happen the day I left Lyonesse. Mark steps out of the shadows from behind Tristan, one hand outstretched, as if bidding me to come to him.

Because not only are we real in the dark, but the darkness is real. And I'm in love with it still.

It doesn't matter that I wake up crying, because usually I've fallen asleep crying anyway.

After another week of this, a visitor comes to New Camelot. He has the kind of ivory skin that probably burnishes into gold in the summer, hair like afternoon sunshine, and dark eyes that burn with some kind of secret intensity. A white clerical collar dazzles from the notch of his black shirt.

He's a priest.

We all eat dinner together in the large but comfortable dining room, a simple meal of steak and mashed potatoes that Maxen makes himself. It's good, but I think of Mark the entire time I eat it, of his absurdly delicate and perfect cooking, like food from a king's hall.

After dinner and after making polite farewells to me, the two men stand to go to the study.

"It's only the usual sins, Father," I hear Maxen tell him as they go.

Father Jordan Brady's voice is so melodic that it's difficult—but not impossible—to catch the dry edges of his response. "So we'll only need two or three hours in that case."

The study doors close, and even though I go to bed late, I don't see either of them leave the room.

The next morning brings with it a blue sky and a mild kiss of sunshine, and after another night of saying goodbye to Lyonesse in my dreams, I'm eager to get out of the house, to enjoy the world without needing a coat, hat, and scarf. I strike out along a riverside path and walk until I reach a friendly clutch of rocks, surrounded by trees and already slightly warmed by the sun.

"Mind if I join you?"

I turn at the sound of the lovely voice and see Father Brady standing at the edge of the trees. I hadn't heard him at all—just a couple weeks out from being a saint, and my instincts are already slipping.

"Please," I say, waving a hand at all the potential stone seats around me. "It's too lovely of a day not to enjoy it."

He climbs up to join me, making it look easy and graceful in his dress shoes and black trousers, and then sits a couple feet away with his legs crossed like a schoolboy.

"I suppose you'll invite me to take confession too?" I ask. I try to have it come off as casual, droll, like Mark would in my shoes, but I've never learned how to turn my untouchable reserve into a weapon of charm and persuasion like he has, so it comes out soft and wary instead.

Father Brady doesn't seem bothered by my wariness. He only closes his eyes and leans back on his hands to tilt his face up to the sun. "I don't even have my stole with me. You are quite safe from being lured into spontaneous reconciliation."

I watch him a moment, fascinated. Even his serenity seems to be lined on the inside with a secret fire.

"So…you know Maxen Colchester is alive," I venture. I know where I want to end up, but I don't know where to start, and this seems as good a place as any. "That must mean you're trusted a great deal."

"There are very few who know the truth," Father Brady agrees. "But by your logic, you must be trusted a great deal as well."

"Nimue trusts me, I think."

"That counts for a lot."

"Do you know…" I hesitate before pushing forward. "Do you know why I'm here? What I've done?"

Father Brady's eyes are still closed as he nods. "I know what you've done, Isolde Trevena."

God help me that I still love the way *Isolde Trevena* sounds. Like it was always meant to be that way, like *Isolde Laurence* was merely a placeholder, a scaffold for the real thing.

"Then you know that there's no amount of reconciliation that can save me."

Father Brady does turn his head and look at me now, his dark brown eyes made only a bare shade lighter by the impulsive February sun. "There is no barrier to forgiveness other than accepting it," he says mildly.

"I murdered the Holy Father."

"Mortimer Cashel was no father," replies the priest. "He was no pope. His election came out of deception, bribery, and blackmail. He saw the role as an opportunity for power, not as a responsibility to lend that power to his sickest, coldest, poorest children, the ones who needed it the most. He was an infection that grows everywhere in the world but thrives in opacity most of all, and while there was plenty of that to cloak him in the Church, in another life, it could have just as easily been a boardroom or a parliament or a battlefield where he spun his webs."

"I had a dream once," I say, not sure why I'm divulging this, because it's so deeply unimportant, "that my uncle and I lived a very long time ago. He wasn't a priest at all but a warrior, trying to run my father's kingdom under my father's own nose. I remember waking up and thinking that version of Mortimer Cashel made an uncomfortable amount of sense."

"Sounds like an interesting dream." His expression is curious. Encouraging.

I shift on the rock. I'm wearing thick leggings and an Oxford sweatshirt of Greer's that she gave me to borrow, and I'm almost too warm, something I haven't felt in so long. "Do you think...do you think there's any kind of hope for me? To be good? I wanted to for so long, you know, to be utterly clean in spirit, to have a heart that would send smoke up to heaven if it was set on an altar and burned in offering. But I can't keep track anymore of what's good and what's evil, and I can't ask God, because he's stopped listening to my prayers. If he ever did in the first place."

Father Brady turns his head to watch the river, silent for a moment. And then he says, "Good and evil have stayed the same, but you have changed. You can no longer unquestioningly accept as good what someone tells you to, and the same with evil. That's not losing direction. That's completion, discernment, adulthood. You saw through a glass, darkly, and now you see face-to-face."

"Maligning unquestioning acceptance is very radical for someone who works for the Catholic Church," I point out.

He makes a face of mock dismay, and I suddenly realize how young he is, how strikingly and humanly handsome. He is so incandescently inspired by God that it's easy to forget he's not a beautiful and terrifying angel come to earth.

"I forgot my theses to nail to the nearest door. But in the meantime, I recommend listening to the still, small voice inside you. It will be a much better judge of good and evil than your uncle."

He glances at his watch and then smiles warmly at me.

"I'm afraid it's time for me to go, so let me say what I found you to say. God aches for your loneliness, Isolde. He wants you to know that you're never truly alone."

The last part sounds like a platitude, something from a sympathy card. "Because of Jesus?"

Father Brady laughs, a sudden and happy sound that brightens everything around us. "No, but you'd be a great Sunday school student with answers like that. You're never alone because you have yourself, Isolde. That's all."

Levity immediately wiped away, I look down at my feet on the rock. "I feel lonely *with* myself, Father. I don't like myself."

"Then that's where you start," he says gently. He gets to his feet. "Perhaps it might be useful to think of when you haven't felt lonely, when you *have* liked yourself. When

451

you felt like you knew your own heart, face-to-face, and not through a glass, darkly."

He touches the top of my head for just a second, a glancing benediction, and then leaves without any further farewell, as if sure we'll meet again. I watch him go, my brows knitted together, my mind burrowing inside itself.

When *had* I last felt like I knew my own heart? When had I last liked myself and the world around me?

The answers come quickly, effortlessly, as inevitably as the river washing oceanward at my feet.

Sparring with Tristan. Playing chess with Mark. The sound of Tristan's voice over rain on glass while Mark stroked my wrist.

Watching Mark in the kitchen, walking with Tristan under the trees of Morois.

Kneeling for Mark. Tristan kneeling for me.

Hearing *I love you* in two different voices.

Hearing my own voice say *I love you* back.

I'm on my feet and walking back to the house before I let myself think about it too much. I'm in my room and putting together my bag; I'm pulling the folder with the divorce application out of a drawer and looking at it once more before I throw it in the trash.

I find Maxen Colchester and ask if he'd mind terribly if I borrowed a car.

forty-two

MARK

"Ah, the great Mark Trevena, laid low by love."

I look up from the folder of reports that I've been unable to focus on to see Nimue come through the door of my office. She's been working downstairs in her own office whenever she comes in, which has been less and less now that I'm back, though I've insisted she keep full ownership of the club. Even with Embry and his stepsister, Vice President Morgan Leffey, quietly squashing the FBI's interest in me, I think it's safer if I remain hidden for now. Organizationally at least.

"I don't look that bad," I say, but the protest is halfhearted. I look like shit and everyone knows it. Side effect of my fun new hobby of crying in the dark—and my other new hobbies: not eating or sleeping.

The only times I even get close to sleep are when I can wrap myself around Tristan like a vine and allow the steady beat of his heart to soothe my own.

"How is the florilegium coming?" she asks as she sits down in the chair across from my desk. Outside, the morning sun is bright and cheerful, apparently having forgotten that it's February in the Mid-Atlantic. It catches the odd silver strand in her dark hair.

I flip the folder closed. "We're almost ready. Next week, I think. Andrea is still working on the mechanism of the leak. We want to make sure nothing can be traced back to the club or our members."

"Good. And don't forget to rest afterward," she admonishes. "Also, I brought you something."

"I love gifts," I say tiredly. Petitcrieu, finally repatriated from Manhattan, snuffles in sleepy agreement from her bed under my desk. She also has a bed by the window, two beds in the apartment, and a bed by the front desk downstairs, as she's taken to following Ms. Lim around the club, drawn away from my side by the sound of clinking keys. She has approximately a hundred and seventeen toys littered between here and the garden, because I can't seem to stop buying them.

Nimue leans forward and sets something on my desk. A slim book bound in yellow leather, with a title in peeling gold letters debossed on the front. *The Tragicall Story of Tristram and Iseult of Lyonesse.*

"I thought you'd find this edifying," says my business partner.

A small needle of amusement manages to pierce the gray haze surrounding me these past two weeks. "My mother's family was Cornish. I'm very aware of the legends we share our names with."

"Quite," Nimue says. She looks like she's fighting back a smile.

I open the front cover and see hand-painted endpapers. Hazel and honeysuckle, a delicate pattern repeated over and over, bright green and pale pink. I run my fingertips over one of the honeysuckle petals, feeling the negligible ridge of the paint. Something hums through my fingers, almost like electricity, almost like sound, but not quite either.

My imagination more likely than not. My dreams these days are strange.

"I'll give it a read sometime," I say diplomatically.

"Good." She seems almost on the verge of laughter now. "What?"

She gives me a look like *you know what*, but I genuinely don't.

"You were like this before too," she finally explains.

"Before what?" When she doesn't answer, I say as I push away from the desk and stand, "You've been with your husband too long. You're speaking in riddles."

"That's a little rich coming from the man who engraved *quarto optio* on the inside of his lovers' rings," she croons.

I study her a moment with narrowed eyes. It's not out of the realm of possibility that Tristan or Isolde told her about the engravings, but it's also not incredibly likely.

She's clearly enjoying herself now. "But what can it mean? What is this mysterious fourth option?"

I continue to look at her. Mistrustfully.

"When diplomacy or war won't do, the president turns to the third option: covert action. But what does Mark Trevena turn to? What does he do when the third option leaves him with a husband to bury and no hope of making amends with the dead?" A smile spreads across her face, fine lines bracketing her mouth. Her eyes sparkle with mischief. "Oh, I know. He decides to burn it all down."

"To the ground," I confirm, but my eyes are slitted now. I haven't told anyone but Melody what *quarto optio* means to me. "And how do you know this again?"

Her brows lift in a picture of angelic benevolence. "I'm a good friend, Mark. That's how I know things. And that's also how I know this: you're absolutely right. You should burn it all to the ground. Today, if possible."

I gesture to the folder in front of me, the latest from Lox

and Andrea about the Scales and their possible whereabouts. "That's what I'm trying to do."

"Great," she says brightly and gets to her feet. "I hope you enjoy the book. It's expensive, though, the only known edition in the world. I'd keep it in the safe for now."

She takes a few steps toward the door, and then she looks back at me. "You know, when I told you that good rulers were merciful, I never meant that mercy only flowed one way. You deserve mercy too."

"Me. Mark Trevena. Deserve mercy." I stare at her.

"Yes," she says.

She's wrong. I shake my head, ready to argue, but she holds up a hand.

"Consider that I'm right. Consider that you'll never be able to temper power with mercy if you don't know how it feels to receive it. If you don't humble yourself enough to receive it."

I make a dry, broken noise that's supposed to be a laugh as I wave at myself. "You don't consider *this* humbled?"

A look that could etch steel. "A humble person doesn't reject what fate has given them."

"I don't believe in fate," I say, but now she's leaving my office, like I haven't spoken at all, like anything else I'd have to say is completely irrelevant. She really has been around Merlin too long.

After my office door swings closed, I lean down to stroke Petitcrieu's ears, and she rouses enough to dozily lick my hand. This morning, she came to lie next to Tristan on the bed, and I was able to pet her while holding him at the same time. It wasn't peace or happiness, but for a moment, it was the absence of pain. Relief from it.

My phone rings, and I pick it up.

"Sir," Sedge says, "Ms. Lim has offered to take Petitcrieu to the vet for you today since the club is closed to guests. Would you like to bring her down?"

Right. The vet appointment. For the dog I got Isolde, which is now my dog, because Isolde's no longer in my life.

As if she senses I'm thinking of my wife, Petitcrieu lifts her head from her paws to lick my hand again. I caress her fur, thinking of how happy Isolde was when I'd brought the puppy upstairs on Christmas. I think of her smiles, her laughter, such rare gems, whenever Petitcrieu pranced or tumbled over or licked her face.

"Thank you," I tell the puppy, scratching behind her ears now. If nothing else, I have more of Isolde's smiles to remember than I would have otherwise. Petitcrieu looks up at me with giant, liquid eyes and then tries to help me scratch behind her ear with a clumsy, oversize paw.

I get her collared and leashed, and before we leave my office, I stick the old book in the safe. And then I walk Petitcrieu down to the lobby, where Ms. Lim greets her with coos of praise and belly rubs.

"Thank you for taking her," I say.

"I'm happy to, and I think you're needed in the treasury anyway," she says, not bothering to look at me while she ruffles the puppy's fur. "Andrea sent me a message saying she couldn't get ahold of you? She's having trouble with the door."

I glance at my phone. I haven't missed anything from her, but the signal from the basement is notoriously terrible, so that doesn't mean much. "I'll go check it out. Have you seen Tristan, by the way? I haven't seen him since this morning when he was going on a run."

Ms. Lim shakes her head as she stands and takes the leash's handle from me. "I got here not too long ago, so I probably missed him coming in."

"Right." There are any number of places he could be, and it's only been a few hours since we woke up together, but I already miss him. Like someone has grabbed something vital from behind my ribs and walked away with it.

He doesn't seem to mind, but I'm aware that I'm exploiting him rather shamelessly, venting my sadness and longing on his body. He's dotted with love bites from the neck down; bruise-colored stripes decorate his skin from his hips to his knees. I can't go very long without touching him, kissing him, pinning him down and feeling his skin against mine, exchanging inhales and exhales and proving to myself over and over again that he is *here*, he is *here*.

He misses her too. He understands. There is no cure, only a treatment that keeps death at bay, and the treatment takes several doses a day to be anywhere close to effective.

See, Nimue? I'm accepting one gift from fate at least.

I give Petitcrieu a final scratch behind the ears before Ms. Lim takes her out the front door to where our new driver waits. There's a fist somewhere below my throat that squeezes and gradually releases as I watch the new driver help Ms. Lim into the car. I'd missed Jago's funeral while being smuggled back into the United States, and I wish…I wish so many things. That he'd been spared meeting me, that I'd never asked him to come work at Lyonesse. That he hadn't been so good at his job, that I'd known the church in Albany would turn into an ambush.

More debts to lay at the dead's feet—bills that can never be paid now.

I glance around the lobby. Dinah is out sick today, and with no guests tonight, we've had the staff stay home with pay, and our security too. It's only Andrea and Sedge and possibly Tristan here, and I can feel it—the emptiness of the space, the vacancy of it. All this vastness, this outlay of wealth and intention, and it might as well be a crumbled Greek theater now, a hollow monument to what used to be.

The vacancy is an extrapolation, a reflection, the kingdom mirroring the king, and while I'm mostly numb to it, I recognize in the staff's faces a certain kind of melancholy.

They helped Lyonesse grow and thrive, their satisfaction was in the satisfaction of our guests, and now all they can do is sit in the stale air of an empty building and wait.

For their sake, I hope this is temporary, that we soon have all the assurances we need to go back to normal. That Lyonesse is filled to the brim with its wicked children once again.

I take the elevator down to the treasury floor, and they open to the usual: a large vestibule capped with glass double doors and lit with blue lights. Beyond is a second set of doors and the server room.

I don't see Andrea.

"She didn't come in today. I'm sorry," says a quiet voice from the corner closest to the elevator doors—the corner I couldn't see as I stepped out. I turn to see Sedge standing there in trousers and a cardigan, his pale hair pulled back into a neat ponytail, his light gray eyes shining blue under the lights. "She didn't text Ms. Lim either. But I'm sure you're familiar with how to spoof a phone number, sir. You know how easy it is to do."

The wrongness of the moment is a veil pulled between us, or perhaps it's a veil pulled back, and now I'm really seeing Sedge for the first time.

My mild-mannered assistant of almost two years, his inscrutable expression no longer closed off but blank; my assistant who should not be down here, who has no reason to be down here, no reason to spoof Andrea's phone number and casually ask for my help in the treasury in her name.

I didn't plan for this. I didn't see it. And I have...nothing for this moment. No favors, no secret armies, no extra information.

Nothing.

My body—used to danger after eighteen years of court-ing it for paychecks and revenge—summons what I need in a scatter of neural sparks. Amygdala to hypothalamus, hypothalamus to sympathetic nervous system. Epinephrine and glucose and cortisol are dumped wholesale into my blood.

"Sedge," I say calmly, meeting his gray-blue gaze as my pulse kicks and my muscles coil.

"I could have used Andrea or Dinah to access the server room," he says, stepping forward. His eternal iPad is tucked neatly in his hand, resting against his hip. "But then I would have been known to them, and there was no reason for them to be collateral damage afterward. Not when I like them both—yes, even Andrea—and you're the problem anyway. You're the one who can't be left alive."

The elevator doors slide closed behind me, but the car stays in place. The elevator and the fire door on the other side of the server room are the only ways out of this basement— I'm not sure how feasible either exit is right now.

"I don't see a gun," I say, "or a knife. So I presume you have a different way of coercing me?"

He nods, his finely worked features catching the gleam of the blue lights. High cheeks, straight jaw. There's something underneath the blank expression, something that I can't quite catch. "The Falstaff routine worked on me for a while, but after the saint's death in Fez and what happened in Albany, I didn't think risking a physical fight was in my best interest." He flips the iPad around and holds it up to show a security feed of the grotto, of an unconscious Tristan bound and gagged next to the pool. Someone stands next to him with a long braid and a scapular.

Veronica.

She's looking down at a phone in her hand.

"She's been instructed to kick him into the water if you don't do as I ask. She's watching us now to make sure you're cooperating." Sedge lifts a hand, and Veronica must see it on her phone, because she lifts her own hand in response. "I felt like this was more elegant than me waving a gun at you, sir. But I am sorry."

I give myself a beat to accept that this is inconvenient, that I won't survive anything happening to Tristan, that I'm feeling terror like I haven't since all those saints came pouring into the church in Albany, and then say, "Okay, Sedge. You have my compliance."

I cling to his *sir*, to his *sorry*. To the thing under his careful neutrality that might just be reluctance or regret, either of which I can use.

Sedge's expression doesn't change. "We're going to access the servers, and you'll show me how to get the information I want."

"And then?"

A pause. "You should understand that you will die no matter what, but your beloved's life is still in your power to save. If we're satisfied, Tristan can live."

"I'll die no matter what," I echo. "And here I thought you carried a torch for me."

Sedge's cheeks darken to purple in the blue glow, and he looks away. I don't press. I have to do this right. I have to do it perfectly, because if I don't, Tristan dies, and I can't—

I can't have that. I won't.

I walk over to the thumbprint scanner, then to the retina scanner. Once upon a time, I could have used my watch to get in, but even before the saints took it, Isolde divested it of the chip that worked as a key, *so*. The old-fashioned way it is, I guess.

"You must work with the saints," I say as the retina scanner flashes. The first set of glass doors click open, and we walk through. "Has this always been the case, or did Cashel flip you?"

Sedge's voice carries just a tinge of sadness. "I've always been faithful to the Church. From the beginning."

There is a fingerprint scanner for the second set of doors, and I slide my first finger against the glass pad, considering my options, my mind flipping through bad idea after bad idea.

Fuck. *Sedge.*

I can't believe I didn't see this.

"The attack on the club, the one that prevented my going to Ireland for Isolde," I say, careful to keep my tone wondering and casual. "Was that you? Who let Drobny's men in via the fake background checks?"

"It was," Sedge admits softly.

I remember the double feint. The misdirection. Sending Drobny's men down to the server room so they could draw away enough security and more easily attack me upstairs.

"It was a good plan, Sedge."

We're walking through the second set of glass doors now. When I turn back and look at him, I see something conflicted in the normally level set of his mouth.

"Adam," he says after a minute. "My real name is Adam."

"Adam," I repeat.

He blushes again.

We're able to step on the pressure-sensitive floor of the server room with impunity since we used my biometric data to access the space. If we hadn't, the system would have sensed an unauthorized user and initiated a lockdown protocol, sealing off the space with aluminum shutters and turning the room into a giant, exitless cage.

As we walk, I give the glass-cased rows of CPUs a fleeting glance, along with the mounted cameras on the ceiling, before I speak again. "So you worked for Cashel from the beginning. As a saint?"

"Not quite," my assistant says.

I lead him to the nearest access terminal, which also happens to be in a row that the cameras can't see between.

Sedge hasn't checked his iPad again since we started walking, I've noticed, and he hasn't waved up at the cameras again either. Like communicating with Veronica isn't all that important anymore. "Not a saint... Perhaps you were purely administrative then? Or clerical? Ah, I see." There'd been a tremble in his mouth at the word *clerical*.

He seems a little irritated with himself for giving this away.

"It must have been quite something to be a priest at Lyonesse," I observe lightly, kindly. "Hard to be further away from holiness than here. Although if you were working for Cashel, I assume you'd already bargained your holiness away piece by piece. A murder here, a theft there, a handful of plenary indulgences for your troubles. It can be disheartening after a while, I'm sure."

Sedge—Adam—doesn't ruffle at my teasing tone. In a way, it seems to relax him, that I'm the same Mark, that I don't seem to hold my impending death against him. His mouth softens the tiniest bit as he shakes his head. "I liked it here," he says a little quietly. "I've been sent so many places— parish churches, army bases, corporations, militia enclaves— and this is the first place where I thought maybe..."

I don't prompt him after he stops speaking. I merely open the case for the terminal and start logging on, taking care not to look in his direction. I keep my face as he's used to it being—cool, unbothered, any wickedness contained to my mouth or perhaps a flashing look—which is harder than it seems right now, when all I want to do is murder anyone who's laid a finger on Tristan. Who'd even *think* to threaten his life.

I'd like to murder myself while I'm at it for not seeing this, for not seeing Adam right under my fucking nose, for being outplayed in my own home yet again. For spending the last eighteen years learning how to block, shoot, grapple, and kill when right now, my enemy isn't a combatant at all but a slender executive assistant who looks on the verge of tears when I glance over at him. Who looks like he'll blow apart like a rose in July.

But I remind myself that it could be worse. Andrea and Dinah aren't here, and Ms. Lim and the dog are out of the building. I only have to save Tristan. I don't even have to save myself.

The soft welcome of my silence seems to work, because Adam finishes his thought as the terminal pulls up the treasury's index.

"I thought maybe there was a different version of myself I could be. Like maybe if I'd met you before I met Cardinal Cashel, if I'd seen Lyonesse before I went to seminary..." He's looking down and away now, and when I dare another glance, I see the blue light caught on his colorless eyelashes. Like he's underwater.

I think of him kneeling in my apartment, the desperation in his eyes when he pressed his face into my lap. Pity rolls through me, hardly perceptible over the anger and adrenaline but there all the same. I can see some of Isolde in Adam, actually, in that inborn need for things that someone in a harness could have given him on a Friday night for free, followed by a kiss and a snack besides. And instead he signed his soul away, quite literally, to the first avatar of power he found, mistaking its votive demands for the actual demands of God, mistaking cruel control for cruel love and order for care. The Church—like the army, like so many things—is just another toxic Dom when you get down to it.

He still hasn't checked his iPad or looked up at the ceiling to check the cameras. Maybe because he knows where they are...or maybe because they don't matter. Maybe because Veronica isn't even watching the feeds right now.

And then it makes sense—God, yes, of course. Adam

already told me that I was going to die, but he'd also told me that he wasn't planning on fighting me. It would be Veronica who'd come to finish things after my obedience was secured with the little display in the grotto. Which means she'd be away from Tristan.

Which means I might be able to have more than Adam's word that Tristan will live—I might be able to personally ensure it.

I'm tapping nonsense into the terminal now, trying to tally up the different variables that would affect the time it would take to get from the grotto to here. The grotto and the treasury are on opposite sides of the club, and you'd need the elevator both ways—maybe ten minutes, going at a desultory pace—but Veronica is shorter than me, and she doesn't know the way as well as I do. So fifteen minutes, maybe?

"We can't change the past, only the future," I say absently, changing the view on the index so that it looks like I'm doing something, then toggling over to the treasury room controls. "Although Cashel tried to change the past, didn't he? Or at least the records of it."

Adam gives me a sharp glance. "You know about that?"

I don't want to implicate Lox, but there's no reason to protect Father Minch. "The Vatican archivist who fled? I took the liberty of visiting him in Fez. And do you know what he said to me as he was dying?"

Adam regards me in silence.

"He said 'it's not real.' At the time, I didn't know what to make of it. It was almost a whim that had me taking his Bible with me when I left Fez, and it was definitely a whim that had me hunting down some of the titles he had written inside. Titles that either hint or explicitly point to the existence of Ys. Except—"

"Except only digitally," Adams interrupts, looking away. "Yes, I know. It's much easier to forge something when it's a small matter of Photoshop and hacking of barely protected archival databases."

"And yet the actual books themselves, the first editions, remained unaltered. No mention of Ys whatsoever."

I've stopped pretending to type now, instead watching Adam as he seems to wrestle with some impulse. Pride, maybe.

"Was it your idea?" I ask.

He slides a look over to me, his bottom lip caught behind his teeth.

"I only ask because it feels like you. You always think of those clever details, of the subtleties other people miss."

It is pride. A shy smile pulls at his mouth. "His Eminence wanted a mythology. He wanted Ys to feel like something that had always been there, under the surface. Convincing people to work with you is always going to be difficult, whether it's moving guns into the Schengen Area or giving you a misinformation campaign for free—but if you invite people into an exclusive ancient club instead, if you make them feel like they've been chosen, like they have secret knowledge only given to the special among us… It's very easy to manipulate people then. But such a club would have a footprint going back centuries, and without it, the allure would be gone. Nothing can be too mysterious—actually secret—if you want it to impress people. It needed to be the kind of rumor that would only seem sturdier the more people tried to look into it."

"So you suggested altering the digital records. A brilliant idea for someone so young, Adam."

The compliment seems to please him. "I'm nearly your age, sir, but I met Cardinal Cashel when I was just out of seminary, so I got an early start. He'd already begun his work when we met, but he was ready to expand, to make Ys into something global and enduring. I helped."

God, how long *can* it take to get from the grotto? Did

466

the elevator break down? I look back to the terminal screen where the room's controls are still pulled up, and I'm about to click away to something else when Nimue's words from this morning slide through my thoughts.

You should burn it all to the ground. Today, if possible.

I press a few keys, hit the Return key before I can think about it too hard, and then say, "But Father Minch saw through it, didn't he? Did you ask him to help with the forgeries?"

Adam shakes his head. "He didn't learn about Ys from us. And for the forgeries, we always used freelancers hired through layers of intermediaries. It was only bad luck that Minch discovered us and then the truth. We've spread our whispers quite far by now—he could have heard about Ys from any number of places. But somehow he found the digital forgeries in our own archives. Stumbled upon enough discrepancies to piece together the truth."

Maybe I was wrong about Veronica coming here, about her being the one to execute me. But I can already feel the new bloom of warmth in the air, notice the fresh hush of half the fans having been shut down. My backup plan is in effect.

"To that end, I'd like everything in the treasury about Ys," Adam requests quite politely, like he's ordering from a menu he's only just had a chance to peruse.

"As you'd like," I say. "But we'll need to move to the server itself and plug in directly. It's isolated from the other CPUs and the terminal."

That's a lie—it's connected to everything, just like all the others—but Adam nods and gestures for me to go ahead and lead the way, so it must sound plausible enough. I grab a laptop from the terminal and a cord and walk into the server cases with enough speed to make it look purposeful. I pick a case deep, deep into the maze, deep enough not to be visible from any of the cameras, and then stop.

"This one," I say.

Adam waits patiently as I open the case and connect the laptop to a CPU I pick at random. A slight mist has begun to shimmer near his hairline. It's noticeably warmer in here now; I think about Tristan being hot as well, bound and unconscious in the steamy grotto, and have to draw in a deep, careful breath. I can't let the anger or fear surface right now. If I'm getting Tristan out of this, then I have to keep Adam engaged until either Veronica gets here or the dormant cooling system sufficiently fucks shit up.

As the laptop comes to life, I turn to Adam and say, "You should know that I think of that afternoon in my apartment quite a lot."

He stares at me, lips parted.

"I think about your offer. How lovely you looked while on your knees."

His throat moves up and then down again.

"I think it must be a special skill of yours, making people crave you." I'm moving closer to him, small shifts forward that have him stepping back too late, too awkwardly. His back is against a glass server case now. "Is that what you did to Aaron Sims when you were his chaplain?"

This is a guess—one I wouldn't ordinarily make out loud without more evidence—but it's ultimately a correct one. Adam swallows again.

"You know about Aaron?" he asks. "How?"

"I knew someone named Father Adam was special to him. I knew he tumbled into Ys's loving arms after that Father Adam left him."

Adam has to look up to meet my eyes now, that's how close I am. I brace a hand on the glass by his head and then use my other hand to hold his hip. I press closer, my thigh between his.

"I don't think Cashel knew how good you were at winning people over," I say softly. "You might have toppled Lyonesse long before now if he'd understood any other human need as well as he understood the need for power."

Adam is breathing heavier, partly from the heat, partly from my proximity. I press closer to him and remind myself—achingly—of Eliot, of how easily he seduced people. Eliot did it by falling in love with them genuinely, if only for a moment, and while I don't know if I can fall in love with someone who's threatened to kill Tristan or who's attacked my club and put my guests in danger, I can try.

I can look down into those pupil-dark eyes. I can squeeze his slender hip. I can let him use my thigh to rock against. I can summon up what I felt that day in the apartment when I knew that if things had been different, if I weren't in love with two other people, I would have had Adam bent over my kitchen table in a heartbeat.

I let him see all that in my face, let him hear the rumble in my throat as his yearning becomes evident against my thigh. I make myself bend toward him and run my nose along his jaw. He trembles.

"Such a meal I would have made of you," I purr into his ear. I keep my eyes on the glass behind him, even as I slide my hand to the curve of his ass to make my point abundantly clear. "If only you would have waited for me. I would have caught up to you eventually, you know."

I move my head to slot my lips against his. A drop of sweat tracks down the back of my neck as he mewls gently into my mouth, and I remind myself to be like Eliot, to summon up every true feeling I could have had for Adam, and I also keep my eyes on the glass. Which is why I see, the moment I flick my tongue against my betrayer's and feel his hips jolt wildly, the reflection of movement behind me.

I duck just as Veronica's knife arcs toward my back,

dropping to a knee and turning as she rights herself and strikes again. Adam is stupefied, I think, kissed senseless, which is something that at any other time I'd feel proud of and right now I can only feel grateful for. I manage to land a kick on Veronica's stomach, sending her back a few feet, and then I take off like a sprinter from both hands and a bent knee, scrambling down the row and then careening sideways at the first aisle so I can scramble toward the edge. Toward the elevator and Tristan.

She's fast though, faster than I plan on, and I go crashing into a server case as she slams against me. I manage to catch her wrist before she strikes out with the knife, and my hands are sweaty, and her wrist is sweaty, and we're frozen for a split second as I try to wrest the blade away from her even though I'm at the worst angle to do so.

"Should have brought a gun," I say breathlessly. I'm stronger than her, but like Isolde, she knows how to twist and squirm in such a way that my strength is matched.

"Didn't want to risk the servers," she says back just as breathlessly.

Adam clears the corner but hesitates. Veronica is a pro—she doesn't look over at him but she knows he's there.

"Father," she bites out. "Help."

I *can* take both of them, especially since Adam is unarmed, but the odds will be much, much worse, and Jesus fucking Christ, what is the point of all these fans and inert gas fire suppression systems if a room full of servers doesn't actually overheat even when you try to make them?

I abruptly let go of Veronica's wrist, causing her to sway backward, and bring my hand down as hard as I can against the vulnerable tributary of her radial nerve. It's a basic move and an ugly one, but the crude defense works. Her hand spasms, weakens momentarily, long enough for the weapon to clatter free and spin on the floor.

The three of us dive for the knife—my knees hit the floor, and sweat burns my eyes—and then fucking finally the sound of overheated glass cracks through the air. Flames ripple up to the ceiling like there's a race, bright orange and licking.

So the servers can overheat after all. Great!

I abandon the knife and decide to tear away to the elevator when I hear a clank and hum, and the treasury's security walls start to whirr down to the floor, something that would trap all three of us in here with the fire.

I'd rather be sewn into a bag of cats and thrown into the river.

I run, feeling fingers just graze my shirt, and I'm almost to the walls, watching them rattle sedately toward the ground, when I'm grabbed, tripped, and then—

Pain.

Gut-deep pain.

I'm on the ground with a knife wedged into my side. The metal walls are all the way down. Smoke is gathering on the ceiling.

I've lost some time...twenty seconds, maybe thirty. From the pain, I think, because I *can* breathe; it's just excruciating. I'm on my back, and I'm looking up at Adam, not Veronica.

The fire is loud. Cracking glass and plastic. It will probably jump server cases, and the continuing heat won't help. I turned off the fire suppression systems when I turned off the cooling mechanisms. I don't remember the metal walls being part of the fire suppression plan, but then again, I zoned out a little during Dinah's last fire safety training session, so my not remembering doesn't mean much.

The hilt of the knife is still sticking out of the left side of my abdomen, the blade entirely buried. I *am* going to die down here, but Adam and Veronica will die down here too. The only remaining question is if Tristan will be safe in the grotto, and I don't have any answer for that. We're in a tinderbox of cables and lithium batteries; it could take the whole club with it by the end.

"Looks like we're going down together," I choke out to Adam. "A shame. I'm sure the Scales would have been so proud of you."

Adam's pale brows lift, as if I've surprised and disappointed him. "Mr. Trevena, *I* am the Scales."

I stare at him. My pain-drenched mind refuses to believe it.

"His Eminence asked me very soon after I took my vows. The last Scales had died, and the cardinal needed someone he could trust, and not just with the work of the saints but his own private work with Ys." Adam's expression is one of pity now. "All that time you spent looking for me, and I was right here, just waiting for you to notice."

Veronica emerges from the glow, her face shining with sweat.

"How do we get out of here?" she asks sharply. "I know you know of a way."

"I don't, actually," I wheeze, then laugh at how little I apparently know my own club, and then scream after laughing. I think that knife is impaling my actual soul, it hurts that fucking much.

Veronica's eyes glint, and she steps forward—to hasten my death or prolong it, I don't know—and then there's a blur. Pearl-haired, in a sweatshirt.

Veronica goes flying, landing on her back and sliding a few feet away, and I drag in an agonizing lungful of air when I realize.

Isolde.

Isolde is here.

There's more fighting. A scream. I try to get up, try to move at all, but darkness ripples over my vision, and I collapse back in nauseous torment.

And then Isolde is kneeling next to me. There's blood on her face, and her honeysuckle knife is in her hand. The flames behind her look like a saint's halo. A real saint. The kind on a holy card. "Mark," she whispers.

I lift a hand to her face. She is everything beautiful in the world.

"The terminal," I manage again. "Might be a way to lift the walls. Get out while you can."

She leans down to kiss me briefly on the lips and then says, "I'm sorry, but I won't do it without you. You can take it out on me later."

I have no idea what she means until she stands up, grabs my wrists, and then starts dragging me to the nearest terminal. I think I scream again, I don't know, because the pain also wrenches the breath from my body, and I lose another chunk of time, coming woozily awake as Isolde is typing at the terminal's keyboard, the air acrid with smoke.

"Veronica?" I ask her with whatever voice I have left.

"Dead," she says, not taking her eyes off the screen.

"Sedge—Adam?"

"Don't know. How do I lift the walls?"

I tell her haltingly—fadingly—my best guess, but even the pain is slipping between my fingers now, along with my focus.

"*Tristan*," I manage to say. "In the grotto. You have to—Isolde!"

My warning comes just in time for Isolde to turn to see Adam. Every inch of his skin glistens with sweat now, his hair has been torn from its neat bun, and there's blood on his hands that I don't think is his.

"At last we get to meet truly, Isolde," Adam says. He

473

puts a polite, bloody hand to his chest. "The Scales. It's a pleasure."

A million emotions flit through Isolde's face just then—everything from shock to anger to hurt—but then the emotions fall away, leaving nothing but determination behind.

With a single graceful motion, the honeysuckle knife is flashing in the light of the fire. Father Adam falls to the floor before he can utter a single other syllable, not even a prayer.

His eyes, by the time I can see them, are completely without life.

Isolde is back at the keyboard, and then after a few more keystrokes, she drops to her knees next to me. She gives me another kiss.

"Hang on just a minute, sir."

Ah, that *sir*. Almost as good as the air it hurts too much to breathe right now. I'm smiling into her mouth as the darkness finally swallows me whole.

And the last thing I hear above the spitting, hissing mess of the fire is a whirr of metal and unseen motors. The walls are coming back up.

———

I open my eyes to a blue sky with puffy white clouds. There's a gentle breeze washing mild air over me—a fool's spring, my grandfather would say. I hear the hungry roar of a structure fire and, distantly, sirens.

I roll my head on the grass to see Isolde kneeling next to me, and Tristan too.

"Sir," Tristan says. He's crying. Isolde is crying too. "Hang on just a little longer."

I press a shaking hand to Isolde's cheek before it drops away. "You came back," I whisper.

"I came back."

"Why?"

Through her tears, she laughs, that rare laugh that should be kept in a tabernacle and venerated on feast days. "Because I love you. Because I choose to. Because I don't want to play the game with you anymore."

Sparks and static frill the edges of my vision; the sirens are so *loud*. In front of us, the club has started to energetically burn, flames licking at the inside of the glass like tongues of fire.

My eyes slide closed; I don't think I can last much longer.

Warm lips find my mouth—another pair, firm and with the rasp of stubble, finds my cheek. Worshipful. Heart-melting.

"I've already lost the game," I mumble as I listen to my life's work burn to the ground, as the internal blood loss pulls—and pulls—*and pulls*—at my pulse. I manage to fumble Isolde's hand in the direction of my pocket, and I feel her fingers close around the crystal chess piece I carry with me always. "You win, Isolde. I want you to win."

"And I have," says Isolde into our kiss, and I can hear the fear and love and stubbornness in her voice. "But I'm taking mercy on you anyway."

Mercy.

But this is mercy too, to have both of them with me, both of them close, and it is the opposite of my dream all those weeks ago, the opposite of standing between their graves in a wretched and desolate garden. This is them alive and together, the way it should be, the way I planned for it to be.

No bitter ending, no tragedy—only the villain dead and the lovers together at last.

The greatest mercy I could grant them, I think.

And it's not the glass-cracking blaze of the fire or the wail of sirens that follow me into the deep, but the kisses of my beloveds—as sweet as the first time I ever felt them, as necessary as air and blood. I hope if they ever stand above my grave, they know that I died in love with them, happy for them, relieved.

More than anything, I hope they know I died wishing I could kiss them back.

epilogue

MARK

TWO YEARS LATER

"YOU HAVE TO STAY STILL, PUPPY, AND SHOW HER HOW GOOD you can be. Otherwise, we'll have to stop, and wouldn't that be a shame?"

Sweat-sheened muscles ripple as Tristan strains against his own urge to squirm. His eyes squeeze shut, open, shut again. Looking makes it worse, of course, but how can you not look?

I let my fingers drift over Isolde's back, across her shoulders, toying with the delicate straps of her lingerie whenever I find them. I lean forward to murmur in her ear. "Lower the candle a little now. That's right."

Isolde tilts the candle in her hand, and pale pink paraffin splashes against the shimmering skin of Tristan's stomach. The muscles bunch and tense as the wax rolls between the corrugations of his abdomen to streak toward his navel, cooling into waxy rivulets on the way there.

"The lower you go, the hotter it'll be," I purr, wrapping

my hand around hers. We've put the candle in a bamboo holder that ends in a kind of spout, meaning it's easier to control where the wax goes. I aim it just above where the tip of his swollen cock bobs above his stomach, a string of glistening precum stretched between the two. "Let's try right…there…"

Tristan moans as the wax spills and burns, and he writhes on the table—not restrained, only commanded to restrain himself. Which is cruel of us, we know.

I'm pressed against Isolde's back, and I can feel her slow, shuddering inhale as she watches him move beneath us, his erection lifting and seeking, his fingers twisting into the plastic draped over the table.

"It's beautiful, isn't it?" I ask her as I nuzzle down to her ear. "Such a simple thing, and you've completely undone everything he prides himself on. His self-respect, his restraint, his need to be good for you… Let's do another, a little higher this time. Let's give him a moment to breathe."

This time, Isolde makes a delicate arc of wax from Tristan's ribs to the shallow valley where his pectoral muscles attach to his sternum. He still pants through it, but he's able to keep his eyes open this time, staring up at Isolde with flushed, desperate worship. His pupils are so big that it's hard to see the ring of green around them, and the sparkle of a tear or two is caught on his lashes.

His gaze slides to my face, and he starts trembling anew. "Please," he whimpers. "Please."

"Please what, baby?"

"You too," he breathes. "I want you to do it too."

"What do you think?" I ask my wife. "Should I play with him too? Do you think he can handle both of us?"

She turns against me, enough to look up into my face. She has her hair up tonight, with a few tendrils having escaped to hang against her neck and wave against her temples, and

I can see every flicker of excitement, nervousness, and sweet, blossoming sadism move across her features.

"I think he can," she murmurs and then drags her fingers up his oiled stomach, over the pink and blue patterns of wax we've already left streaked on his skin. "I think he wants to be good for both of us. Don't you, Tristan? Don't you want to earn a reward?"

As if this isn't its own reward for our little wax tart, but Tristan nods eagerly anyway, lips parted and wet, as if we've extended the promise of clemency to a soul in purgatory. "Yes," he begs. "I do, I do."

I palm the half-covered globe of Isolde's backside and kiss her shoulder. "Climb on the table," I tell her, quietly enough that only she can hear me. "Straddle him and torture him a little while I get another candle ready."

She dips her eyelashes once. "Yes, sir."

I walk over to the far side of the playroom we've rented for the evening, a space in a sleek and glassy club in the heart of London, and squat down to pull supplies out of a well-stocked cabinet. The minute my hand finds a fresh candle, déjà vu laps at my feet like an incoming tide: the foaming memory of playing with Tristan at Lyonesse, of my own stocked cabinets and plastic-covered tables. It's disorienting to feel a candle in my hand, to hear Tristan's soft noises behind me, and then look up to see walls of frosted glass instead of wood paneling. To have the space lit by recessed LEDs instead of hand-finished sconces spilling warm, golden light.

But Lyonesse is gone, burned from the bottom up by its own treasury, nothing but a shell now. A broken crown made of crumbled carbon and shards of glass.

When I woke up in the hospital three days after the fire with a broken rib, a newly repaired gallbladder, and a liver that would appreciate some time off, I knew the truth before anyone had to tell me. I'd felt it even bleeding on the grass between Tristan and Isolde, listening to the sirens get closer. Lyonesse was gone and, with it, eight years of myself, eight years of work and secrets and lies.

Let it burn, I'd wanted to say as the fire trucks wailed to a halt on the shore of the Potomac. *Let it die.*

I didn't need it anymore, and neither did anyone else.

But as I lay in the hospital bed, my broken rib shrieking whenever I dared too deep a breath, Tristan and Isolde collapsed into rumbled, behoodied piles in the vinyl recliners nearby, I allowed myself a twinge of sadness. I missed it already, my expensive sanctum, the wickedness and the sins and the sinners themselves. It had been built as a tool, as a fortress to spit in the face of my enemy, but I had grown to love it for its own sake. For the power and pleasure thrumming through its rooms, pulsing under the glass ceiling of its hall. For Dinah and Goran and Nat and Andrea and Ms. Lim and Evander and Arjun and Christopher and—and Jago.

And Sedge.

One morning, after a final blood transfusion and me shooing Tristan and Isolde back to Blanche's for a shower, Nimue came in wearing a flowing dress and her hair in two long braids. Thin silver chains glinted from the braids, matching the small key hanging just below her collarbone and a necklace with a sword pendant just below that. Looking at her in the daylight, you'd never recognize Lady Anguish, in her suits or sharp smiles.

Nimue sat in a recliner facing the bed, gave all my medical equipment a skimming glance, and asked, "So. Will you build it again?"

There could be no question as to what she meant. "You're the full owner of the club, Nimue," I answered tiredly. "The choice is yours, not mine."

"Then I'll leave it as a ruin and pocket the insurance money." A pause. "How does that make you feel?"

I thought about it a moment and then closed my eyes. "Fucked up. Relieved. Lost."

When I opened my eyes again, she was giving me a fond smile. "Lost is the best place to be found, Sea Hound. Especially for those two to find you."

She wasn't wrong.

Before she left, she pulled a slender yellow book from her pocket and set it in my lap. "It's a good thing you put this in the safe," she said, standing up. "It would have burned in the fire otherwise."

It was hard explaining things to the staff, especially Dinah, who'd loved Lyonesse even more than I had. I gave her everything I could, every contact I had, seed money, my blessing, for her to start her own club. Goran and Nat would go with her, as would Ms. Lim. Andrea had decided to step away from DC altogether, and after she leaked the florilegium to the press, she took a job at Armorica, something like what she did at Lyonesse but more like an actual treasurer this time. Kayden wouldn't have to look at his spreadsheets after all.

Not one of us mentioned Sedge when we spoke. The bodies of Father Adam Wray and Veronica Ramos had been recovered from underneath the club, and Veronica had been taken home by her grieving sister, but no one had come to claim my assistant. He had been so many people—Father Adam, Sedge, the Scales—but in the end, he had no one. Any anger we might have felt for him was tarnished by pity and made brittle by the answers we'd never get.

The florilegium worked, however. By the time I was deemed well enough to be fussed over in a place that didn't have whiteboards on the walls, the revelation that a number of notable people counted themselves members of a secret society whose ultimate aim seemed to be war and mayhem had rocked the news. As had the concurrent revelation that the secret society was, in fact, quite made up. Every single person who had joined Ys had joined thinking they were being inducted into a centuries-old consortium of power and intrigue, an edgier version of the Freemasons or the Illuminati, when in reality, they were joining a troupe of the easily fooled and ridiculously rich, anyone with enough access or enough money to turn Cashel's stratagems into reality. Ys had never been the mysterious, exclusive guild of the most special among us but instead the opus of a clever cleric who understood the allure of secrets and the finer touches of marketing. It had been a Ponzi scheme, where the currency in question was influence and persuasion, and the payday was Mortimer Cashel in red shoes.

The press ate it up.

Embry finally had the leverage he needed to clean house, as did anyone who suddenly found themselves either above or adjacent to these self-important dipshits, and soon anyone who was in the florilegium was being fired, investigated, shunned, or all three.

It meant, among many other things, that Cara Sims was finally safe enough to leave the shelter I'd offered her. She went home to her mother, and after so many years apart, they finally made peace.

As for us, Tristan, Isolde, and I spent a single day at Blanche's before I looked at the two of them and asked, "Have you ever seen Cornwall in March?"

We were at Morois the next day. Two weeks after that, Isolde and I were sitting under a hazel tree while Tristan and Petitcrieu played fetch, and there was an expression of such poignant longing on her face that it pressed on my still-bruised heart until I couldn't breathe for it hurting so much.

"We can stay, Isolde," I said.

She looked at me with a kind of hope that I'd never seen on her face before, not once, not in all the fucked-up years I'd known her.

"We don't have to leave?"

Birdsong was a trill above us, and the newly formed bluebells were a carpet below.

"No," I told her. "We don't have to leave."

Her smile was the first kiss of sunrise over the horizon: life-giving and pure.

———

A few months after we decided to stay, I took a delivery. Tristan and Isolde had gone for a walk, and so I was alone when I signed for Sedge's ashes and then carried the package to the family graveyard afterward. I knelt on the damp grass and opened the box to see a smaller cardboard container inside.

It depressed me: the flimsy container and the plastic bag around it. The Priority Mail Express box hastily sealed with crooked strips of packing tape. It sounded strange, even to me, that I felt like my almost-murderer deserved better, but I supposed that I *did* feel that way. I didn't want Sedge to sit on a shelf for a year because the city interred him anonymously with the other unclaimed ashes. I didn't want the version of the priest who'd come to Lyonesse and had wished he'd found it sooner to go forgotten.

I wanted to remember.

I transferred the container to a small wooden box, and then I spent the afternoon burying it in front of the headstone I'd had made—the only headstone in the graveyard from this century.

It was not at all the first body I'd buried. But I hoped it would be my last.

———

Nearly a year passed after that, and on a hot July day, a visitor came to the door.

It was Nimue, having stopped off at Morois before meeting Merlin and their child in Wales for a long summer stay. She wanted to go on a walk by the sea, and having expected a visit like this for some time, I agreed.

We drove the short distance to the village of Tintagel, parked, and walked northeast, striking for the cliffs facing Tintagel Castle. Or rather the *ruins* of Tintagel Castle, a smattering of half-crumbled walls and isolated courtyards and green, windswept grass. The waves crashed against the rocky walls of the headland, and a stiff breeze waved the coastal wildflowers around our feet—sheep's bit and sea campion and thrift. We sat next to a patch of nodding oxeye daisies and didn't speak for a long time.

"It used to be more impressive," I finally said, as if I'm apologizing to a guest for a messy house. "There were over a hundred buildings on the island alone."

"Larger than London at one time," Nimue agreed.

"There were always sails on the horizon."

"Sheep and cattle on the hills," she added. "Tin coming from the mines."

My eyes strayed up to the top of the headland, beyond most of the ruins. It was impossible to see from where we were, but there was a low stone outline of a long-ago garden, now gone to grass. The bones buried there would be gone now, taken by the acidic coastal soil, and there would be nothing left of the hazel tree that grew on top of one, or the honeysuckle vine that grew from the other.

"Do you remember?" asked Nimue. "The first time?"

The first time.

The life I'd led across the cove, the life I'd led with a sword in my hand.

It was unbelievable in the most literal sense, as in it

couldn't be believed. That there *had* been a Mark in Tintagel, that he had been married to a woman named Isolde who fell in love with his best knight. That the three of us had done this already, the jealousy and the lust and the lies, and it had ended with two petal-strewn graves and a broken king.

That somehow the three of us were here, again.

"Yes," I said. "I remember."

"You read the book?"

I had.

I hadn't planned on reading it—hadn't even planned on bringing it to Cornwall—but I found myself packing it anyway. It had sat on my grandfather's desk for months, through our first summer and the long, sweet autumn that followed, until finally, on a dim winter day, I picked it up.

Something had moved through me then, a slow but urgent current, a sharp and translucent kind of clarity.

When I'd opened the book to the first page, I heard the sea.

"I still don't understand." I watched as the waves broke under a small cave set into the cliff. "But when I remember it, I don't feel like I need to. It just is."

"You're so much like you were then," she said. "Pragmatic to a fault. Uninterested in any fate that you didn't make for yourself."

I thought of the garden above the rest of the castle, haunted by the wind. "I didn't make a very good fate for myself, if that's the case."

"You chose differently this time. You chose mercy. You chose them even when it meant letting them choose each other." She paused. "Will you tell them? Tristan and Isolde?"

"Do you think I should?"

Nimue's eyes had narrowed—not in doubt, only in thought—and as I watched her stare at the sea, I remembered this too from another life. Asking for her counsel as the water roared below and the birds wheeled in a blue sky above us.

"Yes," she said finally, "but when it makes the most sense to you. There won't be graves in your garden this time, Mark. You have time."

———

At the end of the summer, we got a notice from the post office that they'd been holding a package for me for over a year. Baffled, I went to the post office, signed for it, and then took the small box home, where I opened it on my grandfather's desk while the dog snored nearby. The package had been mailed from Rome, but my name had been filled in as the sender's name, and the sending address was a Roman post office.

I opened the box to find a typed note.

I'm sorry, sir.

s

I lifted the note to see what was underneath, and abruptly there wasn't enough air in the room.

A wristwatch was packed carefully in a nest of packing paper. Its silver case winked in the sunlight, and the hands ticked with steady precision under its glass face. There was no blood on it, there were no scratches—no evidence at all that it had been ripped off my injured body after I'd been kidnapped.

The posting date was the day before we'd killed Mortimer. Somehow Sedge had known that my watch had been taken and had arranged to have it sent to Morois, where no one had been available to receive the delivery until after the post office had stopped trying to deliver it at all.

A glitter of airless sparks filled my vision as I tried

desperately to inhale past the ache in my throat.

I'd never thought I'd see this again, this small, beloved piece of Eliot, and it was Sedge who'd given it back to me. Sedge, who'd been ready to kill me but ready to kiss me too.

In a way, this watch had started everything. It had been the flash in the dark on a wet night in Kraków, it had been the reason Tristan knew where to aim. It had been my talisman ever since I'd pulled it from Eliot's wrist with shaking hands, and it had been a reminder every time I looked down at it of what I had lost and what I had left to do.

I stared at the watch for a long time. Heart pounding; sick with relief and also an inescapable kind of regret. And then I walked out to the graveyard, to Sedge's stone, as Petitcrieu followed happily, scampering off between the headstones to chase fuzzy summer bees.

I slipped the band of the watch over the wreath hook fitted over the headstone. It dangled in the middle of the bright green wreath, right above Sedge's name.

Petitcrieu came over and licked my hand and then she flopped down in the grass at my feet. I stood there for a long time, too long, trying to understand what it was that I felt, and then I heard two lovely voices coming from the trees.

My dear ones returning from a walk.

The dog surged to her feet and was gone instantly—off in search of attention—and I finally understood what it was that I felt.

Joy. Peace. Like the rest of my life was currently walking toward the house with a basket of mushrooms and an overeager dog.

I glanced back at the headstone and the watch and took my first real breath since lifting up Sedge's note.

"I'm sorry too," I said to the watch and headstone both.

And when I went to follow Tristan and Isolde into the house, I didn't look back.

In the here and now, I turn with the lit candle in hand. I see that Isolde has listened to me and with pleasing effect: she's straddling Tristan with a knee on either side of his hips as she continues to abuse his stomach and chest with wax and he continues to twist and fret underneath her. Between the hot splatters, she allows her silk-covered cunt to press against his erection. She rubs herself back and forth on it, teasing him as he begs so, so sweetly.

I watch them a moment fondly, covetously, jealous of them individually and then jealous of them together—not in an envious way but like a jealous god. I want to hoard them to myself; I want the earth to shake when anyone dares to approach what's mine.

If I thought time and a safer world would have blunted the edges of what I feel for them, then I was a fool, because time has only sharpened what I feel, and a safer world has only meant that I'm uninterrupted in my obsession, that I can feed it and tend to it and watch it grow like a fire, a funeral pyre for any other life I could have had without them.

They're all I want now. All I live for. I never thought I'd survive, and if I had, I'd always planned on surviving alone, so this—*this*—feels like a treasure too precious to put down. A gift beyond my ability to ever repay.

A mercy, if I were to use Nimue's words.

I play the voyeur for another minute or two, watching Isolde drizzle wax on Tristan with so much affection and lust together in my body that I don't know how I'm able to contain it all. How I'm not ten feet tall with it, how I don't fill every room wall to wall and corner to corner with what I feel for them. It's a wicked thing inside me that can't love without also thinking *mine*, but I can't love them without also thinking *theirs*.

Theirs, theirs, theirs.

I approach and motion for Isolde to stay where she is, still enjoying the sight of her perched atop Tristan like a succubus, and come to the side of the table. Tristan lifts his lashes and meets my gaze with shimmering eyes of green and black.

"Just a little bit longer, I think," I say, ghosting the fingers of my free hand up his wax-streaked ribs. "Can you do that for us, baby?"

He nods, dazed and drugged, his hair tousled and damp with sweat. I stroke it away from his face, practically purring at the feel of it, thick and silken. Isolde and I held a vote, and it was democratically agreed that Tristan was only allowed to cut his hair twice a year at most. Tristan, a believer in democracy, has bowed to the will of the people, and right now his hair is long enough to curl around his ears and neck again. Perfection.

My candle is set into a glass jar with a spout for easy pouring, the wax a pale tangerine that I thought would look nice with the pink and blue already painted on him. The colors of sunrise, of dawn. All the embers buried and nothing left to do but greet the day.

With quick efficiency, I pour a glug of wax over the inside of my wrist to test the temperature—paraffin is miles away safer than beeswax, but it's always good to check—and then I decant a small amount onto Tristan's chest, right in the middle of his sternum. Some wax rolls hotly down toward his abs, and some rolls in the other direction toward his collarbone. He shivers a little but handles it well, and then I nod at Isolde.

She answers me with a small, secret smile, one of edges and darkness, and then together we move our hands, tilting, dripping, flames dancing and wax like rain. We go until Tristan's chest and stomach are covered, his head is tossing,

and the heels of his feet are digging against the plastic covering the table so hard that it looks like it will tear. From underneath Isolde, I see the inflamed head of his cock, ruddy and
miserable looking, dripping uselessly onto his wax-covered
abdomen.

"There." I pull my candle back and admire our creation.
A loose approximation of a flower, rendered in pink and blue
and orange, with ruffled petals spiraling out from a tightly
furled center. "What do you think, darling?"

Isolde blows out her candle and runs her eyes over our
wax-covered hero. Greed, plain as day, and carnivorous
desire are all over her face. "I think I love the way he looks
right now."

"Hmm. What about you, Tristan? Do you like the way
you look, all messy and dripped over? Do you like being so
sweet and pretty for us?"

The knot of his throat works up and down as he closes
his eyes. "Yes," he says pitifully. "I do."

"He's too pretty not to reward," I muse, my fingertips
drifting over the colorful topography of the night. "Shall we?"

Isolde's mouth curves wickedly. "Yes, *sir.*"

She swings herself gracefully off the table, handing me
her candle stub and then retreating into a screened-off dressing area. After I set her candle and mine under the table, I
distract Tristan by caressing the strong lines of his jaw and
neck while I slot my lips against his and slowly taste the
inside of his mouth. He kisses me back eagerly, artlessly, his
hands flying up to find the front of my shirt, feeding me
delicious noises all the while. I'm about to find his wrists and
patiently press them back into the table, but before I can, he
takes my left hand and brings it to his mouth, worshipfully
kissing my palm, giving it little flicks of his tongue and reverent brushes of his lips.

He's kissing the barely visible line of a burn from two

years ago, from the time I watched a candle burn to nothing in my hand while he and Isolde said goodbye in my apartment. A bleaker kind of wax play, but it's one of Tristan's favorite parts of my body to visit. Maybe one day I'll let him drizzle wax on me. If I'm feeling indulgent.

Isolde returns, wearing a harness with a silicone cock fitted into its O-ring, a slender blue length that looks absolutely lovely on her. My body, already all the way awake from playing with Tristan, gives a hot, needful surge seeing her. I hold out a hand to my wife as Tristan keeps the other against his mouth.

"You have the power to utterly unravel me," I murmur as I pull her close. "Looking like you do in that lingerie with a cock between your legs. I'll have to have you fuck me with it sometime. Would you like that?"

"You know I would," she says, eyes glittering.

"I'd like that too. You could make me come so hard, sliding into me and making me take every bit of it."

A short laugh. "Making you take it. As if I could."

I think about this. "You could try," I suggest. "The trying would be fun at least."

We look down at Tristan, who's let go of my hand and is now staring slack-jawed at Isolde. This is new—not because we haven't wanted to do it but because I'd wanted to taunt him with the idea of it for a good long time, make sure that the fantasy of it was a torment all on its own, for no good reason other than that it sounded fun to do.

I was right about it being fun, of course. I usually am.

"Oh, honey," Tristan breathes at Isolde as she climbs back onto the table. "I—I—"

Words have failed him. His throat moves, and there's a faint click as he tries to speak and can't, and he's already restless on the plastic again, so fucking restless. Isolde is kneeling between his legs; she arranges him so that his thighs are slung over hers. Not quite to the point of being able to wrap around her hips but nearly if he wanted to.

I find the lube bottle I'd stashed under the table earlier, and I squeeze a fat dollop on her extended fingertips.

"Rim around the outside first," I instruct, watching Tristan give a start and then a long shiver as the cool kiss of the lube leads to Isolde stroking the sensitive skin there. He tries widening his legs, but his hips are angled upward, and he struggles. "Hold your legs up, puppy. Hands closer to your ankles—yes, just like that, very good. Isn't that better? She can see you that way, get your hole all slick and ready. Now her finger—God, it's a needy hole, isn't it? I can see how eagerly you're taking her, like a wax-covered whore. Shameful. Are you ready for her second finger now?"

Isolde extends her hand once again, and I dispense another pump of lube, utterly charmed by the concentration on her face, the serious frown paired with the blush staining her chest and throat and the raw appetite in her gaze.

I know why she's concentrating though, why she's nervous. Fingers she's had inside Tristan before, but this is something new, and I know she wants to make it good for him. Which is why, when I drizzle lubricant over the blue shaft, I tell her, "He's going to love anything you do, sweet-heart. Aren't you, puppy?"

"Yes," Tristan says, half whimper, his poor erection looking so sore and neglected, his eyes glued to where Isolde is carefully ensuring every inch of her dick is covered in lube.

"And it would be too coarse for a gentleman like myself to mention in detail, but I can assure you that Tristan has weathered much worse."

Isolde's eyes drop to the front of my tented trousers, and she lifts an eyebrow. "I believe you."

I pump some lube into my own hand, set the bottle down, and join in my wife slicking up the silicone before I help her guide the tip to the waiting entrance between his cheeks. Once she's wedged against it, I find her fingers and guide them to the slippery, pleated skin beginning to give under her invasion. "You won't be able to feel for yourself, so it's a good idea to be able to see him, see where you're pushing. You want right in the middle, a good angle—yes, just like that. See how he's opening? The head of your cock will be the hardest, since it's wider than the rest, so give him a little grace here. There's the second ring of muscle, and—oh, very good, Isolde. Stop for a minute now that you're inside, and enjoy what you've done to this poor hero, our supposedly good boy. Do you see how much he's squirming on your cock? How his own cock won't even lie down now? That means he likes it."

Tristan looks like he's being broken on some kind of medieval rack right now—his hands claw at the plastic by his hips, and his head is tossed to the side. His ribs jerk and his stomach moves so much with every breath that thin cracks start appearing in the wax. His balls are already pulled up tight and hard. A vein on the side of his organ throbs with the labor of keeping him erect.

I trace around his stretched hole fondly, a little jealously, and then kiss Isolde, who has to lean down a little to meet my mouth from where she kneels on the table. A sweet novelty.

"All the way in now," I coach her. "Push as slowly as you like, but it should go easier than the tip."

Her thighs tense and her stomach goes firm as she flexes her hips, in an inch, out an inch. In and out, deeper each time, until she's nearly all the way there. I remove my hand so that she can press her lap fully against him, and then they're together completely. Tristan moans, eyes still closed, and Isolde has paused to take it all in: the long, trembling length of him, the shimmer of sweat and the oil we massaged into his skin before we started with the wax.

I unbutton my shirt and strip it off, tossing it over a chair before I toe off my shoes and socks and start on my trousers. The sound of a zipper is enough to pull my two perverted lovebirds from their private moment, and they both turn to look at me, to watch as I open the placket and push the fabric down my hips. To watch me patiently stroke myself as I come back over to the table.

My plan had been merely to observe the two of them, to treat myself to some leisurely self-pleasure as I watched Isolde fuck the cum out of Tristan—perhaps see if I could use Tristan's mouth for part of it and turn his pegging into an airtight fuck—but that all goes to hell now. From here, I can see how perfectly the harness frames Isolde's ass while she kneels like this. I can see her nipples pushing stiffly against the bralette of her lingerie. I want to know if she's wet in that silk underwear, if it gets her wetter to be fucking with a cock, if she wants to fuck *me* with it.

I climb up behind her on the table, pressing my chest to her back and my burning shaft against the small of her back, feeling the firm strap of her harness and silk. I find a breast and squeeze, biting at her shoulder as I slide my right hand between us and tug the silk aside.

"There's my wife," I say to her, dark pleasure curling in my belly. She's soaked, embarrassingly wet, and when I find the tender berry at the top of her sex, it's hot and swollen.

She moans when I caress it, my fingers having to fight for the real estate with the bottom of the harness there, her hands paused on Tristan's thighs, flexing like a cat's as I stroke it. I let go of her breast, take myself in hand, and then seek out the wet slit with a couple impatient rocks of my hips. She moves a little too, which means she moves inside Tristan, and he whimpers.

And then—ah—fuck—yes, yes, it's all slick and hot and like a fist around me, gripping and soft too, and I'm impatient, I can't wait, and I shove all the way home in one thrust. It fucks her deeper into Tristan, who flings an arm over his face, like he can't bear to be alive right now. I find his thighs, arrange them so they're slung over Isolde's, his knees just past her hips. I stroke his calves where they rest by mine and then lean back.

I look down to see my cock pushing in and out of Isolde, glazed with her arousal. I see a hint of blue silicone just beyond it. When I look up, I see the grip of her hands on Tristan's thighs, the side of a pert breast, the curve of her supple back and shoulders. And of course, Tristan, all flushed skin and wax, one hand fisted in the plastic, one arm over his face, and his helpless dick bobbing with every shared thrust between me and Isolde.

"Slow, then fast, then slow again," I croon to my wife, instructing her as I show her how, using her pussy to teach her how to fuck our Tristan. In and out, forward and back, her hot body gripping mine, Tristan taking her cock like a good boy, a ripple of moans and sighs rolling through the three of us as we move.

I find Isolde's waist, cup her breast, and then slide my other hand under Tristan's knee, gripping it firmly enough that he can't move his leg, even when he's jerking and squirming with every thrust.

"What do you think will happen if you touch it?" I murmur in Isolde's ear, leaning forward to look at Tristan spread out in lewd persecution in front of us. It's harder to fuck at this angle—not impossible, just harder—but it's worth it to watch Isolde give Tristan's pitifully hopeful hard-on a vicious little flick, right on the underside.

His leg jolts in my hand, and he groans like he's being torn open. Somehow he swells even more, bobs even higher above his stomach, strings of glistening fluid dripping from the end.

"My cruel bride, my fiendish queen," I purr, nuzzling her. "So mean to such pretty boys." I'm still rocking into her, and she's rocking into him, and she turns her head to kiss me like I've just flattered her. Which I have.

This angle is bad too, but I don't let it stop me from tasting her lips, her mouth, and Tristan makes an inhuman noise in front of us, watching us kiss as we jointly fuck him. "You're both so beautiful," he says on a breath, his eyes fluttering, his chest heaving. "Wish I could be exactly here forever."

I know what he means. It's only because there are a million and one permutations of the three of us fucking and kissing and snuggling and playing chess that we have the courage to pull apart occasionally, to leave each other long enough to shop for groceries or go to the dentist or fall asleep. It's only that we know that we have no limit on each other, cups that will always overflow, that we can bear the limits of everyday life, and even then, we bear those impatiently. Even the time it takes to change the oil in the car is a personal injury; by the time we're done brushing our teeth, we're aching to reunite with caresses and sighs.

There is nothing that I don't share with them, every secret now naked and excarnated between us, and there is *almost* nothing they hide from me. But after years of manipulations and revenge, I am quite content to let them manipulate me, take as much revenge as they want; I find it adorable when they plot against me, conspiring to tie me up or kidnap me away to some small vacation or force me to watch the two of them together and not allow me to touch, even once. If the rest of my life is enduring their revenge, then I'll die with a smile on my face, and if our love always feels like obsession, like hunger and sickness, then I'll pay any price from my past or my future to keep it.

Like the rings we still wear—black and silver, gold,

ruby-studded, etched invisibly but indelibly—our love is mismatched, full of warnings, born of lies, strange and strangely sourced. But it is ours. Scarred as it is, jagged as it is, bitter and burning as it is, it is ours.

We don't last long like this, not that anyone would, I think. There was too much buildup, too much beauty in torturing our Tristan, and now there is simply too much to take in, a banquet of sleek flesh and tight holes and thumping blood and cooled wax and sweat and oil and *us*. It's a banquet of us, wrong and urgent and insatiable.

I move harder against Isolde, pleasure shivering up my erection with every stroke, climbing my thighs and simmering at the base of my spine, and she fucks Tristan harder in response, her blue dick sliding in and in and in, then she reaches down and with admirable clemency takes ahold of his neglected shaft and circles it, masturbating him with hard, brutal strokes.

He is inconsolable in front of her, his arm back over his face, his knees trying to turn inward as if to protect himself from the climax breaking down the door, and then with a muffled moan, with his teeth sunk into his own forearm, he spurts wild and thick all over his wax-covered stomach and chest. We can hear it on the wax, the splattering, heavy and wet, and one pulse makes it as far as his collarbone, a white spatter over the blue and pink and orange petals, and when he moves his arm and sees what he's doing, adding his own hot fluid to the wax on his body, his thighs and stomach shake violently, and another few impossible surges are forced out of him. Also violently, if the noises he makes are any indication.

Isolde and I go still as we watch it, absolute beauty, exquisite filth, cum everywhere and broken sobs wrung from the man in front of us. Isolde lets her hand drop and then slowly curls forward. She presses her mouth to his cum-covered chest and then straightens up to turn her head to mine.

I cup her head and drag my lips over hers, tasting the alkaline tang of Tristan's orgasm, tasting her, and her cunt is so wet, so soft and greedy, and it's the kiss that does me in, I think. A few hard thrusts, and bliss shudders its way up my body, a pumping, brimming ecstasy that rolls over my entire body, electric and urgent and breath robbing, tingling at the soles of my feet and sending bright scatters of light over my vision. I empty myself entirely in Isolde, kissing her the entire time, Tristan's pleasure between our lips. Even after I'm completely drained, I give her a few more desultory thrusts, just to have her pussy around me a little longer, to relish the feel of my cum inside her.

God, that feels good.

The minute our lips break apart, I'm sliding out of her body. I'm off the table and pulling her to the edge so that her legs dangle toward the floor. I drop to my knees and press her thighs as far apart as the table will allow. I'm too impatient to unfasten her harness, so I tear at one side to loosen it and then shove the cock high enough to get at her clit, which I do with a wild, sucking kiss. She moans and stabs her hands into my hair, trying to arch her cunt harder against my face. My orgasm is leaking right back out of her. Her cute little feet hang in the air on either side of me, and when I look up at her face while I eat her, I see that her hair has half come undone, that she still has a pearly streak of cum near the corner of her mouth. Despite how hard and how long I just came, my body gives a lazy stir of interest.

Forever, I remind myself. *You have forever now.*

Tristan, who I'm pretty sure died during his orgasm, has come back to life and is now moving closer to Isolde and kneeling behind her. He kisses her neck and caresses her shoulders and plays with her nipples.

"Bite her," I say from her cunt. I work two fingers into

her wet, wet channel and press up until her toes point on either side of my shoulders. "Bite her until she squeaks."

He bites her.

His teeth dig into the tender place between her neck and her shoulder, and she lets out a high note of forlorn lust, and then with me sucking her clit, she ruptures and comes apart in a flooding rush of clenching release. Her hands are tight in my hair, she's moaning my name, Tristan's name, God's name. Her lingerie is half-off, the still-wet cock is shoved against her thigh, and wax is flaking around us like flower-colored snow.

As Tristan said earlier: I wish I could be exactly here forever.

My wife comes longer than I think possible, and I make a note to put pegging in the regular rotation. God bless.

When she finally slumps back against Tristan, we all look at each other and the carnage of wax and lube and cum, and maybe carnage was all we were every going to be, blood and burned-out buildings and silver wristwatches and chess queens, but we are *fucked*, I tell you, absolutely corrupt and depraved in the same ways, because we like it like that. We look at this room we've destroyed, and we'd do it again. Everything from start to finish, we'd do it all again.

See, you thought it was just me, didn't you? But you must have suspected my little knife wife had it in her. And as for Tristan, well. It's very hard to love two hunters if you're bothered by marrow and blood yourself. If you don't secretly love being hunted.

The smiles spread across our faces at the same time, dark and gleeful. We can't wait to tear each other up again.

But first the hotel. I want to spend the rest of the night pampering the two of them with long massages and even longer baths, and then I want to take them back home tomorrow, to our hidden idyll in the forest. To our dog, to our library. To Isolde's now genuine but mostly virtual job as a religious antiquities appraiser, to Tristan's small herd of sheep and even smaller brood of hens and too-large garden. To my reluctant work as a secret keeper, because people keep coming to me with their secrets for some unknown reason. I don't have a club to offer them anymore, but still they come, hoping for a favor or an introduction or a discreetly placed word with someone influential. Once every few months or so, I leave Morois do things that are best done in the dark, and I come back a favor or two richer or a little less in Embry's debt, with fresh bruises and blood in my hair, and Tristan and Isolde look at me like they wish they could be virgins all over again for me.

It's a good thing, my life.

We dress and do our best to contain the carnage of the room to the plastic sheet and then go downstairs to the lounge to arrange for a car to take us to the hotel. Tristan is still unsteady on his feet, and a florid bite mark is visible above the boatneck collar of Isolde's dress, but it's the kind of club where such things are expected.

We're waiting near the door when the doorman opens it for two men dashing in from the rain. One is tall and pale, platinum-haired and blue-eyed, with a chilling, angelic beauty that makes me think more of Lucifer than one of the good archangels, and the other is lean and subtly tanned and green-eyed, with delicate features under a shock of black hair. He's young, college-age, so he's younger than the evil angel, who looks to be in his midtwenties.

I pause, recognizing the second young man, and his eyes meet mine with a quizzical elegance that is so very Morgan Leffey that I nearly laugh. But if the expression is all his mother, then those dazzling green eyes and the firm mouth are all his father's.

The pale man steps between us, a movement that I clock as more possessive than protective. *He* is taking Lyr Moore upstairs, and he has no intention of sharing, and he'll mark his territory if needed.

"Do the two of you know each other?" he inquires. His voice is as American as mine, which is interesting here in the heart of London.

"No, we don't, I'm afraid," Lyr says politely. His voice is a melody, just a register above his father's.

"I know you," I say with the insufferable knowledge of the old. "Or I should say, I know your father."

Lyr doesn't flinch, but it's a near thing.

"Don't worry," I say, dropping my voice into a confidential tone. "I won't tell him I saw you at a place like this."

"Thank you," he breathes quickly. Still so young, so many glimpses of wounded sensitivity under his armor of poise and good manners.

It makes me slide my gaze to the pale man he's with. I give him the full force of a Mark Trevena smile. Enticing and amoral.

"I'm Mark Trevena. And you are?"

He looks at me with cold blue eyes. "Ryan Bell," he says. We shake hands, both of us too clever to try to outgrip the other, but it's still a handshake of layered meanings.

This one is mine tonight.

I will literally kill you if you hurt him. And then his father and his stepfather and his stepmother and his actual mother and his biological mother and his grandmother will kill you a second time.

We let go and briefly smile, having understood each other.

I nod at Lyr, my hands in my pockets, and he blushes a little as Ryan Bell puts a hand at the small of his back and guides him away.

Isolde watches them leave and says, "Maybe it'll be true love."

"I think that blond one has a few more souls to eat before he settles down," I say. "If he ever does." I know my kind—the heartless and wicked—and it's a rare specimen among us that finds an infatuation that can sustain—or indeed endure—our interest for long.

Somehow I found two such specimens, and for that, I will happily bury my heart at their feet every day for as long as it takes to grow a whole new life around us. A garden of devotion and the unspoiled truth of our deepest selves. A bower of communion and sex. A castle of mercy.

Like the dream I had of the king and the two graves but in reverse, with my own heart as the soil, as the garden walls, as the shelter of hazel and honeysuckle.

Our car pulls up, and I find Tristan's and Isolde's hands as we step outside the club. The rain has stilled for a moment, and the world glistens under a moon just barely revealed by the shredded silver batting of the clouds.

With my beloveds' hands in mine, with the moon looking like truth itself glimmering in the dark, we make our way into the car and then to the hotel.

Tomorrow we will go home, to our woods and our graveyard and our burgeoning little farm, to our dog and our jobs and our unfinished chess game by the fire, to the small little secret deep in Isolde's body that she thinks she's keeping so well.

To our radiant love rare and fathomless.

But as for tonight, we look at each other with magic in our eyes, having seen darkness and lonesomeness and vengeance, having seen death and beauty and pain, and somehow surviving anyway. We sojourned in Lyonesse for far too long, and now we've come back to where we were meant to be all this time.

To where we're real in the dark.

To forever, together.

prologue

THEY FOUND THE ROSES RIGHT AWAY.

The thorns took longer.

First, there was the escape, which wasn't an escape at all, really. The adults were busy with whatever it was that kept them cloistered and murmuring in the library, and the children were otherwise unsupervised, since no one thought any harm could come to them this far into the countryside.

Then there was the maze—which only Auden could navigate with any confidence, this being his house after all—and it only took a single hour to find the center, and in the center, the roses twining around Adonis's and Aphrodite's stone feet, all their blooms white and fragrant and blown.

Fat bees blundered in a drunken crowd. A storm threatened overhead. And only an exploring child would have bothered to crawl under the small fountain at the statue's base to find the secret inside.

Today there were six exploring children.

And they found the secret inside.

Finally, after a dark and damp journey through the tunnel

even Auden hadn't known about, they came to a gate with a latch rusted right through. Saint Sebastian kicked it open.

Becket fretted, and Delphine yelled about the torn spiderweb and the spider that no longer had a home. Rebecca only rolled her eyes and helped Saint Sebastian drag the thing open far enough that all six of them could squeeze through.

Proserpina was last because Proserpina was always last. Not because she was disliked or because she was timid, but because she was dreaming on her feet while everyone else was walking.

The gate led to a path so old that it had sunk into the earth. Trees branched and arced overhead, and to the sides were unbroken woods—oak, ash, birch, and beech. Rowan and elder. All leafy and lush and ivy clad. Between them, blackthorn trees straggled at intervals, their thorns long and cruel, and their branches clumped with the dark pearls of early sloe.

Though it was only just past lunch, the heavy clouds darkened everything to twilight, and the wind tugged insistently on the leaves, making the entire path around them seem restless and alive.

"Auden, where does it go?" Rebecca asked. She and Delphine were both trying to be in the front, but neither of them really knew where they were going, and so their jostling was less violent than normal.

"I don't know," Auden said, bouncing a little.

He knew where everything went in *London*, where his family lived most of the time. Every road led to another road, every car and bus and train had a destination. Every day had a plan, and every plan had a goal, and every goal had a reason.

At Thornchapel, none of this was true.

At Thornchapel, time could slip by unmarked and you could walk places no one had walked in years. Maybe centuries.

This was the first day Auden began to see this, began to see the ways one of his homes was different than the other, even if he couldn't articulate it. He was old enough to feel it, to *feel* Thornchapel, even if he couldn't name what it was he felt, and he was old enough to love it, but not old enough to understand.

And maybe that's why, later, he would grow to hate it.

They walked for ten minutes more, maybe twenty, but so far away from the house and with nothing but trees whispering close, it felt much longer. It felt like they were brave, like they were having an adventure, with the bite of genuine fear that any real adventure is required to have. And then the trees opened up to a clearing.

Nearly knee-high grass waved against crooked standing stones, which were barely taller than the grass itself. They were arranged in a narrow row, and at the end—

"The thorn chapel," somebody murmured. It might have been Becket, but it didn't matter. They all realized it at the same time.

The chapel was really only recognizable by a remaining chunk of wall, on which a glassless window gaped with its distinctive arch. The rest of the walls had crumbled into drifts of stone, barely visible over the layers of moss and grass and roots. Blackthorn trees—more like bushes—pushed up from the ancient rubble. Wild dog roses—just as thorny, just as sprawling—grew everywhere else in hues of almost-white and almost-pink.

It *was* a church. Only the walls had been replaced with thorns and the floor with grass, and where the altar should have been was a large, grassy hummock instead. And everywhere flowers—not only the roses but wood sorrel and foxglove and violets and meadowsweet in restrained riots of white and purple.

Delphine and Rebecca raced to the front while Becket

505

approached the chapel from the side in awe. Saint Sebastian found a stick and started whacking at the flowers to slice off their heads. Proserpina slipped into the stone row—the entrance of which was guarded by two tall menhirs—and began dreaming her way toward the chapel itself.

And Auden stood at the edge of the woods, unable to take a single step closer.

It's really here.

It wasn't a quaint name, chosen on a whim. It wasn't, as he'd once heard his grandfather say, a corruption of a Latin word referencing the thick forest canopy around the house.

There was a chapel.

It was covered in thorns.

Thornchapel.

And he had the strangest feeling that as he thought the name of this place, the place thought his own name back to him...

————

No one later remembered whose idea the wedding was, but it had probably started as a fight between Rebecca and Delphine, since that's how most of their ideas that summer had begun. But once the idea had been voiced, there'd been no doubt that it was a good idea, even to Becket, who was really too old for these kinds of things. There was a chapel, after all, and something that looked like an altar, and weddings were something you did in chapels, in front of altars.

There was a brief fight about *who* should get married because it seemed common sense that Auden, as the sort of lord of the manor, should be the groom, but Delphine and Rebecca both wanted to be the bride and their fight over it grew so heated that Saint Sebastian observed, "You already fight like Auden's parents. Maybe you two should get married."

506

This was not received well, by the girls or by Auden, and then Becket the peacemaker pointed out that Proserpina had already wandered down to the chapel proper and so it might as well be her. Rebecca and Delphine sullenly agreed to be bridesmaid and flower girl, respectively; Becket, as the oldest, appointed himself the priest; Auden turned to Saint Sebastian and said, "Will you be the best man?"

Saint Sebastian sniffed. "I'm already the best man."

Auden rolled his eyes. He did that a lot with Saint Sebastian.

"I'm going to sit in the back and interrupt the wedding," Saint Sebastian declared.

Auden sighed. "What?"

"You know, like in the movies. They say 'speak now or forever hold your peace' and then someone always speaks."

"But that's not real life."

"And this is?"

He had a point, but Auden didn't want to admit it. Something else he did rather a lot of with Saint Sebastian.

No one really could remember the order of a wedding service, except that the flower girl came first. Becket and Auden waited by the uneven lump that had once been an altar, while Delphine scattered hastily gathered rose petals down the center of the ruin. Then came Rebecca, carrying a bouquet of foxgloves because they were tall and interesting compared with the retiring violets and sorrel. Saint Sebastian sprawled in the back, lazily tossing pebbles into the air.

Auden felt strange so close to the altar, like the air around it was infused with an electric charge, or maybe that was merely the oncoming storm, or maybe it was that he was a boy playing a game he hadn't actually agreed to and he was bored. Whatever it was, he suddenly felt the fierce need to hurt something. Or to feel hurt himself. He couldn't figure out which, and the two needs tangled up into an untidy knot in his chest thornier than the chapel around them, and it felt like the knot was all he was, all he ever could be—

Proserpina entered the chapel with a crown of flowers on her head. The knot eased; it untangled some. And when Saint Sebastian decided that Proserpina needed someone to walk her down the aisle and he hopped up to take her arm, Auden quite literally could not breathe for a second. He didn't know why—Saint Sebastian irritated him, Proserpina fascinated him, but he wasn't entirely sure he liked her for having that effect on him—so why now, when the two of them approached the altar and drew near him, did he think of the need to hurt and the need to *be* hurt and why did he want to grab them both and pull them into that need? Grab them and somehow shove them deep into his heart of thorns forever?

He couldn't speak as Saint Sebastian escorted Proserpina right to Auden's feet and then gave her a puckish kiss on the cheek that had Proserpina laughing and Delphine scolding and Rebecca shushing Delphine's scolds and their resident barely teenage priest tutting at the disruption of order.

"I thought you were going to interrupt the ceremony," Becket sighed as Saint Sebastian took a seat on a nearby clump of grass.

"I can do both," Saint Sebastian said in an *obviously* kind of tone.

Becket made a put-upon face, which was only slightly different than his normal pious expression, and then continued with as much as he remembered about wedding ceremonies.

There was a *dearly beloved* and then a story about Adam and Eve, and then he finally said the part Saint Sebastian was waiting for, *speak now or forever hold your peace.*

They all looked over to the boy, who was currently grinning mischievously and was very busy *not* interrupting the wedding. Auden arched an eyebrow at him.

Saint Sebastian arched an eyebrow back but still did nothing.

It seemed like the threat had passed, so Becket moved on to the vows. "Do you, Auden Guest, take Proserpina Markham to be your lawfully wedded wife? You have to say *I do* here."

Auden, still afflicted with that disturbing and paradoxical need, answered in a distracted voice, "I d—"

"I do!" Saint Sebastian jumped in, hopping up between them.

"Ugh, God," went Delphine.

"Shh!" went Rebecca.

"And DO YOU, PROSERPINA, TAKE AUDEN TO BE YOUR LAWFULLY WEDDED HUSBAND?" shouted the young priest above the chaos, and smiling, Proserpina said, "I do," even as Saint Sebastian once again interrupted her vows with his own emphatic, "I DO!" and yanked her flower crown onto his own head as if he were the bride.

Even Auden had trouble not smiling, although those thorns of hurt were everywhere in him now; he felt like he was going to break apart like one of the chapel walls or fall over like the altar; he felt like he was never going to fit inside his own skin unless he became someone else, some*thing* else, some*when* else.

But he didn't need to be some*where* else. He knew that, even if he didn't know how he knew that.

Thornchapel was right. Proserpina and Saint Sebastian fighting over the flower crown in front of him felt right.

It was only him that felt wrong.

"This is *not how weddings work*," Becket accused. "Saint Sebastian, stop it. Give back the flower crown."

"No," said Saint Sebastian.

"You *have* to because three people can't kiss, only two can," Delphine said knowledgeably.

"There's going to be kissing?" Proserpina said, suddenly sounding very, very awake.

"That's stupid," Rebecca said back to Delphine. "Three people can kiss. All six of us could kiss if we wanted."

"Yes, there is kissing," Becket said to Proserpina with the grave tones of one who knows these things.

"We don't have to kiss," Auden said quietly to his bride.

"Well, I want to," Saint Sebastian declared, which surprised absolutely no one.

Becket pinched his nose, looking exactly like an exasperated grown-up. "No one asked you."

Delphine was still fighting with Rebecca, and she wrinkled her nose, which was one of those things that made her look even prettier than normal. "At the same time? It wouldn't work."

"You don't know *everything*, you know—"

Every moment of Auden's unmet destiny bit his skin and punctured his heart, and every second he stood still was a jagged clamp around his throat.

He had...he had to do...

Something...

Thornchapel...

Wounds and dying and fires burning against the night...

Sparks hissing as he was brought back to life...

He seized both Proserpina and Saint Sebastian and pulled them both to his mouth just as lightning cracked across the sky.

A kiss.

A kiss that was almost a bruise, almost a bite, and how he wanted both—he wanted kissing and bruising and holding and biting. And he wanted to shelter them from the rain and force them to kneel in the mud too, and he didn't know what it meant or why it was happening or even why they were letting him yank them close.

510

It was awkward and bumping, and Proserpina had sucked in a stunned breath as Saint Sebastian had shuddered, yet when they stumbled apart to the deafening thunder and the shocked stares of the other three, Auden couldn't bring himself to be ashamed.

He could only feel like he wanted to do it again.

Rain began slicing down before any of the six could find the right words, and there was more lightning and more wind, and within fifteen seconds, it became evident that they'd have to run back to the house. Which they did, and after the long time it took, they were soaked to the bone and shivering, and then they were all roundly reprimanded by the parents, who were not impressed with their refusal to talk about what they'd been doing or where they'd been.

The rain continued for another week and well into the week after that, and by that point, the thorn chapel had become something like a myth or a shared dream and it slipped into the realm of reverence and dares and distance. They instead explored the house and the nearby village of Thorncombe and swam in the indoor pool and put on plays in the attic. Delphine and Rebecca fought, and Becket was an insufferable know-it-all, and Saint Sebastian wandered in and out, and Proserpina dreamed.

And Auden was still everything inside of himself, unbearably everything, every single thing he'd been at the altar when he'd needed to kiss Saint Sebastian and Proserpina and maybe bite them too.

Then the summer term ended.

Author's Note

I first heard Mark Trevena's voice seven years ago while I was staring at a shower wall. I was pondering whether I had the moral courage to shave my legs when I heard Mark explain, patiently, what it was like to kill someone.

(He thinks it's like fishing an accidentally dropped spoon from the trash, if you're curious. He also thinks only a dipshit would complain about doing it, because whatever, it's not *pleasant*, but it's one of those things that simply has to be done from time to time, and so you reach in there and you get the spoon. No one cares about your whining. Stop it.)

I'm not an author who hears her characters very often. I tend to feel them more than I hear them, and honestly, I can't say I love it when I do hear them! It's usually a sign that they're going to insist I park the car after the first chapter and let them drive instead! Not cool!

But Mark's voice was so clear, so striking—immoral and irreverent and a little bitter—and I remember turning off the shower and running still hairy-legged into my office to write down what I heard, and what I now knew about him. And then poor Mark—poor, mean, murdery Mark—had to wait his turn while I wrote three *Misadventures* books and Thornchapel and *Saint* and some Christmas Notch books, while I noodled over his story.

And noodle I had to, because as deep as my fascination with Arthurian literature ran, I really only knew of Tristan, Isolde, and Mark as they intersected with my precious baby boyfriend King Arthur. The Lyonesse trio typically pops up as a kind of messier, unlovelier foil to the Arthur-Lancelot-Guinevere triangle, and honestly, I'd always found Tristan and Isolde's story to be fairly shallow waters, creatively speaking. (I mean, a love potion? Really?)

Mark, however, I usually liked, even though he's painted as the old, ugly husband-monster who deserves to have his hot wife cheat on him. Some stories even give him the very, very realistic condition of having been born with the ears of a donkey, just to really hammer home how unfair it would be to have to marry him or serve him as a king.

But also imagine you're a king and you're just trying to do a good job at having a kingdom to run and then half your day is spent batting away advisors who want to burn your wife and knight at the stake because your wife and knight are *so bad* at affairing and can't illicitly bone with even a fucking morsel of decorum. Instead of, you know, spending your day on actual king shit. I'd be annoyed too, and so I decided that I was going to fix this for him. He deserved a happily ever after without donkey ears or having to die alone because of a love potion on a boat.

The oldest versions of this doomed love triangle were composed in French and German, but they always set the scene in Cornwall, and so I began there when it was time to flesh out Mark's character. I started in Tintagel, the seat of King Mark's power, and I put myself in the fur-lined boots of a post-Roman British king. If you know me, you know I like thinking about kingship (not the actual political system, just the metaphorical expression of power and responsibility), but King Mark represents a very different kind of kingship than the one most of us picture when we think of *kings*. Not gold but tin; not jewels but Mediterranean glass; not horses but boats and boats *and boats* bearing away ore and bringing in luxury.

Imagine this—you're in the sixth century, at the far edge of the post-Roman world. The Pax Romana is gone, the roads are slowly crumbling, and everyone wants to be the lord of their own muddy little hill. You've got pirates biting at your shores, and your British kinfolk are pushing closer and closer as the Saxons continue their trespass westward. You're staring at the Dark Ages rolling toward you, and here's what you've got to keep your people safe: a fortress that's impossible to take, and tin.

What kind of person can take those two things, and for a generation—maybe two—create a semblance of a kingdom? What kind of person could corral all the ambition and desperation and vendetta-seeking and scattered acts of brilliance or courage into the powerhouse population center that Tintagel became?

My king Mark was that kind of person. Someone canny and sly and also quick and bold when needed. Someone who wasn't afraid to trade in secrets as well as tin. The kind of someone who wouldn't hesitate to lie, cheat, and rip open his own stitches. Someone who buries the embers at dawn.

Unlike Maxen Colchester's White House in the New Camelot trilogy, Lyonesse is a jagged, whispery sort of place, designed to gratify and influence. There'd be no gleaming turrets and snapping pennants, not for my tin king. His castle is like this version of the story—dark, depraved, and a hazard to everyone's good sense.

But what of our two wayward lovers? From the moment I heard Mark's voice that night in the shower, I knew Isolde needed to be able to hold her own with him—survive him—and I knew that would be something he'd absolutely adore about her. In the legend, Isolde is an Irish princess, and so I replicated the idea of her being from another kingdom via her vocation in the Church. I wanted her lonely and reserved and guilty. I wanted her sharp and efficient. I wanted to believe that she could one day beat Mark at a chess game.

As for Tristan, I'd known since *American King* that I wanted to unravel that moment where Mark confesses to Ash that one day he'd like a submissive just like him. Tristan is indeed a green-eyed Army hero, but where war clarified something for Ash, it complicated something inside Tristan. Where Ash has generated certainty inside himself, Tristan can only find doubt. The Tristan of legends who plays a harp and just can't help falling in love—I translated him as our singing bodyguard, who feels his natural tendency toward obsession like a sickness.

I liked the idea that Tristan and Isolde shared something in common with Mark, and that was the experience of dealing death, and I also liked the idea that Tristan and Isolde were both fresh from relationships with bad dominants. Except in their case, the bad Doms were the Army and the Church, and what made these Doms so dangerous was their ability to *partly* recognize certain needs and fill them. To be partially seen is a very dangerous thing—but to be fully seen, as these two are by Mark, is a gift so rare most people never receive it.

They face a common enemy by the end, one of my larger deviations from the original legends. In those, Isolde does have an asshole uncle (named Morholt), but he dies early in the narrative and his primary job is stressing Tristan out. But the bad guy uncle opportunities were too great to give up, and so I made him my villain, the head of the fictional Ys.

Ys, obviously, is not real, nor is it based on anything real, but I was inspired by the origins of the Illuminati in eighteenth century Bavaria. I was fascinated by how the Illuminati was simply *made up*, half-plagiarized from Freemason customs in the 1700s, half invented by Just Some (anticlerical) Fellas. I wanted this for Ys. I wanted the actual conspiracy about the evil secret society to be that there wasn't an evil secret society at all!!! At the end of the day, Ys was more like a marketing plan than anything else; turns out that the narcissistic hunger and ambition of one soulless man can cause just as much suffering and mayhem as an ancient consortium of shadowy patricians. The real conspiracies are happening out in the open—we don't have to look for secret sects or hidden symbols or invent corruption. The crimes are visible to us all, reported in the news, evident in how we treat the sick, the poor, and the stranger, in how billionaires consolidate power and control, in where the bombs fall, in where people die of diseases that we have the medicine to treat. I don't want to get too radical here, but I feel very strongly about this. You don't need any secret information at all to spot the malfeasance; it's happening in the headlines.

Sedge is another deviation from the source, and one I didn't necessarily plan on. To me, one of the central antagonists of the legend is not a single person, but a group of people—King Mark's court. These courtiers are backbiting, vicious, and manipulative, and almost eerily determined to destroy Tristan and Isolde. And so I created Sedge knowing he'd be the Scales, thinking it would be a clever way to connect that suspicious, undermining vibe of the court to its ultimate end, which is the destruction of Lyonesse. *Unfortch*, I wound up really liking Sedge. I'm not sure why? I do try with my antagonists to find something inside them that I *like*, so that I can more easily access why the characters around them might like them—Mortimer, for instance, looks like Jared Harris in my head. I love Jared Harris! If he were my uncle, I'd trust him too!

But I didn't do anything on purpose with Sedge. He just walked quietly onto the page with his cardigan and his iPad, and by the end of it all, I was very sad that I had to kill him. Much like Tristan and Isolde, he'd had a bad Dom. If he'd found a good one before Mortimer found him, the world would be a different place, and there wouldn't be a new headstone in the graveyard at Morois.

While I took liberties with Mortimer and Sedge, I did try to bring in my favorite moments from the legends and translate them to our contemporary setting while still honoring what purpose they served. Tristan and Isolde still have a tryst in the garden, they still escape to Morois, where Mark is moved by the sight of them sleeping next to each other. Mark is Tristan's step-uncle, and Tristan is still tasked with getting Mark's bride for him. A few things I changed even more: rather than exchanging swords when Tristan leaves for Brittany, they exchange rings; there is an Isolde of the White Hands (Isabella) but she and Tristan never marry; my black and white sails are instead a black and white folder of divorce papers.

I've always felt bad for Isolde of the White Hands, by the way. She's another person who's totally hosed by the circumstances, and as her reward for putting up with her husband's occasional adultery, she's made into the ultimate villain of the story, the person who deprives Tristan and Isolde of any chance at a happily ever after. So I decided to give her a chance to redeem herself. With honesty and with comfort, even though she's comforting Mark instead of Tristan.

I even fixed the love potion! Mark's yacht, the *Philtre D'Amour*, is a love potion unto itself, filled with all the wicked little tricks Mark built into it to make sure Tristan and Isolde came together.

The problem with writing two kinky, polyamorous legend retellings is that it's impossible not to compare the two. As a writer, I have to find the need to tell a story—it's not enough to know that I can make it work mechanically. I also can't go back. I can't write New Camelot again, because I'm a different person now, a different author now, and I'm different *because* I wrote it. The process of writing it changed me, and now I can never tell a story in exactly the same way again. (Even if I could, I wouldn't want to!)

But it was a blessing that it took me so long to start writing Lyonesse after I first heard Mark's voice in the shower. It meant I had time to ask myself how Lyonesse was different from New Camelot, and how I now felt about war and power and obsession and desire. If New Camelot was about good people doing their best, then Lyonesse is about bad people loving each other despite what they've done at their worst. If New Camelot was about a hero and the people he loves, then Lyonesse is about a villain and the people he can't keep.

If New Camelot is about sacrifice, then Lyonesse, in its own dark, strange way, is about mercy.

The mercy that King Mark should have shown his knight and queen in the legends; the mercy that they should have shown him as their betrayal tore his kingdom down stone by stone. The mercy that Isolde of the White Hands should have shown the two lovers at the end of the story.

The mercy that the old king should have shown himself while standing beside the hazel tree and its blooming, sweet-smelling honeysuckle consort.

I'm glad I was able to give Mark that mercy at last. I'm glad that I was able to make Isolde capable and Tristan selfless. I'm glad that all of you took this twisty, angsty journey with me, that you followed our trio to the end, and sojourned at Lyonesse with our brave puppy, our knife wife, and our tin king. I hope you've come home with magic in your eyes. And I hope you come back again.

xoxo,
sierra simone
April 2025
Olathe, Kansas

ACKNOWLEDGMENTS

I really put the *dead* in *deadline* with this one, and I'm profoundly grateful to everyone who *Weekend at Bernie's*-ed me into extracting Mark's story from my brain.

Thank you especially to Christa Désir and Gretchen Stelter, who both had the patience of Job as I kept promising that I was so close to the end, like *really, actually close this time*, and it was never true. (Now that you've read the book, you can appreciate why…let it never be said that I abridge myself.) And eternal gratitude to my stalwart cinnamon roll agent John Cusick, who graciously let me panic at him multiple times.

I owe a huge thank-you to the entire Sourcebooks team, including Katie Stutz, Madison Nankervis, Pam Jaffee, Susie Benton, Carolyn Telesca, and Dominique Raccah. And a big thank-you to Hang Le, Antoaneta Lisak, and Sabrina Baskey for making the book beautiful inside and out.

I couldn't have functioned this year without Ashley Lindemann, my bestie and second brain. And probably the only reason anyone knows what I look like is because Flavia

Vazquez patiently reminds me to occasionally take a picture of myself or whatever. Thank you both for putting up with me.

Thank you to Erica Russikoff for all the comfort and warm words, and making sure Mark has his best suit on for the girlies, and thank you to Michele Ficht, for making sure everything is nice and tidy. Thank you to Serena McDonald and Candi Kane for all the behind the scenes support, and thank you to Chiara Panzeri at Folio for helping my messy trio find loving homes all over the world.

Of course, all authors are only as productive as the people who patiently listen to them complain allow them to be. I owe Julie Murphy a profound debt for listening to me wail, fuss, and groan over Mark's insistence on having A Plot. I'm also grateful for my author buds for talking shop (and gossip): Tessa Gratton, Adib Khorram, Nana Malone, and Natalie C. Parker. And everyone else who endured my TikTok links, listened to my rambling VMs, or gently petted my hair in the last year: Aubrey Bondurant, Megan Bannen, Kenya Goree Bell, Jo Brenner, Becca Mysoor, Kennedy Ryan, Nisha Sharma, Nikki Sloane, QB Tyler, Rebekah Weatherspoon, Julia Whelan, and Julian Winters, along with the Bu, who were the very first people to witness me rolling around on the floor about words I had to write. (In the Olathe North newspaper room. Sorry, Gail Brumback!)

Thank you to Noah and Teagan, who are the coolest and funniest and smartest.

I don't think a *thank you* is enough for Josh and all the comfort and stability he poured into me over the last year. (I promise we'll catch up on all our shows now.)

Finally, thank you to all the readers who went on this sojourn to Lyonesse with me. I know it was a long wait, but I'm honored by your trust. Mark's still not sorry, but he's awfully charmed that you hoped he would be.

ABOUT THE AUTHOR

Sierra Simone is a *USA Today* bestselling former library employee who spent too much time reading romance novels at the information desk. She lives with her husband and family in Kansas City.

Sign up for her newsletter to be notified of releases, books going on sale, events, and other news!

thesierrasimone.com